9 780812 553857

50699>

EAN

# THE SULTAN'S DAUGHTER

## ANN CHAMBERLIN

## Praise for *Sofia*

"This is a brilliant novel. Ann Chamberlin is the master of crafting exciting realistic historical fiction."

—*Affaire de Coeur* (five stars)

"Blends absorbing historical detail with a lively, romantic plot about two Italian teenagers sold into slavery in the Ottoman Empire. . . . Fascinating descriptions. . . . Compelling."

—*Publishers Weekly*

"Lyrical prose. . . . The era in *Sofia* comes brilliantly alive. Chamberlin is a master storyteller."

—Kathleen Dougherty, author of
*Moth to the Flame* and *Double Vision*

"Magnificent! *Sofia* is a breathtaking story of love, betrayal, and heartache, with captivating characters, set in a fascinating and exotic time period only Ann Chamberlin could so skillfully bring to life."

—Charlene Raddon, author of *Forever Mine*

"*Sofia* is a fascinating story, beautifully told. It captures the imagination and holds it firmly in hand from page one to the finish. Ann Chamberlin succeeds in blending passion and humor, joy and pathos, to produce a Turkish delight of a tale."

—Kate Cameron, author of *The Legend Makers*

## Praise for *Tamar*

"Ann Chamberlin tells her story with authenticity and depth. . . . Chamberlin is a great storyteller." —*Affaire de Coeur* (five stars)

"Engrossing. . . . The characters are believable . . . [and] brought vividly to life." —*Publishers Weekly*

"A tale of passion, loss, and fated retribution. . . . [A] meticulously researched, well-crafted novel." —*Booklist*

"A stunning story that sweeps you along. . . . A brilliant evocation of a strange and fascinating world with dynamic and believable characters. This is a book that will live in your memory."

—David Nevin, author of *1812*

"A provocative new writer." —Anne McCaffrey

"Evocative and vivid. This is the finest debut novel I have ever read. This is one of the finest novels I have read, period. I envy Chamberlin's talent."
—Jennifer Roberson, author of *Lady of the Forest*

"Rich and subtle, woven of threads brilliant and dark, Ann Chamberlin's *Tamar* is a story of dignity and courage in the face of outrageous betrayal, wisdom, and selflessness."
—Merry McInerney, author of *Burning Down the House*

"The vibrance of *Tamar* catches what so much of fiction misses these days—reality. Chamberlin's succulent details and glittering humor engulfs us. She showcases a great secret of historical writing: that history isn't over."
—Diane Carey, *New York Times* bestselling author of *Best Destiny* and *The Great Starship Race*

"Ann Chamberlin brings the ancient realm of King David to startling, thrilling life in this tale of a time and place where God was called Goddess, and dwelled in the secret groves protected by the knowledge of women. *Tamar* is a one-of-a-kind adventure of the mind and soul."

—Molly Cochran and Warren Murphy, authors of *The Forever King* and *Grandmaster*

"*Tamar* is brilliant—luscious, evocative, honest, and moving. I've seen a dozen authors try to write in similar millieus, but none has succeeded better. In my estimation, Ann Chamberlin isn't a name to watch, she's a star that has already risen!"
—Dave Wolverton, author of *The Golden Queen*

# The Sultan's Daughter

## ANN CHAMBERLIN

A TOM DOHERTY ASSOCIATES BOOK
NEW YORK

This is a work of fiction. All the characters and events portrayed in this novel are either fictitious or are used fictitiously.

THE SULTAN'S DAUGHTER

Lines on page 15 from *Harem: The World Behind the Veil* by Alev Lytle Croutier, published by Abbeville Press, 1989.

Lines on page 169 from "The Inferno" from *The Divine Comedy* by Dante Alighieri, translated by John Ciardi. Translation copyright © 1954, 1957, 1959, 1960, 1961, 1965, 1967, 1970 by the Ciardi Family Publishing Trust. Reprinted by permission of W. W. Norton & Company, Inc.

Lines on pages 234–37 and 268 from "Paradise on Earth: The Terrestrial Garden in Persian Literature" by William L. Hanaway, Jr., in *The Islamic Garden*, published by Dumbarton Oaks, Trustees for Harvard University, Washington, D.C., 1976. Reprinted by permission.

A Forge Book
Published by Tom Doherty Associates, Inc.
175 Fifth Avenue
New York, NY 10010

Forge® is a registered trademark of Tom Doherty Associates, Inc.

ISBN: 0-812-55385-3
Library of Congress Card Catalog Number: 96-44192

First Edition: April 1997
First mass market edition: September 1998

Printed in the United States of America

0 9 8 7 6 5 4 3 2 1

*This book is dedicated to*

*my cousins*

*Kourkan Daglian*

*and*

*Ruth Mentley.*

# ACKNOWLEDGMENTS

MUCH OF THE list is the same as for the first volume of this trilogy, but repetition should not indicate a lack of appreciation, rather the opposite.

My cousins Kourkan Daglian and Ruth Mentley, to whom this volume is dedicated, Harriet Klausner, Alexis Bar-Lev, and Dr. James Kelly all unstintingly shared their expertise with me. Again I'd like to thank the Wasatch Mountain Fiction Writers Friday Morning Group for their support, patience, and friendship. Teddi Kachi, Leonard Chiarelli and, in the Middle East Section, Hermione Bayas at the Marriott Library, as well as all the Whitmore and Holladay librarians, never stinted in their assistance. Gerry Pearce is new to the list, but cannot be surpassed as a sounding board.

I owe a great deal to the friendly people in Turkey, especially the guides at the Topkapi palace who hardly raised a brow as I went through the harem again and again. I'd like to thank my in-laws for their support and my husband and sons for their patience while my mind was elsewhere.

There is another woman to whom I owe much but she didn't want her name mentioned. She knows who she is. She doesn't approve—except of good spelling and grammar.

None of these people are to be blamed for the errors I've committed, only thanked for saving me from making more.

And finally, of course, there are Natalia Aponte, my editor, Steve, Erin, and all the other folks at Tor/Forge, and Virginia Kidd, my agent. Without them *The Reign* would have existed, but never in the light of day.

## Part I

# Abdullah

# I

*"I am a harem woman, an Ottoman slave.*
*I was conceived in an act of contemptuous rape*
*And born in a sumptuous palace.*
*Hot sand is my father;*
*The Bosphorus, my mother;*
*Wisdom, my destiny;*
*Ignorance, my doom.*
*I am richly dressed and poorly regarded;*
*I am a slave-owner and a slave.*
*I am anonymous, I am infamous;*
*One thousand and one tales have been written about me.*
*My home is this place where gods are buried*
*And devils breed,*
*The land of holiness,*
*The backyard of hell.*
*I am——"*

ESMIKHAN SULTAN STOPPED her song, a song she might have learned at her nurse's knee or from any of her childhood companions, it was that popular among Constantinople's women. She sang it for the sweet, plaintive melody, I hoped, and not because it was true.

Well, some of it was true. She was a slave-owner. She owned me.

*She owns me.* I had heard rapturous stage lovers sing such declarations—but in a previous life.

And sometimes the word "love" flitted through my mind when I looked at Esmikhan Sultan and thought of our relationship. An unnatural thump of the heart accompanied the word: here was something I feared to lose. Perhaps more than life itself. She is not just my mistress, I thought in unguarded moments. Or she *is* my mistress indeed, my mistress in the other, beautiful sense of the word. We have been through much together. Yes, I have faced death for her sake. She is my best and only friend in this foreign place. . . .

But no. I rejected "love," the breathy whisper of *"amore,"* all the lushness my Italian childhood had taught me to expect. One cruel cut had put all hope of love forever beyond my grasp.

Esmikhan Sultan owns my body, I reminded myself. But not my heart, not my soul. My still-raw pain told me I would die before I gave those to anyone.

Esmikhan Sultan turned to look at me. Her face flushed to match the scarlet tulips she had been readjusting for the twentieth time that morning in their Chinese porcelain vase on a low silk-draped table in the center of the room.

"I hear their sedans in the yard!" she exclaimed. "Oh, Abdullah! What will they think when you are not at the door to greet them?"

Esmikhan made the much-older Vizier a better wife than he made her a husband, I thought, not for the first time. And they were both better at their allotments than I claimed to be at mine: my lady's chief and only eunuch.

None of us had had any choice in our fates; we learned to make our choices elsewhere.

Every harem in Constantinople knew Esmikhan Sultan was with child from Sokolli Pasha's brief nights of duty with her. Viewing the decor of her new winter rooms was the ostensive reason for this long-awaited visit. But quite plainly, the women of her father's harem came for no other reason than to see how she fared in her condition.

As only a female, albeit the granddaughter of Sultan Suleiman the Lawgiver and the Magnificent—"richly dressed and poorly regarded" as the song said—any son she bore would not be in direct line to the throne. Nonetheless, given the right circumstances, the right personality, the right play of fate, the will of Allah, this combination of royal Othman blood and a Vizier's cunning could make things very interesting twenty or thirty years hence.

Women, I was beginning to see, start calculating such things before their first missed blood time. On the other hand, a promising youth appears full grown at the edge of the world of men and the men treat him like a bothersome gadfly—often until it is too late to properly account for him in their calculations.

I looked down into that round little face, rounder still with the pregnancy, those round, dark eyes, that round little chin, the dimples when she smiled, the mole by her nose—all the supreme pleasantness of her that I'd come to take for granted. She was like a pearl in this velvet-lined case, the walls inlaid with mother-of-pearl and ivory in the olive wood wainscoting. A pearl with the pink tint of tulips.

I laughed gently at her fluster. *These sessions of display with your family are not all that important,* I wanted to speak along with my silent brush at a black curl that strayed into her face. *When they have gawked their fill and gone home, I will still be here. No matter what their sharp tongues invent, I am your slave.*

"Abdullah," she protested, shoving my hand away with her own little dimpled one. "At once!"

So at my lady's bidding, I strode down to the courtyard and helped the visiting eunuchs hold up the silken canopy. This canopy allowed their charges to slip into our harem without the gardeners catching a glimpse of so much as veils and outer wrappers.

I was getting good at distinguishing women and their individuality through such covers. I'd originally come to the Land of the Turk as first mate on my murdered uncle's trading ship. Women had seemed altogether invisible to me then. I was learning to use other senses more now, as a blind man does and sometimes fares better than the sighted.

Today, I went by the scent they wore, and Prince Selim's harem presented a whole airy palette to the nostrils.

This first one, smoky with the musk of ambergris, was Nur Banu Kadin, my lady's stepmother as well as mother to the son of the heir to Suleiman's throne. My lady's unwed sisters were cloying in attar of roses, sandalwood, cloves. Their maidservants were the usual giggling bouquet of violet, mimosa, and orange blossom.

Ah, but here——through the silken corridor I held up to one edge of the sedan and the eunuch next to me held to the harem door——here passed an odd one. I couldn't recognize her, nor her clumsy way of moving in her veils, as if threatening to shed them all off at any minute. Some new slave, I thought, for I'd never known any native-born Turkish woman to be so clumsy with the burden of her sex. Some new slave, perhaps, whom Nur Banu would soon train to her usual rigorous elegance. The surprise was that Nur Banu would let a recruit of such raw manners come with her on any outing.

Still, violet- and mimosa-scented bundles held back and let this package go in first. And there was an odd smell to this one, the smell of quinces set to ripen in the midst of winter bedding. This odor proclaimed no artifice but straightforward practicality: every drug known to man and some known only to women, medicinal bitterness disguised with the flavor of quince.

*Suppose this was some interloper, some threat to the peace of my lady's harem?*

I told myself that this was a petty sort of concern—for a man bred to the wild adventures of the sea, indeed! But the manhood left to me was not considered the equal of pirates or shipwreck anymore. I was meant to have no purpose other than the protection of this sanctuary behind the grilles. So I couldn't help that my mind entertained such possibilities, fretful though they sometimes seemed.

That thing I lacked—manhood in vague generality—was the very threat against which I wore a jeweled, ceremonial dagger. Could this be a man in women's veils? Or could some other invasion I had yet to imagine take feminine form?

Again I dismissed the ideas. Anything Nur Banu Kadin allowed into her sedan must be allowed into Esmikhan's harem.

The mystery would unwind itself soon enough, and the scent that brought up the rear of the cavalcade, too proud to jostle for position among the rest, gave me more important things to worry about. Jasmine. Heady, overpowering, sweeping away all before it, jasmine assaulted the nose with a fragrance to which the senses could never grow numb. That jasmine could only be Safiye—Sofia Baffo she had been once, before she learned eastern fashions in perfume. Safiye was my lady's brother's odalisque. Instinctively, I stiffened, hating always when she had the advantage of veils over me: I could not read her eyes to warn me which way to jump.

Safiye swept on into the narrow doorway and ascended the steep staircase without a sideways glance. At the top of the stairs, however, as she kicked off her outdoor shoes, she gave me a momentary—purposeful, I thought—glimpse of white ankles under ballooning red *shalvar*.

I turned to make the visiting eunuchs comfortable in my lower sitting room. I helped them fold the silken curtains neatly back into the sedans. With a pang, I remembered helping sailors with the sails; these new mates of mine would never scramble up masts. And the way their thick and heavily jeweled fingers set upon the fried pastries dripping with orange water and honey, they were bent upon keeping such activity an impossibility.

A pair of Nur Banu's eunuchs unabashedly loosened the wide silk banded about their middles as they settled into my cushions for the afternoon. They struggled with the sweat-soaked furs of their long, heavy, blue robes and the high cones of their white turbans, releasing very feminine perfumes to the room, though they were perfumes pickled by greasy perspiration. Then they launched into the sherbets I offered.

Well, extra flesh distracted from the other deformities eunuchs were prone to—the barrel chest, the long, dangling, apelike arms and clawed hands. As eating and drinking distracted from invisible distortions within.

So far I had avoided the outward mutations, but I feared it was only a matter of time. Slackening into cushions on a warm afternoon seemed one sure way to hasten the inevitable, so as soon as I saw my colleagues settled, I left them. Their reedy voices pursued me, like the fragile notes of a ship's flautist on the night air, up through the stairwell. Here, over the neat rows of discarded feminine footwear on the threshold, the scent of jasmine still lingered, trapped.

"Alas, the day is too warm to show off the braziers," was the first thing I heard my lady say over the preliminary oohs and ahs of her guests. Esmikhan had been fretting over that all morning. "But you were right, Nur Banu Kadin. I was just telling Abdullah."

"About what, my dear?" The ambergris's question was still muffled by the white gauze that rode over the bridge of her nose and scrunched into the black sharpness of her eyes.

"I should have started with the summer rooms. Here it is,

too hot for braziers, and we must spend the summer in this velvet-lined chest without a single cooling fountain."

Absently, Esmikhan smoothed the buttons down the front of her *yelek;* she was already leaving three undone as her belly grew. "Summer" had become synonymous with "baby" for her. "It is hard to think of summer when you're cold."

"Allah willing, all will be well, my little mountain spring," said Nur Banu.

*"Inshallah,"* Esmikhan echoed.

"It is warm, lady," I agreed as I nudged our still ill-trained maidservants forward to remove the guests' wraps. We could ease their heat that much in any case.

My lady caught my eye. I read gratitude there—for covering for the stupefaction of the maids. I'm not certain how much of my concern was towards Esmikhan and how much that Safiye should not find too much amiss in our house.

But Esmikhan's look also carried her empathy to me.

Earlier that morning, during the last hectic rush of preparation, Esmikhan had caught me staring out the window at this sudden warmth of spring. Touching my arm folded across my chest in a eunuch's habitual attitude, she'd murmured, "It's been about a year, hasn't it?"

I didn't need to say. My lady sensed how the spring air with its bath of light, warmth, and birdsong, reminded me of my first days among the Turks. How the exquisite opposition of such beauty and new life with remembered pain and death of all hope in a dark house in Pera sometimes came close to tearing my soul apart. How a year ago, through the machinations of Sofia Baffo—or my own stupidity and youth—I had lost family, homeland, manhood, more than most men could lose without considering their lives at an end.

My lady was aware of my pain now, even with the pressure of friends and family upon her, and I was grateful. Then I caught Safiye's scrutiny upon our silent communication. Our little maid had pulled back Safiye's veils as if they were curtains on a theatre act in which some heinous murder lay revealed.

That face had not changed from the first time I saw it—and settled my own fate in the same instant. If anything, Baffo's daughter had grown more beautiful. The convent garden where we'd first become acquainted had provided an ill medium for the cultivation of women's appearance when compared to the imperial harem. Still, she stood out, even among women scoured from an empire for their loveliness.

Her glorious golden hair and almond eyes had intensified during the year of our acquaintance like a quarter moon coming to its full. The cold demonic nature of that moonlight could turn a man's reason. Time was when it had turned mine. Knowing of what she was capable, using that breathtaking beauty as her weapon, I looked away in horror. And Safiye's exquisite alabaster features quickly covered any signs of disapproval at what she had seen pass between my lady and me.

Still, I vowed to keep an eye on her. And hoped, for once, that the castrator had done his job well enough to make me immune to her infection.

Now the admiration of the rooms, which had hardly even started, was interrupted by Nur Banu. "Do you remember our Quince, Esmikhan Sultan, my dear?"

The Kadin gave over her veils and wrappers to our slaves with a flash of her commanding eyes. She was a handsome woman still, her formerly raven-black hair now wearing the bronze cast of gray-covering henna, but those eyes, demanding obedience, were as bright as ever.

"The harem's midwife?" my lady asked. This woman I'd never met before with the medicinal smell of stored linen bent to kiss my lady's hem. "But of course. Madam, you are welcome." And

Esmikhan returned the kiss of honor with a nod of deference. "You delivered my mother of me, I believe."

"Indeed, lady, I had that honor."

Few women own as much power as the midwife in a harem. Of course, this explained the woman's awkwardness. A midwife alone is included in a harem not because of her beauty and grace but because of her intelligence and skill. I was ashamed of the threat I'd felt from this woman at first and was glad I hadn't acted on it.

And how apt her nickname! Never had the exigencies of womanhood swollen out a more bulbous shape. Her skin had a yellow, quincelike cast to it, exaggerated by the olive green of her coin-trimmed head scarf and a great deal of facial hair she had not the self-absorption to remove. Not to mention her stored-fruit smell.

"Nur Banu Kadin has decided the Quince ought to stay with you, my dear Esmikhan, until your baby is born."

This was Safiye speaking, diverting attention from the cloud that had imperceptibly passed over the conversation, for few had forgotten that my lady's mother had died with her birthing. Did I owe Baffo's daughter a debt of gratitude for this consideration? I doubted it. How could Safiye know of something that had happened in Turkey fifteen years ago? Or care?

"For me, Auntie?" Esmikhan turned to Nur Banu.

"It was Safiye's idea."

"No one can deny the Quince's skill," Safiye said.

"Bordering on magic," Nur Banu concurred.

The room was warm. Why did I shiver?

Nur Banu continued: "The Quince well deserves her place as attendant to the births of princes and princesses."

My lady said: "To have the Quince sent to my lying-in, even just for an hour or two, even if she did no more than hold my hand . . . Why, this is an honor."

"Honor for a woman," Safiye said, "equal to the honor for a man if your husband the Vizier puts in an appearance at the circumcision of his son."

"Well, you shall have her," Nur Banu said. "In your house as a permanent guest, working her magics day and night against miscarriage and injury from these very early months."

"Auntie, this is an honor indeed."

"For the Sultan's first great-grandchild, you should have expected no less."

Was there a subtle jab here by the older woman at Safiye's continued childless state? Safiye turned with dignity to an open window, above such pettiness, and my lady moved quickly lest any offense be attributed to her failure as a hostess.

"Thank you," my lady said. "And thank you, Quince. We can make room for her, Abdullah, can we not?"

Before I had time to reply to my lady's deference, Safiye ingressed, "Oh, my dear Esmikhan. You don't ask a *khadim* if the arrangements are to his liking. You tell him how things are going to be."

Where I had seen no difficulty with this extended visit before, with Safiye's snipe I suddenly had a most desperate one. But how to express my unease? The rummage through my brain left me speechless for a moment.

"You will see, Abdullah, that the Quince is made comfortable in the room next to mine." Flawlessly, my lady took her cue from Baffo's daughter.

"As you will." I bowed with stiffness as if I'd never made such a movement in my life before. Desperate for excuse, I continued, "But I must remind you, lady, the workmen for the summer rooms have stored their tiles and plaster there. It would take all day to clear it."

Safiye's glance read, *Well, then, you'd better get started right away, hadn't you, eunuch?*

She said nothing, however, as if yielding graciously herself to the Sultan's granddaughter, who said, "Of course, Abdullah, you're right. But then the Quince must sleep with me in my room. You won't mind, madam, will you?"

"Not at all. This way I can better judge the instant, Allah forbid, anything should go amiss."

"It is most gracious of you."

As she spoke these words, my lady failed to see a glance that passed between the Quince and—of all people—Sofia Baffo. I was more determined than ever to stop this new arrangement in our home, but I could think of no way to do it. By this time, too, Esmikhan had already slipped her arm into Safiye's and was leading the way toward the divans and the lattices thrown wide against the heat.

Safiye said: "If you'd like, Esmikhan, the Quince can tell you right today if it's a boy or a girl you're carrying."

"Can she?" Esmikhan turned with such excitement to the midwife that the gauze of her head scarf stuck to the pink flush on her windward cheek. "Can you really do that, madam?"

"You doubt my skill, lady?"

"No, no. Of course not."

"Because such predictions are the easiest part of a midwife's work."

Esmikhan caught a reproving glance from me, swept her hand in a studied gesture of welcome and said: "But first, you must all sit down. Make yourselves at home. Please. Welcome. Guests belong to Allah as well as to the hostess."

So the women draped their skirts around their feet as they tucked up on the various divans according to their status. My lady, however, who'd been pressing her hands together in order to contain her excitement, could no longer. She blurted out: "I should love to have you read the signs for me with your art, madam, if it is the will of Allah."

Having seen that thrill in my lady's face, how could I begrudge her her midwife?

# II

FROM A SAFFRON-COLORED square of silk the midwife had given her, Safiye sprinkled a good cook's measure of salt into the pale part of my lady's dark hair. The well-ground crystals—none larger than the head of a pin, not a cook's coarse lumps—glinted with anticipation, like sequins in her curls.

Meanwhile, Esmikhan sat and blushed and squirmed to have every eye on her with her head uncovered, as she usually only bared it in the bath. Her locks were still sweat-damp and -dented into the shape of the cap she twiddled now between her fingers. She hadn't been on such display even as a bride.

"She squirms," the Quince diagnosed.

"She is only nervous," Safiye protested, putting an arm about her friend's brocaded shoulders. "Aren't you, my dear?"

Esmikhan made the effort not to be, and only blushed the more.

"She doesn't itch," Safiye declared.

"She does, but she restrains herself with a princess's restraint," the Quince countered.

"The salt doesn't itch your scalp, does it, Esmikhan?"

"No, no, not yet," my lady replied, as though determined to create an itch if that would please.

"You see? It should itch like lice, didn't you say, Quince?"

"No, it doesn't itch. Is that bad?" Nervousness washed from my lady's face to give place to a pallid fear.

"It's been long enough now," Safiye urged the midwife. "She doesn't itch."

"She doesn't itch," the Quince conceded with a shrug. "She carries a boy."

The company let out its bated hope in an audible sigh. "A boy! *Mashallah!* A boy!" They exclaimed all round and took turns congratulating their hostess.

Over this pleasant confusion, I saw Safiye shoot slivers of almond eyes at the midwife, some sort of stern call to duty. The Quince shrugged without commitment, but asked me to fetch her a pair of scissors and a knife.

*These are sharp blades,* I thought as I handed them to her with a complaisant little bow. *Imagine them sinking into my flesh—or worse, my lady's.* My hand found the hilt of my own dagger and shifted it somewhat out of my sash, just in case.

The happy bevy of women brushed the last of the salt out of Esmikhan's hair and replaced her cap, its veils and its ruby-rose ornaments. While they were so distracted, the Quince slipped behind them to my lady's vacated cushion on the divan. I followed the healer closely, saw her secret the two cutting implements behind the cushion, and got a firmer grip on my dagger. I had faced a pack of brigands in defense of my lady's honor; I would not hesitate to face a midwife.

"She sits to the left, she sits to the left." Safiye's declaration after having observed Esmikhan's attempt to settle back down on her cushions brought me up short.

Wondering, delighted with surprise, Esmikhan withdrew

the hardness she felt through the figured velvet and wool stuffing of the left side of her cushion. It was the knife.

With another shrug, the Quince announced, "A boy. She sat on the knife. That means a boy."

Only another harmless divining device. I really did get too jumpy when Safiye was in the room.

"*Mashallah,* a boy for certain." Over all the renewed exclamations of joy, Safiye's was the only one that seemed to contain a hint, not so much of sorrow, but almost of doom.

"*Mashallah,*" my lady echoed her guests. "Oh, but I grieve to have you here, Quince."

"Esmikhan, lady, why say you so?" Nur Banu asked.

"Because her presence is a clear indication that no baby more royal than my own is expected in the coming months." Esmikhan reached for Baffo's daughter's hand. "Dear Safiye, can't you give me word that my child will have a little cousin to play with?"

Safiye, it seemed, had so little hope of becoming pregnant that she couldn't even hunch her shoulders and say, "If Allah is so pleased."

One of Nur Banu's slaves, Aziza, began to accompany the conversation and the feasting with the same haunting tune my lady had sung earlier:

"*One thousand and one tales have been written about me.*
*My home is this place where gods are buried*
*And devils breed,*
*The land of holiness,*
*The backyard of hell.*"

Aziza had a lovely voice. She was a pretty thing, too, but now consigned to the rank of menial since Prince Murad had rejected her in favor of Safiye. I suppose she sought to ingratiate herself to the company in the best way she knew how. She would show *she* was not unpleasantly aloof.

After Safiye had achieved her purpose—the entrusting of Esmikhan and her unborn child to the astringent mercies of the Quince—Baffo's daughter had completely turned from the society of the room. She gazed absently now through the latticework of polished olive wood. Even a guest who'd been to two weddings and a circumcision before she entered our rooms would have shown more interest in the dainties that Esmikhan presented. It was nothing short of ill-mannered to ignore platter after platter, crowded rim over rim beneath the tulips on the room's three low tables.

My lady personally supervised the kitchen and was not averse to getting her velvets dusted with flour as she turned out the various Turkish sweets as delightful and voluptuous as their names: "Woman's Navel," "Ladies' Thighs," "Lips of the Beauty." There was lokhoum, that fruit paste that called for the stirring of two pots over the flame simultaneously, in white grape, mulberry, apricot, and quince jelly flavors. And of course, my lady had turned out hundreds of deep-fried "Little Bonnets of the Turks," one entire extra tray for no other reason than that they were Safiye's favorites. But these, too, Baffo's daughter seemed to ignore that day.

I surprised myself by taking Safiye's negligence personally. It wasn't presumptuous to include myself in the credits for the stacks of treats with which we dazzled, honored, and rather overwhelmed our guests. I had done what was asked of me to make these trays for the palate what the intricate inlay of mother-of-pearl and ivory of the new rooms were to the eye. No, I realized as my offense grew. I took pride in my part, though a year ago I would have scoffed at it as being something "any housewife can do." Of course, any Turkish housewife was confined to that house. She needed her eunuch to make things run smoothly, and I had done it. Why else was I hovering around up here with the women instead of downstairs with my cronies if not to see how it all went?

If I say so myself, my lady and I were learning to work well together. Economy meant nothing to her, as a princess first and now a Vizier's wife. She was used to having any desire appear at the first thought, and it became my challenge to work that magic for her. Spurred by her taste and delight in the best the world had to offer, and the world's best marketplace, Constantinople, out our front door, I had shopped. When desire to disparage the skill had crept up on me, sometimes just to keep my self-respect, I had remembered my training under my dear dead uncle. To haggle, bargain, and trade was done by the richest of merchants as well as the lowliest housewife.

So I gave credit to myself, even if the ladies gave it to their hostess. All my trips to the bazaar for fabric swatches before she finally settled on that figured magenta velvet for the divans that ran around three walls. All the purchasing of skilled seamstress-slaves for the gold work on drapes and coverlets. All the hauling of Persian carpets back and forth as they failed to please in the salon's afternoon light. Not to mention the simple logistics of letting workmen into the inner sanctum while at the same time giving the ladies some sort of privacy. All the trips to the latrine—which were frequent at this stage of my lady's pregnancy—had to be negotiated, for the only route lay through this salon. And there was the master's mother, a gnarled, deaf blank most of the time, but apt to disorientation and immodest wanderings when her environment was disturbed.

I begrudged Esmikhan none of her guests' delighted praises for the accomplishments of either interior decorating or the kitchen. In the service of the kitchen, too, I had risen to the challenge, aiding the success in ways that a secluded woman cannot imagine.

Who saw to the quality of the olives, the honey, shrewed the merchant for his rancid oil? When this sudden warm snap made the icemen's usual cartloads melt, who arranged for the horseback riders? The riders had raced the nearly twenty *farsakh* from the mountain the Turks called Olympus, vying with the ancient Greek place of the same name, where the snowcap is stored over summer in caves. The riders had raced back with their panniers of ice wrapped in flannel and cooling vines showing only the first hint of dampness. I had paid them what such a chase was worth so our guests had to give no thought to the delicious coldness of their sherbets. They had only to make a choice of flavors from the assortment with which my lady dazzled them—rosewater, aloe, linden, ambergris, or gardenia.

Esmikhan had worked on the blending of syrups like an Alto Adige vintner with his wines. These oversweetened things with ingredients I was used to calling perfumes and medicines were hard for a Venetian to take in the place of his daily libation. Sometimes I wanted a glass of the basic old Bardolino in the worst way. And I often thought that, given the present state of my life, I would quickly and easily drown in my cups—if cups were available. That was one more void for which to damn Islam.

But at Esmikhan's hand I had learned to appreciate the tang of lemon-almond with a little linden—innocent of intoxication. And to appreciate that sherbet could sicken if it wasn't cold. I saw to it that every glass she served was very, very cold.

I did not mind that our guests gave Esmikhan the credit, nor even that she took it to herself with blushes of pleasure. That was the form of Turkish manners; watching the quiet satisfaction of others was a new sort of triumph for me.

When I was a man, I had disparaged such things, and would have turned away to look at the view as if I were above food and drink, even as Safiye was doing. Her disregard shamed me and, when I saw through the shame, I was infuriated. Baffo's daughter was a woman; she should know better.

Her negligence was almost as if she had written off Esmikhan. The world of power and politics might write off my dear, sweet lady, might not even know that she existed. Because Esmikhan had no wish in her heart but to please—and particularly to please Safiye, whose beauty, liveliness, and daring held my lady entranced—men would take my lady for granted. Would Baffo's daughter do the same?

Or would Baffo's daughter reject another woman just for having a baby? In Safiye's almond eyes this condition seemed almost to remove my lady from the cycle of living instead of entrenching her all the more deeply in it.

"Ah, she dreams of her prince."

The Quince spoke, watching Safiye's detachment with a long, warm, bubbly drag on her pipe. The midwife had brought her own wad for the bowl and I couldn't distinguish its smell over all the other odors compressed in that hot room.

The lattice work at the window mimicked the room's new inlay, with the gleam of blue-gray sky in place of mother-of-pearl. Over a fringe of pine and cypress, the height of the house's situation revealed a prospect of the sea, its islands and the blue-hazed Asian mountains.

No chance existed that Safiye would see Murad through that window. At her feet bloomed no more than a quiet spot in the harem garden where the tulips, in profusion, remained oblivious or even defiantly careless of the power ploys of men. I suspected her mind was not on Murad, but that was because mine was not.

Lawn was being cut somewhere by men with scythes, hard, but sweet-smelling work. These spring sights and sounds reminded me once again that a year almost to the day we had first come to this city, Safiye and I. She had told me once how she

had passed regiments of tulips to enter "the belly of this beast"—
as she'd called the imperial harem—for the first time.

But I should have known better than to think that Safiye's
thoughts had time for any such sentimentality. Still less were
they, as Esmikhan's compassion made her weep to think, cen-
tered on prayers for a child of her own.

Safiye did not speak to defend herself, however. Curiously,
it was Nur Banu who did, leaping into the silence after the
Quince's statement rather more hastily than necessary.

"Allah preserve him, my friend, but do you remember the
night my son was born?"

"I do indeed." The midwife smiled, nodding at Esmikhan to
listen now and gain a young woman's education for her own
birthing.

"We had a time getting him to suck, didn't we? Four wet
nurses we went through, and all the time it was his own per-
versity."

"Yes. The little lion refused to suck for three . . ."

"Four days. It was four."

"Yes, it was almost four days."

"I was sure he would starve."

"All he needed was to get hungry enough. Then he sucked
like a leech."

"Praise Allah, he did all right then."

The midwife continued thoughtfully, "I always take omens
from the birth of a child and his first few days."

"Are such omens trustworthy?" Esmikhan asked.

"Of course," the Quince replied. "Your brother—he has been
the same with affairs of state as he first was with sucking. For
years we wondered if he would ever latch on. But this past year,
we have seen a marvel. He is everywhere—in the Divan, inviting himself to the counsels of the viziers, speaking his mind
when the most reverend of religious judges hold court."

"*She* puts him up to it." Aziza had stopped singing and stepped out of place now to express her resentment.

Safiye took, or seemed to take, no notice of the accusation and Nur Banu did her best to silence the other girl, even if she could not nullify her.

"He does it to prove himself a great man," Nur Banu said, "worthy of the sword of his ancestors."

"Worthy of the Fair One's love," the Quince purred cattily through her smoke.

Aziza seemed more comforted to find her suspicions confirmed by the wise old woman than she had been when they were simply brushed aside. At least she did not think it out of place to give one more comment. "He even takes liberties with Suleiman, the Sultan—may Allah preserve him—all at *her* instigation."

"Suleiman is a far greater man than his grandson has yet become," the midwife said. "He takes little notice of Murad's pretensions."

"He does indeed take notice," Nur Banu defended herself through her son. "He is proud to have such a grandson."

"Well, he may be forced to take notice at this latest request," the midwife admitted, "as one must take notice of a mosquito when it bites." The Quince was perhaps the only woman in Islam who could speak her mind freely to Nur Banu and get away with it. "Murad has bitten the teat, we may say, and the wet nurse must turn from her pleasure at the candy tray to slap him, be he prince or no."

"He asked for a ship to take him—and Safiye—back to Kutahiya for the summer," Nur Banu continued her defense. "You are staying here with Esmikhan this year, else you would remember, my dear Quince, how wretched that journey overland is."

"How dangerous and full of brigands," Aziza added with a look at Safiye.

"And how one cannot be blamed for making every attempt to avoid it," Nur Banu concluded.

"But to ask for a galley when the Faithful are now in open war against the infidel of Europe and every vessel is needed for the defense of our shores?" the Quince said. "Add to that the fact that as the mainstay of his harem Murad has a Christian girl, the daughter of a very powerful governor of the Venetian Republic for whom great ransom has been offered. No, the wet nurse Suleiman must be doting in his old age if, besides letting Murad suck at his power all winter, he lets the boy now take a bite."

Safiye turned from the window to the company with a smile that startled us all with its indication that her mind had not really been absent, but had carefully and with deep scrutiny overheard every word of the recent interval's conversation.

"Then the Sultan *is* doting, may Allah preserve him," she said, weighing her words for just the right measure of disrespect and surprise, and watching like an alchemist for the various reactions they caused in every face present. "For my lord, the prince, sent me word just after morning prayers today. I am to meet him quayside on Thursday in the afternoon. He has been promised the galley, and we shall have such a luxurious cruise down the coast at this time of year!"

Nur Banu rejoiced in the sharp-stroke victory of her protégée as if it had been her own, and those who lost the foray sank quietly into their cushions.

Only the Quince ventured a "Well, we shall see" afterwards, and the talk moved hastily on to other, lighter things.

As a matter of fact, the Quince was said to take omens from her smoke, and she was no less prophetic this time than at others.

# III

"DOES MY GRANDSON think he invented love?"

Suleiman's magnificent fuming found its way to the depths of our harem. The Sultan's own love for Khurrem, of blessed memory, was the subject of popular poetry throughout the empire. He could not be outdone by a mere boy.

"Allah willing," Suleiman concluded his tirade, "Murad will learn some sense before he ever comes to the throne of Othman, our ancestor."

What Murad found at the quayside that Thursday morning, there in the presence of Safiye, ready in her traveling clothes, with all her bags and servants, was an old, leaky ketch that barely stayed afloat to carry them across the Bosphorus. They had to make their way back to Kutahiya the same plodding way everyone else did.

When this tale made its way through our lattices, I had to laugh out loud. I had, after all, been on board a ship with Sofia Baffo and would regret it the rest of my days. My laughter, however, grieved my lady endlessly, and three full days afterwards, she was still scolding me for one word of torment I'd side-cast at Safiye during the party.

"I merely suggested to Sofia Baffo that her childlessness may not be only in the hands of the Almighty," I defended myself.

"But I asked you specifically to be nice to Safiye when she came."

I stiffened and she felt it. "I am always nice to Safiye," I said.

"No, you're not."

"As nice as she deserves. And infinitely nicer than she is to me."

"Just try to ignore all that."

"As Safiye ignores me?"

"When she's in a good mood."

"Like a rug beneath her feet." As if to emphasize the phrase, I began to pace our new, deep-piled rugs. The subject of Safiye always made me nervous.

My lady watched me from the divan where, dappled with lattice-strained light, she was teasing a kitten with a peacock feather. "I'm afraid it's a *khadim*'s lot in life to be ignored much of the time."

"And what about when she is restless and irritable?"

"You two do have some spectacular exchanges."

"She starts them all."

"She only has to look at you wrong and you're off."

"It's those eyes of hers."   .

" 'Almonds dredged in poison,' didn't you once say?"

"And that hair."

"Butter."

"That picks up the odor of whatever onion of a man handles her."

"Abdullah, you know she's perfectly faithful to my brother Murad."

I snorted without comment and flung myself to the divan next to her. I know it is not proper form for eunuchs to sit in their ladies' presence, but ours was not the usual mistress-slave relationship. Since my refusal to go by the ridiculous name she'd always wanted to give her first eunuch—"Lulu"— Esmikhan had never tried to mold or even order me. She was too used to being molded herself; there was no older woman, as a harem usually has, to take me in hand.

And I had come too late, too recently to my slavery and sex-lessness to accept the pinch of their molds about me. So rather than being her gossipy *khadim* and a talemonger, I knew it was no use—and no kindness—disabusing Esmikhan's innocence with the truth.

My lady laughed, let the kitten rip the feather away, and took my face gently between her hands so I'd look at her. I closed my eyes against the shame that not all the smoothness I felt was her plump little palms. In the past year it had become clear that I would never grow more beard than I had. I would always smart under this charcoal smudge which had so mortified me when I first met Safiye—Sofia Baffo then—so long ago and far away.

"Ah, sweet lady," I said with my eyes still closed. "You refuse to see malice in anyone."

I caught one hand just before she pulled it away and held it there, to my spayed, stripling cheek.

She declared: "I think your squabbles give you great pleasure."

"You laugh out loud and clap for joy at our antics as if we were baby kittens play-fighting for your amusement."

"Aren't you?" She tugged at her hand and I let it go. "At least, if you must squabble, I wish you'd stop slipping into Venetian all the time, you two. I always feel I'm missing something."

"So you should let me teach you my native language as I've been longing to."

"Perhaps, yes. After the baby . . ." She let one more button out of her *yelek*. "I'll bet even if I knew Italian, I'd be missing something."

I looked away. "I assure you, lady, you are not."

"I get jealous."

"Don't," I said. "Don't ever be jealous of Sofia Baffo."

"Does Safiye ever get the best of you in Venetian?"

"Never."

"Even when she prepares her comments in advance?"

"Does she do that?"

"I think so."

"Never," I said doughtily. "She never gets the better of me."

"That's good."

"Still, I wish . . ."

"You wish what?" Esmikhan urged, resting her little round chin on my shoulder. "That I wouldn't invite her at all? Safiye, who is my dearest friend in the world?"

"No, I don't wish that."

"I can't not invite her." My lady removed her chin and looked away. "Even for your sake, dearest Abdullah."

"I will never say her presence is unstimulating. I always take care not to drowse, no matter how late the hour, when she is here. I'm certain to find myself the brunt of cruel jokes while my eyes are closed."

"But she has lost the ability to consume your every waking thought?"

"Sofia Baffo never consumed my every waking . . ."

I stopped because Esmikhan's glance, gone sideways with perception, made me sound ridiculous.

"She does not make you miserable anymore?" my lady asked.

"That, I thank Allah, is no small victory."

"I hate to think of you miserable, for any reason."

"For that, my lady, I thank you."

"So please, please, treat Safiye with the utmost tenderness."

"For your sake, I will try."

"For *her* sake, Abdullah. It grieves me so much to have this child, this wonderful child, growing within me while she, who has been with my brother months longer than I've been with the Pasha, should have none."

"Ah, so that's what this is all about." I laughed.

"And why shouldn't it be?"

"My dear, tender-hearted little lady." I slipped a hand under the head scarf at her neck and rubbed the tension there.

As I turned her face to me with the pressure of my hand, I could see Safiye's condition pained my lady to speechlessness. How could I let Esmikhan's features—and especially her soul—grow mundane to me?

I changed the subject and turned away as if admiring the room for the first time. Actually I'd been consulted and reconsulted on every chip of mother-of-pearl and ivory inlaid in the olive wood wainscoting.

"Even without the braziers, you were right to be proud to show it to your sisters and friends," I said. "You can be proud of what you've done."

"What we've done, Abdullah. I am sensible that I couldn't have done it without you."

"In any case, it's a vast improvement over what we found here on our arrival," I agreed.

"Oh, yes. Do you remember that first night, Abdullah? 'A palace built by the great architect Sinan,' you promised me."

"Well, it is, isn't it?"

"Yes, but the plaster wasn't even dry. And no furnishings at all. That first night we slept on rolled up rugs in the smell of damp and empty echoes."

"It was an adventure."

"I've been having adventures ever since I met you."

I turned from her look as from a brazier that had grown too warm. "Progress has been made."

"And now that Safiye's gone for the summer . . ." My lady's thought lost itself in a sigh.

"You will miss your family and friends, won't you?"

Esmikhan let out yet another button on her *yelek*—then fastened it back up again. "But I will have the Quince. The baby, *inshallah*. And you."

*"Inshallah,"* I repeated, more because she always said it than because I believed, "If Allah wills." And I smiled at, but didn't provoke, her naive faith. I thought, but didn't say, how my protecting her ability to say *"Inshallah"* 'til death overtook me had very little to do with any will but my own.

# IV

AND THE QUINCE, too, put little faith in anything outside herself. I knew this because several days previous, I'd helped her to set up a whole pharmacopoeia in some of the cupboards concealed within the wainscoting in the new winter rooms.

"No, no, the drugs used in poultices must be kept separate from those taken internally," she had instructed. "I always store them on a separate shelf, else an assistant I send in the night might fetch the wrong item. If nothing worse, precious time may be lost."

No mention of Allah in that, though I wanted to say "God forbid" against the mere idea of such an accident. The Quince went about her business with the perfect assurance that if she put her jars in their proper places, nothing could possibly go wrong.

I gave up trying to help and only watched, fascinated by the confidence she displayed towards these powerful simples. She greeted each with tender strokes and embraces as she unpacked it, sniffed their aromas as a mother breathes in the fragrance of her newborn's hair. She understood where each wanted to sit and how it might best serve and show its peculiar attributes. Few people know their most intimate acquaintance better.

When I exclaimed over the quantity of drugs we were to host, the Quince waved her hand in dismissal. "These are only things I may need here. When I agreed to come and stay with your household, *khadim*, I did not mean to give up my practice with the main harem at the serai, those who are not packing to go with Nur Banu to Kutahiya, or with Mihrimah Sultan, our master's daughter, to Edirne, or just to the Princes' Islands to escape summer's heat. I have my herbs to tend in the garden, see that they get plenty of water through the hot months and are picked when their virtues are at the peak. I must engraft the new girls against the smallpox, help the faithful old servants with the aches and pains of their years of service, the *khuddam* with the ills their particular station is subject to."

"You cannot—you cannot restore one who's been cut such as I—?"

By God, I hated myself when I sounded so pathetic.

I was almost glad when she brushed this question aside as well and scoffed, "No, I can't. And don't you, *khadim*, ever fall prey to those who, when your position makes you rich and powerful, will tell you they can help you. I've treated too many *khuddam* who've believed charlatans. I've treated them for burns—trying to burn back what was lost, can you imagine? I've treated poisonings— Aconite, just think! Aconite is called 'love poison.' People hear the 'love' part and go deaf for the rest. All I've ever seen aconite do is kill the gullible, the desperate, with horrible delirium on the way.

"There's maid's ruin, savory, pepper internal and external, dragon bones . . ." She gestured her list on and on. "Not to mention that five-leafed plant the Chinese like to kill each other over, which they say glows in the night and rises above the ground— I've cuttings in my garden and I've never seen such a thing.

"Charlatans will tell you any or all of these are beneficial, and I can tell you, you'll be lucky if you only waste your wealth and not your health. If you're not belly-cut, yes, there can sometimes—rarely—be a remedy. If the cutters left you something to work with, I could prescribe. But what usually happens is the desperate urge without the ability. No, don't waste your life looking for the cure. There is none."

By heaven, I was almost relieved to hear it, her sentence of lifeless life. A sort of desperate panic that had been eating at my heart—most would have called it hope—took love's poison and died.

She continued: "The same as there is no escape from death. I make those Allah has marked comfortable with pain-numbing draughts, but I never give false promises. I cannot raise the dead. I cannot grow your parts again. No one can. And if the pain of that terminal knowledge is too great for you, I can recommend opium. You won't be the first *khadim* I've ordered it for. All I can say is, it's too bad to ruin a life so young as yours with a poppy haze. I've seen it happen, but it's a shame when the only lack in your life is a bit of flesh between your legs. I might as well take to the pipe myself, for being female. There are those who do, but it's a great waste.

"Oh, by the bye," the Quince continued, having come across our scissors and our knife during her straightening and handing them to me. "I think these are yours."

"Yes," I replied. "Thank you." I swung away on my heel to return the implements to their places, but then came back to her, holding the knife foremost. "So it's a boy?"

"How should I know?" The midwife now found her herb pots better company than myself.

"But you said, if my lady sat on the knife side of her cushion, it was a boy. And she did."

"Old wives' tales. Hocus-pocus."

"But you do it."

"I do it because it's expected. Safiye in particular wanted to know." I tried to read more out of her face on this theme, but she wouldn't give it. Heedless, she continued: "Knives and scissors behind a cushion, salt in the hair—these things, these charlatans' ploys, they're harmless. Not like what the quacks might do to you."

They'd already done their worst to me, I thought, then said: "Such hocus-pocus might make a woman hope for what is not to be."

For the first time, the Quince looked studiously away from me, almost as if she couldn't meet my eye. "Well, usually the readings of such idle tricks are ambiguous. Or one trick contradicts the other. I guess you could say I always try to read 'eunuch.' "

She laughed at her joke at my expense and went on. "Your lady's readings are, in fact, the first time I've ever had two unequivocal readings both say 'boy.' And part of that was Safiye, pushing me for a definite answer. Usually I try on purpose to leave some doubt or push the answer towards a girl child in one or both cases. That way the mother can always be pleasantly surprised.

"Though why," the Quince concluded, "I can't say." She passed her hand lovingly over the swollen belly of her angelica jar; angelica, to promote women's courses. "I've always been much more partial to females myself."

After this conversation with the midwife, I was completely at ease to have her in our house. I might have accepted Italy's birthing-demons if I'd stayed in my homeland the rest of my life, never knowing any others. But I was much more skeptical when confronted with a new, different, conflicting demonology. The Quince's unsentimental dashing of my secretly held hopes strengthened rather than diminished my trust in her. I liked her hard, no-nonsense view of the world and, while trusting souls to her might cause scruple, I had no problem about bodies, either my lady's or my unborn little master's.

It seemed clear that the sense of threat I'd gotten from her came rather from Safiye. And now that Baffo's daughter was *farsakh* upon *farsakh* away—whether by land or by sea made no difference to those who stayed behind—the threat was gone, too.

FROM THE FIRST twinge of life she felt inside her, my lady loved that child of hers with a love women dream to find in husbands; later, thwarted there, in lovers, and most are lucky if they are content to find it in fairy tales. It was a passion that did not consume, or turn the possessor inward, but gave her a quiet, joyful strength and compassion for those in the rest of the world who were not blessed as she. So Esmikhan would not allow me to take the mirth in the episode of Safiye and the leaky ship I would have.

My lady's joy and strength were like a sore thumb that seemed to catch on everything, and she took great, cautious steps to avoid injuring the weaknesses of others.

Her new, sublime compassion fell short of Madonna quality in this, however: it did not prove to be immortal.

Her babe, a boy, though he gave a healthy yell when he entered the world that midsummer, left it again within the hour.

At first I took comfort with the thought, *Time will heal this. She is young. She is not the first mother to lose a child. With time, she will conceive again.*

But instead, that time extended into a hellish eternity for Esmikhan Sultan, who conceived, bore, and then immediately lost another small son.

I knew nothing of birthing rooms. I only saw the tiny white

bundles hastened off to the graveyard with hardly a wink from religious authority. I saw the Quince's hard, grim look—in want of baking and sugar I thought. And I heard—helplessly—Esmikhan's grief. My lady, though always patient and submissive to the will of Allah, could not come through this tragedy unmarked.

During this time, I almost came to believe in the malicious old jinn-hag who was said to haunt birthing rooms seeking to steal infants or their mothers. I heard some of the women speaking of this witch in hushed tones. And though Esmikhan wouldn't let the hag's name pass her lips at any time lest she call the jinni to her thereby, I could tell by her fearful glances to dark corners that she, too, believed.

But the Quince's hard look did not believe. *That's life,* was all I read there. And because she had forced me to accept my life, I accepted her word. Safiye, after all, was never anywhere near our tragedy.

Yet, there are days, midsummer days, when the sky over Constantinople is a thick, dusty, putrid yellow. Many such days I suffered when I was being unmanned. On just such a day my mistress' first son was born and died. On such days, the city, usually so divine, shows her mortality like capers, growing in every crack.

# Part II

## Safiye

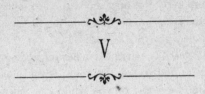

# V

Safiye unfolded herself from the confines of the carriage and, though veils and wrappers still burdened her, she stretched her long limbs to rid them of the cramp. They'd just been visiting within the city. The cramp, she knew, was not so much from being cooped up with three other women in the velvet-lined box for the short ride as it was from seeing yet another winter pass. Yet another martial parade of tulips was splitting its green sheaths with vibrant color in the courtyard of the serai. Yet another winter had passed with the power she had sensed and craved upon first entering the marble harem beast still eluding her—or at least, not growing as quickly as she liked.

It was the end of winter in the year of Our Lord 1564 as the Christians tell the passage of time. Safiye was sixteen years old; she had been among the Turks now for a full eighth of that time, the oldest, most vigorous eighth.

Every passing day confirmed her understanding of the workings of this system into which she'd thrown her lot, her appreciation for the magnitude of power it could give her, outstripping anything she'd hoped for in Venice. But the heedless passage of time exaggerated her frustration at the slowness with which she could make that power hers.

Yes, she knew that paying calls, binding the highest-placed ladies to her with gifts and acts of graciousness was necessary. She exerted herself in this direction; there wasn't a woman among the Turks now who wouldn't take seriously her most offhanded comment. But how she wished to pierce the gauze of this veil, to reach—more importantly, to affect—the hard reality of the men's world beyond!

How to do this? The tenseness in her limbs demanded some action, but her mind couldn't name it. It was like sitting passive, immobile, for hours on end while a friend painted your hands with henna paste. Most Turkish women—perhaps because they'd experienced having their hands painted since they were children—were content with such endless waiting. Safiye thought of Esmikhan Sultan as the prime example. The girl might as well be a cushion on her own divan!

No doubt most women in Venice were the same. Safiye remembered the aches in her knees after a long convent vigil and remembered, too, that she must not think of "home" anymore. As long as inertia was expected of her, she could never really be settled in either place.

She tried to think where the blocks to her action were. The old man, surely. Sultan Suleiman, after a reign of over forty years, showed no signs of dying.

Idly, but not for the first time, Safiye wished him dead, just to see how the pieces might fall with that great keystone gone. Interesting chaos, ready for the swift and clever to form at their own will.

Her thoughts moved to the next step. Poison was the most obvious means for a woman to use on a man: quiet, easy of access, needing no physical strength or even incriminating contact.

And the Quince would provide.

Safiye, in the past months, had even checked on the dishes the Sultan preferred and how they were served—only to discover that he had incorruptible poison-tasters.

Damn these veils that kept her from using her wiles as lavishly as she'd like!

Then she'd learned about the celadon porcelain on which every morsel the great lord ate was served. The pale grayish-green of its glaze would reportedly turn an incriminating black if it came in contact with anything the least bit unwholesome. Poison Safiye could consider, but her mind balked to face such magic.

Nur Banu used the same priceless ware.

In any case, having watched Suleiman as well as lattices and curtains would allow, Safiye—like most of the vast empire—could hardly imagine the world with him dead. The magnificent Shadow of the Faithful roved from one end of the greatest empire in the world to the other with an energy that would have worn down many a younger man. Indeed, it taxed Safiye's intelligence to keep up with him in her mind. This season he was north, battering at the walls of Vienna. Next she heard, he was east, beating the insolence out of Persia's Shah, the Grand Heretic, then ordering the movements of his corsairs out at sea and against her homeland. Now looking 'round the Pillars of Hercules towards restoring Spain to his Faith, now south, against Yemeni or Ethiopian rebels. Or taking on the Portuguese for control of the Persian Gulf shipping routes to India.

Well could this magnificent man boast in his inscriptions: "In Baghdad I am the Shah en-Shah, in Byzantine realms the Caesar, and in Egypt the Sultan. Allah's might and Muhammad's miracles are my companions."

She had observed him in procession on several occasions. Of course the face was not always easy to see within the press of crowds. Often she saw only the turban, the great turban which, in the blaze of sunlight, assaulted the eyes with the purity of its whiteness. Topped with royal heron feathers, it was nearly a third the size of the man himself. This bulbous creation was formed from fifteen lengths measured from the tip of the monarch's nose to the end of his outstretched finger, fifteen lengths of the finest silk and linen woven together. And a duplicate turban was also wound around the end of a pole and carried before him as he progressed, carried by some honored aga who made it bob and nod in recognition of the cheers so that everyone could think he got a good view.

But she had actually seen the man full on. Then his sharply hooked nose, eyes deeply sunken with wisdom into the tough, bony face, the sparse beard just graying that hid nothing of the force of his mouth and jaw——these had set her heart fluttering to the martial beat of his accompanying drums. Gossips told her he covered a sickly complexion with a red paste makeup, but she saw no sign of it, only a ruddy, healthy glow, tanned with the out-of-doors and vigorous activity.

And such splendor surrounded that face for the press of a hundred men in any direction that, it was said, more than a few men were made rich each time he passed. This was just from the gems knocked loose of their casings and casually left behind in the dust for the fortunate to bend and claim.

Although Safiye called him "the old man"——and worse—— disparagingly and aloud any time she chose, to herself Suleiman was, in fact, an astonishingly magnificent piece of manhood. Even so little a thing as his arrival in Aleppo the previous fall for overwintering reverberated glory from the inner heart of the harem to the end of Christendom. She would leave the keystone in place, as a pattern of what she might attain. He deserved every honor the world showered on him——nay, more. How she wished to honor him herself——personally. If only to selfishly drink his splendor to her own.

"I wish I'd been bought for *his* bed." Safiye sometimes couldn't help but openly contradict herself. "Instead of just for his grandson's, so now I can never know him."

"No, you don't," Nur Banu always reminded her with a snap when such words were overheard. "He already has a son, a grown son, old enough to be your father. And a grandson. *My* son, and your lord and master. You just wait your time and do as you're told."

That was the hard part, the waiting. And waiting for this glorious Sultan's death . . . Why, any son of his was much more likely to die first. Suleiman had, in fact, already buried three sons and the single heir left to him, Selim, didn't seem much longer for the world.

Ah, here was the weakness. Prince Selim was a much more profitable chink to pick at in the bastion of Allah's will. Upon first glance and, again, from a distance, Safiye had also been impressed by this presumptive sultan of forty as well as by his father. But now she saw easily through the trappings of his inherited station to his short, corpulent figure and the unhealthy flush under his wobbly turban. There were even rumors he was not Suleiman's son at all, that Khurrem Sultan had smuggled in a lover, and this was easy enough to believe, looking at the man.

But that such a splendid woman as the splendid Suleiman's consort was rumored to have been could have so debased herself was difficult to believe. Safiye found it more reasonable to remember that every litter has its runt and, the more vigorous specimens in this case having torn each other to pieces in their rivalry, Selim was what remained.

There was no need to consider poison in this case; Suleiman's heir was busily poisoning himself.

Here, among the Turks, where indulging in wine was a capital offense, Selim was openly given the epithet "The Sot." The Sultan wrote to his son over and over again, urging him to "relinquish that mad red thing." To no avail. Safiye had never known such a serious drunk even in Italy, where wine replaced mother's milk on a toddler's tongue. Perhaps, she thought—and prided herself on her wisdom—the religious prohibition added to the drink's attraction, created the very evil it sought to eliminate. And surely, having grown into his prime and past it, waiting for his father to die—surely this aggravated the prince's condition as well.

Selim being what he was, yes, it was best to be loved by his son, Murad. Safiye folded herself more firmly in her wrapper, pressing the memory of love's attentions to her breast to keep it safe, a prisoner there. Here, at the bottom of power's ladder, she could mistress not only carnal needs, but the young prince's education and political interests as well. She had turned Murad from the opium, to which he'd been a slave when she'd first been given to him, to the equally alluring but more influential inner workings of the Divan.

Even Suleiman, the most powerful man on earth, had sat up and crinkled his eyes in pleasure to see this change in his grandson. The Sultan's letters to him, which Murad shared with her, contained no scoldings or fatherly threats, but were written man to man and concerned the most urgent affairs of state. If Selim was the weakness, Murad was the tool with which she had to work.

Someday she would have a son, too, of course, to be her tool. But there was no need to look so far ahead yet. The getting of children was for the less resourceful, the more desperate. Those who had no looks that pregnancy might erase. In the meantime, the Quince's pessaries of medicated tar and sheep-tail fat conspired to keep Safiye's present powers unburdened.

The request to sail down the coast had been a setback. That was Murad's doing: he frequently let romance clutter his desires. In his wish to delight her, he had pushed too fast too soon. And in a totally irrelevant direction. Murad never fully realized that if he wanted to please Safiye, he should seek the Sultan's favor and trust, not occasions for voluptuousness.

Safiye felt herself blush with shame at the memory of the leaky ketch floundering in mid-Bosphorous and was glad, for once, for the concealing veils she wore. She had learned a lesson: she must always keep a careful rein on her lover's propensity. Every sign now read, however, that the more sober behavior she had demanded of her prince since that escapade had restored him in the old man's good graces. Perhaps even elevated him higher.

Mentally, she washed the blush from herself and returned to the question: How best to make use of this favor for Murad's benefit? And for her own, of course. A young man could grow bored, indolent—self-destructive like his father—if his prowess wasn't continually challenged.

So might a young woman, for that matter. This particular young woman, anyway, Safiye thought, hugging herself again.

"Why won't you let me buy you a eunuch, my love?" the young prince would always ask her whenever she hinted at these concerns to him. "I'll give you the money. Get yourself a eunuch, the best money can buy. Then you won't have to be so beholden to my mother and her *khuddam*. Anything you wanted, anyplace you wanted to go, wouldn't have to be screened by those watchdogs first. It would be very liberating for you."

"Liberating" seemed an odd word when it was not less she wanted, not *out* of the harem, but more, deeper, into the controlling heart. Still, she'd agree, "It would be nice. If I could find the right eunuch."

Murad would say something like, "I'm sure you could if you'd only look." He'd nuzzle her neck so she couldn't tell exactly what he said, other things on his mind. "You're the cleverest woman I know." Some such nonsense, stating the obvious.

She would return the nuzzle, just enough. Then she would hint, "Your sister Esmikhan Sultan has a eunuch. That Venetian Veniero."

"Who? Abdullah?" Maybe he'd say it. Or maybe he'd start on her buttons with his teeth.

"He has some intelligence." *He could even be dangerous, with what he knows.* She'd keep that part to herself. *What he could tell you about me—* "—My love." That part aloud, with the proper groan of desire as Murad found her breast.

Everyone considered Veniero a mistake of the cutter's knife and of the marketplace. They pitied Esmikhan his youth, his unsettled nature, his lack of experience. But compared to everything else Safiye had seen—*and, my dear princeling, I have looked*—Veniero-Abdullah had promise.

She'd have to be careful: Murad would be in her now and each thrust would bring a new descriptive word to her mind: *whiny, shrill, gossipy, silly half-men like so many geese. They were worse than the lay sisters in the convent.* Of course she meant the eunuchs.

He'd hitch up her thighs awkwardly, so it hurt, with no thought beyond the best and swiftest striking of his immediate goal.

And then the prince would collapse across her, and she'd toy with the cinnamon topknot on the crown of his head and say, "They must cut away part of their brains with the rest of it, my wonderful, glorious master and lord."

But she'd think, *That's where all you men keep your brains. One cut takes it all.*

Esmikhan also had the best of luck with her husband. The Vizier, unlike Prince Murad, was already at the peak of his powers. Sokolli Pasha often held meetings of highest state right there under Esmikhan's innocent little nose. That's another reason why it was good to visit the princess as often as possible.

It was just as well that Esmikhan was no more sensitive to her blessings than to call them "the will of Allah." If she were, poor girl, she would really be a force to reckon with. More than courtesy visits and a midwife would be needed to deal with her.

Safiye had offered Murad's sister a great sum for that eunuch. She'd had her prince offer even more. Esmikhan had merely laughed a silly little laugh and refused to sell him "for anything in the world." Safiye wouldn't be at all surprised if the eunuch himself had something to do with that refusal. Esmikhan, left alone, would do anything to please. Anything.

On the other hand, Veniero, though smart, might not prove biddable enough. Indeed, he showed only signs of rebellion. Towards anyone but Esmikhan.

No, Safiye decided, she had better keep looking. She would find some *khadim,* intelligent but perfectly beholden to her as well. Courage, too, would not go amiss; he should be willing to die for her. Such criteria were easier expressed than met. Her beauty, the key to most of her power over men as well as women—women usually made quick treaty with her open threat—seemed to have but uneven effect on the sexless.

With such thoughts—and a sigh—Safiye made herself move from one velvet-lined box to another, the harem roomier but no less confining than the sedan.

From the sedan through this long passage, a woman had to remain veiled. She took them blind, these uneven stone floors and surprisingly stepped thresholds, plunging from the light of the yard into the narrow, windowless corridor. Safiye negotiated it only by the knowledge of frequent use and by passing from hand to flaccid hand of the ever-present colonnade of eunuchs.

And by the sounds. The brassy, open, official, *tantalizing* sounds of the Second Court milling for the session of the Sultan's Divan grew fainter and more unreal as if being gargled by this throat of marble and tile. And then swallowed completely by the rhythmic lash—heard almost as frequently—of punishment dispensed in the eunuch's courtyard.

Then Safiye realized what sound was missing today. The whistle and beat of the scourge was unaccompanied by any lament from the tortured.

Brushing aside the next pair of guiding hands, she took an unguided turn to the left. Stopping to adjust her eyes to a return to light as she stepped to the edge of the eunuch's courtyard, she watched. The shadow of a plan condensed in her brain.

# VI

SIX FREE-STANDING COLUMNS opened onto the eunuch's yard. Their gray stone capitals, sharply, newly carved with lotuses in relief, declared them to be the exquisite work of Sinan, the imperial architect. Incongruously, a rough wooden canopy hazarded against them, protecting the tilework and the dormitory rooms on the southern wall from extremes of weather. And under this canopy, Safiye saw a pair of great black eunuchs, bulls more than men, rhythmically executing the grim punishment.

The other eunuchs, whites, who were supposed to be guiding Safiye forward to her own rooms, had a keen interest in their black brothers' proceedings. With their tall, sugarcone hats, fur-lined robes in cinnamon red and candied-violet blue, their too-sweet smells, they seemed to be confections, left in the sun and melted to the spot. They ceased paying any attention whether their other veil-wrapped charges tripped and fell while scurrying through the dark passage to the inner chambers. And they made no grunt of protest when Safiye stopped to watch along with them.

One of their own, lying on his back at such an angle that Safiye couldn't see his face, had his legs hoisted up and caught in the wooden bastinado stocks. The black eunuchs laid onto his naked soles with thin, whiplike canes.

This was a preferred form of punishment for odalisques: they might not be able to walk for a month afterwards, but their beauty remained intact. Ten blows was a good number for women; the most recalcitrant rarely required more than fifteen to learn proper obedience.

But Safiye counted twenty lashes as she stood and watched before she gave up counting. The victim was not a black man. White, or rather, earth-colored, tawny, like a lion. His punishers' reeds caught bits of bruised and swollen pink flesh. Tiny droplets of blood arced up and behind the bullmen's dark, felty heads with each swing of their great black arms. But still there was no sound from the victim. The shudders that ran through his prone body seemed due more to the vigor of the blows than to his own quailing.

"Come away, my Fair One." Nur Banu was at Safiye's elbow, speaking gently. "This is not a scene you need to watch. It may linger with you and spoil you for my son's bed tonight."

This concern for the sensibilities of Murad's favorite was something Nur Banu hadn't shown in a long while. Jealousy and competition had welled up too divisively between the two women; Safiye knew Murad's mother could see her only as a supplanter. Safiye, in one part of her mind, knew she should accept the overture with open arms. She had been waiting for just such a move, looking for the chance to make one of her own. It was not helpful to have the harem's head woman so constantly at odds with her, suspecting every move she made.

But the spectacle before her wiped all good intentions from Safiye's mind. "Who is he?" she asked, and budged no more than the beating's victim in response to Nur Banu's pressure on her arm.

"Hyacinth. You remember him, a *khadim* that belongs to

Mihrimah Sultan. Ah, well. She is lax in her discipline, that daughter of our master."

Yes, now Safiye remembered the man. She hadn't recognized the topography of his stripped, well-muscled chest—its valleys and high, flat plains—nor the tangle of mousy brown hair on his head. These features had always been hung with furs and capped with white linen before.

And that mincing name! Hyacinth, for such a figure of a man! It was enough to confuse anyone.

"But what's he accused of doing? Deflowering Mihrimah's virgins?" Safiye nearly laughed at the notion.

"They found him with Selim's current favorite." The subject put bile in Nur Banu's voice.

"When I said 'virgins,' I only half jested. I'd believe this particular *khadim* not only capable but anxious to do so."

"Not with Selim's *girl*," Nur Banu fairly spat her disgust. "With his *boy*."

Now, Safiye made it her practice not to let anything surprise her. Surprise was the first sign of an irredeemable weakness.

So she said: "I can't imagine this sordid little affair can please our master the Sultan's ears." She looked at the older woman with a hard pity. To be unable to wean her man from his drink, let alone a *boy!* "His heir a bugger as well as a drunk. Or . . . ? Yes, perhaps it is better to keep quiet about it."

Nur Banu answered the barely concealed threat in Safiye's words with a look such as a potter might give a vase that displeases and shames him just before he dashes it to the ground. The older woman restrained herself, however, and Safiye swallowed her own spittle into meekness.

There was no reason, Safiye realized, why she couldn't be standing here waiting her turn in the stocks rather than just observing. Her relationship with the harem's first woman had disintegrated to the point where it seemed only a matter of time before Nur Banu decided this pleasure was worth incurring Murad's wrath. Of course Prince Murad was the only male his mother had any control over anymore—this sordid affair with the boy was proof of that. Nur Banu would attack Murad's beloved—and risk his wrath—only with the greatest caution. Still, restraint was best, Safiye decided. It was no use frightening off the game by making it too jumpy too soon.

In spite of her prudent thoughts, Safiye couldn't suppress her next comment: "I for one doubt he's guilty."

She meant her words to more than defy authority. She timed them carefully to the quiet between two blows. They'd carry.

"He says he's not," Nur Banu confirmed, settling her anger with dignity. "But they all say that."

"I believe him." Safiye punctuated off the pulse again.

"He says he only let the boy crawl into his bed for comfort after the rigors of my lord's passion."

For a moment, Safiye imagined herself crawling into that bed. Though she would never confess to the need of such comfort, she felt the pleasure of that warmth, the silent dark, those enfolding arms.

Nur Banu continued: "Hyacinth says he only let the lad cry on his shoulder. But again—they all would say that."

"By Allah, I believe him."

The eunuch in the stocks shifted his tawny mane, ever so slightly, to fix Safiye with a pair of icy, feral blue eyes flecked with green. And she, in return, ever so slightly dropped her veil. He'd recognize her when next they met. If the pain he then shut those eyes against were not too numbing. She hoped it was not.

"Come, Safiye," Nur Banu said. "They won't be at it too much longer. He's bound for the Seven Towers as soon as they've finished here."

"The Seven Towers." Safiye had a hard time telling whether she felt fear or thrill. She often did.

Safiye had never been to the Towers. She had never even seen them, though she knew the ancient fortress, dating to the Christian era, was within the vast palace compound, off where the land walls and the sea walls joined. There, far from—and yet always at the edge of—the mind of the world, prisoners moldered. And there was equipment for more serious tortures than this mild caning. There, only the torturers could hear the screams and extracted confessions over the sounds of the sea and the silencing distances.

The sea also provided a quick and discrete disposal site for those prisoners who did not survive their stay. Most of the rest walked—or were dragged, broken men—to the blocks before the Executioner's Fountain where soon enough their bodiless heads would be displayed as an example to others.

"Yes, take him to the Seven Towers," Safiye said, turning to comply with Nur Banu's urging that she move on. "This bastinado is child's play to such a man."

But she was careful to say this away from the courtyard and under cover of the sound of the lash.

# VII

WITH THE HELP of a mirror, Baffo's daughter could always shut a lattice in her mind against the noise and brilliance of the harem just as the harem shut its lattices against the world. The Quince's green headdress with its gold-coin fringe flashed for a moment in the mirror, but Safiye adjusted the angle and then saw only her own face. The reflected oval fit the mirror's gold enameled rim perfectly.

Tight oval echoes were also formed about her person by the hummingbirds'-egg emeralds in her ears, the matching wren's-egg at her throat—new gifts from her prince. The reverberation of shape gave her pleasure.

Even dearer than pleasure was the image of concentric self, like rings round a pebble dropped in a pond but flowing inward instead of out. This image helped her to focus her being which otherwise, in the harem, was liable to dissipate. Dissipation happened to too many other women she met, women otherwise intelligent and firm of purpose. Such women lost concentration to the diversions of this place, became as silly and vacuous—as it was hoped they would become.

*We are kept here for just this reason,* Safiye mused. *Shortly Murad will send for me—if the Sultan does not keep him too long tonight. My entire day's purpose is for this end. At least they mean it for this end.* But she concluded this thought with a brief consideration of what she had in fact accomplished that day—and of her new eunuch, Ghazanfer, who proved useful in that accomplishment.

Having thus established her sense of purpose—if not to say superiority—Safiye allowed herself to reach out. She took an oval fingertip full of almond and jasmine cream and rubbed it into her face, releasing the cloying scent into the air about her like curls of blood in a warm bath. The alabaster of her face firmed and whitened under the cool smoothness in further layers of perfection.

*When one girl's complexion is praised as being like feta cheese,* Safiye thought, *another's like Turkish delight, I still rejoice in the alabaster of my own. Cheese is too spongy, Turkish delight too tinted and transparent—both too easily dissolved, digested.*

Confirmed in the solidity of her being as well as in its centeredness, Safiye reached out again, letting her attention go further, to the delicate blue glass phial that held her beauty cream. Glass made in Murano, she noticed with no twinge either of homesickness or self-banishment, but rather with an affirmation of the state of trade and policy between her old homeland and her new one.

She looked beyond to the hands that held the vessel towards her, the Quince's greenish knots of knuckle. Then she allowed those hands to take up their own daub of cream and conform it to the oval. Safiye knew that while she herself was alabaster in response to that touch, the midwife's hands, otherwise so confident and calm, would quiver.

They did, like stone-scraped flesh.

Prince Murad's reaction was the same when he caressed her.

The linger of the Quince's fingers grew so long as to annoy. But Safiye took care to keep her annoyance shut behind her mind's grille.

Nor did she bother to break the boundaries of her own oval perfection to wonder about the older woman's fascination. Safiye only knew that the midwife—otherwise so incorruptible—remained vigilant at Esmikhan's. And returned again and again to sit on the cushion next to Safiye with new Venetian glass filled with this new potion and that.

Baffo's daughter wasn't convinced of the efficacy of beauty rituals. She never had been. In this as in everything else she felt self-sufficient, above a groveling slavery to fashion. She was certain she had won Murad and continued to hold him not because of any human concoction but by a touch of God.

Safiye had the feeling that her face had, in fact, been made in much the same manner as divine fire honed the prophets of old. She had an innate right to be beautiful, and heaven would allow no hindrance to the authority beauty gave her, that same heaven's open gift. This was perhaps the extent of her theology in either her native religion or her adopted one. If pushed to a corner, however, or even on the rack, she might confess nothing more: Safiye Baffo recognized no divinity beyond the rim of her own face.

Still, if cloves and ginger were no fail-proof way to attain irresistibility for those God had not blessed, Safiye saw no harm in the spices. She saw no harm in any ritual—whether prayer or fasting or feasting—she discovered here among the Turks.

The tingle in the Quince's fingers: Well, it might be the burn of cloves, of ginger, nothing more. But Safiye needed very little convincing to see that these rituals did serve beyond the surface. Their rare ingredients did have efficacy greater than merely translating her God-given gift to the Turkish vernacular.

And then the Quince let the quiver affecting her olive-green fingers move to her tongue. "Pepper is cheap in the spice market," the midwife said, following the curve of Safiye's cheek down to oval chin as if touching holy relics and uttering prayer instead of venalities. "It's so cheap, I'd almost scrub my pots with it in place of sand. A pity there's little beauty benefit in pepper, my sweetest mountain flower. But I've stocked up on enough sacks of the stuff to poultice a hundred winters' coughs."

"That'll be the twenty thousand *quintals* of pepper Sultan Suleiman's ships have confiscated from the Portuguese in the Indian Ocean." Safiye spoke, and watched in the mirror how entranced the Quince's fingers were by the slightest movement of her lips.

"You care a lot about the source of your spices," the midwife commented. "More than about the spices themselves, I think."

Safiye smiled and condescended to speak some more. "This cargo has been brought to Alexandria. Thence some comes to us in Constantinople, much to the Venetian traders for an excellent price."

"You favor the traders of your homeland, fairest of the fair?"

The Quince asked it as if she would willingly capture the moon for Safiye if that would please as well as a coup for Venice.

"In this case, what helps the Venetian Republic helps the realm of Islam, too. I do not pick sides except against the Portuguese who, ever since their ships rounded Africa, have had unfair—uncustomary—advantage of the Indian seas."

"No wonder the cooks have been over-peppering the sauces lately."

"Your ambition, my Quince, extends no further than your belly?"

"While yours, my fair one, encompasses the entire earth." Was that a note of exasperation in the midwife's tone?

" 'Where the pepper goes, there goes the gold,' was a saying when I was a child." Safiye unfurled her eyelids and drawled, letting the midwife think she was half aswoon with caresses. "I remember the smell when, as a child, we'd pole through the canals where the richest merchants warehoused. Sometimes cloves, sometimes cinnamon, but always, always pepper. The smell of wealth. The smell of power."

"Come to my surgery, heart of my heart." The Quince quieted to a whisper in her intensity. "Leave this silly, garish communal hall. You shall smell that smell again."

Safiye pushed a smile up into the cream on her cheeks as if the offer were a great temptation. She was, in fact, delighting in another brief reverie of her new eunuch. Finally, she had found a *khadim* of her own, and such a one as might be an extension of herself. It seemed to be the Quince's touch that thrilled her. But it was in fact a more mystical thrill, a sharing with Ghazanfer of what she knew he must be accomplishing at that moment.

Safiye didn't reply to the midwife's invitation. Instead, when the tantalization of clairvoyant union with her eunuch had past, she spoke in another vein. She retained in her voice, however, the note of husky desire which, she knew, drew the midwife to her like a lodestone.

"How the war with Portugal goes will affect how willing you are to slather my face with any of your concoctions, my dearest Quince."

"Fair one, I would not hesitate to do so if almonds were as dear as gold."

Safiye sighed as if the entire world conspired against their mutual attraction. "I wish——" She let the Quince's imagination fill in the wish voluptuously, then continued, glancing at the crowded room about them as if that alone thwarted the mutual granting of that wish.

"——I do wish our lord the Sultan would free enough men from other arenas to complete construction of that canal joining our Mediterranean Sea to the Red Sea at Suez. That would defeat the upstart, renegade Portuguese once and for all, have them on their knees before us to spice their sausages."

"What can a ditch through some desert possibly have to do with you here, my heart?"

"Sometimes you do surprise me in the narrowness of your thinking. You are an intelligent woman, my Quince. The most intelligent in this harem."

"Do I take that as a compliment?" The Quince struggled a bit with her veil, the first effort in that direction she had evidently made all day.

"Of course."

"I'm not certain. Sometimes I'd rather hear you call me beautiful."

"Well, my Quince, you're clearly not . . ."

Safiye bit her tongue and was much relieved to hear the midwife laugh, as if this were no matter.

"Sometimes I think you equate beauty with wisdom," the Quince said, "as if anybody with any sense would chose to be beautiful if she could."

"Well, certainly, any woman . . ."

"And so this makes you not only the fairest in our harem, but the most intelligent as well?"

Safiye was glad to hear the other woman laugh again, although it was a fuzzy, bitter laugh, like her nickname, the Quince. Safiye did not trust herself to make a reply, however. How could she, without offense? Or without striking the phial from the midwife's hand.

The Quince spoke first. "I'm not so certain as you are. Oh, not that you aren't fair and intelligent, my Safiye, but that the two keep good company most of the time. Or that beauty is to be preferred above intelligence. And both outweigh a certain sweetness, kindness, concern for one's fellows. Love."

"Oh, my Quince! Who are you to speak of loving kindness and tender mercy? You have a heart, we all know, as hard and tart as your namesake fruit."

The midwife shifted on her cushion, clearly made uncomfortable by the barest hint of accusation, of blackmail.

"But do the narrow walls of this harem cramp your mind as well?" Safiye continued.

"My Safiye, does the lure of a distant mirage blind you to what is here, this that is more real than realms and principalities?"

"What can be more important than the spread and security of our master Suleiman's empire? That empire that will be Murad's. And our son's."

"And yours?"

"Yes, and mine."

"Allah willing."

"Allah willing, of course."

After a pause spent conforming the movement of her heavily used hands to the ellipse of Safiye's skin, the Quince's cause, whatever it was, subsided. The midwife regained her contentedness to give Safiye anything, even her topic of conversation.

"In spite of the distance," she said, "I understand our lord receives ambassadors from Calicut, Malabar—as far away as Sumatra—pleading with him in the name of that Islam we share to come to their defense against these heathen Portuguese."

The Quince took up no more almond cream on her fingers, for Safiye's alabaster was already slick with it. But she kept working on that face. From temple to lips, from bridge of nose to point of chin she slipped, as loathe to part contact as a lover at dawn.

Safiye closed her eyes and sighed, trying to set the tone between the satisfaction the Quince was hoping to evoke and the disappointment and frustration the conversation made her truly feel.

Safiye said: "And to each supplicant our lord gives a cloth of gold coat of honor, a sack of silver aspers—but not the artillery and master gunners they want. They deserve."

"I suppose a man, even a sultan, cannot be everywhere at once, and must pick and chose his battles."

"And the harem, a woman's country, denies a woman the right to be anywhere."

"But that same denial allows her to be much more omnipresent than a man's world allows him."

*This again. What was the midwife driving at? Let her keep to her potions and magics, things she can understand.* But for an instant, Safiye felt herself drawn in by the sweep of the hand across her face and she kept her thoughts to herself.

The Quince continued, lulling: "A woman is invisible, yet the touch of her finger is everywhere."

"Like Allah?" Safiye purred.

"Like Allah," the Quince replied.

# VIII

SAFIYE SMILED AT the notion of an invisible woman as God. She saw her smile shoot through the midwife's body, the Quince's eyes half close with the rigor of emotion.

"But I—no less than the Sultan—must pick and choose my battles," Safiye said. "I think—if it's Allah's will—I shall know better than the old man how to choose, when I am there.

"In the meantime, the site of the old man's war with the Portuguese is so distant, the hostilities so scattered, it takes forever to hear word of what has happened and even longer to decipher what it may mean afterwards."

"What it means for the Sultan. For his grandson."

"For *me*. Your price quotes from the spice markets are as good—and as rapid—an indicator as any other I've discovered."

The Quince seemed to take more compliment than Safiye had meant. But it was a sign that, secure in this ally, Baffo's daughter could expand her attention to the rest of the room.

Here, harem walls contained the brilliant splinters of life created by close to two dozen young women yet uncontained within themselves. The young women's native integrity imploded under the pressures of grille and veil. Although beautiful, indeed chosen first for this beauty, they were not naturally favored quite enough to be free of beauty's thralldom—and all the other slaveries fashion brought in its wake.

The Quince sighed. "Your prince will call for you soon."

Safiye hummed a half-attentive response.

"Too soon."

After another circle of Safiye's face, the midwife said: "Will he love the smell of jasmine on you as much as I do, my doe?"

Safiye could tell her lack of attention galled the Quince. Speaking would help, even if it were mindless repetition of thoughts she'd shared before.

"On my first visit to the harem," Safiye said therefore, "before I'd even been bought and guaranteed a place here, I felt the pulse of power in these inner rooms. It was as if, in a body apparently dead, there had been this forceful sign of life. Can you appreciate that, my Quince? Have you ever come upon a body like that?"

"No. Mostly what I find dead is genuinely dead."

"It was not just life, but a vigorous, splendid life, the most glorious life I could imagine." *And I claimed it for my own,* she told herself with a fierce glance in the mirror.

"There is something in the harem I have tried to explain to you, my Fair One, but words have failed me. Something—between women. Was that what you sensed?"

Safiye shook her head, not so much at what the midwife said, which she hardly heard, but at her own discovery. "I realize now that the power I sensed came from Nur Banu."

"Well, a woman and her mother-in-law are always at odds."

"Mother-in-law?"

"That is what Nur Banu—Murad's mother—is to you, though I suppose 'law' has nothing to do with this case. These troubles are proverbial among us."

Safiye decided to humor the midwife and follow that train of thought for a while. It took less thought; the words came of their own accord.

"In Venice as well. 'The husband's mother is the wife's devil,'

I was warned. Still, for much of my life my aunt and her fellow nuns were the women I knew. They would have had the Blessed Virgin Mary as their mother-in-law, wouldn't they? A curious concept. I never thought of that before. I don't suppose they could complain about *her*. Or aspire much to her position, do you think?"

The Quince said something about heathen Christendom and its abuse of women, so formulaic Safiye assumed she was not required to listen.

"No," Safiye reverted the conversation to the line of her own thoughts. "I felt no repulsion from Nur Banu that first time I met her. Envy, perhaps. But I certainly thought we could be friends."

"You didn't know then that you'd have to share one man's affections." The Quice dropped her voice to her whispered intensity again. "You don't have to, you know."

"I wanted to be friends. I did. I wanted it desperately. I wanted to share her power, you see. The power of this place I sensed from her—in this carcass—like blood beat from the heart."

"The other girls—women—they were not worthy of your attention?"

"The other girls, Nur Banu's slaves, were mere veins through which her heart's power coursed. Even when she was not in the room, she dictated their purpose. Why, it is the same tonight as it was then. Look around us. A girl might chat to a parrot or take individual joy in these last tulips of the season."

Safiye gestured towards the closest vase, one of many, ladening the close harem air with their metallic scent. "Still," she insisted, "every girl's purpose here is dictated by the first woman."

"The *bash kadin*. Because she has borne a son. Shall I stop making you the pessaries? Shall I make you a fecunding charm of coriander seed and salt crystal instead?"

"Just look at them this evening! Every girl's main focus is the packing of chests and trunks, the rolling of mattresses and rugs for the spring journey across the bosom of Turkey for summer quarters in Kutahiya."

"You yourself do not join in this project."

"It's not required of me."

"No, it's not."

"I'm not a menial slave, after all. Must I appear before Murad all hot and sweaty?"

"That will come soon enough after you meet him, I warrant." The Quince did not conceal a sigh—and a smile. "A pity, however, you do not lend some of that effort to things in here."

Safiye said nothing but looked in the mirror, feeling the point taken.

The Quince elaborated: "I mean socially, with the other girls, it would be helpful to join in. And to solidify your relationship to Nur Banu."

"But since I have laid claim to Murad's heart," Safiye said, "I am a heart of my own."

"Are you certain you are not too much *his* heart? Such dependence on men is common among your countrywomen, I understand. But you need not transfer it here. The harem helps us escape that."

Escape in the harem seemed nonsense to Safiye, so she made sense of her own. "I have weaned Murad from his mother as surely as I weaned him from his opium. It is for this cause that I am at irreconcilable odds with Nur Banu. There is no reason to pretend otherwise."

"Can you imagine, my Fair One, that I could have the freedom of my work if it were exposed to the men's world? My work—my art would be taken over by men. If they let me practice at all, it would be according to their rules. It would be men telling me—and you—when to have a child and when not to."

"Any other woman's whims—like another heart's veins are a mere distraction from my own."

Safiye was relieved that the Quince interjected no more of her endless refrains. Here in this self-same harem room where she had snatched destiny, Baffo's daughter could now feel little more than annoyance—at anything and everything.

The packing, the bundling up of a smooth, seamless life into any number of various, separate bundles—that annoyed her.

And there was the women's chatter accompanied by two competing musical renditions, one vocal and sad, the other an instrumental for lively dancing. The plash and purl of an indoor fountain, in play for these warm spring evenings, contributed a third rhythm, all its own.

There were the crazily mingling scents of tulips and perfumes and sweets and sherbets, and a brazier smoking with sandalwood chips and ambergris at which three or four women were fumigating the folds of their garments.

The glint of jewels collided with rich fabrics and the explosions of color and noise that were the pet parrots—

All this tossed together, all collided, jarred, intensified, then was thrown back at the observer with double the force from the walls of tiles and mirrors.

The Quince spoke with an indulgent smile, as one might warn a child: "Nur Banu must call your retreat rudeness if not out and out insubordination."

"At this moment, I don't care."

Safiye retreated into the mirror. Was this self-defense as she waited for the call from Prince Murad—and dissipation of another sort? Perhaps it was true, but she wouldn't hear the Quince say it.

"Two years ago, Prince Murad's mother paid four hundred kurush for a Venetian girl of breathtaking beauty, outbidding the

Sultan himself. This is an investment Nur Banu hoped—in a most irreligious way—would gain value with the years, not slip from her control like so much quicksilver through her fingers. Insuring such devotion was no simple task. You must know that, having undertaken to work for loyalties among the women yourself, behind Nur Banu's back."

"I have to do something with my leftover garments: Murad, like his grandfather, is shown the honor of never seeing me in the same dress twice. I give them away."

"Does it become tedious after so many months, this nudging of a man towards endless fascination?"

"What? Don't you like tonight's outfit? I liked the green flowered damask particularly well when I first saw it. But now you mention it, that was by daylight. Those saleswomen! It does lose something by lamplight. The colors muddy, somehow."

"My heart, you would look beautiful in anything, and rags turn to riches by your touch."

Safiye was silent, enjoying the sound of that flattery.

Presently, the Quince had to coax her out of her silence. "On whom will you shed tonight's used petals, beloved rose of my garden?"

Safiye whispered, no louder than the sound of her hand over the damask's nap: "Even with such gifts, I know never to trust over much beyond the rim of my own being."

"The girls who are not favorites of one Ottoman male or another—with their own sources of riches—they have to dress in strict livery every day but holidays, don't they? Novices in green, menials in a rust."

"Nur Banu can tell at a glance who's who, who's out of place. A woman has to be in harem service a very long time before she's allowed fur trim. Look! Those who have it wear it even on a warm evening such as tonight, to show off."

"You are beyond that stricture in any case."

"But I know most of what I give away has to be sold outside the palace for a little spending money."

"Not what you give me. Everything you've ever given me I have still, in a special place, treasured."

"You never wear them."

"Dear heart, I never even wash them. They smell of you."

Safiye laughed her knowing skepticism at such flattery. "When my gifts are sold, that limits their effect. And in any case, none of it has effect outside the harem."

"Are you sure?"

"None that I can see."

"Perhaps your own treatment of your lover's mother teaches you that gifts are no hedge against treachery."

"You don't like Nur Banu, either."

"No. An old—difference of opinion. Your dislike seems more tinged with—remorse or guilt, shall we say?"

"I am simply reminded that Nur Banu never sees Selim—her son's own father—at all anymore. She cannot afford to be so self-sufficient. And her influence dies at the harem's grate. Ah, when I am mistress of a harem of my own . . ."

All at once, Safiye found herself in the center of a profound hush, as if a gale had suddenly dropped. The parrots had reduced their chatter of Koranic verses and "Who's the fairest of all?" to sporadic chuckles, throaty with the tension even they could feel. And Safiye knew that she had been addressed from somewhere outside the circle of her being and that she had failed to respond. Perhaps even her alabaster face had betrayed more of her thought than she usually hoped for. Or had the splash of fountain failed to keep her conversation to the Quince's ears alone—?

Then Safiye saw what the intense concentration on herself

had allowed her to ignore: that Nur Banu——who had left the entourage to twitch without her for a while like some beast with its heart torn out——Nur Banu had now returned to claim her place in the room.

# IX

NUR BANU CLAIMED the central seat on the divan——always left vacant in her absence——leaned back and draped one arm on the cushions to either side of her. Bracelets swagged with the elegance of silk from her arched wrists, one pearl-seeded slipper dangled with studied nonchalance from a single toe. Nur Banu was no longer young, though she seemed younger tonight than she had for a while, Safiye thought. And the cords in her neck, the slight sag of her cheeks——attended to, though no longer much aided by almond cream——commanded in a way tauter flesh could not.

The girls on the floor to either side of Nur Banu had turned towards her, their feet tucked up under their identical green robes in attitudes of enthrallment. So did Murad's mother impose focus on the shattered fragments of sight, scent, and sound in the room——and was intent upon sucking Safiye in with them. Nur Banu had said something; the entire room awaited the Fair One's reply.

Somewhat cautioned, Safiye said, "Beg pardon, madam." The humble inclination of her head was not too much to ask. Newly confident in her own purpose, Baffo's daughter could afford to give this consolation to her rival. "Forgive me, but I'm afraid I did not attend your words."

Nur Banu snorted with sharp disdain, her obsidian eyes flashed. But Safiye was pleased to see that the older woman was full of news that pounded toward success too assuredly to use much caution.

"I said, insolent miss, that we shall all shortly know the pleasures of a sea voyage."

"My prince promised me one, yes."

"This is thanks to *my* prince's father, not to yours. As we can all plainly see by your disgracefully flat belly, you have no prince."

"Life and death are Allah's will," Safiye said, working on her humility.

"But some things we on earth can, with the help of Allah, effect. Like the promise I have extracted from my son. He will never marry you. He has promised me, as he loves his mother."

"You have taunted me with this before, lady, but I have known promises to be broken. With the right allurements."

"He will certainly never marry you as long as you remain childless."

"And I have made an oath of my own, lady. I shall not have a child until I have the full power of a wife."

"How can a Sultan marry himself to a childless woman? It would be an omen of dearth and sterility for the entire realm. Even Khurrem Sultan had proven herself with several fine sons and a daughter before our master Suleiman made her his legal wife."

"But this old, tedious threat is not what you came in here to tell us," Safiye said, winning the room's gratitude that they did not have to hear it all again. "You said something of a sea voyage, I believe."

"Yes, the entire harem, not just one selfish girl, is to have the pleasure."

"This is good news, my lady." Safiye saw no cause to let up on her self-effacement. "We are all to sail that part of the trip to Kutahiya we can take by water, then?"

"Not to Kutahiya. No, not to Kutahiya, to which you so selfishly aspired. And for which pride, I thank Allah, you were justly thwarted by our master Suleiman's great wisdom."

Safiye didn't flinch. Nor did she disguise the fact that she had been studiously avoiding any packing herself. "Have you come to tell these girls they must give up their packing, then? Are we to spend the unbearable heat of the summer right here where we are, in Constantinople?"

Nur Banu's voice glowed with triumph. "I am pleased to say we shall journey, and that most of the journey shall be by sea."

The predictable murmurs of wonder and delight sparkled throughout the room at this. Safiye smiled to herself. This reaction among the harem's inmates demonstrated that she had made the older woman show more of her hand than before.

*Careful,* Safiye warned herself. *Forcing a mere slip off balance into imprudent speech is no triumph.*

Safiye turned what was left of her smile into a fealty gift to Nur Banu. Then Baffo's daughter waited 'til the echoes of the harem's pleasure at this announcement had slipped off the tiles and sunk into the plush of the room's carpets before she spoke again. She wanted no ear to miss what she would draw from Nur Banu next.

"Where are we to go, then, my lady?"

"Magnesia."

The announcement had the force of a swordman's parry and the room flew up before it in all directions like leaves before the wind of a passing blade.

"Magnesia!"

"By sea!"

"Oh, do you remember . . . ?"

"How happy we were there!"

"It was before my time but . . ."

"I have heard such wonderful things!"

"All praise to Allah, the source of good."

"But this is wonderful news."

Safiye let the others take their pleasure. They'd thank her for it later, long after they'd forgotten whom they were thanking now.

But at the first lull in the chatter, she interjected: "Lady, this is wonderful news indeed. At least——I pray to Allah that it is good news."

"Whatever are you insinuating?" Nur Banu turned to her with a lash of whip black eyes.

"Nothing——I hope, as Allah is merciful. But your master Selim——he isn't shirking his duty, is he? I thought we went to Kutahiya to join him where he must serve his father and his lord as *sandjak bey*——as provincial governor. And as I know you would not shirk your duty to join with him, my next thought is . . ."

Safiye felt another blow of those eyes, but she refused to stop.

"We all know Selim is sometimes——how shall I say it?——apt to be drawn from his duties by the lure of—— No, forgive me. I forget myself."

"You do indeed, girl," Nur Banu hissed. "Let me set you straight at once. Selim shall not be *sandjak bey* of Kutahiya any longer."

Since the only reaction among the rest of the girls was a breathless silence, Safiye volunteered to fill it. "Oh, Allah save us. Then it's as I feared!"

"As you feared, simple girl? As I prayed! No more Kutahiya, where we were banished when Selim, in the heat of youth, fo-mented civil war against his brother."

"Brother Bayazid is dead, a traitor's death these two—three years. Since before I came to the realm of Islam, lady. If reprieve were assured, I, for one, would have expected it sooner. But"— Safiye was cautious to conclude—"Allah knows best."

"Allah does indeed know best. You expected it sooner because you don't understand the just deliberation of the Shadow of Allah on earth. But this is the very news I bring. The *sandjak* of Magnesia has always been given to heirs apparent."

"Because it lies the shortest distance from the City of Cities, Constantinople." Safiye held her own. "In case—Allah forbid— something should happen to our Sultan, his inheritor in Magnesia is poised to gather up the reins of power as hastily as possible. But several years have passed now since Suleiman has been left by Allah's almighty will with but a single son—and Selim has, in all this time, still not been given that plum of a *sandjak*."

Nur Banu waved the protest away as ineffective. "Selim did have Magnesia once. It was in Magnesia, lovely Magnesia, where Selim loved me and where our son was born."

"But he was removed—remember?—at the Sultan's severe displeasure for brawling with his brother. Another, a mere bureaucrat, has been considered more worthy to hold Magnesia in recent days."

"Since you think you know so much, it may please you to learn that Sultan Suleiman—may Allah shield him—has finally decided it's time to end this tedious interim. And that's all it was, an interim, while Selim cooled off."

"Cooled himself with wine."

Someone—not just a parrot—tittered. Nur Banu was growing livid—and, Safiye noticed, careless.

"You will not say so! It is against Islam to drink the Christian's poison, and Selim was born to rule the faithful."

"It is Allah's will," Safiye said. She liked this formulaic way to avoid committing one's own opinion. She kept her calm.

"Suleiman has now declared himself ready to replace that—that fellow he set in the *sandjak* during the interim."

"Ferhad Bey."

Safiye caught yet another snap of Nur Banu's eyes. She knew she annoyed when she demonstrated more knowledge about the empire's workings than the older woman had.

But Safiye deliberately misinterpreted the threat in the glance this time and continued: "Ferhad is the name of the man—a cavalry man, I believe. Capable, but young. Not too long out of the palace school. That's who's been governing Magnesia since Selim's disgrace. So Ferhad Bey's been displaced, then?"

"Only removed for advancement." Nur Banu struggled to show that she had useful knowledge, too. "He is a particular favorite of Sokolli Pasha, I believe, and the Grand Vizier has decided to reward this bey's capabilities with a post closer to our lord and to the center of power."

"Closer even than the heir apparent," Safiye mused.

"Such recalls for consultation as we have enjoyed with Selim's presence in Constantinople these past few weeks are uncommon and must mean something. It isn't customary for Sultan and heir to spend too much time too close together."

"Too much temptation for rebellion?"

"Lest one disaster under the same roof—Allah forbid it!—take both at once. It isn't our custom to tempt Fate so."

"Ah, yes," Safiye said, with the shiver down her spine she got whenever she knew she was playing too simple. But it was necessary, to drive this skirmish to its conclusion. "So, Magnesia, now being empty—"

"Is in need of a new governor."

"It's settled, then? The new bey is to be our master Selim?"

Safiye lost control of her heart's beat—just for an instant. All this news of Ferhad Bey and the heir's vacant *sandjak*—she'd already been mistress of it for the better part of a day, entertaining its rumors for nearly a week. She had Ghazanfer's skills—not to say his perfect devotion and his own thirst for revenge—to thank for this. Ghazanfer ferreted for her in places where other *khuddam* would blush or grow faint—certainly give themselves away.

For one moment, Safiye wished Ghazanfer in the room with her. Sharing this triumph would go far to assure his permanent enclosure in the tight oval of her will. She needed this assurance—for the next success. But then her mind gave him his feet again. She was more certain he was with her than she was even of the Quince. For the next success, he must be where those great eunuch's feet carried him.

Then the thrill of fear came back again, just one more instant. Suppose Nur Banu's eunuchs had been working just as hard? There were more of them; they could work more directions at once. Suppose Selim were already declared *sandjak bey* of Magnesia—?

*No declaration cannot be annulled by another declaration,* Safiye dismissed these doubts. Nur Banu's *khuddam* were not half so devoted as Ghazanfer was. And never so motivated by intent of their own. The confidence Nur Banu exuded was only because she had not thought through the entire matter quite so far as she, Safiye, had. And because Safiye had—for the pure desire to fight and win, the more publicly the better—teased the older woman into an extremely exposed position.

So, then, in for the kill.

"Our master Selim has been granted the heir's *sandjak?*"

Ah, the trapped look in those black eyes! Did ever Suleiman the Magnificent take so great a victory from so slight a wave of surrender?

Nur Banu betrayed herself to the rest of the room only by losing the casual drape of her arms and playing with their bangles accompanied by a slight twitch of nervousness.

"Selim has not, no. Not in so many words, he has not. But he will. Who else is there?"

"Who else, lady? Who else, indeed?"

Satisfied with this capitulation, Safiye settled back behind the defenses of her mirror's rim. She let Nur Banu and her ladies fall unharried into their disparate bursts of satisfaction at the news of Ferhad's elevation, or rather, of Magnesia's vacancy. Let them think she had pushed them into only a momentary and tactical retreat—for the time being.

❧

SAFIYE HADN'T TOO much longer to wait before Ghazanfer entered the room.

She sensed rather than heard him first: a wonder how like a cat he could move on those torture-flattened feet of his. The hands he laid across his chest in the eunuch's attitude of patient waiting—every finger of them had been broken, too. The nails were only just beginning to regrow, far down at the cuticle beneath great expanses of scabby quick. Every move must give some painful reminder.

She turned her mirror to catch within its rim the feral green flecks buried within the blue ringing the eunuch's narrow pupils. Over a twisted, broken nose, only those eyes remained the same as she had seen under the bastinado less than a month before. For the sake of those eyes she had rescued him from the Seven Towers—in the nick of time.

Even his name was changed. Instead of that silly Hyacinth, she now called him Ghazanfer, "Bold Lion." She doubted whether even Mihrimah Sultan would recognize her old *khadim*. But in all his ugly ravagedness, here, at last, was the eunuch for Safiye the Fair.

Safiye smiled at him, ever so slightly, through the mirror and across the room. His green eyes missed nothing, not even a flash of light on glass. His reply was slighter still, too slight to be called a smile. But then Ghazanfer never did smile, even for great provocation. His mouth was too gapped with missing teeth; some self-pride remained intact.

His glanced reply was enough, however. Safiye felt the wild darkness of the night in it more clearly than had she crossed to him and felt its lingering freshness on the flat of his cheeks. No, she could not have gone out into the dark and felt the night's freedom sharper on her own face.

Safiye knew the deed was done, and done well.

And then Murad sent for her.

## X

EARLY THE NEXT morning, Aziza and another girl, Belqis, ran in panting and awakened the room, still languid from a late night spent celebrating. The pair went everywhere together, inseparable companions in their beauty and in its rejection by Prince Murad several years previous. Now they stumbled and clung to one another in a new distress, and that distress instantly magnified off tiles and mirrors and riveted the room's splinters to attention.

"Allah shield you." Nur Banu looked up at once from the rough beginnings of a conversation on how to alter a wardrobe planned for dusty roads to suit the pleasures of a ship's deck instead.

The girls' words stumbled over one another as their feet had done in their agitation.

"We've seen him."

"Seen his head."

"On a spike."

"Allah shield us!"

"He is dead."

"When we saw and guessed . . ."

". . . We sent the *khuddam*."

"They confirmed."

"At the Executioner's Fountain."

"As we passed, lady."

"Past hope."

"Past life."

"Allah save us."

"Dead!"

Nur Banu finally got a word in edgewise. "He's dead? Girls, calm yourselves. Who's dead?"

Safiye folded her hands calmly over the mirror in her lap that still revealed her hair in lover's disarray. She watched Nur Banu instead of the girls as they tried to tell more, watched how the older woman's face rinsed of all color. The only word Murad's mother had heard, that anyone had heard of the next jumble was the name of her child's father: "Selim."

"Selim? Allah shield me, I am ruined." Nur Banu's words came from the very edge of a faint.

"Oh, no."

"Not Selim, lady."

"Allah forfend."

"Allah bless you, lady."

"Selim lives."

"Allah be praised."

"But it's Lufti Effendi."

"Lufti Effendi, our master Selim's companion."

"Lufti Effendi is dead."

"Executed."

"By the Fountain."

"His crime?" The color had still not returned to Nur Banu's face and her voice betrayed her.

"Drunkenness," Belqis choked.

"Oh, lady!"

"Everyone knows."

"The Sultan knows."

"Lufti Effendi was drinking—"

"—Drinking with our master Selim last night."

"Within the very palace."

"Celebrating the bey's elevation from Magnesia, I fear."

"Lufti Effendi was discovered."

"On his way home afterwards."

"The Sultan fairly tripped over the Effendi, lady."

"Dead drunk he was."

"His body, dead to the world . . ."

". . . Where the Sultan could not possibly miss him."

"And now he is dead indeed."

"And shall abuse our faith no more."

"For that we should praise Allah—perhaps." Belqis dropped both voice and head in the helpless sorrow her words belied.

Nur Banu struggled for control. "Selim? What of my lord Selim?"

"We think he lives."

"Allah be praised."

"It is difficult to tell from this women's country."

"But the eunuchs think so, lady."

The watching *khuddam* confirmed these hopes in their own

silent way, though Nur Banu sent one of them out instantly for better assurances.

Belqis continued: "It seems this public execution was meant as a warning."

"To no one more than our lord Selim."

"A sign of the Sultan's deep displeasure at his son's habits."

"A warning to improve."

"And improve he will," Nur Banu said. "He must." She found her feet but nearly lost her voice on these words. Then she regained speech enough to say, "I will find him a new girl. The most lovely girl. Or a boy, too. I'll give him a boy if that's what it takes."

Safiye caught a pair of green-flecked eyes across the room, but rested assured that so changed was her Ghazanfer in appearance that she alone in the harem shared the secret of his past.

"All shall be well, Allah willing, girls. We must calm ourselves."

Nur Banu then gave more orders to more eunuchs. But though she urged calm, and Belqis and Aziza bolted themselves to cushions in compliance, the head of the harem herself continued to pace.

A girl in novice green piped into the churning silence: "Does this mean, lady, we are not to have a sea voyage?" The still weight that followed let even this girl know herself a fool.

Safiye watched the look that passed between the rigid faces of Aziza and Belqis. She saw Aziza chosen for the nasty task. She saw the girl chew on her lip until surely blood must mingle with her words.

And finally the word came: "Lady."

"What is it, Aziza?" The girl flinched as Nur Banu snapped, the older woman impatient to have her desperate maneuvering disrupted yet again.

"Lady, the Sultan has declared a yet sterner warning."

"Warning? What warning?"

Aziza gasped for breath. "The Sultan has decreed . . ." Then she looked frantically to her companion as the judgment failed to leave her throat.

"The *sandjak* of Magnesia will not go to our lord Selim," Belqis finished the tale when her friend's words failed her. "As a sign of his severe displeasure, the Sultan has given the governorship to his grandson, Murad, instead."

For one brilliant moment, Safiye felt the lash of Nur Banu's black eyes on her. It thrilled rather than chastised, as some of his reported perversions must Selim. With one deliberate finger, Safiye drew around the oval of her mirror's rim.

Then the room exploded with fury which tile and parrots amplified, feathers flying like bits of sound.

"Get out! Get out of my sight! Get out!" the older woman screamed at her.

Shortly there were other things flying. Nur Banu caught up pots of beauty cream and launched them through the air after her words. Murano glass shattered, loosing the scent of a spice market within the narrow confines of the harem. Other pots thudded dully into the cushions close—too close—to Safiye's love-disheveled head.

"Get out!"

So in defiant, tight control and slow, deliberate dignity, Safiye fulfilled the order. And even the Quince, who had come, hoping for a chance to comb out Safiye's golden hair that morning, did not dare to follow.

Nonetheless, though Safiye did not hear it, she knew she was not alone. Confidently she sensed the shadow of Ghazanfer's feet behind her. She saw no more than his hands as they opened the intervening doors, but she felt their surety as they closed those doors behind her against the harem's chaos.

She wondered as she walked, about the strength of such hands. Such hands, so solicitous, could overcome a man stumbling home drunk, even empty of any weapon. Such hands had forced more on the man's unconsciousness with a Quince-provided potion. Then those hands had hoisted that Effendi up to broad shoulders and carried him through the fresh palace night to a place where the body couldn't be missed.

"I dowsed him with more drink afterwards," the great eunuch had reported in the laconic, hissing way the lack of teeth and outward masculinity forced him to. "A whole bottle of raki."

She saw gratitude in his eyes then as he spoke, perfect gratitude. She knew if she cared to look back she would see it now, flooding the hard green with their only softness. She had given him revenge—as he had helped her to take her own ambition by the horns.

"Get out!"

Nur Banu screamed, out of all control. But the eunuch's torture-scarred hands gently closed one final door and the sound dropped to nothing.

Then Safiye could set words the older woman didn't say— that she would never say—into the calm of the oval of her own mind.

*So you have won, you bitch, you demon from hell. You have won the heir's sandjak for your lover. My son, whom in your presence I can no longer control. You've won it for him, for yourself. Along with the sandjak you gain your own harem to add to your new eunuch. A harem free of my scrutiny. It puts my Murad—and your own accursed self—even further from my reach. We remain in Kutahiya, you go alone to Magnesia. Murad grows even closer to his grandfather, to his grandfather's throne when the old man should vacate it.*

*And I? I am condemned not only to that fiendish overland journey and the desolation of yet another summer in Kutahiya, the end of the earth. But all my future is condemned to dependence on this man, this Selim, who forgets—in his drunken stupors and love of boys—that I ever existed.*

This is what Safiye heard, all she cared to hear. Still, the ears of her mind could not help but hear one further echo off the face of the naked tile, the echo of accusations Nur Banu had once actually flung at her.

"This you have won, this battle, you they call the Fair One, you whom I bought on the slave block. I might as well have purchased an afreet from the depths of hell. But the war is not over. Not by far. Do you know why?

"You have no son, you selfish slut. Murad may always tire of you, as Selim did of me. But unlike my good fortune, *you have no son.*

"And we have yet to see if you can conceive. May not the Quince's potions destroy you as readily as they destroy others? May they not rot out your insides? If not in the original formula, in one she may be bribed to concoct?

"And if you can conceive, you know girls are born into this world as frequently as boys. More frequently, it seems to be Allah's will, when their presence is least desired."

Safiye denied all this, then as she did now. Heaven would never so betray the beauty it had given her. Would God betray holy writ? Still, her mind couldn't shake the words.

"As long as you have no son, Fair One, you must know. You are vulnerable. You are more vulnerable, even, than I."

# XI

THE SEA JOURNEY to Magnesia was everything harem envy promised. The time did not dawdle away in the same spirit of languid indolence that most of the inmates imagined, however. She wouldn't have liked it, Safiye supposed, if it had.

For example, she delighted in the sight of the Turk's naval might from the vantage of the Sea of Marmara, the all-important shipyards, the arsenal on the soft, southern underbelly of the city's peninsula. She counted five new war galleys under construction, like the skeletal ribs of beached sea monsters. On the water itself, she tallied every hull crested with Saint Mark's banner. She nursed no interest to escape to them, but debated if she might know a captain or an owner and what he might be sailing for. She weighed their presence against the arsenal's production.

Lacking more direct information of the Venetian vessels, she made Murad tell her the names and capacities of all the crescent-flagged ships in the harbor instead, their tonnage, their armament. She made him find out their captains if he didn't know them, then entertain the cream of these corsairs—in a place where she could hear everything from behind a screen of sailing shroud—while they yet rode at anchor.

Then, at the Dardenelles, Murad took her ashore and together they inspected the two solid fortresses, built by the prince's ancestors, that guarded the waterway from either side of the narrow strait.

"So you need never fear, my Safiye," the prince said, "or worry your pretty little head about an attack on the heart of our empire, Constantinople. You see the approach is impregnable."

Safiye picked her way around the forts for a while with no reply. She knew her veils gave her the attitude of silent wonder at men's accomplishments. But presently she had to speak what had been obvious to her even from on board the ship. She might have chosen to keep her knowledge to herself, sell it to the next Venetian galleon they happened on.

But "Impregnable?" she asked her prince instead. "Perhaps, yes. When your ancestors built them and hoped their crossbow bolts might reach the decks of invaders' ships."

"Now we have cannon in each fort and so that much less to fear."

"But the enemy has cannon as well. Not as in the days when Muhammed the Conqueror, your great forefather, turned firepower against the Byzantine Greeks who were as yet unarmed with guns."

"But, you see, my sweet—" Murad took the tone with which one explains things to a child.

Safiye didn't mind. She flattered him where she could. The prince still even thought he was responsible for his own advancement to *sandjak bey.*

"A cannonball has much less difficulty falling down"—the prince's tutorial continued—"as, say, from those battlements, than flying up."

"Precisely my point."

"I don't know what you mean."

"In their effort to reach the invaders' decks, your ancestors failed to claim the highest points on either side for their fortifications. See the precipice here—and across, there. Naked and unprotected as newborn babes—and peering right down into the fortress's yards. An enemy would only have to get his guns up there—no light task, certainly, but perfectly possible in a single dark night—and he would control both forts and the strait."

Murad ran from vantage point to vantage point in a paroxysm of denial until he could deny it no longer. Then Safiye helped him compose a letter to his grandfather the Sultan delineating the problem—as if the prince himself had discovered it, of course—and urging immediate action to remedy the situation.

At Izmir, Safiye saw the harbor, still silted up from the rapacity of Tamerlane.

"After over a hundred and fifty years, they might have redredged it," she suggested.

"But we don't want too many foreign ships coming to Izmir," Murad said, the blush of a sea breeze riding above his beard.

"Why ever not? Foreign trade will make the region bloom."

"The region feeds Constantinople and, most importantly, the armies of the faithful. If unbelievers help themselves, Muslims will go hungry."

Safiye remarked that there were plenty of foreign merchants scrambling for bargains of silks and cottons, figs and malmsey, in Izmir's bazaars anyway. She liked to stop the sedan and overhear the talk of Venetians with Genoese incognito. And she noted the species she had never seen before but learned to recognize as Englishmen. Those Englishmen who had not adopted Turkish dress sweltered irrationally in heavy woolens. Their faces were sunburnt and burnt again peeling, pink as fresh fig flesh.

And everywhere, everywhere along the coast were the classical ruins. Colonnades of teeth-white pillars leered down on the sea from deserted promontories. Great bowls of theatres echoed emptily against their drab hillsides, still able to seat tens of thousands in comfort. Agoras and villas and streets and temples were empty save for the occasional shepherd with his flock. Yet, the permanence of their stones, glaring an impervious white under the best efforts of a malevolent sun, seemed to need only the quick addition of a few softening touches: awnings, strings of laundry, cushions, a few potted plants, perhaps, to make them thriving metropolises once more.

Ruins such as these defied the word "ruin." They would stand for as many generations again as they already had, generations, Safiye hoped, which would not be slaves of such prudery as the present one. Sometimes Murad found the stuff of their sightseeing objectionable. There were so many shamelessly naked figures with marble skin and unveiled beauty that no conqueror since their making had had time to chisel out all the eyes and privates to suit his higher standards of modesty and iconoclasm. Safiye pleaded with her prince not to complete the task for which his predecessors hadn't had time.

"Not this one," she counseled. "But consider—if the polytheistic Greeks and Romans could sustain such wonders on this land, there is no reason why the Turks cannot as well."

And she felt the force of his concurrence in that night's love.

# XII

TIME PASSED. FOR lovers, it was but moments. And regular mortals knew it as seventeen or eighteen months, sometimes long, sometimes short in perspective.

It was late summer 1565, according to how Christians tell the years, and now in Magnesia, rides in sedan chairs had lost the odium for Safiye that they had for the harem in Constantinople. For one thing, Murad nearly always traveled with her, in the roomy, double chair he'd ordered.

He traveled with her now, on the hunt, urging open the sedan's shutter to get as much of the early morning sun as possible on the day's dispatches.

"You will not take Safiye on a hunt with you, my son," he read from the top missive. "To expose yourself to such censure!" The mischievous sparkle that filled his eyes and the mimic in his voice told Safiye this letter could only be from his mother, Nur Banu.

Murad continued, or rather, Nur Banu did: "Safe in her harem, nothing a woman can do brings shame on her man. But in the public eye, one ill-timed giggle, and people will think not just her, but *you*, silly and frivolous. One slip of a sedan bearer, one twisted ankle as she passes from sedan to tent on uneven ground and in her veils, as she must. My dear, a twisted ankle, and folk will never let the prince of my heart live down the name as one who has no care for his women. Have we yet lived down the shame of the brigands, even though all of them were killed, and your indiscretion was neatly covered by saying your grandfather—may his realm last until eternity—made the roads safe for travelers?

"If you insist on taking her, the hunters will say you are one who is addicted to women, even if—Allah willing—no ill befalls her. 'He is a man who cannot leave his harem behind, even to go into battle. What sort of Sultan can he make?' they will ask themselves. And, 'No wonder he cannot get a—' "

"Well, go on, my love," Safiye prodded, knowing full well the word he could not read was "son." "What else does she say?"

"More of the same," Murad said, taking his own voice again.

"And then she closes with her usual effluence: 'Allah's mercy keep your eyes. . . . May he exalt you as the exalted constellation of the Big Dipper. . . . This worthless slave. . . . Your eternal mother.' "

"You read that very well, my love," Safiye said. "I could almost hear her in the sedan with us."

"Thank Allah she's not."

And the shutter, which Murad had earlier opened, now slammed decidedly shut behind him. Over her own giggles, Safiye heard the chair's bearers curse. The prince had made a lunge for her and the men outside struggled to keep the conveyance upright against such a heated shift in the balance on their shoulders.

Perhaps it would be better to say *she* traveled with *him*, to any place the governorship took them. She was pleased to think that she was never further from the *bey* of the entire *sandjak*—and hence its most inner workings—than the bearers could bring her.

And often much closer than that, as they were at this instant, rocking the chair in a lover's embrace.

Safiye hitched her hips, hindered by Murad's weight and the deep nap of the sedan's velvet upholstery against her layers of summer silks. That Murad could read her his mother's letters in the midst of defying them was a reassuring sign. It was so reassuring that she smoothed her henna-stained fingertips up under Murad's jacket and down into his waistband.

She pressed his forehead to her lips as she urged, "Your mother writes such things and you defy her?"

"Let her rail all she wants," Murad punctuated with kisses, on Safiye's throat, on her eyes and cheeks. "This letter's two weeks old or more. What does it matter what she thinks, here where I am *bey* and her notes but one scrap of paper out of a hundred?"

"And yet you won't defy her in the one thing that is most important to me and . . ."

Safiye didn't finish the sentence. She felt Murad's whole torso stiffen and withdraw. The topic of marriage was a constant between them, though she tried to avoid it precisely because of this reaction. She often feared she nagged, though she never meant to. She sounded like a parrot trained with but one phrase.

*And like a parrot who doesn't please,* she thought, *I can just as easily be sold.*

"I've never promised Mother anything—anything but that," Murad bit back on the full voluptuousness of his lips, making them but a thin line between moustache and beard. "She is my mother. She must be content with that. And you, too, must learn to be content, my fairest one. You are with me all the time."

"That only makes it harder, not to have the dignity of being your wife, being something people only snigger at."

"Perhaps they snigger at you in Venice. Here, no one would dare. Please, love, be content that there is nothing I would rather do than make you my legal wife before all the world, as my honored grandfather made my grandmother—Allah's blessings on her."

"Do it then."

"I gave my mother my word."

"Break it."

"I—I can't."

"You won't." Safiye turned from him sulkily. "And no woman would ever be good enough for her precious boy."

Even without looking, Safiye knew he winced at the word "boy." "But she does have a point," the "boy" defended himself. "The reason the sons of Othman do not usually marry dates back over a hundred years . . ."

"I know. Tamerlane."

"When we were but a small people, Tamerlane overcame us."

"And you still haven't redredged the harbor at Izmir."

"Tamerlane carried off the beloved wife of my ancestor Bayazid the First in chains. Did unspeakable things to her. It took his sons years to overcome the shame of that and win the respect of their people again. Now that we are great, there are no princesses in either Europe or Asia worth polluting the royal bed for the political alliance . . ."

"Pollution! I like that!"

"I didn't mean you, my love." He touched her shoulder and she shook him off.

He tried a different tack. "Slaves don't offer the threat to our honor that a wife does."

"You are telling me you are so weak—now, under your grandfather whom the world calls magnificent—that you must fear a Tamerlane's chains?"

"No, I swear I would die rather than let such a thing happen to you. But even in such a time, there are things . . ."

"What things?"

"You forget the brigands who took you from me? I was prostrate with grief all those ten days."

"Brigands will not happen again." The promise in her voice might have suggested that she herself had been responsible for their capture and could have prevented it.

"As Allah is my shield, they will not. But it was during that time of grief that my mother extracted this vow from me. I have only to remember how sharply my honor was cut at that time to recall the feelings—and renew my vow. Allah witness, my love, I cannot break it while she lives."

"You want a child first," Safiye accused.

"I'd like a son, yes. What man does not? But such is my love for you that I'd as soon have my brother ascend to the throne at my demise . . ."

"Allah forbid it!"

". . . Than to abandon you, whom I love more than life. She *is* my mother, Safiye."

"I see." Safiye knew the ice in her voice would fire him.

"Perhaps—perhaps I may talk her into rescinding the vow she made me give her."

"If I don't go hunting with you, perhaps." Safiye felt Murad squirm uncomfortably as she retreated from him.

"Perhaps, if you, Safiye, with your gift of words, may help me compose another letter."

"You're the poet, your majesty." He hated it when she gave him that royal title. "She will not allow it for jealousy. Your father never married her. She could not bear to see us happy where she is not."

"Perhaps."

*She could not bear to see me a queen in my own right rather than attendant on my sons,* Safiye thought but didn't say.

Murad mused aloud, "Perhaps if Allah were to give us a child . . . She could not then contain her grandmotherly joy."

"Yes, that's what it would take."

"Or maybe when she knows you better."

"I fear we know each other all too well now."

"She doesn't know you as I do."

"For that I'm glad." Safiye planted a kiss on the point where Murad's turban met his brow and began to wind him back from this distraction.

"So until then, love, please . . ." Murad fought to resist her touch but failed.

"Until then. Or until she dies."

"Allah forbid it!" Murad turned the passion of this prayer back onto Safiye, eliciting another curse from the bearers.

And Baffo's daughter knew she should drop the subject there. She worked her fingers up into the prince's tightly bound turban, over the familiar bumps and planes of his meticulously shaved head. *Until then*. Until then there was no reason not to lie back and relax, enjoy the love of her prince, how her every touch made him gasp and sigh. They had a long ride to get to the Boz mountains where the army encampment and the hunting would be. It would take the better part of the day at bearers' pace.

Safiye took a moment to fumble behind her among the sedan's folds of velvet for her silver cases of *farazikh,* the compounds the midwife had taught her to make that would prevent conception. The trick would be to get one inside before Murad got there first, and without his knowledge. This had presented challenges before, but she'd always managed it. Murad was naive in such matters—and, in the heat of passion, oblivious to the point of distraction. Of course, night provided good cover, and she always took care to go prepared whenever she was called into the prince's presence.

Daylight had its drawbacks, even in the gloom of the shuttered sedan. But she got the proper case open and one of the medicated sticks in her hand without detection. The sheep's tail-fat, very soft in her fingers, released the familiar scent of powerful drugs—rue and myrrh predominated. Their odor must also stimulate Murad, for his passion stiffened against her thighs. She gave a groan of encouragement and thought she must only wait 'til he loosened the tie of her *shalvar*. She doubted he'd bother with anything else this time.

Meanwhile, with her free hand, she returned to work on his head. Under his turban's muslin she found first the fine linen undercap and then his topknot. She twisted the shock of hair between her fingers till the scent of the musk he used filled the cramped sedan to every seam of its paneling, covering her telltale drugs. Safiye reached up to meet Murad's lips, swollen again and panting in his ardor. She drew those lips to hers with her tongue as though on a leash, but as the kiss began, the flex of her hands knocked the turban free.

Murad sat up with another jolt and yet more blasphemy from the bearers. He might have had cold water thrown on that naked scalp of his and that single, dangling hank of rusty, Russian-red hair he'd inherited from his grandmother. Safiye thought this, but could not imagine what the matter was.

"My love, what is it?"

With a lurch, then, she felt the chair sink to the ground beneath her.

"We're here." Murad panicked.

"Here? Where? The mountains are *farsakhs* away. My love, in truth you must find new bearers. These who can't mind their own business and keep discreet about a little—"

"A plague upon this infidel turban," Murad said, quite forgetting in his distress that nothing was, in fact, more of the Faith than a turban. "I will have to rewind it without valets while those fools of bearers hem and haw and smirk out there."

"Let them smirk, then get rid of them."

"I never meant for this to happen."

"Oh, didn't you?" Safiye asked him, taking a passing squeeze at the stake of the tent formed in the lap of his *shalvar,* betraying just how urgent was the desire from which the cursed turban distracted him.

The sedan was suddenly full of white muslin. What had fit so tightly and neatly on Murad's head before now left room for little else. She tried to lend a hand, but a royal turban—each extra span a sign of higher nobility—demanded the length of an audience hall to achieve the proper tautness, the interweaving of layers in a smooth dovetail over the brow.

"Forget the turban for the moment." Safiye lost an important tuck at this juncture. They would have to start again, either turban or love, and she'd rather do the second one first, so as to have the trouble with the turban but a single time. Love was better with efficiency. "Just yell at the fellows to move on. We'll get to it later."

"But I told them to stop here," Murad said, finding one muslin end and determined to start the winding once again.

"We're nowhere near the mountains. You can tell. It's getting too beastly hot in here and the muslin is taking up all the air."

"Not near the mountains, no. But they are waiting for us. I have to get out. And I can't go like this!"

*He's about some governing business,* Safiye thought. *We haven't even left town yet.* But nothing too important, she decided, or she would know about it already.

Murad said: "There's something I wanted to show you first."

"Here?"

"I assume it's here. They wouldn't have stopped before. They are good men, for all your complaints."

*Winding a turban is something like braiding,* Safiye thought. She picked up quickness in the task, once she'd tucked the *farazikh*— the heat of her hands had melted this particular dose too much in any case—secretly under a cushion and wiped most of the stickiness there as well.

When the pass of palm over smoothing palm freed one of his hands for a moment, Murad used it to open the wooden shutters a crack.

"Yes, we're here," he announced, breathlessly.

Safiye helped the prince tuck the end of the muslin in at the back of his head. Then she brought her fingers forward and let them dawdle, still hopeful they could change his mind, on his neck where the thick body hair turned into even thicker beard. Thwarted in this, she hurried to fasten the aigrette set with diamonds and its three rust brown pheasant feathers over an unsightly bulge of fabric in the turban's center front. Finally, she shoved the prince out the door and settled back to wait, hoping he wouldn't be too long as the sedan grew hotter by the minute.

"Hurry up, Safiye," he hissed.

His turban seemed dangerously close to the verge of unraveling, grotesquely large and lumpy, for they'd come nowhere near the tight, compact ball of which such fine fabric was capable. The feathers wobbled. It was all she could do to keep from laughing.

"I thought I'd just wait here until you're finished. Please your mother."

"No," Murad insisted. "I mean to please *you*. I mean for you to see this as well."

So the two of them undertook yet another scramble with fabric, this time with the heavy outer wrapper, head veil, and none-too-fine gauze for the face necessary to make Safiye presentable.

And then Murad stepped aside to let Ghazanfer be her eyes. For even if she was veiled, it wasn't seemly for the public to see a virtuous woman too close to any man, not even her husband—if she were legally married. How much more so when she was not?

Any other woman in a similar position must have shrunk conventionally back into her veils for shame at such thoughts. Safiye felt her determination harden instead, her ambition piqued rather than thwarted.

# XIII

THE MIDMORNING SUMMER air burned like clear, unwatered raki as it went down the throat. The sedan's iron fittings throbbed audibly, expanding, creaking like live things. Even through a veil, her dark-accustomed eyes found the great expanse of sun on naked soil too brilliant to stare at directly. Safiye bowed her head—some would be pleased to read modesty there—and kept her attention close by, no further than the dust-trimmed hem of Ghazanfer's skirt.

Just outside the sedan chair, she sensed rather than saw the bearers squatting at rest, passing a skin slick, almost obscene, with seeping water among them. Those six bearers from the poles on the other side had already taken the liberty of coming around to the door, for they had thoughtfully placed this facing west. All twelve of them now crowded together in the little bit of shade allowed by a sun rising rapidly over the sedan's roof.

So tight was the press that Safiye felt her wrapper drag across one bony knee. She sensed that the man was fully aware of the difference between her body's active heat—encapsulated as it was, concentrated—and the surrounding world's passivity. The quick exchange of husband for eunuch couldn't have fooled the bearers. They knew what sort of lurching rubbed their shoulders raw. No doubt they'd make some comment among themselves once she was out of earshot. She'd told Murad horses were better.

Still, after all, what was the discomfort of a few bearers to her? The lower sort of humanity existed to carry the upper, both physically and as the burden of their tongues.

*We must be in a desert,* Safiye thought, considering the heat, the glare, the total lack of vegetation, and the puffs of yellow dust that pillowed every step she took. She did not know Magnesia—or any place in Turkey for that matter—more than descriptions of land rents in the Divan or the view between a sedan's slats or from a lofty upper-floor lattice allowed her to imagine. That such sources might tend to an illiberal view of the world seemed impossible to her mind. But she knew of no desert in the provincial capital's environs.

She might have known from the sounds that this was no desert, though: the ring of metal on metal, the thud of iron on dead earth, the call of many men to their fellows like the chorus of some unmusical lyric. And as her eyes adjusted to the assault of light and singing heat waves, she began to see things no desert would contain. Numerous crews of men populated the space, not just ordinary men, but well-fed, well-muscled janissaries. She could tell because, though they had mostly stripped to the waist for the work they were doing, they maintained their white headgear with the telltale drape down to their shoulders at the rear.

The work entailed digging, deep digging in at least two spots that she could see. Relays carried the fill away in baskets and dumped it off the hillside. Lines of little donkeys also tiptoed up under great weights which, when unloaded, proved to be blocks of fine white building ashlar. Other janissaries stacked the stone here and there, in readiness.

"This must be the site of his mosque." Safiye adjusted her original judgment away from "naked desert." "Ghazanfer, ask him if it is."

The eunuch hastened to comply and brought back an affirmative.

Safiye had heard of the project, of course, although when Murad flushed with aesthetic details, she listened less. Like his evenings with poets and scholars, she let him indulge alone. The legal battles challenged her more.

"This buying up enough land to clear for the scheme is taking an inordinate amount of time," she had commented to Murad on several occasions.

"I don't want it so far out of town that no one will pray there," had been the prince's reply. "It must be close to water as well, for ablutions. That makes a suitable plot difficult to come by."

"Who are these people holding up the business, then?"

"Just small landholders. Old families with too many children, not enough land."

"I thought they must be great lords or something, by the trouble they raise. If such people will not sell at a decent price, surely they can be removed by force."

The idea had clearly shocked Murad. "Many of them have lived here—their families, at any rate—since time out of mind. Who's to say but that their ancestors were here to watch the Greeks sail in to avenge Helen at Troy? Long before we Turks arrived on the Gediz River, in any case."

"They're not even Muslims?"

"Many are Greek Christians, yes."

"What is your compunction, then? At home, in Venice, it happened all the time, particularly on the mainland. Water projects, you understand. Any small holders would have to move if the Council determined it was necessary—for the good of all, of course."

"That's barbaric."

"Sound business sense, my dear prince. A sense of progress."

"Against not only the spirit but the letter of our most merciful law." Murad had smoothed dignity into the feathers of his aigrette. "As you've just heard the mullah declare—if you were listening, as I'm sure you were, behind the Divan door—'Being an orphan himself, the Prophet—blessings on him—would never sanction the removal of property from the unwilling and underprivileged.'"

*You are the law in Magnesia, my prince. Can't you act like it?* Safiye had said this, but not aloud.

The convulsions of circumventing this law took up Divan time second only to the most contentious thing: trying to stop the locals from turning their grapes into wine or from selling their raisins, grape syrup, and dried figs to any but the empire's agents. Of course the farmers wanted the high prices red-nosed Englishmen and other foreigners would pay for these commodities that were luxuries in their distant homelands. But the Turkish laws were unstintingly clear—and annoying—about the evils of "tulip-colored wine." Since Magnesia was close enough to Constantinople—one of its attractions, Safiye reminded herself—the law could not be circumvented; the capital demanded and consumed all the fresh produce at fresh, local prices. Domestic workshops required local cotton, too, if Ottoman subjects were to have work. So the *sandjak bey* had to see that selling abroad was severely punished.

Such cases made up, along with the usual petty thefts, tawdry adulteries, and inheritance squabbles, the majority of pleas that Murad—and Safiye curtained behind him—heard day in and day out. That, and the efforts, often maddeningly futile, to get a decent-sized plot on which to build a mosque.

Seeing this hard-won plot of dirt now in heat-seared substantiality was gratifying. There were some holdouts who still clung to the orphan Prophet's mercy; Safiye saw their physicality now, too, their ramshackle houses making uneven tumors at the edges of her sight. But she was certain they'd soon be brought to bay—or at least Murad would be brought to see his legitimate rights as a ruler—and she could easily erase their existence from her mind's construction of the projected edifice.

"The man to whom the prince my master speaks is called Mustafa Effendi," Ghazanfer bent to inform Safiye. "He is the head architect."

"But I thought Sinan, the Royal Architect himself, was to build my master's mosque."

Ghazanfer obediently queried Murad on this point as well and then passed the following dialogue back and forth.

"Sinan did draw the plans with his own hand. But the Royal Architect is old and so has sent his disciple Mustafa instead. Sinan is older, even, than my grandfather the Sultan—Allah grant that his reign may last to the end of time."

Safiye knew the prayer was formulaic, but still she wished her prince would not ask quite so fervently for something that was so decidedly against his own interest—and hers.

"The only traveling Sinan thinks of doing," Murad continued through Ghazanfer, "is the pilgrimage. Perhaps if he goes this year—if building projects in the City of Cities do not keep him yet again—perhaps he may stop in Magnesia and see the site. Allah willing, he has promised to try."

"So what are these two holes the men are digging?"

"For the minarets, their bases. A group of craftsmen skilled in the special art of raising these fingers of stone that point towards heaven is directing the work. These men rove from town to town throughout the empire, wherever they are needed. Mustafa Effendi had news of this gang with a few months free so he thought he'd get them while he could and set them to work. We will have galley slaves to help as well, but only when the shipping lanes close for winter."

"Two minarets, my love?"

"I know." Murad blushed more than the sun would have caused. "Only a sultan's foundation is allowed two. Perhaps I tempt heaven."

"Your aunt Mihrimah's foundation in Üsküdar has two."

"That is because, in theory at least, her father built it for her. Still, it was her money. And certainly her taste."

"You think perhaps you will be Sultan by the time the building is completed?"

"Allah knows best."

So, whatever his pious and filial veneer, Murad would not really be content for the Angel Israfil's horn to blow before he got to be Allah's Shadow on earth. Safiye was pleased he harkened to her in this much, anyway.

At that moment, Baffo's daughter stumbled over an unevenness in the ground. Another woman might have thought her pride caused the difficulty. Safiye only knew it was one or the other of her many obstacles preventing good sight. Ghazanfer quickly reached out a hand to stop her and prevented a spectacular tumble.

"This is quite a severe slope you're forced to conform to," she had the eunuch comment to the prince.

"All Magnesia is steep," Murad replied. "Either coming up or going down."

Safiye already knew this geological fact by the slipping first one way and then the other inside her sedan. Shifting her veil the tiniest bit, she now got a clearer idea of just how truly Murad spoke. Two mountains whose tops she could hardly see pinched the settlement at their feet as though in a vise. Behind each rocky peak, rank upon rank of other precipices followed, much like mosque domes themselves, only steeper. Each one shimmered hazier than the one before it, bluer, until the sky hit the final, purest degree. Magnesia was a divine setting for a memorial to defy the ages.

The town was blessed with another imperial mosque already, the one Suleiman had built for his own mother, Murad's great-grandmother. Safiye caught a glimpse of it now across the edge of her view and knew the architect had been no Sinan. A heavy, primitive thing, the low dome seemed but a flattish blister such as days spent hiking up and down these hills might well raise on unaccustomed feet. She hoped silently that Sinan would have more success in dealing with—and matching—the terrain.

Murad had every confidence in his grandfather's man. ". . . Sinan says that a severe rectangle cutting straight across the slope will be the best plan." His parallel hands gestured the direction.

"A rectangle will not be too mundane?"

"The light angelic touch of Sinan with arches and domes will remedy that. Then, there will be room behind on a different level for a *medresse*—a religious college—a public kitchen to feed the poor—"

Safiye happened to catch the eye of an old woman watching them with dull interest from the closest of the hold-out houses. Silently, the prince's favorite tried to send a message across the distance that separated them: *See? You'll be perfectly well cared for if you give up that shack of yours. A public kitchen! Peasants in Venice never had such fortune.*

Behind her, Murad was still cataloguing the wonders of this child of his inspiration. ". . . Costly tile from Iznik throughout the interior."

"You'll let me have a hand in their choosing?"

"Of course. And the façade will be pierced by a thousand thousand holes, more light and air than dead stone."

"You will fill these holes with glass, I suppose."

Murad looked a little crestfallen, an emotion Ghazanfer couldn't translate. "The plan specifies only open air, spaces small enough to keep out birds, large enough to let in refreshing breezes."

"It should be glass," Safiye insisted.

"Well, bottle glass was mentioned as a possibility. But unfilled holes would be lighter."

"Bottle glass! Why not real stained glass? From Venice, say. The best glass in the world."

"That would be nice," Murad sighed. "But then we'd have to put a second skin—bottle glass—on the outside to protect such treasures."

"Common houses have glass where I come from," Safiye said, on the verge of taunting.

"Terribly expensive. On a *sandjak bey*'s salary?"

"You are getting the local people to save their souls and contribute a little, I hope?"

"Yes. And my aunt Mihrimah, having already built a mosque of her own, is helping as well."

"And you will not always be limited to a *sandjak*'s income."

"Allah willing."

"Nothing at all will ever happen if you wait on Allah." Safiye was glad Ghazanfer censored out that part of her comment. But he did faithfully say the rest. "If you can have two minarets, I would not dismiss stained glass as out of the question, either. And you forget, my prince and my life, you were born in Magnesia. This monument is in honor of that. But Venice is *my* home. You should let me see what sources I can tap before you settle for a wall of empty holes." It wouldn't do to get any more specific about Venice than that.

"I take it the project pleases you, my Fair One?"

Murad spoke directly to her now, for, having seen what there was to see on a site but newly leveled, they had returned to the sedan. And it was high time to escape the punishment of the sun.

The bearers unfolded themselves and recovered their places as reluctantly as ratted hair. And Ghazanfer stepped aside with his usual silent tact to let the conversation turn immediate again. Until the sedan door closed behind them, their talk could not claim the intimacy of touch. Yet touch was the only way Safiye could think of to express her true delight at all she had seen and heard.

"It pleases me more than I can say," she exclaimed and, feeling that her effluence sounded too insincere, she defied convention and reached out a hand to her prince to substantiate her words.

Murad stepped beyond the contact in order to serve modesty, but she could tell that the mere attempt impressed him.

It was Ghazanfer's arm she felt instead as the eunuch helped her up into the bloodred velvet lining of the sedan, now as hot as oven bricks. Soon, soon veils and constrained hands could be discarded.

"That's good." Murad continued the dialogue behind Safiye and her servant. "And I must give the Venetian glass some thought."

"Give it no thought. Simply do it." Safiye was impatient with heat and veils as much as with the prince.

"Yes, because, in a way, I'm building this great mosque for you."

"For me?" Safiye hoped her new purr tone carried through the veiling. She fumbled to remove the white silken gauze sweat-plastered to her face——in order to breathe, if for no other reason.

"In a way, yes. For Allah, of course, first of all. But I have made a vow and offer it to the Creator if He will but grant us a son . . ."

Murad's voice foundered——not from heat, but from emotion.

And Safiye stopped what she was doing and kept her face covered, just a little while, until the door was shut upon them and the chair lurched up to the bearers' shoulders. She did not want the emotion in her face betrayed, not even to Murad.

A mosque for herself, she had been thinking. Nur Banu could claim no such honor. Only the greatest men had mosques of their own. And the women? You could count them on one hand: Suleiman's mother; Haseki Khurrem, his beloved; Mihrimah Sultan, his daughter. That was privileged company indeed. Of course, this mosque would probably not wear her own name. They'd call it the Muradiye. But she would know, he would know—he'd just confessed. God would know. Perhaps most important of all, Nur Banu would know. Safiye would see to it that Murad wrote his mother this much—in his very next letter.

Now this talk of divine vows—that put a new spin on things, a spin Safiye couldn't hear without a sting of tears in the corners of her eyes, threatening to betray her. She couldn't afford to let such gestures flood her with emotion; she might lose sight of more important things.

Nevertheless, it touched her. No matter what he protested aloud, having an heir was as important for Murad as it was for any other man. Perhaps more so. Murad was willing to go to the fabulous expense of building a mosque—with Venetian glass, even—in order to attain it.

Safiye had to look at the absurdity of his ill-wrapped turban to temper her swelling emotion with reality. It also helped to remember a recent scene.

"Mother says you are doing something to keep from having a child," Murad had accused her at this time. "I don't know about such things, but is this possible? How on earth is this possible, my love?"

"Your mother has a bitter, jealous tongue," Safiye had replied with a tight coolness.

She struggled to regain that coolness now as the sedan door closed on them. "How can she think I'd deny you anything, my lord and prince?"

"That's what I told her."

"And you believed her?"

"No. No, my love, I believe you."

But if this mosque was being built to petition the One who could give the prince a son—well, Allah's will had nothing to do with it. The great Muradiye mosque and its complex of pious and charitable buildings was, in fact, built to no one else's honor but her own.

# XIV

FAR OFF TO the west, white clouds marked the horizon where, although she couldn't see it, Safiye knew the Mediterranean lay. The clouds swelled and clustered—like the ripening grapes on the vines they'd passed in the valleys below. But for the sky, this was just practice. It would be a month, probably, before such a sky actually ripened, full of white wine, before it marshaled its drunken troops to march inland with the season's first rain. For the moment, most of the vault was unveined lapis lazuli, too rich, too weighty, too parched for use, or for the use of anything under it.

The land in all directions panted under waves of heat, reflecting off that sky and yearning towards harvest, towards the olive press and the satisfied smell of fresh-filled granaries. Safiye looked over it all to the clouds, thought *Mediterranean,* thought beyond, to Constantinople, then had to force her thoughts back to the present. Magnesia wasn't Constantinople, but it was a step in the right direction. She must perform this stint well, no matter how impatient she grew, in order to earn the next one.

Ghazanfer had set up a lovely little spot in the shade with cushions, rugs, and a repast of stuffed grape leaves; sliced cucumbers in salted, vinegared olive oil, flecked with sweet basil and pepper; napkin-wrapped flat bread, still warm and puffing at the black blisters; honeyed yogurt; fresh peaches to close. It was too hot to eat. Mostly Safiye concentrated on the pomegranate sherbet, tanged with lemon. No matter how much she drank, it still crunched with ice. How Ghazanfer managed that on such a hot day did not concern her.

That there was enough of everything for two was a little more disconcerting. The fluff of the lining velvet still itched on her sweating skin, but Safiye knew there would be no return to the stifling sedan after this rest. Thankfully, Magnesia, its prying eyes, its tattling tongues, was far enough behind them; it would be horses from now on. Murad had gone to see to the horses and then sent word back through Ghazanfer that the officers of the corps had detained him. He could not refuse their invitation to eat with them.

From time to time she could hear their coughs of rough male laughter carried around the intervening outcrops of limestone. She longed to overhear what sparked those flashes of merriment, the solid kindling and fuel beneath, almost as much as she wished to be back in Constantinople where the magnificent heart of the empire beat.

But the longer she sat where Ghazanfer had set her, the quiet, rustic pageant curling about her feet distracted her more and more. At first she thought the eunuch's sole purpose in placing her here was the shade. She certainly had to crane her neck to see those clouds over the Mediterranean and she was maddeningly far from Murad and the officers.

But then Ghazanfer presented her with a handful of flowers

he'd plucked from the wayside: asters, mostly, the lavender blossoms tiny, pale, dusty, brittle, weedy with drought. And then she realized that the spot gave her an excellent view of a shady grotto let into the steep side of the hill. A small stream trickled from the rock here, pale and thin as her heat-bleached flowers.

And within the grotto was a white stone the size and shape of a woman.

Safiye shifted from one end of the rugs that bounded her space to the other. No matter at what angle she sat, Safiye could not escape the impression that this was a real woman, her hair veiled, standing rigid with her arms pressing to her breast in a tight, hopeless grief. The fact that the source of the little stream was out of the rock near the woman's head and that it pursued its ageless trickle across her hardened person—this exaggerated the impression of sorrow.

The hand and chisel of man had aided the natural form of the stone, roughed in a waist, the edge of an arm, a chin. This artifice was much older than the Greek and Roman sculptures she had seen, cruder—but this made it all the more compelling in a wild, barbaric sort of way. The individual moment of beauty captured by the classical style was superseded here by mere suggestion that encompassed every woman, indeed, the universe itself in a shapeless, basic anonymity.

"Niobe," Ghazanfer said. "All tears."

At first Safiye didn't ask for any more explanation, no more than she asked her attendant how he happened to know this or how he kept the sherbet icy. She was used to giving explanations, not asking for them. But the longer she sat before this stage she had the distinct impression her eunuch had set for her, the more compelling it became, the harder to pretend omniscience.

Safiye was not alone in her attraction to the site. A stream of local women as thin but as steady as the fountain on the stone female's face found its way to the primitive shrine.

"Greeks?" was the first thing she asked.

Ghazanfer's sugar-cone turban nodded.

The twinge of regret she felt at this reply surprised her. She had suspected this would be the answer: most peasants in the neighborhood kept their ancient faith. But now she knew for a fact that she would not be able to speak to her associates at this revered spot. Whereas Greek men might learn enough Turkish to make their way in a man's world, their women steadfastly spoke nothing but their ancient mother tongue. She'd never regretted her inability to speak to Greek women before. And she had seen them, standing on their balconies or low tile roofs, placidly dropping their spinning whorls into the courtyards below to get the right tension in their wool. Or—particularly the old ones—sitting on their doorsteps, knitting their weatherproof stockings, the traditional patterns inside out on five hooked needles, and crooning to the small children about their feet.

Greek women were not as secluded as Muslim women, but she didn't envy them. This was doubtless because they were poorer, not from any lack of desire for the status of seclusion. And there was nothing like a sedan chair accompanied by janissaries—the conquerors' army—to send them scurrying.

But suddenly, here in the grotto's shade, Safiye wished for communication.

Although some of the visiting women wore the striped skirts, white with deep blue or red, traditional to the race, most were widows. Like crows they flocked, every garment down to underlinen and pocket handkerchiefs having been sent to the dyer's on that fateful day and returned a unanimous black.

*What have I to do with those on whom heaven has thus turned its back?* is what her usual reaction to widows might have been. *Whose lives are, for all intents and purposes, over?*

But for the first time she saw them as individuals and saw that not every petitioner was irredeemably old. A woman could be hardly more than a girl, and pretty, too, when an awe-full heaven—St. Agnes preserve us!—might plunge her into black and send her praying to springs and rocks for her solace.

Many of the petitioners brought offerings. Some brought only flowers—asters like hers—and left them in little lavender clouds at the impassive stone's feet. Copper trays of boiled wheat were more popular. Even cold from a long hike on some black-swathed head, the dish exuded an earthy fragrance. And when the covering kerchiefs were removed, Safiye could see that designs of leaves, flowers, and inscriptions in colored sugar, almonds, basil, cinnamon, sesame seed, raisins, and dried figs ornamented the tops of these vulgar heaps.

"A dish for the dead," Ghazanfer said. "It harks back to Mother Ceres and Persephone, her child."

Mostly the petitioners ate the grain themselves with one or two friends and a skin of wine, quite joyfully al fresco, then returned with the copper tray, empty, balanced on their heads as they had come.

But an ancient woman begging among them saw to it that there were no leftovers. *She is much like the rock itself,* Safiye thought, though her clothes, in rags, did not have the luxury of a single color. Inevitably, this mendicant shuffled her way with an incomprehensible, singsong whine and a head sunken into her shoulders in a caricature of humility to the edge of the royal rugs. Then Safiye surprised herself by handing those wizened hands all the *dolmas* and gesturing that the old woman should keep the platter, too. Giving away a large part of her meal was the only way Safiye could think of to achieve the communication she craved.

The woman pulled the gift to her, bowed once, getting her clown-colored bodice in the dish's oil, muttered blessings as in-

comprehensible and fretful as the begging, then scurried off like
a mouse to her den with a prize.

"Lady—"

Safiye started from the abnormal glow charity gave her,
something like eating too much spicy food. The usually silent
giant beside her had sucked in his breath with unmistakable horror.

"Ghazanfer, my lion? What is it? You feel there is something
wrong with my largess?"

"Not at all, lady." The *khadim* was tight-lipped.

"Well? What is it?"

"Only *this* charity."

"Explain yourself."

"Don't you believe, lady, that ill fortune will follow a gift that
goes directly from your table to the beggar's hands? Didn't you
see how careful the other donors were to set the old woman's
portion in a neutral place for her first?" Such a long speech spoke
to the earnestness of the eunuch's words. "You don't believe—
or fear—you may become as destitute as she?"

"I've never heard of such a thing. No, I don't believe it. I won't
believe it. And I order you not to believe it as well."

"*Mashallah.*" Ghazanfer bowed in compliance.

But Safiye didn't like the panic which stung her own eyes as
she watched, helpless, her disappearing tray.

She breathed once or twice, deeply, until she convinced herself that this was only a foolish superstition of her eunuch. He
was so solicitous of her that he sometimes went too far; she
would have to keep the head of reason between them. When
they cut a lad, they often left him a child in more ways than one.

But in spite of such wisdom, she couldn't shake herself free
of the spell of the place, a spell of which she was quite certain
Ghazanfer wasn't totally innocent. She had to ask: "Ghazanfer?"

"Lady?"

"Who is she?"

"An old woman Allah has blessed with poverty. I know not, lady."

"Not the beggar. I mean the stone."

"Ah. Niobe."

"Niobe." Yes, he'd said so earlier. Safiye felt she should know the name without the eunuch's help, from some fresco imitating the classical in some rich relative's entry hall at home. But at the moment she couldn't remember and hoped Ghazanfer would answer her implied question without her having to actually raise the last syllable herself.

He did. "Niobe was a woman. A mortal woman." She couldn't expect Ghazanfer to warm to his tale like the best of wayside storytellers. "Niobe was blessed above the usual course of mortals."

"Blessed with riches? She was a princess?" It wasn't too self-effacing to urge the story on like this, else they might be at it all day.

Ghazanfer nodded but added: "The gods had given her many children, seven boys and seven girls."

*"Mashallah!"* Safiye exclaimed in spite of herself, not at all certain that this was indeed a blessing.

"But she forgot."

"What did she forget?" The eunuch had to be pulled out of his usual infuriatingly laconic style again.

"That it was the gods that had blessed her in the first place. She had the temerity to boast that she was greater than the goddess Leto, whose only two children were Apollo and Artemis."

"So what happened?" Safiye tore nervously at the eunuch's gift of asters and their brittle foliage.

"Leto's children avenged their mother's honor by showering their divine arrows down on Niobe's offspring so they died, all fourteen of them, all in an instant."

*"Mashallah!"*

"Niobe, in her grief, could not cease weeping until the great Creator took pity on her and turned her to stone. She weeps still, but at least she no longer suffers."

"And this is the stone?"

"So they say."

Having been chided once in an afternoon for superstition, Ghazanfer was not going to commit himself so readily. It was all Safiye could do to resist ordering him to do so at once. Such was the compulsion of the place, a power she desired, like all power. Unlike other power, however, she didn't know how to claim it. Thus unnerved, she wanted to leave the place, but couldn't begin to imagine where she might go to escape such a spell or even, she realized, how to get to her feet to begin to try.

Murad's appearance with the horses was a great relief. The officers must have helped him to rewind his turban. He looked as neat and attractive as the entire meal she had failed to eat.

"My love, what's the matter?" the prince asked as he helped her to her feet, helped her to rediscover what those appendages were for.

"Nothing. Nothing at all, my heart's desire. Only missing you."

For once, her lover's patter was true and heartfelt. And her clinging to him somewhat embarrassed Murad in such a public place.

Fortunately, at the prince's approach, the black flocks of pilgrims had taken flight like crows before a sling stone. Safiye suspected they and the spell would return as soon as Murad was gone, and she wanted to leave, with him and as quickly as possible.

Leaving Ghazanfer and a menial or two to pack up the remains of the meal, she let Murad lead her to the horses. She greeted her dappled mare with a hand to the muzzle and filled her head with the smell of horse, the smell of freedom—escape from the harem, the sedan. The smell, finally, of power.

Murad held the stirrup for her, promising all of this, but just before she lifted her foot to claim it, Ghazanfer interrupted.

"Lady?"

"What is it, *khadim?*"

Oddly, he approached no nearer, carefully keeping the horse's flank between him and the prince as if he had something to hide. Safiye had no choice but to join the eunuch on the other side, leaving Murad with a little reassuring pressure on the arm—but was the reassurance for her lover or for herself?

"Yes, Ghazanfer, what is it?" She began with an exaggerated show of patience, indicating that patience was about to run out.

Ghazanfer closed the green of his eyes as he looked down. Following that look, she saw what the matter was. In each hand the eunuch held one of the silver cases in which she kept her pessaries, the *farazikh* that prevented conception.

"I found them in the sedan while I was packing up," Ghazanfer elaborated.

"Of course. That's where they ought to be. In case—" Did she have to spell it out for this sexless creature?

But now she saw more. The eunuch held the cases, protecting his flattened hands from the metal with the ends of his sash. Both cases lay open. The sheep's tailfat in one, the black tar in the other, had melted in the sedan's heat leaving no body-ready fingers, but large, shapeless, useless puddles of swirling simples instead.

"Is everything all right, Safiye?" Murad called over the horse's flank.

"Just fine," she assured him. Then to the eunuch she said, "Never mind, Ghazanfer. Keep them safe. With the sherbet ice, perhaps. I'll reform the mixture later."

*"Inshallah,"* she heard her attendant say as she swung up onto the horse.

The saddle leather, smooth and sun-warmed, embraced her legs and soothed her cares. Finding the bunch of asters still burdening her hand, she tossed the flowers from her, grasped the reins, and gave the dappled flanks a good nudge with her yellow kidskin slippers.

# XV

ACROSS HER REACHING shoulder blades, Safiye felt the rousing whip of the ends of her six braids. She'd dropped the stiff golden brown outer wrap off her back perhaps half a *farsakh* ago, hardly out of Niobe's tear-bleared sight, and brought it around to rest in front of her over the horse's neck. The golden crepe extending her braids allowed her hips to feel the stimulating lash as well. The wind made by her ride on an otherwise still day penetrated the thin shirt over her forearms and breast until gooseflesh rose and her nipples bunched as if wrung of sweat.

She felt her breath competing with the sun for enough moisture to find any scent in that late summer countryside. All she did smell held the dryness of tinder and, as it filled her head, she felt herself ready to burst into spontaneous flame. She rode harder—to escape that potential? Or to ride directly into it?

Certainly she felt the wind carried her veils behind her like a banner on the battlefield and Murad, she knew, would follow like the good soldier he was. Did soldiers, she wondered, feel such urgency as they rushed towards the enemy? And was glory what they longed to embrace? Or the beautiful maidens, the houris of paradise?

The idea the Koran gave her that she might be riding towards a celestial court full of doe-eyed and divinely insatiable page boys pressed a groan up from the warmth of her saddle leather. For she had never attended to religious discussion carefully enough to know if this pious promise was meant for her or only for the appetite of a Selim. Used as she was to making the world over in her own image, Safiye assumed she led the ranks of the blessed herself, and the thought brought a rigor to her thighs. The horse, a sensitive, spirited creature, took this pressure as an urging to go forward faster still.

Attendants, guards, and hunters dropped like the sun behind the west-riding hills at her back. Ahead rose the Boz, the Gray Mountains, her destination, but untrue to their dull name in the golden afternoon sun.

There was no rush. They planned no more than to reach the encampment by nightfall. Slaves were even now setting up the tents and seeing to supper, others sorting out the hawks and hounds, jesses, pistols, pikes, beaters, and net men. Her haste was unwarranted.

She knew she wasn't trying to escape from Murad. Through Murad's power lay her own. And she remembered how handsome he had seemed, his turban neatly retied, fresh from the inspiring company of officers. She could look over her shoulder now and see him still as attractive, pursuing just behind the screen of her dust.

But she also knew the urge she felt was not toward the highly staged world of the hunt, either. In spite of her direction, didn't she long for escape from this actor's box where the prince could hardly prove himself a prince? Didn't she long to have him succeed in a world where mistakes were not impossible?

At that moment Safiye saw an opening in the trees to her left. As if in confirmation of her theory, she spontaneously dragged the bridle in that direction, off the cart-sized and rutted road, onto a path that quickly closed chestnut branches over her. The foliage was close enough to stroke her hair and pluck at the red silk *shalvar* on her knees.

"Safiye, don't." Finding that first order useless, Murad, behind her, amended it. "Wait!"

But the throb of horse hooves in her ears overrode him. Over her shoulders along with her braids, she threw the prince a laughing dare to follow.

The warm, leathery smell of tannin bit her flirtatiously on the nose, for besides the still-green burrs on chestnuts, the sky was erased by oaks and the ground by thickets of sumac. It was perceptibly cooler here in the shade than on the road, and the sudden half-light threw a second veil over her face.

Thus half-blinded, an unexpected scramble in the underbrush made her think either Murad had closed quickly or her own horse was scrambling on the tangle beneath her hooves. But when, five steps later she still had her seat, she knew it was neither.

Before either panic or confusion could touch her, the shadow she heard more than saw took on definite form, and that form was a deer. A stately fallow doe leapt off at an angle towards her right. A good omen for the hunt. But even with so quick a glance, Safiye saw the velvety nose, quivering with terror, and the big, sad eyes—*the eyes of a paradisical houri.*

Such a vision was enough to make her breath pull up sharp

and her heart stop, not for fear, but in wonder mixed with desire. *The doe has a fawn with her somewhere,* seemed an obvious thought. *One still young enough to hide while she draws the hunter's attention off.*

She pulled up at the perfect awe of such a thought and her mare sidled to a halt. Safiye had seen deer before on other hunts, both dead and alive. But mother love and self-sacrifice were otherworldly wonders to her. She sat frozen, matching her heavy breathing to that of the horse beneath her, and fought to overcome this debilitating reverence enough to go on. Mother love and self-sacrifice she would condemn as weakness in a fellow human, but in a dumb animal it was difficult to disparage.

Safiye couldn't fathom the instinct. She could never accept it, but she couldn't deny it either. This instinct, like the ancient weeping woman of stone, plunged her into confusion. She'd ridden on the horns of that confusion since she'd left the shrine. Confusion was the enemy she battled.

The sight of the deer was powerful enough to make her sue for a momentary truce. She would turn the mare and go back, comply with the world's expectations until morning renewed her strength.

A ride like she'd enjoyed today would never have been hers in Venice. She took consolation in this thought. She had done some riding in her youth, but never as much as in the past five months. Even if the nuns had approved, she would have had to go sidesaddle in order not to tangle her skirts.

*And never on such a lively little mount as I've had to work with since coming to Magnesia. Intelligent, yet so willingly obedient . . .* She relished the use of these horseman's terms which six months ago she could not have appreciated. *Yes, I know. Ghazanfer would have me say "Thanks be to Allah" after a thought like this.* But with a final restorative turn to her rebellion, she refused to do so, even in her mind.

Then, in the middle of this thought, and the middle of drawing the bridle off to the right, the horse beneath her suddenly screamed and lurched up and out from under her.

The last thing Safiye saw was a stand of sumac coming up fast.

# XVI

SAFIYE WAS NOT badly hurt. More than two breaths could not have been knocked from her before she found both breath and senses again. Broken sumac twigs were sticking into her at odd places, clinging to others, hampering movements, rendering any action uncomfortable, filling her nose with their sharp, bruised smell. But a few tentative maneuvers, though they sank her deeper in among the foliage, and the sumac deeper into her flesh, revealed nothing serious.

The first thing she saw when she was half upright again gave her a serious setback, however. Safiye found herself in something of a hollow and, almost level with her eyes, her mare's legs thrust towards her like four gray ashwood lances. Even as she watched, the top rear leg quivered once, twice, and then lay still, deathly still.

Unable to grasp what could possibly have happened, Safiye lay back again, gasping for breath and consciousness.

"Allah! Allah! I've killed her!"

Murad, having left his own horse at the edge of sight, rushed to the mare. Then, moaning "Allah!" once more, he lifted up

Safiye's gold-brown wrapper that draped the horse's shoulders—along with the broken nock end of one of his own arrows. The rest of the shaft was buried in the mare's heart. Now Safiye's senses truly did spin from her.

She awoke with an ache of black, tightened vision clogging the bridge of her nose. She was caught in her prince's arms. He didn't carry her far, only out of sight of the attendants who had rushed up to see to the fallen animal, away from the heavy sound of flies that had already found the place.

He carried her to a less treacherous embankment where he knelt and set her down. As if from far away, she heard him offer praises to his God for her survival. Closer were the protestations for the innocence of his mistake: He saw the deer. He thought to start the hunt early without the crutch of beaters. Such an easy shot. He lost the deer for a moment. He thought he saw it again. He realized, just the instant he released the arrow, that what he saw was his lover's wrapper instead. And he couldn't remember that she had shrugged it off.

And now he was closer, promising her a new horse, promising her twenty, promising her the earth and paradise as well if she'd forgive him. *There's always marriage,* she thought, but before she found breath to make the suggestion aloud, an ache of hunger crawled through her limbs for the beauty of his speech. And it was hunger, not for a tray of pastries, but for a most basic and hearty pilaf.

And now he was very close indeed. Murad felt her for injuries she'd already dismissed and her veils had vanished somewhere, tangled up in her exertions. Instead of faint and sumac, bruised masculinity now filled her nose.

When he'd convinced himself her worst injury was a scratch on her cheek, he kissed it better. He unbuttoned her jacket to check her ribs, her breasts—desperately seeking more, hidden ruptures in her love for him.

*How Murad is changed since the first evening I saw him,* Safiye mused, considering the change her handiwork and loving it for that reason. He was much handsomer now with flesh on his bones. His cheeks—no longer sallow—were glowing from the day's exercise like oil-filled lamps of which his eyes were the flames.

*Marriage,* she thought to press again.

And then she saw him no more as a separate being, but as herself. For he was rooting kisses from her like weeds and the soil of her being crumpled in his hands.

Safiye gave a little yelp of surprise as the loss of self swept over her. She was surprised to find all her manifold ambitions focused so suddenly on the hard underridge of her pelvis—she always was. She, who made an effort to avoid being taken unawares.

Once ambushed, however, there was no time for retreat. She was indeed a prisoner, a slave. She groaned that her platform was never firm, or never firm enough. Never enough for the hard press up a hill that love drove her to—either frantically towards something or away. Whatever the desperate goal of that moment was, she didn't know because she'd never reached it—or escaped its pull.

Oh, she knew orgasm all right, but whenever it came, it seemed a pallid return for the desperation driving her. Some unnameable game beyond tantalized. She never managed to demand quite enough before the softer heart beyond was pierced and the scalding urgency lost itself in a blur like a warm water bath.

Knobs of acorn and chestnut burred under her. She rammed her flesh onto them hard, desperate for the leverage silk on silk failed to give, with no time in the midst of her hunger to remove any garment completely.

Murad's consummation was quick and bruising, even more

so, perhaps, than being thrown from the horse. Safiye was hard-pressed to turn her cries of pure pain into those of a satisfied lover. She bore the fierce weight with patience, however, convinced this was still the path on which her own desires would be met—sooner or later.

A gap of hurtful, brilliant summer indigo hummed with insects over Murad's turban, which was unraveled once more. Fringes of dagged oakleaf hemmed the blue, like some Venetian dandy's sleeve.

Safiye felt the acorns and chestnut burrs again, more mortifying than before, though now in her mind they provoked images of deep winter afternoons by the fire, roasting nuts and wine. Imagining such surroundings instead of the present ones, she gently stroked Murad's red hair, twisting it about her fingers.

*Now is not the time for my wants. How to give my prince the words he needs to leave the violence of this place and go on?*

She asked some crooning, innocent question, then let him talk.

It was not the first detail he mentioned, but Safiye knew at once by the sudden drop in his voice that it was the one she should set off after in wild pursuit.

"There was the doe . . . ," he said.

When he seemed reluctant to continue, Safiye said, "I saw her."

"Yes. She was very beautiful."

"My heart stopped to see her, even from a distance," Safiye agreed.

"You should have seen her up close. Those eyes!"

"The eyes of a paradise houri," she coaxed into his hair.

For one brief instant, she assumed he would kiss her on the eyelids, bridging the metaphor without words. She even closed her eyes for the moment.

But then Murad leapt to his feet as if her touch burned him. He began to dress in a fever. The sight of her might almost have disgusted him.

Safiye prodded yet more carefully, rising on an elbow and reaching a hand to narrow the space between them again. "I . . . I suppose she has a fawn in a thicket nearby. She will return to it . . ."

This seemed precisely the wrong thing to say. Murad sank into a crouch on the littered forest floor as if her words were arrows. The prince hugged himself into a ball, nursing the wound she couldn't see. In his gold and rusty colors, he seemed a premature autumn there.

On hands and knees Safiye crawled across the verdant summer floor towards him. The fallen fruits and twigs concealed by grass and infant trees were harsher on her knees than they had been on her buttocks, and she was shaking with the pain of it by the time she reached him. Pain, and a good deal of distress. Still, she pressed through the tightness, like the moment of lost virginity, in order to lay a questioning hand upon the brown and yellow summer silk of her lover's shoulder.

The prince shuddered, as from a hurt rather than a comfort. He was weeping.

Safiye was taken aback. Murad had railed, whined, even struck her before. But he had never, never cried. She hadn't known he could cry. She herself had cried but once since the Turks had captured her, and then only in secret. A man in tears turned her stomach with disgust. And this man . . .

Safiye fought down her nausea. Much as she wanted to slap him, shrew him into finding his lost manhood, shame him forever for such tears, she could not. Perhaps it was the dead horse, the living doe. Perhaps it went back even so far as Niobe, solid rock, weeping for eternity. Safiye could only crouch and stare with awe, and when that grew awkward she had no other choice but to crawl around to a different angle and take the shuddering ball of silk, brocade, and tender, tender flesh into her arms.

The violence with which Murad returned the embrace frightened her, but she couldn't flinch. Nor would she confess, even to herself, that she was daunted. Soon the fabric on her shoulder had turned hot and wet, like a poultice.

"So easy to take life," Murad said eventually, when he thought his voice would hold. But again control failed him as he continued, "So easy. And yet, so hard to give it."

A cuckoo called, its mate responded, and in the silence between, the other birds they cuckolded. Safiye could feel her lover's heartbeat like an inflammation in her own breast.

She said nothing, but waited until, in a few minutes, Murad began again. "Forgive me. Say you forgive me, my love."

"Forgive you? Whatever for?"

"Forgive me that you are fated to a man who can never give you children."

"No children?" Safiye exclaimed gently. "But that is Allah's will, not yours, my own sweet love."

"It is my fault. I know it. He punishes me because I fretted away time with the opium, and created worlds for myself that He did not create. That is blasphemy. I took opium and let it steal Allah-created desire from me. Most men blame their women for their childlessness, but most men are fools. And most men are not blessed with such a faultless creature as yourself. I have grieved much over this. Others may blame you, but I do not."

"Your mother . . ." She didn't know how to finish the phrase herself.

"Yes, I know my mother made your days in the harem a hell because she would have a grandson in her old age. But rest assured that I do not love you one whit less. I know it is not your fault. I saw this clearly today. Today, when I thought I'd struck you—Allah forbid! When I pulled up the wrapper, thinking to find your death-shriveled form. When I pulled my arrow out of the mare's warm, dark insides, I brought forth only blood and death. What else do I do to you but that? What else have I only just done? In my anger against Heaven and myself? Served you no better than the poor, poor horse."

"My love," Safiye said with a thrill in her breast that was only contained by pressing Murad's head to it. "Be at ease, my cool summer rain. For surely, if there is guilt here, we share it, as we share everything."

They loved again, slower, deliberately this time, sharing guilt as much as they shared delight.

Near sunset, Safiye relinquished her lover's arms for her eunuch's. Ghazanfer had recovered her veils and stood with them placidly draped over his arm. The *khadim* had kept his faithful watch, even there in the woods, preserving the lovers' privacy inviolate.

And it wasn't until that moment, until she met his green eyes as he laid the ridge of silk to ride chafing over her nose, that she remembered. She remembered what she had forgotten in the midst of the horse's death. She remembered she ought to have pressed her advantage and gained the legality of marriage.

And she remembered what lay melted in ornate silver cases, back in the overheated red velvet of her sedan.

# Part III

# Abdullah

# XVII

"Good morning, madam."

The Quince sailed into Esmikhan Sultan's harem, trailing Bosphorus damp and cold after her. Winter lingered in earnest in the capital.

I prodded again: "This is a pleasant surprise."

I really didn't look for an answer. I had only ever had one good conversation with the midwife—the day she assured me no power on earth could restore my lost manhood. Otherwise, she had always been one of those women—the majority—for whom *khuddam* were just one more item of harem furniture. Like cushions and divans we were, there to make life comfortable, but never expected to intrude upon her business with conversation.

The Quince had presided closely over my lady's health for over two years. I was familiar with the midwife's quirks, as she must have been with ours, that my lady and I did not hold to the usual formalities between eunuch and mistress.

My lady's little slave girl took the midwife's veils and wraps as I'd taught her and hung them on pegs to dry. But even before her pinched, sour face was revealed, I could tell our guest's manner was even more brusque and agitated than usual.

So I spoke to set her at ease. "We didn't hope to have you back with us in Constantinople for many months more." Though, if I'd thought about it, I would have done better to serve with the impassivity of a pillow—something she was used to—if I truly sought her comfort and not my own.

Frankly, curiosity put decorum the furthest thing from my mind at the moment. The last time we'd had the bustle of this woman in our house had been just before the sea lanes closed for the winter. At that time, Esmikhan had been daily hoping for Safiye's return for the season. Such hopes had been dashed, then quickly dispelled by even happier news. Safiye's condition forbade her removal on any long journey; my lady's child was no longer the most royal expectation in the empire.

"Of course you must go to her," my lady had told her midwife.

"Safiye isn't due until three, four months after you, lady," I'd interjected. "The midwife could see you, *inshallah,* safe and have plenty of time to travel on to see to your brother's child."

Esmikhan had chosen to ignore me and spoke exclusively to our guest. "Safiye will need you. And I—I have done this so many times I can manage with another midwife."

The Quince hadn't needed more convincing. She'd packed her things in an hour and caught the final ship out of the Golden Horn—to see to Safiye and the royal child she was expecting.

"My brother's child, *inshallah,* will be heir to the throne," my lady had said wistfully when at last we'd been alone. "It needs the best midwife, not I."

Now, here was the Quince, back after only three months, no more. My lady was yet undelivered. The sea lanes had hardly opened again. Perhaps the midwife had even come by land. Or perhaps she'd not made it to Magnesia at all.

What could it mean? Curiosity prodded me to attempt one more speech. "Are we to expect you for an extended stay, madam?"

If she did plan to move back in with us, as had been her custom as long as Esmikhan carried her ill-fated children, I would need to know so I could make arrangements. The Quince could hardly deny me an answer to this.

The eye she turned on me simmered with impatience that I, the cushion, had forced any pronouncement from her at all. "I just come for a little visit," she said in clipped tones.

And then we were in my lady's presence, so I retreated to my post by the door of the room and trusted Esmikhan to draw out the details.

My lady sat on the floor before the low table on which lay one of the seven or eight dainty meals she ate a day at this stage of her pregnancies, when the huge mass of child pressed awkwardly on her stomach. Earlier that morning, I had placed a metal brazier packed with fresh coals under that table and a heavy rug over the top of it. My lady had gone directly from her nighttime quilts to this rug. Though other pregnancies in the ninth month had prostrated her with the heat, so grim and cold was this day that she kept all of the lower half of her body tucked under the insulating rug, her knees and feet almost touching the room's only source of heat.

The light was bad through the window. I'd lit a lamp or two but considered lighting more. Unpainted olive-wood lattice was difficult to distinguish from the gray of the sky beyond. Many other details in the room were obscured as well, but in the darkest corners the sweet smell of the sandalwood I'd put along with other fuel in the brazier snuggled the nose. The weather outside, vacillating between a drizzle and an even damper fog, hissed in the ear. The entire mood, close to sightless though it was, remained safe from the world's cold blasts. As usual, I liked to see my lady as a gem—perhaps dull onyx today—in a setting of my own design.

But the effect was lost on the Quince.

Esmikhan's reaction upon seeing her guest was much as mine

had been. Even our words were identical, though the Quince
eked this rehearsal out with greetings in return and a salaam as
negligent as her usual attentions to such forms.

When my lady reached the part about the length of her stay
with us, the Quince repeated, "Just a little visit," but added, "Just
long enough to see my prize patient and the new child, *mashallah.*"

"I am fine, thanks to Allah," my lady replied. She shifted her
attitude and the rug so the midwife could give her hem a cur-
sory kiss, as royal blood demanded. "The child—well, that is
in the hands of heaven. I am doing my best for him. And yourself, madam?"

There was no reply. As she raised herself from the obeisance
and got her first good look at my lady in the half-light, the
Quince started. She could not have been more shocked and
surprised if Esmikhan had pulled a pistol and shot her. The midwife's usual color grew yet more pallid and green, and that pronounced the fuzz on her face more as well.

"Madam, what is the matter?" My lady attempted to raise her
awkward bulk to assist, for her guest suddenly seemed to demand it.

"Nothing," said the older woman in a tone that betrayed a
bold-faced lie.

"What can I get you? Some watered yogurt? Sherbet?"

When the Quince managed no reply to this but a weak gesture, Esmikhan sent for both, and a warming broth besides.

"Madam, please, have a seat." My lady was on her own feet
now and caught her guest by the elbow. She signaled everyone
else still in the room—including me—for cushions and rugs.

I was just behind the quince-shaped hips, plumping pillows,
when the midwife found the strength to put up a little protest.
"Your child has not been born yet, majesty?" she choked. And

I saw that, in nervous hands, she was fingering a large gold coin—such as one might offer an infant as a birth gift—too distracted at the moment to find a place to hide it.

"*Mashallah,* no," Esmikhan replied. "But let's not worry about me right now."

"But we figured . . ."

"Yes, I figured it would be here by now, too." Esmikhan shrugged, other concerns on her mind. "This one is tenacious, that's all. Allah willing he may be of life as well."

"But—but they told me you'd delivered."

"Who told you that? Madam, you must relax."

"Some . . . someone."

"Allah's will, I wish they were right. I'd have no complaint if I'd finished with this business a fortnight ago, as we'd thought."

"But she said, clear as day, 'Yes, the princess delivered.' "

"She—whoever she is—must have confused it with another time. It is easy to do, I suppose. *Mashallah,* there've been so many . . ." Esmikhan's voice faded as her concern for the Quince reached another peak. "Madam, what ails you? Can I send Abdullah for a physician?"

"No physician, no," the Quince said with a sudden vehemence that gave her the aspect of returning health. "Those charlatans. I'll be fine, a good deal better than if you send for a physician. Just a momentary . . . a momentary weakness, I assure you. I'll be fine."

She closed her eyes and took a deep breath, then seemed to resign herself—to death? Something just as momentous passed before the bitterness of her face. But when she opened her eyes and breathed again, the midwife seemed almost herself.

"Madam?" my lady asked.

"I'll be fine," the Quince repeated. "Maybe a little pilaf."

Esmikhan quickly set the rest of her meal and a napkin before the other woman. The napkin afforded, I felt, no use for its station, encrusted with gold thread on every crossing of warp over weft as it was.

"*Khadim?*" the Quince said then through one mouthful, her fingers reaching after another.

"Madam?" I had almost regained my post after the flurry with the pillows but stepped from it once more with a little nod.

"Down in the sedan chair is a green and gold kerchief of comfits. Fetch it for me, will you? I think—I think they may help. My heart . . ."

"Of course, madam."

"Oh, and *khadim?*"

I turned back at the door. "Madam?"

"I will be prevailing on your hospitality. Until the child is born. You can send the men back to the palace for my things."

"Madam?" I stopped and asked only because I couldn't believe my ears had heard such a complete aboutface.

"Abdullah, at once," my lady ordered impatiently, still very much concerned that any vexation of her guest might exacerbate the frightful condition once more.

So I went, found the kerchief, and gave the orders. I had no doubt I'd found the right bundle. It was the only thing in the sedan, no medicines, no spells as a midwife on anything more than a social call must surely carry. I wondered at this, but not overlong. The bundle I found exuded the heavy smell of an evergreen forest—mastic gum—and seemed innocent enough.

Somewhat less reassuring was the conversation I had with the bearers. We exchanged small talk as they prepared for the trek back to the imperial palace. I had seen to it that they were offered refreshment and narghiles to warm themselves in the lower rooms while they waited out the Quince's return and I hated to see them torn from such comforts in any rush.

So I said something innocuous like: "It was certainly nice of the Quince to come so soon upon her return from Magnesia. She can hardly be rested from her journey."

The head bearer was a Greek, with brows that met in the middle of a heavy forehead over a hooked nose. He gave this reply: "Not at all. The midwife's been in town these two, three weeks. She did seem to want to keep her presence a secret, but nonetheless she delivered a set of twins in that time—*mashallah*—and two or three others. All wonderfully healthy babes, thanks be to Allah. Cured a few rheumatisms and fevers as well. Now if she could only cure me of the life of a bearer . . ." The fellow shifted his shoulder muscles in his own form of cure.

I didn't know what to make of this information, so I followed the drift of our pleasantries from there in their usual fashion. At length the men sloshed off in ankle-deep mud and were soon lost from my view in the fog.

But I stood staring at the spot where they'd disappeared for some time after. It seemed odd to me. First, that the Quince should be back in Constantinople so soon before Safiye's time. By St. Mark—or whomever one prayed to in such events (I was beginning to forget things like that)—this didn't bode well for the empire's heir.

Even more disconcerting was the notion that the midwife should have been avoiding us once she did return. Although it was clearly her place to be with the princess throughout the confinement, the Quince had given priority to other cases instead. She had purposely stayed away from my lady until— well, until some informant, confused in her facts, had said the baby was already safely delivered. The Quince didn't want to deliver this baby. Was she afraid she might fail us again?

By the time I returned to the brazier-snug room, the first part of the mystery, at any rate—how it was that the Quince had returned to Constantinople when Safiye's child wasn't due until late spring—was in the process of being unraveled.

"Safiye? How is she?" My lady felt her guest was so far out of danger now that she could begin the inquiry. "Pray Allah she is well. And the child—the child was not untimely born, Allah forbid—that you left her so soon?"

"Safiye is well."

"Thank heaven. And the child?"

"Just as well as could be when I left them. No thanks to its mother, I must say."

"Whatever do you mean?"

I tendered the kerchief towards its owner, who snatched it from my hand. Her fingers shook with something akin to greed—this was weakness, indeed—as she unknotted the bundle. She would not answer the question until she had popped one of the golden balls of sugar revealed by the kerchief's petals into her mouth to chase the pilaf.

"I mean," the Quince said over her sippet, "I hadn't been in Magnesia through a single hour of prayer before Safiye was asking me to get rid of it for her."

My lady looked almost as ill as her guest had not long before, which was a greater drop from her accustomed blooming health than from the Quince's sallow. "You don't mean . . .?"

"I do mean." The midwife made a face around her chewing as if at some bitter medicine, then continued. " 'I won't carry it,' that Fair One says. 'He hasn't married me, I am not a legal queen. I won't have a prince unless I am a queen.' "

"Madam, you refused."

"Of course I refused," the Quince snapped.

"I didn't mean to suggest, madam, that you could be capable of such a crime."

The Quince gave her hostess and her patient an even, unflinching look, then popped another comfit in her mouth. She seemed to wait until the candy masked her words before she spoke them.

"I've emptied many a womb before," the midwife said. "Don't think I haven't. And don't look so scandalized, majesty. I think it no sin at all for a poor woman who already has too many mouths to feed; for a woman whom another pregnancy might well kill. When a rich man calls me to clean out his slave girl so he doesn't have to free her or her child, well, I usually refuse then. And in this case—as Allah is my witness—I wouldn't do it. The heir to the throne? Safiye's own child? I wouldn't do it."

The Quince looked at my lady across the table under which their knees must nearly touch. The look was almost a dare. "I do have my limits, princess."

"Of course you do, madam." Esmikhan retreated from what had been an attitude of subservience in the first place.

" 'Why else do you think I tolerate you here?' the Fair One tells me. Me, her Quince! And 'Then I will get someone else to do it.' And she did. Tried a few old wives' concoctions. They didn't work. Made her good and sick to her stomach for a while, but never a spot of blood nor a single cramp. Amateurs they are out there in the provinces."

"So she will keep the child?"

"The Fair One has no choice. For the first time in her life, perhaps, Safiye Baffo has no choice."

"It is Allah's will."

"Yes, and she hates it." The midwife gave a thin smile, sour in spite of all the sweets she'd eaten. "She was much too far along, anyway, when I got there for even my methods to work in perfect safety. Why, she'd already got herself the hardest little round belly." The Quince popped another comfit, having studied it as if it were a swollen belly, too.

"My brother, then, can't be ignorant."

"Oh, he is fully aware of her condition, yes."

"But what would she have said to him if she'd lost it?"

" 'I miscarried. These things happen.' " She captured Safiye's very shrug in that quote.

"And does Murad threaten to leave her, as she always feared he would, now that her shape is vanishing?"

"Of course not. I've never seen a man more thrilled about his heir than your brother the prince. On his knees in thanks to heaven twenty times a day, pouring money into that mosque of his, showering his love with gifts, scratching out stacks of poems as the spirit moves him."

"So when you wouldn't do as she asked, Saifye dismissed you?"

"There was that, yes."

"And something else?"

"As long as your child, majesty, was yet unborn, she wanted me here with you. I was ordered—yes, ordered to attend you. 'There'll be plenty of time, afterwards,' Safiye said. 'Months and months. You can deliver . . . deliver the princess and then return and see to me. And should you not make it back? Well, there are good women here. I'll be fine.'

"Good women?" The Quince grunted with scorn. "Women who don't have the first idea about getting rid of a child. So how can they hope to save one?"

Esmikhan murmured something kind and full of confidence in the midwife's skill. "And I am also most grateful that you would make this long journey—at this time of year—to attend me."

The midwife grunted again—she often did—as if to say, "Yes, thank me when you've reason to." Then she leaned back into her supporting cushions, suddenly overcome with exhaustion. She closed her eyes like one in the throes of some dream.

Esmikhan had no desire to disturb her guest. As she always did when in doubt, my lady reached for something to eat instead. Having had her fill of everything else on the table, she thought to help herself to one of the two or three comfits left on the Quince's kerchief. They were of a variety not usually fabricated in our kitchen.

The morsel was just before her lips when the Quince suddenly bolted upright and knocked the candy violently from her hand. "My lady, you mustn't," the midwife exclaimed, as close as she'd come to an apology. "These candies—though wholesome for . . . for some of us—are very bad for a woman with child."

"I see," whispered my lady, the fear of how close she'd come to harming her child strangling any other response.

As if my lady had accused her of having something to hide, the Quince lighted on what must have seemed the most harmless of creatures—me—when she assured further: "*Khuddam* like them. I mix up these goodies for *khuddam* all the time."

And the dialogue moved to other things.

Not too much later, the Quince's belongings arrived.

"Oh, they've forgotten my best garments—and most of the drugs," the Quince sighed out her exasperation. "I shall have to make another trip myself."

"But another day," my lady said. "Surely you've done enough for today and can rest until tomorrow. Anything that's mine belongs to the guest of Allah as well."

"Yes, it can wait," the midwife agreed.

So, in the meantime, the women got up to see what could be done about getting her settled before the noon call to prayer was heard. This left the menials and me to clear away the remains of the meal. The girls took off the trays of pilaf, as they'd done any number of times before, to go and eat the leftovers themselves in the kitchen. The Quince's kerchief, the only unfamiliar thing on the table, remained for me.

For all intents and purposes, the midwife had finished off the whole lot herself. Still, there were some fair-sized crumbs left among the gold and green threads. Out of idle curiosity—and being hungry myself, since the midwife's arrival had disrupted our usual schedule—I licked a finger and brought it to my mouth covered with crumbs. Well, the woman had said—hadn't she?—that this concoction was good for a eunuch's ills.

I dropped my hand at once—and the kerchief as well.

"Good God!" I couldn't help exclaiming aloud—and in my most basic tongue.

Under all the coating of sugar and mastic, a familiar buzzing sweetness filled my mouth. My gorge rose to meet it. In my memory, the taste was too closely tied to an ineffective attempt to strip me of my senses as the cutters stripped me of everything else in the dim little house in Pera.

These candies contained opium in an edible, concentrated, candy form instead of the more popular and milder smoke.

The midwife must have just ingested enough to fill a thousand and one nights with heady dreams.

# XVIII

WHEN THAT THIRD infant son was born, taken to Paradise and buried all on a single cheerless winter's day, I truly feared for my lady's sanity. The Quince departed for Magnesia after nursing Esmikhan through but three weeks of indifferent recovery. I cannot say I was sorry to see her go, having caught her with her golden comfit balls on at least two other occasions and having noted a decided distraction in her attentions as well. But I wasn't certain I could bring my lady out of the serious slump into which I saw her sliding. I would have liked some sort of second, just so as not to feel so helpless and alone.

The moment the midwife and her veils were out of the door, however, things improved immediately. I would have suspected some sort of slow, wasting poison went out the door with her—if I hadn't taken to tasting my lady's food myself as a precaution. And if Esmikhan didn't instantly explain the reason for her rally herself.

"Why, I must go as well," she said, clapping her hands with the thrill of it.

"Beg pardon, lady?" I could hardly condemn what I thought she meant when she grew so suddenly cheerful. I hadn't seen her eyes so brightly polished with excitement—no, not since those first few days I knew her, before her marriage, I decided.

"I must go to Magnesia as well."

"My lady? In your condition?" Although at the moment her condition seemed much improved, not harmed, by the prospect, this might be the frenzy of delirium. The journey she suggested was certainly madness enough to jump to that conclusion.

Before I could protest further, Esmikhan made her purpose clear by saying, "And what is my condition but that of a childless woman? Didn't you tell me my husband is in Magnesia?"

"Yes. Yes, I believe that's true." I'd told her when the dispatches came, but then she'd seemed to spare not the slightest care for Sokolli Pasha. Because she didn't remember, I didn't bother either.

"I had no reason to remember," she said now, reading my thoughts, "before the baby—Allah preserve him. My need was to stay here then, to give him the best health I could." She swiped impatiently at a tear or two in her sense of repeated failure—and at what she had tried so single-mindedly to do. "But now . . . now I remember that you told me this."

"Yes, Magnesia is indeed where the master is. He, along with my lord your brother, is charged with mustering the troops and reserve units from that western portion of the Empire at Bozdag. Later, he is to march them northward and meet up with the rest of the army under your grandfather's direct command. Together they will undertake this summer's campaign against Hungary and Austria."

"You see? I must go to him at once."

"My lady, is it advised? When the master will be so occupied and you . . . ?"

"And on his march north, won't he be even more occupied? How many days do you suppose he may spend in Constantinople?"

"Two, perhaps three. You know how it goes."

"I know. And you are trying to placate me, Abdullah. I'm no fool. I've been the wife of Sokolli Pasha too long. He'll be here one day at the most. If he doesn't send word that he must not leave his men for 'his own personal pleasure' while they are already sworn to battle. And what if I should be suffering my time of uncleanliness on that one night he may deign to give me? Abdullah, in that case I may not go near him. Don't you see? That means I will not see him—even if Allah favors me—for nine whole months or more. I could not bear all that time without hope of a child."

She caught my hands in the desperation I had expected all along, considering the tragedy she'd just been through. "If I can have—oh, just a week with him in Magnesia, I shall know I have done my best—and the rest is Allah's will, whether I conceive or not."

"Lady, he will be much occupied with the affairs of the army in Bozdag."

"Of course. But he will not refuse me. He cannot, when I have gone all that way, just to be with him. When you tell him . . ."

"It is a long journey. You may not feel well enough to see him at the end."

"The journey's by sea, as Safiye always likes to gloat. Not nearly so strenuous as by land." Esmikhan withdrew her hands now, sulking—which she knew had its effect on me—rounding her face, pouting her lips. Had she been clamoring for *my* bed, there would have been no more discussion. "Besides, any discomfort is worth the hope of getting a child that might, *inshallah*, live."

"The Quince has already departed. We will not have the comfort of her company on our way." Remembering the buzz of opium on my tongue, I wasn't at all certain that this was such a bad thing. It didn't deter my lady either.

"We may catch up with her in any case—if you aren't too slow. If not, she at least will be there when we arrive to provide—*inshallah*—some fertility drug that may enhance the prospect of those few days I will have with my husband."

"But lady, you are still in your time of uncleanliness." I feared more for her health, her soft little body put through yet more all-consuming pain and exhaustion without a moment's rest. But I couldn't deny that the very idea of this stress—to which I could compare only one thing in my life—seemed to enliven rather than intimidate her. She had learned all her life to take her greatest meaning from the fruits of such torture, I guess. Whereas my torture had been the means of removing that meaning from me altogether.

"I won't be unclean by the time we get there. Certainly not if you persist in dawdling so."

With that, I ran out of excuses. And when a scouting trip down to the wharves restored my arsenal, my lady's exuberance soon dispelled that as well.

"The Golden Horn is quite ominously full of ships," I told her. "The Kapudan Pasha, Piali, is amassing a great flotilla to sail against some benighted enemy of the Faith. I counted eighty galleys while I stood there. Come to the window. You can see some of them, at least, for yourself."

Esmikhan looked disinterestedly through the lacework of lattice in the direction I pointed and shrugged.

"As Allah is my witness," I persisted, "I wouldn't be anywhere on the seas with such an armada about."

"But these are my grandfather's ships, Abdullah. I need have no fear of them. Besides, we are only sailing to Izmir, never losing sight of Turkish coast the whole way. Piali Pasha sails to some distant land, of that you may be certain."

"Perhaps my lady is right. I did hear a rumor that they mean to lay siege to Malta, the lair of the Knights of St. John, to punish those pirates' depredations of Turkish shipping." I did not mention how this intelligence made me feel: almost a Turk myself, for it was in large part due to a Maltese knight—under the influence of Sofia Baffo, of course—that I found myself in my present shadow life.

"The bastion of Malta defied them last year," I elaborated. "Yes, I wouldn't be surprised if Piali Pasha meant to renew the assault with reinforcements and better weather."

"There. You see? Piali Pasha's galleys mean nothing to us. I've thought it all out while you were gone."

"Lady?"

"My brother and Safiye are in Magnesia, as well as my husband. I will rely upon their hospitality of course so I won't have to consider camping out primitively with the army. And after my husband leaves about his duties, I can stay until Safiye has her child, *inshallah,* and help her with that."

Yes, I saw that the reasons my lady could produce to go had multiplied in my absence while mine to stay had only increased by the vague unease caused by Piali Pasha's ships. And that discomfort might only be the last reflexes of my former life I couldn't quite shake, the sudden leap of the heart in the throat, the charge of desperate energy to every limb. The Turkish crescent would probably always cause that, no matter where they cut.

If anything, the planning offered Esmikhan distraction, filled her with hope and life in place of loss and despair. I couldn't line her empty womb for her, but I could do this. I was a fool to oppose her.

"Abdullah, you waste time. Find us a boat to sail on—at once. I will go to Magnesia."

So down I went to the docks to try again.

# XIX

I SUPPOSE THE lodestone of nostalgia drew me on. Like an addict with his drug, I had avoided the sights and sounds of the sea with sober success for four long years. But now, one breath of the spray-thick air and I was hopelessly intoxicated again.

How many times had I made this very promenade at my Uncle Jacopo's side? Is it any wonder that the call of the sea is legendized in sailors' minds as the mermaid or siren, the most beautiful image men removed from their doxies for months on end can imagine? And I had tried to deny this pull which was, after all, my birthright and my very weaning. For four long years I had denied this lost world, knowing that the first sip would make me feel the pain of the cutters' knives all over again.

Indeed, it did. But having now, at my lady's insistence, endured the first harrowing of memories, the sea's addiction had me numb under its spell once more. And as I wandered up and down the salt-sprayed hem, heedless of exhaustion and the futility of my search, I wondered how I had stayed away so long.

I think I had truly been ashamed for the sea to find me in my maimed state. But I knew the moment I saw the sun, just past its pale spring zenith, silvering the wavelets like streaks of age in a mother's hair, that she would have me any way at all.

The wharves and docked ships tamed the sea's hair like a lace cap. The red Turkish flags—and no one dared fly either cross or saint's emblem under Piali Pasha's nose—pulsed in the wind like a mother's heartbeat. They were the throb at her temples, the blush of pleasure on her cheeks. The creek of planking, the whisper of empty rigging, and the cry of gulls between them—these were a mother's songs, her lullabies. They were her call of encouragement to her toddling child to take the narrow leap over the vacillating slash of dark water between wharf and deck. To escape from the weight of earth. To take the canvas wings of flight.

Whenever I reminded myself that we were going to attend the motherhood of Safiye Baffo, the image lost some of its poetry. What I should be doing was reclaiming what Safiye had stolen from me. *What she has stolen from Esmikhan.* That was a bitter, unfounded thought. It only rose because it rankled: *Why should she become a mother and my lady not?* That was like asking why Murad should become a father and I not. Simply because there was no justice in the world—never had been, never would be any.

Getting my lady to Magnesia, however, grew perceptibly more difficult by the moment. Piali Pasha's admiralty drew every available bark to it by sheer mass. Provisioning skiffs and flat-bottomed ferries as well as the more substantial craft for which I sought were all detailed to outfitting the master of Allah's seas.

The last of the seaworthy ships owned by the harem of my lady's grandfather had just departed, bearing the midwife to attend on the birth of Murad's heir. I supposed this was an errand equal to the supplying of Piali Pasha. We could wait until that one returned, but I knew Esmikhan—and her empty womb—would give me no peace until it did. Otherwise, the demands of war had requisitioned every chunk of wood that could float within two days' sailing.

My lady owned a neat little caïque, like all women of her station, for pleasure outings on the Bosphorus. She didn't use it much—seasickness came quickly when she was with child. Instead of finding the ship I wanted, I got incredibly inflated offers to use the caïque for the provisioning instead. I could almost hear my lady accepting every one that came along with an irrational flush of partisan enthusiasm. There are reasons women stay in the harem.

I resisted these offers, not requiring much imagination to picture what one trip out and back with a load of gun grease or leaky flour sacks would do to the velvet curtaining and the mother-of-pearl inlay. But this didn't help me to find the transportation I needed either, for which the caïque was equally unsuited.

There were foreign ships, of course, skirting the arsenal's menace warily, trying to stay invisible lest they be suspected of spying out what Piali Pasha might have in mind for those at home. I rejected these out of hand. It would never do to entrust a princess of the blood to an infidel hull. Nonetheless, desperation finally brought me to the foreigners' wharves at Pera. My legs were beginning to ache, unaccustomed as they were to hours of fruitless wandering about the wharves.

Wherever boats gave an arm's length of space between hull and prow, fishermen grounded because their boats were with the navy dangled their lines. The black of their doublets clanged with the metal of their trade: hooks, scalers, knives. The offal of last week's catch sloshing in the gray-green water below their feet offered the predominant smell to the place and attracted mangy cats who slunk about for their own share.

But such smells might have been a mother's perfume to me. And the great baskets of fingerling *hamsi* fish—anchovies, we called them at home—appeared to me in their silver sheen like a princess's dowry.

A man could take his pick from the top of the heap, still wriggling, their eyes popping, mouths agape at death's surprise. The fishermen would thread your choice on a skewer—with yet more wriggling—and shove them over the coals of his brazier. In a moment, the fish were smoky, blackened, fragrant, and delicious. That might have been mother's milk to me.

I was downing my second *shish* of the day, aided by sea-whipped appetite, chased by tall glasses of minted yogurt drink. The yogurt vendor was wiping out the glass from the last customer with the corner of his sash to pour me another when that last customer introduced himself to me.

"You won't be drinking and eating like that in a day or two, will you?" he asked, winking.

"Ramadhan." I nodded, not knowing what to make of the wink in connection with the soon-to-begin holy month. Perhaps the man only had a tic.

"Yes," he said carefully, as if to say "Make of it what you will." And he repeated, "Yes, Ramadhan."

Watching the shipping, but mostly the hypnotic roll of the sea, we fell to talking, and the cryptic messages fell away.

The language we used was the traders' patois. My companion expressed no surprise that I, a *khadim,* should be conversant in the jargon, mixed like the bastard blood in any Mediterranean port of Turkish, Arabic, Greek, and Italian. Perhaps this fellow's experience of the Ottoman realm, circumscribed by water and wharf as it must be, made him believe the patois was indeed court Turkish.

His habit of falling back on the Italian whenever a word failed him helped me to place him in the patois' stew. That this Italian had Liguria's whispering silibations and horror of consonants helped me place him even closer. The man was from Genoa. I couldn't hear that duplicitous dependence on vowels without painful jabs echoing on my person. Such an accent would always recall the man who took my manhood and life from me, the renegade Genoese who called himself Salah ud-Din, with exquisite irony. But even before that, my family had held the Venetians' traditional hatred against anyone of that city which was our keenest rival.

I tried not to let my past color my dealings with this man in the present. As always, I dreaded anyone knowing what I had been. And besides, he didn't seem to hold it against me that I was a eunuch as many another of his kind would. Or did he perhaps not know our costumes?

Then the sail of my mind recaught his name—Giustiniani—and I navigated to the realization that he was not really Genoese at all. He hailed from the island of Chios which, since Muhammed Fatih's conquests, was the one eastern outpost remaining to that city across the spine of Italy from my homeland. All Italian Chians called themselves Giustiniani whether they originated from the first colonizing couple or not. I wasn't certain the name actually had imperial Roman roots, as it sounded. In any case, it gave their settlement and their trading organization a certain familial solidarity. They were a force to be reckoned with in foreign parts.

My guess was quickly confirmed. My new acquaintance described how he had set sail with the first clearing of the lanes that year as part of the escort for Chios' ambassador, come to pay the island's annual tribute money to the Porte.

"Actually, he comes to negotiate terms," Giustiniani confided. "Even with trips to the usurers, there is no way Chios can pay the forty thousand ducats owing."

After some exclamation of disbelief and sympathy, I assumed to myself that I had misheard. Such a vast sum was clearly impossible.

But, encouraged by my sympathy, Giustiniani went on, explaining that since their first offer to buy the Turk's oversight for a handful of silver less than a hundred years before, the annual dues had steadily risen. The present sum was the culmination of three unpaid years of that steeply inflated tribute. And it was exaggerated by the fact that, whereas the Chians were counting by the Christian calendar, as was their custom, the Porte was expecting payment according to the Muslim book of days, which came round just that much faster every year.

"And I will not hesitate to tell you—because it cannot be kept a secret anymore—that we have been raising this money for years on the backs of bad investments. No Giustiniani likes to remove fee from his own purse when he can take it from the moneylenders'." The wink his obsidian eyes gave me imitated the glinting gold cross that dangled from his ear, asking for sympathy if not conspiracy.

So I hadn't heard wrong at all. The debt really was forty thousand. And all this posturing after ancient honor was a sham. Whenever we used to anchor in the smile of Chios' harbor, my uncle had always warned our men to be careful how they cursed the name of Genoa in the taverns on shore. But there had been contrary rumors even then: "Drink up now; you don't know how long before this harbor is as dry as the rest of the Turk's realm."

Such rumors were closing in on confirmation, then. The Empire which held the rich and strategic bit of soil bracing the Izmir coast was hardly Roman; it very nearly belonged to the Turk, in deed if not in name. But I kept my thoughts to myself where politics were concerned and spoke of neutral ships instead.

"Ah, I can see you are a good judge of seaman's timber."

Giustiniani was now showing me the ship, rather pretentiously christened *The Epiphany,* of which he was master. And some comment I had made in passing caused him now to rub his chin, appraising me as thoughtfully as I had been appraising the keel. I'd seen that the ship was quite unladened, the keel bobbing high out of the Golden Horn's very ungolden scum. The seams were excellently made and pitched, with a new coat of tar and tallow against shipworm on the hull.

I wondered what he saw when he looked at my chin, equally smooth and growthless.

Then he told me. "You can take the sailor out of the sea, but not the sea out of the—"

The look I gave him was enough to freeze him up like a European river at Christmastide. But I couldn't hide my knowledge that he was justly proud of his little craft. Though small, no larger than a caravel, she was solid and round-hulled as the best of northern cogs.

"You're not looking to sell, are you?" I said in my most solid Turkish. "Because if you are, I must set you straight. Don't waste your time. I'm not—"

"By God's Mother, of course I wouldn't sell her!" Giustiniani's emotion confirmed that he was the true seaman I took him for: a true seaman would sooner sell his own mother than his bark.

"Just idling here," he said when he was calmer. "Just hoping to scare up enough cargo to fill my hold. To make it worth hoisting her sails once more and be off."

Well, I'd certainly spent enough days of my life at that same task to sympathize.

"And in a day or two Ramadhan will be upon us," my companion continued. "A Christian man can't hope to get anything done for a whole month then, once those cannons start going off every cursed night." And there was that wink once more.

But my pulse was already racing with other possibilities. If Chios was not really a foreign port, after all, if it was so close to Izmir, our destination, as in fact I knew it to be, if he were looking for custom . . .

I blurted out my quest.

"So it *is* a ship you want." He smiled and the ring bobbed with pleasure in his ear.

"Only one way. With captain and pilot. For my lady."

"I'm sorry. I'm already quite full now. Too full to take on a passenger of quality. I'm only looking for cargo."

And for a moment I'd thought we were bargaining. For a moment the *Epiphany* had seemed almost perfect. I nodded my comprehension, however, as well as my disappointment, and watched the never-disappointing sea.

Under the *Epiphany*'s prow, a tender was loading. It was headed out to a French galleon riding at anchor, the wharf for foreigners being so circumscribed that not a third of the commerce could expect an actual berth. I supposed anyone who knew anything about ships was with the Turkish fleet. These fellows were inexpert enough. It was a wonder how they'd ever found their way here, or how they hoped to find France again, considering how unstably they were loading the little craft and their clumsiness with oars and lines. Finally, in a gesture of exasperation as well as instinct, I interrupted the conversation— which seemed to have reached a dead end in any case—to help out with the tangle of one of their ropes.

When I returned to the *Epiphany*'s master, his eyes were measuring me with unabashed amazement. Well, I suppose it must have been odd to see a figure in eunuch's skirts handling ropes. Then I chastised myself, realizing perhaps I'd been a little too expert. If my past were known, how much more shameful was my present state!

But I read no scorn in those olive-black Chian eyes.

And suddenly he was talking about how he probably could farm out most of the tonnage he'd already acquired to compatriots. I heard a quick catalogue of his cargo, destinations and alternatives, that meant little enough to me but which culminated in this:

"Yes, I think that, save for those spices bound for Chios, I can offer you an empty vessel. A stop at Chios to unload should give your mistress no difficulty, I think?"

"We would do that anyway, wouldn't we? On the way to Izmir?"

"Exactly. And a few crates and sacks of rhubarb and cloves in the back of the hold, these won't bother your lady, will they?"

Speaking directly about my lady to a stranger and a foreigner besides was hardly good form for a eunuch. But by suggestion I let him know Esmikhan was of such a modest demeanor that she would never wander down in his hold. Why, he would hardly even realize she was on board. I might have been describing a pet.

And suddenly, there I was on the *Epiphany,* feeling the rock of the sea below me, gentle and comforting as the rock of a mother's arms.

We spent an hour or more discussing the arrangements. Accommodations must be prepared. I needed to set up a sort of tent so my lady could enjoy the feel of a watery journey without the loss of privacy. Where might her luggage go? Her provisions? How soon could I send workmen to see to this and that? To see that she had every comfort she wouldn't even notice unless it were missing.

In fact, once I felt the sea below me, everything was settled. My tongue engaged these dutiful topics, but my mind was ever and again distracted by a thrill that matched the rocking of my feet and pounded with an excitement no more articulate than this: *The sea! The sea! I'm coming home!*

Over the Horn, then, from Aya Sophia and the city's comb of minarets, the fine hair of the muezzins' voices drew, mournful, distant as the call of gulls. I gave them as much mind as gulls, caught in the moment's deeper compulsion.

And the moment I did ignore the call to follow Allah's will, it seemed the very wind began to blow a new direction. Certainly Giustiniani began to speak a different tack, laying yet another offer on the table of our bargain. Before I understood quite what he was driving at, however, I remembered one last thing for which his native harbor was world-renowned.

Chios, sitting as it did at the Turk's doorstep, yet solidly part of the Christian west, maintained an actual public office which existed only to help Turkish slaves to freedom. Uncle Jacopo and I had never had a fear to anchor there. The Chians wouldn't help the other way, a Turk off our oar benches. But we knew Turkish ships would demand a very serious storm before they'd be forced into that bay.

Not only that, but Chian agents were known to wander through the Muslim empire, helping to plot escapes wherever they could. A slave on the run could light a fire on the Asian shore, be seen by the boatmen on Chios, vanish from Turkish lands before daylight. On Chios he'd be hidden where no passing janissary could find him. He'd be fed, given Western clothes, hastened home to the bosom of his kinsfolk. The Chians accepted gratitude, the blessings of Lord Jesus, His Holy

Mother—and whatever partial ransom payments the families had raised to offer the Turks.

"I'm out a mate," Giustiniani hinted broadly now.

And I returned with equal candor, "Signore, you cannot want a eunuch for a mate."

Giustiniani shrugged one worn-leathered shoulder up to his earring. No, my condition wasn't news to him. "It might keep me from losing you like I just lost my last one. Run off with his tart, if you can imagine. Decided her thighs were better than the sea and food on the table." The master's eyes twinkled. "I don't suppose I'd have that trouble with you, now, would I?"

Even I had to chuckle at the notion.

"But I cannot very well push off with you now," I said. "Not with Piali Pasha and his flotilla riding like a hurricane upon the Bosphorus."

"Of course not," Giustiniani said, winking.

Now I understood what the winking was all about, and I winked myself, just at the wonder, the danger, the excitement of it. "During Ramadhan, the Turks will be less watchful."

"Less watchful, but more full of heathen demons when they do get a glimpse."

I nodded, and winked again. And Giustiniani took that as encouragement to speak of me and the spices off at Chios, after which he would take my lady to Izmir, then come back to reclaim me, in an Italian sailor's hose and doublet once more.

*And a codpiece?* I wondered. *I can never wear Italian clothes again without a codpiece.*

He spoke of no greater remuneration than a handful of my lady's jewels I might steal. When I looked a little seasick at the thought, he came down: "Just work for nothing but your board for three years, and you'll be a free man. We must only take care that our voyages are all to the west for a while. Yes, a free man with a first mate's job, standing to inherit this ship and all it contains, for I've only daughters waiting with my wife at home."

*And at home I have my lady . . .* I suppressed the longing that welled up in my own heart at that thought.

Night was quite fully upon us when I shook his hand to go. We shook on the deal as well as in friendship, the arrangement to carry my lady, her staff, her belongings, safely to Izmir in a timely and seamanly fashion.

About the other, I told him, "I'll think about it."

# XX

"BY THE BLESSED Virgin, who is this lady of yours?" Giustiniani exclaimed as I took over his ship to Esmikhan's needs.

Somehow he learned—or guessed—the truth. I know this because of what happened later. At the time, however, my only reply was the eunuch's cultivated, tight-lipped smile. Such information was my secret. And, in this case—anticipating Esmikhan's delight—my pleasure.

The most spontaneous purchase I made during the hectic week that followed turned out to be the most fortuitous. Amidst the dealings with carpenters and drapers, porters and victualers, I happened upon a Turkish seaman who'd set up such a stall as a square of old gray serge afforded him in a corner of the grain merchants' port at the edge of the Golden Horn. Under orders to be ready to sail with the Kapudan Pasha at a moment's notice, I suppose, he wanted to liquidate his holdings to more convenient cash. And he wanted it done without making the trek clear to the bazaar, for Ramadhan was now upon us and everyone on the Turkish side of the water at any rate moved as little as possible in their daily lethargy of hunger.

If, in my own stupefication, I had been looking for what he had to sell, I certainly would have gone to the bazaar, where I might have found any number of his fellows with similar bargains to choose from. Or I'd find pawnshop owners who'd have saved both of us trouble.

Of course, I wasn't looking for such wares at all. But on the stretch of serge between his often-patched knees, the Turk had a silver crucifix, a rosary of Murano beads, a wooden drinking cup, a tool kit with needles and an awl, and a leather-bound book. These were the effects of a Western sailor—my uncle might have had the same about him when he went down, though nobody had bothered to pluck him clean.

I couldn't help myself. I stood and stared at the display while behind me the crowded sounds of the port shed from me like beads of water over a duck's feathers. The hull after hull of grain it took to keep the Turk's navy afloat, the Turk's city alive, hissed like swords being drawn. The slap of sandals on the packed earth in between, the squawk of bargaining—all these might not have existed.

But I did hear, as always, the compelling creak of rigging and masts that bristled at my back, currying my spine as if I were a horse about to show. It was my name the combined rigging spoke: "Giorgio, Giorgio."

Abdullah? Who was he?

Hardly stopping to bargain, I bought the book from the sailor. That seemed the least likely of all his wares to sell: the crucifix was worth melting down; the rosary's millefiori glass, attractive without religious connotation. But the book, with its split, salted leather, was worthless on this side of the Golden Horn, worthless to one who couldn't read the chopped Italic of its letters to find the treasure there.

I opened my purchase briefly, enough to see the imprint, Aldus Manutius, the famous Venetian house. It was a new translation of Homer. Then I left the place quickly before the pirating Turk should read by my face that he'd given me the bargain.

I bought the book for myself, of course, an act of reclaiming my native tongue, my patrimony, my former life in the midst of building a future for my lady. But then my life got confused with hers. While I was distracted with other details elsewhere, my lady came upon the book packed in a bundle of new purchases I'd made for her.

And, "Abdullah, what's this?" she had to ask.

I couldn't tell her what I was plotting—Giustiniani and I solidified the details more each time I saw him. And I had pestered her to learn Italian since I'd first known her; she had sometimes expressed curiosity. So that's the tack I followed.

Quite to my surprise—and soon, delight—the book rekindled her interest. The little ditties and proverbs I was accustomed to say when occasion demanded, I found she could recite them back to me. Lullabies, folk songs I didn't even know I'd sung in her presence, she knew them and their vocabularies. And she even remembered most of the alphabet I'd once hurriedly sketched for her: Italian's sturdy building blocks so different from the winding vines of the Turkish, Arabic, and Persian with which she was already familiar.

Once we were under sail, I came to realize that what I'd taken for disinterest or witlessness before was neither. Childbearing simply consumed her, heart and soul, and the time between pregnancies had been so short. Now there was no child. We had done our mortal best to put ourselves in Allah's hands to acquire another, but we couldn't hasten the ship, bring more favorable winds, or call Sokolli Pasha from his duty to the Sultan. So she abandoned herself to me, as she did to the will of heaven.

The ferocity with which she yielded was sometimes frightening, hollowed of infants as it was. But what at first I couldn't begrudge I rapidly came to crave. And how could I be jealous of the ill-fated mites that had distracted her before?

There was, besides, the separate, sacred time created as much by the novelty of sea travel as by the holy month of fasting, Ramadhan. There was never any question that Esmikhan would keep the fast, for, although believers on journeys are exempt, pregnant women are also exempt and she had been pregnant the past three years. Fasting days missed would have to be made up later—when, it was hoped, she would be expecting again. So it was best to do it now.

The past three years I had kept the fast with the rest of the household—to please my lady, who was required to deny the blessings herself. I began the fast with her this year as well, the complete and strenuous refusal of food and water from sunrise to sunset. And then I didn't stop, for all Giustiniani's winking. The holy month has a sort of compulsion with it, an addiction, especially when shared. With loved ones.

And there was the particular leisureliness of our voyage, at least compared to the merchantman's pace I'd always known before. We took the luxury of setting in at any and every port, at the first sign of seasickness on my lady's part or at the first inkling to sightsee. The anchor was always dropped to allow the servants to light proper cooking fires for each evening's fast-breaking meal, as they would not have been had we been rolling and lurching under full sail.

So sometimes it seems we spent more time ashore on that

journey than afloat, for all that getting there was a major undertaking. I had to insist the sailors move below decks or to the seaward side of the ship while I helped Esmikhan to negotiate the ladder down to the tender in all her veils. For better seclusion, I usually did the rowing myself, after the serious ship's business had been taken care of, with at most one or two of my lady's maids joining us. But it was easier—more pleasant—when just we two went alone.

In such company, the shore of Asia Minor was gentler, more feminine than I ever remembered from my past. Esmikhan never bathed in the sea as I had done as a lad, for—not to mention her modesty—my lady was convinced that bathing in salt water while she was still unclean from the birth would harm her fertility.

But, hungry, lightheaded together, Esmikhan and I read of "Troy's proud glories" and the "white-armed Helen." As Fate would have it, we were right there in the springtime fields of Ilium even as we held the book in our laps. We read of Penelope's unstinting devotion, Poseidon's unslakable wrath with the very heave of the god and his nereids below us, the drumbeat of Leto's fair-haired son above.

Because it was Ramadhan, we lived much of our life at night, sleeping while under sail and fasting during the day. For fear of fire, we couldn't light a lamp to read by. But even when the light failed, Esmikhan hadn't had enough of my past—of *me*.

I didn't know any Homer by heart, but I did have a dour childhood tutor to thank for my Dante. I did not recite to her verses from the very pit of hell, where the poet placed Muhammed the Prophet next to Judas Iscariot. But the tale of Francesca di Rimini and her Paolo, more pitiable than damnable, was particularly applicable to our state, what with its eternally unsatisfied swirling. Or at least, so it seemed in the moments of our deepest hunger-induced melancholia. Esmikhan had me recite it to her over and over until she could recite it to me:

*"And this, I learned, was the never ending flight*
*of those who sinned in the flesh, the carnal and lusty*
*who betrayed reason to their appetite.*

*"As cranes go over sounding their harsh cry,*
*leaving the long streak of their flight in air,*
*so come these spirits, wailing as they fly."*

But in spite of her tortures, Francesca offered no regret, no apology, only this:

*"Love, which permits no loved one not to love,*
*took me so strongly with delight in him*
*that we are one in Hell, as we were above."*

For happier times, or when my voice gave out, Esmikhan had her Persian poets:

*"Awake! for morning in the bowl of night*
*Has flung the stone that puts the stars to flight:*
*And lo! the hunter of the East has caught*
*The Sultan's turret in a noose of light.*

*"Come with me along some strip of herbage strown*
*That just divides the desert from the sown,*
*Where names of Slave and Sultan are forgot,*
*And pity Sultan Mahmud on his throne.*

*"A book of verses underneath the bough,*
*A jug of wine, a loaf of bread—and thou*

*Beside me singing in the wilderness—*
*Oh, wilderness were paradise enow!"*

Well, no loaves were allowed us when we did take early-morning or late-afternoon rambles to explore the shore. And certainly no wine jugs. But there was a blessed communion in our shared denial that is difficult to explain to someone who hasn't experienced it. More than once, the Christian crew of the ship tried to slip me something while my lady slept and the sun rode high.

"She would smell it on my breath." I thanked them, but refused.

I would lose more than what she might sense. The poet, denying himself the freedom of rhymelessness and plain, straightforward speech, is pushed into the sublime almost without trying. Such was the drive of hunger—and more—between Esmikhan and me.

We were two halves suddenly one, the failed single sexes suddenly whole. Or if we were whole the way we were, which her presence often made even me feel, together we had double the space in which to stretch our humanity.

One evening we returned to the ship hand in hand after a taste of Khayyam's paradise more real than bread so fresh it can burn the hands. The soil between more sober rocks puddled with hyacinths or anemones, difficult to distinguish, save by scent, in the growing dark. The world was so green and quickened by the seeming death of winter, I couldn't help but think of Easter, resurrection. And what I thought, I spoke, and spoke until tears came and I was glad for the dust of twilight between us.

"What would your grandfather think?" I said by way of apology, an excuse to escape thoughts of hope or joy when reason told me I must expect none, ever.

"What do you mean, what my grandfather thinks?" Esmikhan laughed, teasing me with a tickle to the ribs.

"Here I am reciting *Il Paradiso* to you, speaking in glowing terms of Christian feasts and beliefs."

"Well, what is the harem if not to keep such things?" She bent to the ground and then I saw she had plucked yet another hyacinth to stuff into a turban-free curl on my head.

"What are you saying, lady?"

"Exactly that. The harem is to keep such things close to the heart. Where the Shadow of Allah cannot touch them." And with a palm she pressed the part on my anatomy where such safety might reside.

There was another, different safety in a scholarly detachment. I took it. "Allah's Shadow. I suppose the term comes from the Arabs in their deserts for whom a shadow is always a blessing. But for us, who have just suffered such a bleak winter, 'shadow' is a mixed image. My lady"—and I groped for her hand again—"I fear you speak heresy."

"And if I do? Who is to know?" She leaned towards my ear to whisper it, close enough to touch my loosened curls with nose and lips. "Only my eunuch, my servant of Allah. Not a soul more."

And then it was time to replace my turban, replace her veils, rejoin the world before the tumbling night. I let my fingers linger on her face as I helped to drape it from profane view. I hungered for the curves of her cheeks and her eyes' flashes of delight, even as darkness was clearing the sight from my table.

I couldn't help myself. Just before I dropped the gauze, I had to dip and kiss the dimple in her pudgy chin, or I felt I should burst with emotion, gelded from all other outlet.

I fully expected her chastisement. It was deserved. I was a fool. But no chastisement came. Instead, I felt the briefest pressure of her hand on mine. And then she moved with me, to return those gems of hers we brought out for play within the confines of their purse, secured.

And I had to return—to do double duty as the *Epiphany*'s mate. For I was forgetting my approaching freedom, an approach I was more and more apt to let slip my mind.

# XXI

THE NORTHERN SPUR of Chios floated lightly off starboard, belying its heavy, rocky appearance. We'd hit a becalming lull in the wind; we drifted more than sailed towards the harbor. But the scent of the island was perceptible, even a quarter of a league offshore. I'd have known Chios anyhow, even if it'd been my eyes Turkey had taken from me instead.

Clear from the Campos to the south came the fragrance of citrus bloom, resinous mastic, bemusing dust, triggered to life by the passing night's dewfall. Above the creak of the timbers, the shiver of rigging, the hush of water slipping away from the prow, the sky panted like punctured bellows and glowed the flame-blue color found at the center of a low fire.

And was that cicadas I heard over the deep breath of other sounds? It seemed too early for those creatures to be singing to one another, but maybe Chios always had cicadas. The sound rolled off the island like the opening of prison doors, the rattling of rusty keys. It was the promise of freedom.

For all the pleasures of sight and sound that sent trills of expectation down my spine, the island's capital looped about the bay like a grubby, well-worn linen collar. The red tile roofs bleached out to drab. Few of the whitewashed walls had been renewed in some time. They offered little contrast to the fading patterns of beige or brown, the repeating friezes of triangles and circles, triangles made of circles and vice versa, with which Chian walls were traditionally decorated.

As a whole, the city exuded the depressing corruptibility of a grasping merchant who'd made compromise after compromise, giving up all he held most dear in the process, until he could no longer tell the difference.

And with this city I must throw my lot in order to gain freedom?

I looked away, off the port side, where mainland Anatolia dozed like a gypsy's shaggy bear spring had not yet wakened. But only a fool would think the beast dead so that nothing could rouse him.

A sudden pealing of bells from the island made me start. *What are they thinking?* pulsed the panic through my brain. *They will awaken the brute. He will discover what we are about.*

But Giustiniani walked up beside me on the forward bulwarks then, as calm as the wind that slackened our sails.

"It's Easter Sunday. The heretic Greeks will have theirs in a week or so, but this is ours. Did you forget? Too much Ramadhan?" he asked with a twinkle in both eyes and earring. "If we did not ring, the Turks would suspect. Good day for rebirth as a Christian, eh?"

I nodded vaguely. Certainly during these past glorious days with Esmikhan my mind had been yearning towards the meaning of Easter in a primal urge no renegade's knife could cut from me. The very countryside clamored for it, but in ways that made bell towers quite redundant. I had been feeling "Easter" in no way so precisely defined as the ultimatum that rang out from Chios that morning.

Had the ability to feel Christianity been cut from me along with the rest? Or were there things about Christianity's compulsion that I had forgotten until this reminder?

"This will do." The captain shoved himself from the rail with the carelessness of command, more immediate things on his mind. "Why don't you, my mate, give the boys the order to drop anchor. Then go gather your things and—and you're a free . . . you're free."

I couldn't fail to notice how he avoided saying "A free man." I could never be that. And since I couldn't be that, was there any use in freedom at all?

I suppressed this doubt and others like it, however, and went to do as Giustiniani bade me. Orders are easier to follow than to think about.

The anchor carried its cable to the bottom with a plunge that seemed to take my heart with it. Now I had to go get my few belongings from the cubicle where my lady lay. But I lingered on deck as long as I could, contemplating how not even a bubble arose to show where my heart had gone down.

I thought—I hoped—Esmikhan was still asleep. It was her fast-day custom, after taking a sustaining meal before dawn, to sleep again as much as she could into the long, hungry day. But perhaps hearing bells in place of the muezzin startled her as much as it did me. As I quietly pulled back the damask curtains to slip inside, she roused and sat up on her cushions, stretching with lazy luxury.

"Morning, Abdullah," got swallowed in a yawn.

"My lady."

*Say as little as possible,* I told myself. But every word I did say seemed awash with gall. *Look your last,* I advised again. But I couldn't. To have her read betrayal in my eyes?

"Ah, Abdullah," Esmikhan said in another yawn. "Up so early? You sailors are a hardy bunch."

"Yes, lady." I had my things now. I could go.

"Today is the day we rest at Chios, isn't it? Yes, I remember. Does it look like it will be a good day?"

She tried to hold me with her idle chatter, but it was the sweet smell she stirred when disturbing sleep that held me more. With an explosion of breath that came close to a groan, I snapped free of the spell.

I even choked on the word *"Inshallah"* as I fled.

꧁

OUTSIDE, THE MORNING air, though breezeless, cleared my head. The ship's boat lowered smoothly. But Giustiniani seemed somewhat agitated. I fell alongside his stride of nervous pacing at the rail.

"Something's amiss," he said, twiddling his earring.

"What is it?"

"I don't know."

Giustiniani shook his own hand from his ear as if it were an invasion. Then he pointed out a flock of little local boats drawn up on the Chian strand. The natives were among them, almost frantically decking out the crafts with rugs and garlands and bunting.

"An Easter custom?" I offered, though I realized as soon as I said it that one didn't suggest an ancient custom to a native. But the islanders' actions did seem quaint and harmless enough.

"No," Giustiniani said. "The only time we get up a little flotilla like that is to greet incoming Turks."

"Turks?"

I was certain the captain must hear the thud of my heart. Or perhaps he was deafened by the thud of his own. I raked the horizon all around but saw nothing.

"They come once a year to claim some men and ships for their navy," Giustiniani explained. "It counts as part of the tribute. We put up a little pomp for them when they do. Seems to make them satisfied with less of a material nature. But it's fall when they usually come, on their way to shutting down for the winter, as it were."

"And they already came last fall?"

"They did."

"So what can the actions of your countrymen mean?"

"I don't know." With disgust, the captain once more found the cross in his earring gave him no comfort. "But I think you'd better stay put for a while 'til I find out."

I nodded my compliance. I might have tried to logic him into the position that the sooner I got onto the Chian shore, the better my chances of freedom were. But haste didn't seem to be his first instinct. I trusted to his instinct and to my own, which at the first sign of danger was "My lady." But was it her safety that concerned me, or my own which I sensed would be greater if I stayed with her?

For all at once my mind couldn't place Piali Pasha in the Bosphorus where we'd left him anymore. The numbers of men-of-war we'd seen on our trip down the coast suddenly added up to stragglers of the armada rather than the oddities for which we'd previously taken them.

I saw Giustiniani over the side and off towards shore until I couldn't hear the groan of his boat's oars anymore.

And then I went to do what I'd thought I'd never have to do again: I went to face my lady.

# XXII

It was a long, quiet Easter-Ramadhan day when, to the long numbing weight of hunger was added the stupefaction of doubt. It was a day much, I suppose, as that first Resurrection Day must have seemed to the Three Marys who found the Holy Sepulchre empty but as yet had no proofs as to what their discovery might mean. They knew only the emptiness.

Perhaps I could expect a miracle for which nothing yet in personal experience taught me to hope. Experience taught me that even the most beloved of life's companions assaulted the mortal senses with corruption when they turned to corpses. Was it possible that beyond this time of doubtful waiting, beyond the proofs of sight and sound, a scenario was playing out that would bring a freedom for which all previous freedoms in this vale of tears had not taught me to hope?

Or was what we stood before only, as I had once heard Muslim clerics argue, an empty tomb? The body was stolen. Or the worms worked exceedingly fast. Or the man hadn't died in the first place, as was reported, but recovered and walked away from his ordeal on the cross. In any case, Isa ibn Maryam, Jesus the son of Mary, was not the Son of God. God—when he was called Allah, at any rate—didn't work that way. Saints He allowed, and prophets. But life went on as before, unpeopled by divinity. And resurrection was for another plane which never touched this one at all.

Esmikhan sensed my desire to avoid her, although she didn't

(I hoped) appreciate the reasons for it. But I couldn't avoid telling her in terms as terse as possible—which was easy enough since I knew so little—what was about.

"Turks?" she repeated innocently.

"It's only a rumor." I did my best to calm her.

Esmikhan was quite calm already. "You mean Ottomans? We have nothing to fear from Ottomans. I am a princess of the Ottoman blood."

"Exactly." In my mind, I was thrashing myself for the lack of care that could have lured me into this position. Had the desire for freedom blinded me so to the dangers? "You are an Ottoman princess on a Christian ship in a Christian harbor."

Her calm was quite unnerving. "We need only tell my grandfather's men who we are. We need not fear them."

"A stray cannonball may not stop to ask for introductions. And it may come from the fortress there"—I indicated the three gray stone turrets marching out to the sea on the right-hand side of our vista in easy firing range—"as easily as from any Muslim ship."

"Muslims won't fight without discussion first. My grandfather's servants will hear the other side with reason."

I'm afraid my scoffing at that idea was loud enough to offend her. "The time for discussion is past, lady, when there are forty thousand ducats to answer for as well as a small army of runaway slaves."

"But what has any of this to do with us?" Esmikhan may have been less naive than I had hoped to keep her about the Chians' latter infringement, for she looked at me hard.

I looked away and ended the conversation with: "Well, it is probably nothing. I see no Turkish ship."

Not long afterwards, however, we saw a ship leave the island under sail. Only single-masted, it depended heavily on oars in the calm, but the bunting and banners decking it purported some official mission. At first I thought we might be its destination, but the vessel quickly passed by, touching us only with a gentle surge of wake.

"Isn't that our captain on board?" Esmikhan asked.

I had to agree the man did have the same air, but then every Chian shared the blood. The man who caught our interest along with all his fellows on board this launch was dressed in brilliant red robes of an ancient cut and didn't spare a single glance in our direction.

Eventually we lost them in the blur over against the mainland coast, which was only visible if you knew what you were looking at. Then the tomb was empty again.

No Christian bell rang at midday, which I found disconcerting, particularly on Easter. Esmikhan was more distressed that we had missed her hour of prayer, but we said them late. I kept hoping to hear bells, and she didn't want to cheat lest her anxiety to make the hungry day pass quickly leave her a greater burden of leaden hours at the end.

Rising from the prayers gave us the view of the launch returning under the same press for haste, under the same labored power. It dropped anchor near shore, then shoved off again in less than an hour. It followed its wake back to Asia again with a different, even more noble-looking group than the first time.

"Look," my lady said, our first exchange of words since the brief discussion of prayer time. "Aren't there quite a number of ships across the straits there?"

Indeed, the lowering sun did seem to pick out more detail on the far shore. And the sleeping bear did suddenly seem to have all claws unsheathed in a bristling of masts.

"I'll climb into the crow's-nest to see," I offered, blinking up the long height against the sun.

"Up there? Oh, don't. Abdullah, you'll fall and kill yourself."

Her concern sparked a determination that caught at the pit

of my empty innards. I determined to refuse the image of the eunuch, the wounded boy in need of mothering she tried to press on me with a squeeze of her hand.

"But I'll have to get out of these first."

I shed her hand along with my robes down to only the loincloth. In order not to have to think about the pain and shame beneath that for long, I was on the ratlines in a moment.

Less than a quarter the way up, I knew I'd been foolhardy. My feet were as tender as an infant's, my balance skewed by the lack of practice, my head light from fasting and, with the perverse way it has of doing so, the wind seemed to pick up just to welcome me aloft. But I wouldn't back down at this point, not for anything, not with Esmikhan's eyes on me, tearing with sympathetic effort over the hands she clasped across her veil to hold back a scream.

"*Ustadh*." Esmikhan let out her breath when I returned to the deck. She used the most reverential form of address she could for a eunuch, the one that means "master." "*Ustadh,* that was very brave."

I wish I'd something else to tell her, for all that bravery. But I could no more deceive her than my eyes could deceive me— except perhaps as far as my bravery went. "It is," I had to say, "it is Piali Pasha over there against Çeşme. The entire fleet."

This did not seem to concern her, however. Something else did. "I . . . I've never seen a man without . . . without . . . ," she stammered, gesturing to the upper part of her body.

I laughed skeptically. "Lady, you have Sokolli Pasha for a husband."

"It's always dark then." She blushed, but she didn't stop staring at me. "And I keep my eyes closed."

"I am not a man," I reminded her, and quickly sashed my body out of her sight.

The first thing I decided had to happen was that the long-tailed banners—red crosses on a silver ground—had to come down from the main masts. The white-checkered Genoese flag and the Three Kings in procession had to be hauled in off the stern.

Now the five rather indolent seamen who'd been left on board to keep an eye on things decided to question my actions, as they hadn't bothered when it was just a matter of a sprint up to the lookout's basket. The men hadn't any fear of mutiny; my post as ship's mate had only been informal at best. They delegated the gruffest of their number for the task and for a moment I thought I'd have to fight him for access to the banners' ropes.

But all I really had to do was to say the word "Turks" and suggest, "Go up and have a look for yourself if you don't believe me." A few blinks towards the east and all five of them were hauling in the Magi at once.

A quick glance over the other options in Giustiniani's flag cabinet disappointed me. Something about the captain had made me willing to bet he had a Turkish flag on board for such occasions—or for when a little pirating seemed too good to pass up.

"Giustiniani, you're more honest than I gave you credit for." And I cursed him as I stuffed the too-blatant flags into the empty cubicles.

Now I had to ask myself whether, Turkish banner or no, the six of us together could get the anchor up and sail this tub out of harm's way. The anchor seemed the most difficult thing, but I wouldn't despair until an attempt was made. The shrouds would only take a little more time than usual, that's all. I'd shed my robes again and risk their stares in the direction of my vacant crotch to lend a hand.

But then I realized that these men had families ashore at Chios. They were frantic for the return of the ship's boat so they could go to them. One of the men—the youngest and strongest—even risked the charge of desertion and the chance he simply wouldn't make it to dive overboard and swim. I don't know whether he made it or not. I do know that without him my hopes of sailing away diminished, even if I could have talked the others into the idea, which one look in their shoreward-yearning faces told me wasn't worth the risk.

At the first sign of possible confrontation with strange men, Esmikhan had crept back under her draped awning with her maidservants. Although I had nothing good to report, I took a peek in there as my fruitless pacing brought me nearby. I told myself I went to reassure Esmikhan. But the sight of her, lounging calmly, bravely, trustingly fasting among her cushions, seemed rather to reassure me—or at least fire me with determination to think of something to do to help our situation.

And it did, in fact, give me an idea. Or rather, her *shalvar* gave me the idea, for she had kicked the white-and-silver-figured fabric of her *yelek* off her knees as she lounged. And a great expanse of the red silk of her gathered trousers was exposed. She was still wearing a very large size of this garment, as her body had yet to shake all of the effects of her pregnancy. There were plenty of cubits of good fabric about the hips and above the crotch, which didn't begin until below her knees.

I sank to my knees before her cushions and caught her ankle, partly from emotional and physical exhaustion, partly to feel the fabric—which was as excellent as I knew it would be—and partly to beg before I knew begging was necessary.

"Lady," I propositioned. "Would you be willing to sacrifice these *shalvar*?"

"My *shalvar*?"

"Yes, and whatever white stuff you might have to spare. Take your needle and make us a banner. Proclaim your faith to the world."

Where the thought of facing eighty galleys of Turks did not move her, banner-making as a pious Ramadhan activity did. Or perhaps—and why, at such a time, did I delude myself with the thought?—it was the earnest touch of my hand on her ankle.

In any case, I had no sooner stepped out of sight when I heard the unsettling sound of ripping silk. It was too reminiscent, especially under the circumstances, of the sounds of rapine and looting. So I let my pacing carry me farther away, assured that if once we did get under sail, our topmast, at least, would be prepared.

Pacing stirred the thought up to my mind that I had reason to be grateful I wasn't depending on Sofia Baffo in this strait. I remembered the Fair One's vain attempts to make a shirt for our slave Piero—in a time so long ago that I had had slaves. But circumstances were otherwise quite similar. Or Baffo's daughter had persisted in making them so dangerously similar soon afterwards by her irresponsible actions.

The contrast of Esmikhan heartened me as the sun set in bleeding bandages over the roofs and rocks of Chios. She and her helpers had made good progress and continued without pause to coax a white crescent and star out of red silk with pinpricks of needles. Riding at anchor lessened the danger of fire. I hung up a chained lamp from the roof so they need not fade as the sunlight did.

The women stopped to pray, to break their fast on ship's biscuit, the dregs of an olive barrel, and tepid, stored water. The pleasanter things promised by Giustiniani and even the citric air of this port itself had come to naught. But Esmikhan allowed no complaint among her women and they went back to their work the moment they were halfway satisfied.

No matter how the four Chians divided the night among them, I determined to keep a watch myself. I certainly hoped the quiet and loneliness of the wait wouldn't let me forget what ominous portents hung in the air. Fasting urged me towards sleep already. But the menace was clear enough that it spared me that shame, at least, by coming early.

The night's first watch cannot have seen two hours before I picked what was more than the moon's reflection out of the gloom. This yellow lantern light approached rapidly with the creak and slip of oars.

An "Ahoy" brought up Giustiniani's familiar vowels and limited consonants. The Chians threw him a line and soon his shadow and those of six or seven others—enough to raise the anchor, I determined—joined ours on board.

"What's the news?"

"Is it truly Piali Pasha off the mainland there?"

"Saints help us, have negotiations availed anything?"

"Our wives and children—are they safe?"

But the men's pleas for tidings went unheeded. Giustiniani's first no-nonsense words were, "Where's the capon?"

He had never called me that before—not within my hearing. But I stepped forward to claim that abuse and whatever else he had to give me.

Discovering me made him change the address but not the tone. "Veniero, get your lady and bring her to the boat."

Certainly his voice meant business, but to save my soul I couldn't fathom what that business might be. "Beg pardon?"

"You heard me. I'm taking your lady ashore. We'll keep her in the fortress. Piali Pasha turns away all our suits. He says we Chians have nothing left to bargain with; we must surrender. He underestimates our willingness to fight. Let's see if he says we have no bargain left tomorrow morning when we send him the delicate gem-studded ear of the Sultan's granddaughter as a present."

# XXIII

"What are you squawking for, Veniero?" The *Epiphany*'s captain snapped at me. "Your fate remains the same. The slave-freeing network still operates. At least it does as long as Piali Pasha stays out of our harbor." Even against the dark I could see how his look grew keener. His earring itself seemed to sneer. "Or do you *want* the Turks on Chios? You *want* this escape route for captives to dry up? You *want* to remain a slave?"

Each "want" was a scourge upon my soul. It had been so long since anyone had consulted my desires in anything, perhaps that part of me had totally atrophied. Did I even know how to want anymore? The heavy disgust in Giustiniani's voice loaded me with self-doubt. Even if I could distinguish what I really wanted from all that had been foisted upon me, would Giustiniani let me realize it any more than slavery did? His stance—patience contained with difficulty by the arms crossing his chest and backed as he was by a dozen sea-toughened men—this hardly lent me hope.

And the violence so thinly veiled in his word "capon." My head still rang with it.

Somehow I knew I must speak, and speak I did, repeating my first words, but managing a lower register this time. "I cannot let you do this to Esmikhan Sultan."

My fingers danced on the hilt of the dagger stuck in my sash, the symbol of my office. But I knew from experience that, like most symbols, it was of little practical use in the real world.

"We will do this with you or without you, eunuch. You may stay with her or go. Go to your freedom."

Giustiniani took a solid step towards me and I countered, backwards, brushing up against the curtains that, besides my emasculated person and showy but useless dagger were the only things that stood between my lady and Chios' fortress.

"Our families are on that island——" Giustiniani explained the obvious and echoes of agreement rose from the men behind him "——and we will do whatever we must to protect them."

"By God—and, yes, by Allah, too—Esmikhan Sultan is the only family this world has left to me." I said this with more firmness than I felt.

And when this raised snickers from my opponents, I added with desperation, "At least she never thinks me inferior for a loss that is not my fault. She thinks I have gifts to offer, even as I am. Exactly as I am." I realized I sounded like a child facing bullies in the alleyway, and my voice rose until it squeaked again at the thought.

Giustiniani's voice dripped with exaggerated pity. "Yes, well, any man who'd rather live life as a ball-less slave doesn't deserve to be called a man—whether he is or not."

"Freedom." I breathed the word and closed my eyes as if life itself were fading from me into heaven behind layers of cloud.

Times like this before, a dervish had whirled in to save me— a dervish who was really my friend Husayn. A friend of the family since before I could remember, the Syrian merchant had stepped in to godfather me when others had failed. He had taken the ultimate vengeance on my castrator and so was forced to live as an outlaw in a holy man's disguise. In such disguise, the teeming land of the Turk had disgorged him when I had need before, in the face of both pirates and brigands.

But I couldn't hope for such a deliverance now, far off in Christian waters. I was on my own.

Isn't that, after all, what freedom meant?

My eyes remained closed. Without having to strain in the dark to catch sight of the threatening moves of my opponents, my mind opened to other things. Beneath my feet was the comforting rock of the timbers, the lullaby they crooned in answer to the tide. This was the mother I longed for. I felt the tide itself pulsing through the narrow boards. It was rushing in now, towards Fate. The very breath of God in Creation.

My life, the entire world, seemed to teeter there in the balance. But that world also contained—I couldn't forget—my lady's life as well.

And then my nose, unconfused by sight, caught the smell of bilge water coming up from the hold. "Strong enough," as my uncle used to say, "to make a blind man see." A putrid "hellhole" made sailors rejoice. It meant the hull was sound; there'd be no back-breaking bailing this voyage. Dwellers of the most congested, filthy cities would clear the decks of such a ship. My lady countered it with ambergris and clove-stuck oranges. But seamen were willing to put up with the stench for a little peace of mind and "freedom"—so they called it—from pumping.

I felt crushed by the swells of that freedom. In their loneliness was a hidden enslavement.

And then, still with my eyes closed, I could see. I saw the threat of Giustiniani's earring. The cross branded itself red in the back of my brain because, along with little else, it had caught the single lantern's light.

And then, in the darkness of my still-closed eyes, I saw the simple jewelry of the other men. I remembered their trinkets, rather, from the many times I'd seen them before: combing through an enviably hairy chest as the anchor heaved, dangling from the fingers in an idle moment. Perhaps I had even seen some sign of chafing when the Genoese Giustiniani ordered a psalm read.

Whatever I remembered, bits and pieces, they all came back to me now, whole and in a flash, on the breath of the incoming tide.

In spite of the show of unity, at least half of the men before me, if they wore crosses, wore the symmetrically armed crosses of the Greeks.

Four years ago, if I'd registered this detail at all, it would have been to condemn these men as benighted heretics. Four years had taught me more sympathy for other points of view, though I could never recommend my way of learning compassion. Genoese were Roman Catholics, in the Pope's pocket; they ran this island. But the majority of the inhabitants followed the Greek rite. What of them? They made half the ship's crew. And they had chosen their Greekness no more than I had chosen castration, nor was it much easier for them to shake.

I remembered once having heard the question asked, "How shall we tell Greek from Turk if the matter comes to blows?" It was during some threatened fray in my uncle's ship along the Adriatic.

To this a Venetian seaman had replied, only half in jest: "Just kill them all. The fact that the Greeks are overrun by Turks only gives positive proof that God is displeased with their blind heresy. This is their deserved punishment."

I wondered just how much of the Turks' success in these lands where Catholics had once lorded was due to the Greeks' displeasure with this ascribed status. At least, they might not care one way or the other who their masters were, Turks being, from their point of view, no worse than Catholic Christians; conceivably quite a bit better.

Genoa, I further remembered, for all her talk of democracy since Andrea Doria's reforms but thirty years ago, was now little more than an arm extended eastward from Spain. And Spain bespoke "Inquisition" to my mind. Had the Genoese been using *these* tactics to rule this island?

Such twists and turns of logic came not from my mind, not by reasoning, but all at once, in a flash of inspiration, I could only say, or in a panic of fear, and in a much shorter time than I took to tell of it. When reason returned, I clung to this lead; I had nothing else. I opened my eyes and gave it a try.

"Yes, I will go with you. I will bring my lady and go with you."

Was that a gasp of pain I heard from the curtain behind me? Esmikhan was listening? Esmikhan, who could understand a little Italian? I couldn't think of that now. I had to forge ahead before the vision left me, before all courage did.

"Yes, for I would certainly rather have the fortress's walls between her and Piali Pasha's guns than this flimsy timber. And much rather the fortress than your plaster houses and simple tile roofs under which your wives and daughters cower. For do you think the Genoese are going to let your wives and daughters have a place in the safety of that bastion? Not unless your name's Giustiniani."

Good, good. I could feel the shift of that half of the men, as subtle but as perceptible as a change in the tide. And under the awning behind me . . . No time for that now.

"Or perhaps," I continued, warming to my subject, "they'll find you a cozy place in the dungeon—when they've charged you with heresy for no greater crime than following the faith of your fathers. Then, who is your torturer? The Turk? Or the Giustiniani?"

I felt another, stronger wave of support, strong enough to urge up a murmur with its motion.

"You think Piali Pasha comes with eighty vessels just to check on things in Chios? That the Giustiniani can fast-talk their way into yet another compromise? That the Turk may be satisfied with other promises? You know what such promises are worth. You've listened to them yourselves, but only because you have no choice, not because you are fools enough to believe them.

"The Turk is no fool, either. He knows these are empty promises when he hears them, empty because they are based on the pockets of moneychangers. Will the infidel forget his shame at Malta? I assure you, he will not. Or . . ."

I swallowed for spittle—desperately—then pushed on. "Or do you hope you can hold off all those galleys full of circumcised janissaries until a fleet can be brought from Genoa to aid the situation?"

"They will come!" Giustiniani barked. The high pitch in his voice pleased me.

"You see? I knew that was part of your captain's business on shore today, to see a ship off to Genoa. And who's on that ship? Not your wives. Not your children. Giustiniani's."

"He lies. My wife and daughters are still on Chios, sharing their fate with yours."

"I'm certain some great lords found room for their loved ones. No room for yours."

"The Genoese fleet will come."

"Oh, they will come. But that's a two weeks' sail, my friends. I've done the run myself in better days. Two weeks to Genoa, two weeks back—if there are no delays. A month. How many times can your wives and daughters be raped in a month, my friends?"

I let the murmur rise and caught it on the crest. "Of course, a month is optimistic. The Genoese in the mother city, like Genoese everywhere, prevaricate. If they cared what became of Chios, wouldn't they have sent funds to buy off the Sublime Porte before now? They've had three years to do it. You should be glad the Turk, unlike the Genoese moneychanger, is no usurer. Will the Genoese risk the blood of their sons when they wouldn't risk a few sacks of ducats? I know how the Genoese love their ducats. You know it, too."

Hatred for that other Genoese, Salah ud-Din in the little house in Pera, spleened my voice. But that man was dead. *Remember, you washed his mutilated body yourself. Be satisfied.* And, I realized, such untempered hatred might make me seem the madman instead of the voice of reason. Half of my audience, I recalled, was Genoese, too. I did what I could, with my next words, to wash the bitterness away.

"But the Genoese do love their sons. Even they are not so inhuman."

For some time, Giustiniani had been countering me with only rough guffaws and steps in my direction that alone made me flinch, so certain was I that they'd end in blows. At some point I'd heard him order: "Grab him, men. Stop his Turk-loving mouth."

As long as nothing came of such defenses, though, I kept my mouth going——like a man swimming against an undertow for dear life.

But now it was clear he could allow me to blather no longer. He must enter the fray or lose it, such was the palpable countercurrent of my words swirling among his men.

"Don't listen to the damned renegade," he said. "You all should know what Piali Pasha told our delegation today. He comes only to enjoy the Campos here, our pleasant landscape on Chios."

It was my turn to snort with scorn. "And you believe that?"

"It's what the Turk said."

"You trust such leaders, men, when they believe such things? From the mouth of a Turk, no less."

"Yes, I believe him." The man's voice cracked with desperation. "Why do you think they waited against the Turkish shore all day today if their words aren't to be trusted? We were all prepared to give them the usual welcome with flowers and banners—you men saw it. But no. 'I will not interrupt your Easter solemnities,' he said."

"The Roman Easter, men, mark. Nothing was said of the Orthodox holy day. Just where will the Turk be in a fortnight's time? Having turned your churches to mosques and your wives to odalisques." That was a shot in the dark and without much basis in logic, if I'd stopped to think about it. But I had to keep stirring the pot, even as I seemed to let Giustiniani have his say.

"That's what he said, on my honor."

"But what of the Turk's honor?"

" 'We are finished with our solemnities,' we assured him. 'Come ashore in peace.' But he wouldn't—and it's clear he hasn't. 'Tomorrow is time enough to come and enjoy your green gardens and flowing fountains,' he said."

"It is true," murmured one voice in the dark. "Our eyes see for themselves. The Turks linger at the other side of the straits. What is the meaning of that?"

I grasped at straws. "Perhaps they mean to come by night, to have the element of surprise."

All on board fell silent for a moment, straining to hear confirmation of my words. What seemed confirmed by all the senses proved to be only echoes of our own noises as our ears picked through the silence.

Another murmured in favor of Giustiniani's view. "Piali Pasha wouldn't disrupt our solemnities. That shows some civility, surely."

"What? That he didn't come and take your virgins in their holiday best? The Turk's not interested in what your women wear. He'll take any garment from them fast enough, for what he has on his mind. He—he simply wouldn't have your souls go straight to heaven, newly Easter-shriven. That's his plan. The man gives you at least one night in which to commit new sins to taint your eternities. Of course, the Greeks must go un-shriven altogether. I hope, men, you've kept an extraordinary Lent."

The fact of the matter was that I could not explain the admiral's hesitation. All I knew was, when Giustiniani reiterated, "He comes to enjoy the countryside," that was ridiculous.

"And can you see it?" I scoffed. "Piali Pasha and all his men, armed to the teeth and picking orange blossom in the Campos to stick behind their ears. Be serious, Giustiniani. I assure you the Turk is earnestness itself. And—and to let you know just how earnest he is, let me divulge some knowledge I am privy to that the Genoese are not."

My own heart had begun to race the instant the idea came to me. I spoke quickly now to transfer that same palpitation to my audience.

"You face not only Piali Pasha in his eighty ships, but my master Sokolli Pasha as well. That was my business in your harbor, to bring my lady to her husband, who waits at Bozdag with half the Turkish army. He waits only to see Chios fall."

The more I said, the more I came to believe it. This was how I would run a world conquest, anyway.

I elaborated: "Chios must fall before Sokolli Pasha can march north to join the Sultan in Hungary. And I don't think the Sultan wants a full half of his army too far behind when he crosses the Danube. Piali Pasha won't wait long. With this intelligence, have you any doubt as to what his purpose is? He is not come a-maying. Piali Pasha's reinforcements are much, much closer than yours are, my friends. I wouldn't be surprised if Sokolli Pasha was already at Izmir, perhaps even at Çeşme. My master and his hordes are just waiting for the first ships to vomit their loads of men and arms on your shores, then to come back and pick up more, ever more janissaries to swarm through your streets and your homes.

"And when the Turks enter your streets, as I promise you they must—tomorrow, dawn, at the latest—do you think they'll spend much time worrying about my lady? I don't. I know how Turks treat their women. Don't you? They trust them so little they must put them in the care of creatures like me—and would sooner see them dead than have a whisper of dishonor about them. So—go ahead. Do what you will with my lady. But trust me. Tens of thousands of janissaries will do what *they* will with your mothers, wives, and daughters."

And I couldn't resist this last little turn: "Gentlemen, wouldn't all of you welcome the protection of a eunuch for your women at times like these?"

# XXIV

THEN I STOOD panting, backed against Esmikhan's curtains, out of breath and out of words. I had painted a picture so grim that even I balked at it. But having exhausted my brain on this, I had no mind left to plan a remedy to the situation.

It was into this faltering that my lady stepped. Out of the curtains she came, only the very careful, strict draping of her veils let me—and me alone—know just how much such a move cost her. To step thus before a crowd of strange men and demand their attention on herself? I was silent a while longer just at the wonder of it.

And she did attract their attention, she certainly did. Of

course she looked like little more than a bundle of fabric, but she had taken great care that it was her very richest fabrics that showed. Sparks of gold and silver threads caught the lamplight. A ruby glowed like blood upon one exposed finger.

But more than the impression of costly treasure, her appearance was striking in its indefiniteness. And in this indefiniteness, each man's mind created its own particulars. My lady in all her distinct plainness of face might have appeared ridiculous, at best not worth fighting for. As she'd moaned herself as we stood on Ilium, "Allah, in His wisdom, made me no Helen."

But as she now stood before us as no woman, she was Every Woman. Each man put aside that swath of silk and in his mind's eye saw his mother's face, his sister's smile, his wife's tender breast.

And draped over all, Esmikhan carried the Turkish star-and-crescent banner.

I could see signs of hasty completion. The stitches began as tiny and neat as any Esmikhan had used—too many times to bear the thought—to make garments for an infant prince. But towards the end, the lengths of thread extended until one hook of the moon and most of the star were merely tacked on. They would serve—through the first gusts of wind, anyway.

And they served very well now, in the lamplight, in the hand of a woman who was every man's dearest.

"Sirs," Esmikhan said.

My heart was in my throat. She spoke Italian—*Venetian*—my own mother tongue. They must understand her, although her thick accent and sometimes stilted or over-poetic choice of words lent a musical, exotic, almost otherworldly quality to what she said.

"Sirs, your flag is ready. Sail with it, and under it, as Allah is my witness, your families will receive no hurt at the hands of my grandfather's slaves."

The men couldn't guess, but I knew. My lady had just about reached the limit of her impromptu vocabulary as well as of her courage. So, with miraculously restored vigor of my own, I stepped into the breech. I took the flag from my lady's shaking fingers and placed one reassuring, thanking hand at the small of her back, the place only I in all the world would know where to find beneath the bundle of wrappers.

"Go," I said. "Fetch your families, your valuables. Enough to start a new life, but no more than you can carry. If Giustiniani won't sail his *Epiphany* to safety, if he's too proud, too Genoese to accept an Ottoman's gift of protection, I'll sail her myself. I'll sail all of you and yours to safety through the very heart of Piali Pasha's armada. This, by the word of Sokolli Pasha's eunuch Abdullah, Giorgio Veniero."

SOMETIME DURING THE hectic night that followed, between hastily rowing men to shore, hastily rowing boat after boat of disoriented women, squalling infants, ill-sorted belongings back and stowing them, I found a moment alone with my lady. The moment I did, I fell to her feet in gratitude.

"Allah alone can recompense what I owe you, lady. What a brave and timely deed you did."

"Nonsense," she replied, her hand on my turban, then on my chin, trying to raise me. "Abdullah, what you said, when you said I was the only family left to you. Look, I weep now at the thought of it. How could I not do all in my power to aid—what was really an attempt to aid me. Abdullah, what you did, standing up to all those men who would have killed you and then—cut off my ear in a dungeon . . ."

She got my face so she could look at it, then pulled away her veil so she could laugh through the tears that lamplight embroidered with gold upon her cheek. "Abdullah, you really must stop all this groveling at my feet. You owe me no such obeisance. You never will. And you know it."

When I still wouldn't rise, she collapsed her form to kneel and bundle beside me. "I owe you," she said, the instant before our lips met.

What a lovely, lingering moment was then, each touch untainted by sense of payment due, by looking towards some future goal. All was glorious in and of itself. Each fondle, each caress held perfect existence for itself alone, each touch an independent climax of its own. When lovers promise "for eternity," they mean only 'til the need is spent. Then they will roll over and sleep on it. Our ardor, appetite, and food all at once, knew no such conclusion . . .

. . . But then the world coughing for admittance outside our door intruded. With one last swirling taste of her chin, I rose to go, letting her know there was more freedom in serving her than in all of Christendom, letting her know in truth my service as well as my love was forever. There was nothing left about my person that could even stir for any other.

＊

AND SO, AS the Chian sky began to silver, we weighed anchor and unfurled the sails. The predawn breeze was brisker than the previous day had promised; the canvas overhead filled with the crack of whiplash. But still the movement was sluggish. We were terribly overloaded, daredevil toddlers and weeping old women to the gunwales.

Giustiniani had command. When he'd succumbed to our plan and brought his wife and daughters on board, I thought that

was enough assault to his pride. I didn't need to captain a ship.
I had all I'd ever want in the safety of Esmikhan behind her curtains and her veils.

When my lady had invited the captain's family to crowd
under her awnings with her and her maids—well, that was
fine. No time for dalliance in such a throng. Besides, I should
keep a watch on deck and on the water before us. I'd have
Esmikhan to myself plenty of time in the years to come—
*inshallah,* for the rest of our lives, and even in the unphysical-
ity beyond.

So I came to mate our desperate sail to safety that morning.
Exhaustion fairly nauseated me. More ship's biscuit to prepare for the long Ramadhan day ahead didn't help the stomach.
But I would sooner cut my own throat than cut ties with
Esmikhan by breaking the rules of her fast now. And in their
scramble for possessions, few of the Chians had thought to
bring any food. I'd eyed a number of chickens and a milch goat
with interest—less interest now that I'd stepped in their drop-
pings a time or two. Besides, I'd promised safety to these for-
lorn souls, and until I was certain Piali Pasha wouldn't despoil
them, I couldn't very well do so myself.

Until then, I found distraction in the wind upon my face and
a detached scrutiny of Giustiniani's style and skill. I was glad
the smooth hand of God in wind and sails prevented our means
of locomotion from picking up their captain's style, which at
the moment was as rough as cullet with guilt and nerves.

"We've got a good start. We know the sandbars in the dark,
we native Chians. And the Turks, the Turks are all asleep. We'll
be past them before they have an inkling."

He kept muttering things like this over and over as he paced
among bundles of belongings and sleeping Chians along the
Turk-ward, starboard side of the rail. He said it to anyone who
asked, anyone who'd listen, sometimes just to himself. He said

it with the inflection of an *Ave Maria*. Well, those tones were easy enough to pick up. Anyone awake on deck was saying it, if they weren't murmuring some Greek prayer in its place.

Had I been captain, I'd have soon put a stop to both of them. The same wind that blew us alongside the Turks would carry the cant ahead of us. But of course I was the irredeemable skeptic. I'd *Ave*'d myself 'til bile rose in the dim little house in Pera— and saw that heaven did as it damn well pleased, for all our petitions. Still, how could I begrudge people their comfort where they could find it?

As long as they left me mine, I thought with a protective glance towards my lady's curtains, drifting with the same breeze that propelled us.

All this "they sleep," however. This "the Turks are still asleep" was delusion. Giustiniani deluded himself and anyone who believed his prayer. The Turks were awake, filling their bellies for whatever they had planned for the day, filling their hearts with Ramadhan fervor. The coating of biscuit and—did I taste it?— weevil on my teeth told me this was so. Indeed, before I could even tell sail from sky, I was certain I heard the Ramadhan drums across the straits, louder than both Christian prayers. The drums roused the faithful early, roused them so they could eat before sunrise. Made them alert.

I thought in good faith I should tell Giustiniani what my communion with the Turks—in my stomach at least—told me. After prayers, I thought, was soon enough. If I could find an inch of deck on which to spread my rug. Maybe without Esmikhan to share prostrations with, maybe I didn't care about prayers.

But then I overheard another verse to our captain's prayer: "We'll pass them by. Yes, we'll pass the flotilla by and then, with the princess as our cover 'til we're far beyond Greece, we'll make it safe to Genoa. As God is my witness—Genoa."

He wished us dead, that's what he wished. Overloaded and

underfed as the vessel was, I knew a trip to the mainland was about all we could hope for. My lady and I would be destitute if not enslaved in Genoa. Genoa was not a port for which I'd ever set the helm. Let the man pray "Genoa" if he liked—after our prayers were answered first. So I never told Giustiniani of what nerves, his own eyes, and his God failed to inform him.

Then what I knew would happen without bothering to pray for it did happen. The Ramadhan watch saw us. We were now close enough to see the men ordered from their breakfasts to scramble over the sides of Turkish galleys, into ships' boats to row and drag the larger vessels at the circumference of the flotilla around so their guns could face us. This was unnerving.

"More coastward men," I heard Giustiniani call. "Yes, cut the bars as close as you dare."

I heard the sickening brush of wood on shallow shoal. Miraculously, the solid timbers held. The *Epiphany* slipped on.

"Closer!"

Closer? By God, we were far too close already. I was glad to see the man at the helm was in no hurry to fulfill that order. He knew, if the captain didn't, just how low the load pressed.

For the love of Allah, couldn't the Turks see Esmikhan's banner? We weren't out of firing range yet, not by a long shot.

"Closer. Trim the sails—"

I craned my neck up the mast behind me for reassurance—and then I couldn't see the red banner, either.

I obliterated the captain's orders with an outburst of my own. "Giustiniani, the banner. You're a damned fool, man. To hope to sail without my lady's banner."

"I will not captain a ship under the infidel's colors."

"Then, by God, you'll captain no ship. I will." I yanked the *shalvar* silk out of an undecided Greek's hands and ran it up myself.

Perhaps it was only the communion of predawn food, but once the wind caught the women's stain of red, I was almost certain the Muslims at the fuses relaxed their hands a bit. At any rate, instead of the cannonballs I fully expected, the flotilla at last sent a little yawl towards us. A number of larger ships, too, had dropped their sails and began to move like the dawn out of the east towards us. I didn't like that so well. The wind was with them, our cargo decidedly against us. So close to Chios as we were riding, our sails grew slack between gusts, panting like an overweight man near the top of a hill.

"Get off from land. Starboard, hard starboard," I hollered to the helmsman. He was only too glad to comply as we brushed yet another rock, although his twist of the shaft brought us, for a moment, straight at Piali Pasha's forces.

"They're closing, you fools!" Giustiniani hollered. "Back port. And get these women and children out of the way." Where they might go but packed tighter and tighter into each other's arms, he didn't say.

Then Giustiniani ordered: "Men, man your guns."

"No," I countered, knocking the first gun I came to out of its stand. "No. No, these are women, children, old folks we have. Giustiniani, we parley."

"I will not parley with a God-accursed Turk. Not when women and children are at stake." Dawn glistened on the man's mad skin of sweat as he peered over the barrel of his own gun, the best little falconet on board. "We'll all die martyrs first. I've got the damned yawl in my sights."

And martyrs we would have been if a single gun had blown. But I said, "We parley," reining my voice down as low as it would go. And, out of the corner of my eye, I saw powder stay where it was, even behind the falconet. At the moment, that was the best I could hope for.

"Ahoy!" I heard then from over the bulwarks. While command of the ship was in debate, the yawl had slipped close enough for speech. But the Turks still suspected. The call came in very bad Italian. "Friend or foe? You fly the Sultan's colors, but your actions—we do not trust."

Giustiniani didn't move. His face under the sweat and the sky's reflected colors had frozen to the white of ice. So I moved instead, stepped from his side to the ship's.

"Ahoy," I replied, little concerned now that my voice betrayed me in a squeak. The Turks had easily as many guns in that yawl as we had with us. And they were also manned and primed.

"Ahoy," I repeated, and the next came in Turkish. "I am—I am *khadim* to Sokolli Pasha."

*"Khadim?* To Sokolli Pasha? Don't believe it." I heard a mutter among the yawl's crew. Their weapons, bouncing with the waves, caught dawn like kindling to fire.

"His harem is on board, sirs. Believe me, as one who fasts this day with you. Believe, by my manhood which heathen dogs devoured in the streets of Pera, believe. I am charged with their safety. Please, let me bring them to the vizier. Let me bring them out of the punishment you plan for Chios."

"You ride awfully low for one man's harem, *khadim*. Even for a vizier's." Their skepticism was not without humor. I took that as a good omen. Some of the guns sank out of sight.

"Yes. Yes, sir. You're right. These are . . . women and children, women and children who have been kind to my lady. For these kindnesses, my lady has chosen to throw the protection of her veils over them." *Quite literally her shalvar,* I thought, but let the yawlers have time to think about what I'd said aloud.

"We should board and see," ran the Turks' discussion. "There may be treacherous Giustinianis among them."

I heard a groan of fear behind me and realized the captain understood at least enough Turkish to know his own name when he heard it. I pushed my voice to cover his involuntary betrayal: "Sirs, you will not pass a vizier's eunuch. For Ottoman honor and for the Faith, you will not."

And, in the end, they didn't. No man swears by the fast who doesn't keep its rigors. Even less does any man feign a lack of manhood in a eunuch's dress—unless he's nothing left to lose.

And so the yawl escorted us around the headland and into Izmir, my lady's original destination, while in our wake, the rest of the fleet sailed into Chios.

That day I turned my long-robed back upon the sea. Easter had come and gone. There were no miracles, only luck awarded to courage, perseverance—and love. The tomb remained empty, and the Resurrection—somehow it no longer mattered.

Now I must concentrate on getting my lady a child. I couldn't perform the honor myself, though heaven knows I wished it. There was only one thing heaven had left to me: to get her to Magnesia, to Sokolli Pasha—and, incidentally, to Sofia Baffo.

# XXV

IN HISTORY, SAFIYE was the fairest of the Prophet Muhammed's seven wives. Sofia Baffo's harem naming was a co-incidence of the similar sound in her given, Christian name and the popular Arabic appellation. The name *Safiye* means "Fair One" and the matriarch's namesake was the fairest in the imperial harem. But *Sofia* in its original tongue means "wisdom" and I have always considered the combination, the conflict of beauty and wisdom in one mortal body, like the kiss of powder and fire.

I have never seen a woman bear a pregnancy quite like Safiye the Fair One did hers. Esmikhan's every attempt—and it grew worse with each successive one—seemed to overwhelm her, like some great parasitic fungus sapping all the strength from the trunk of a tree. My lady had to devote her every waking thought to the matter of the child within her; there was time for little else. As I had seen, she spared little time even for me.

Safiye, on the other hand, perhaps because she was so tall, never lost the supple grace that was hers by nature. Though it did require her to go about in jackets with but the first two little pearl buttons fastened under the breast, the bulge itself seemed tightly bound to her as a barrel is bound with hoops of iron. It never got in her way. She was always in complete control, and she had plenty of time to fill her mind with other things.

So befell that day in the month Christians call May—for Muslims it was the first decade of Dhu 'l-Kada in the nine hundred and seventy-third year after the Hijra of the blessed Prophet. Leaving my lady alone with the dregs of Safiye's harem in the governor's residence in Magnesia, I made my way to the army's encampment on Bozdag. Safiye herself hadn't been in the residence since the four days of Bayram at the end of the holy month of fasting. In spite of her condition, she would not leave Murad's side, and Murad's place was with the empire's battalions.

There is probably no location on the face of the earth where a eunuch feels more out of place than in an army camp—unless it be a battlefield. I know creatures like myself in the time of the Greeks did actually lead men into combat, but that is a calling I cannot imagine. I can only speak for myself, and Bozdag was discomforting enough.

Spring had almost faded from the countryside in ripening grain. Trees stood in the silent state of potential between flower and harvest. The fruit hung undistinguished from leaves and buds unless you cared to look closely.

In camp, however, spring had been pounded from the earth

weeks ago. Clouds of artillery practice sulphured it from the hillsides. The overused latrines and cavalry pickets dunged all growth senseless. One phalanx after another of yellow and indigo janissaries or violet spahis marched spring into summer dust on the parade ground. Following their horsetail standards, the troops perfected the martial step: left, right, twist face to the right; right, left, twist face to the left. This gave the impression of stern and constant vigilance to the impassive features under regiment-precise headgear that, acre after acre, held no seeming distinction or individuality.

My master had never had to leave Bozdag to come to Piali Pasha's aid on Chios. The Chian annexation to the realm of the Faithful was an accomplished fact of a month's standing. And, much to the credit of the Kapudan Pasha's patience, the island got off much easier than it deserved. Let it never be said that Suleiman punished unjustly, for the Giustiniani alone suffered, as we in Magnesia heard the tale. Save for those the *Epiphany* brought safe to Izmir—and the man I knew had only daughters—all the rest went in slavery to Constantinople.

Here, a number of Giustiniani sons between the ages of eight and eighteen died martyrs rather than turn Muslim, though they'd already been forcibly circumcised—the worst part of conversion—as an introduction to their tortures. Some of their mothers and sisters still wept over their tale on our return to the imperial harem.

But there are harder things in life than death. I can testify to that.

Thus died the Giustiniani name as artificially as it had, to that point, been growing. The rest of the Chians had already, within that month, been given more freedoms than they'd enjoyed under Genoa and encouraged in every way to bring their industry to the benefit of the empire as well as to their own. That was the tale as we heard it.

At any rate, all these soldiers still blotched Bozdag. All these men, primed to the peak, waited just to be shown the enemy—and needed him pointed out quickly before they began to crumble in on one another. I made my way through circle after circle of them. At each sentry I stated my master's name and was directed closer and closer to the eye of the storm, as it were, the pivot around which all that might spun.

Though Chios hadn't immediately called him to duty, it was in the springless realm of camp discipline that Sokolli Pasha felt most at home. More than a eunuch's natural awkwardness in the place, I felt graceless calling the Grand Vizier to a duty he clearly would rather ignore.

I wished my lady would be content, like other wives, that her husband would come when he chose to come. Unfortunately, for all our effort to travel this far, the master had only spent four nights—the same four nights of Bayram as Safiye and brother Murad had—with Esmikhan in Magnesia. Then business had cropped up, then the deep disappointment of her unfilled uncleanliness. But there were times when she would defy her upbringing for patience and claim a princess's prerogatives. This was one of them. And I already knew I couldn't deny her.

I made my way thus far through acre after acre of nothing but men, carrying no more news than that my lady had bathed this morning and was once more willing, anxious to receive her lord. And these were the manliest of men who smoothed their chest-long moustaches protectively as they watched me pass. They guessed my message. This embarrassed me to the very root of all I was missing.

But I was determined to help Esmikhan to her goal in any way I could, and for the moment this seemed the only way to do it.

So at length I approached the field commander's tent. I distinguished it from all the rest by size, by central placement, by fabric. Rugs and thick brocades of the finest make, patterned all over with stars, moons, stylized flowers, Koranic inscriptions in blues and greens and reds and gold patched together in a busy but harmonious and respect-commanding whole. Pillars of inlaid gold and mother-of-pearl propped the roof up well over the height of the tallest man. My master's standard dangled seven horsetails in front. This was the place, but a swarm of petitioners and janissaries three deep, planted like so many tulips in their beds, blocked my further advancement.

"Sokolli Pasha?" I asked one more time.

I'm not certain my voice carried to the turban-brushed ear over the buzz of humanity around me. Though the janissaries were perfectly disciplined in silence, the petitioners, a motley crew, were not. In any case, I was directed around to the rear of the pavilion and around to the rear I picked my way.

Here, indeed, the crowd was much less and, to my surprise and sudden comfort, I found another *khadim*. I walked over to him at once, remarking only after the fact that it was Safiye's monster, Ghazanfer, a creature in whose presence I never had felt at ease.

"Your lady . . . ?" I meant it only as small talk.

But without a word, Ghazanfer drew back the section of tent he guarded and ushered me inside.

Safiye Baffo nested in a cocoon of rugs and cushions swaddled especially for her between the pavilion's double walls. The prince's favorite took up nearly all the space there was, stretching out as she did to better accommodate her larger bulk in comfort. I stumbled clumsily on a rucked up corner of rug. There really was room for only the two—Safiye and her unborn child—in there.

But the Fair One made no protest at my presence. Indeed, she seemed quite pleased to see me.

"Ah, Veniero. This will interest you." Her succulent lips mouthed the words.

And she quickly curled up her feet to make place for me on a cushion next to her.

"I came looking for my . . ."

Safiye stopped me with a quick firm hand upon my jaws the instant they had sunk within her reach.

"What is this place?" I hissed a whisper of Italian as soon as my tongue was free to do so.

Safiye held one finger to her own lips.

"This is the Eye of the Sultan." She mouthed the words only, with no pass of breath, and with one hennaed fingertip, parted the curtains in front of us the meanest crack.

I caught my breath when I recognized my master's back so close I could reach out and tickle the creases in his nape if I'd dared. The Grand Vizier sat cross-legged on a heap of cushions; Prince Murad reigned next to him. Sokolli Pasha wore a high turban of fine white linen that gave him a neat and efficient appearance, and his green robes, though flashing with threads of pure gold, were in other respects purposely somber and restrained so as not to detract from the business at hand.

Between the men's two shoulders, fine, spring sunshine filtered through the side of the pavilion opened for air across from us. Janissaries lined the tent room, blue and yellow like shadow and light, at attention like so many pillars, these troops whose very name could make all Christian Europe quake with fear. The Vizier's Divan was receiving foreign ambassadors this day, ambassadors who would be duly impressed by the might and wealth of the Turks and send effusive and cautionary reports home to their rulers.

The total impact of this glorious scene upon my senses and my sensibility kept me from noticing any particulars. Safiye, to whom the pageantry of all this concentrated power was obviously a common spectacle, had noticed at once all the details that made this day different from any others. She caught my arm and pointed. With this force of concentration behind me, I was able to discern that the delegation now being received, struggling with their clumsy white Turkish robes of honor, was that of Venice.

The Venetians bowed with the stiffness of coaching still behind their movements, and presented gifts: lengths of plush velvet, mosque lamps of fine Murano glass, a casket of pearls. They came to protest the actions on Chios, actions which, in my mind at least, were a foregone conclusion.

I found it more interesting to watch Safiye than my former countrymen whose friendship and influence I was now far beyond. A flash of palpitation had come to her cheeks. Did the child move within her? Or was it the memory of the child—herself—and the free, sunny days she had spent in the republic of St. Mark, hitching up her little girl's skirts, and climbing for apples in the convent orchard? Did the sounds of our native tongue ring in her ears like a call to devotion for the tears of homesickness she had secreted away?

I was distracted from such thoughts by a ripple in the smooth flow of decorum before us. "I protest, my lord vizier," a young representative of Venice said, oblivious to the scowls of his superior, the actual *bailo*. "I understood we were to be in the presence of the Grand Turk himself, yet here are only viziers."

The face was familiar—round, soft, and effeminate. It didn't take long to realize where I'd seen it before: the young man passing out notices about the ransom her father was offering for Safiye's return. The face behind a black mask at a long-ago carnival, as like my own as a mirror. So he had come up in the world the last four years. He was no longer running errands in the marketplace, but was among the first rank of diplomats to pay their respects. Of course, he was from such a prominent Venetian family that his career was assured.

What was his name? Oh, yes, Barbarigo.

Young Barbarigo must have received some clue by now that he had spoken out of turn. This was not the Kremlin or some other court of barbarians after all, but a land with the strictest and most ancient etiquette in the world; still he would not keep quiet.

"No insult meant," he hastened to apologize, "but Suleiman has always received us himself before, and the people of Venice, hearing rumors of the Grand Turk's health, are very interested to learn of him personally."

I could only see the top of his fine white turban, but I could imagine the sort of half-smile with which my master would meet such insolence.

"But you are in his presence," Sokolli Pasha said, and pointed with one long finger behind his head to where Safiye and I sat. "Behold," he said, "the Eye of the Sultan."

Barbarigo had to be content with that.

In Constantinople, the Eye of the Sultan was an institution Suleiman had set in mortar and stone. Khurrem Sultan, Suleiman's beloved, legal wife sat often there, close to her lord—or so the romantics had it.

My master must have known full well, as did everyone else, that Suleiman was nowhere near that place, that the Favored of Allah, no matter how long the shadow he cast, was halfway to Hungary by now. The convention was mere symbolism, used to suggest that wherever the Sultan's servants were, there Allah's Umbrella was as well.

But did Sokolli Pasha know who sat here instead? Probably not: he took little interest in the harem. My master, I suppose, considered this seam at his back as empty of all but symbolism. And he would have fumigated the place if he'd suspected what larvae wriggled there.

Now Safiye's reaction interested me more once again. She drew herself up firm and regal, as if she were indeed the magnificent Suleiman himself instead of just the slave mother-to-be of his heir.

I looked at that curious anomaly in lavish, feminine silks, far-gone with child, round, soft, beautiful, but inside was something with which one's eyes dallied painfully as if with a razor hidden in a vat of new butter. And Safiye looked at the young Venetian with a smile that was at once self-satisfied and lustful with her usual lust for nothing but what would lend her power.

"You just watch," she murmured then, neither to me nor to the Venetian ambassador in particular, but rather to the world in general, or, in defiance, to God Himself. "I will do as she did," she proclaimed. Before I could wonder who "she" was, I was answered, "No, I shall even outdo Khurrem Sultan, the beloved of Suleiman."

And then I realized that thoughts of Venice never touched Safiye as they did any other mortal born along its canals and touched by its sea breezes. To her, Venice was the city that had thought her only a silly, headstrong girl and determined to marry her to a peasant on the isle of Corfu. It was a place that would slap her hand from any work save stitchery and letter writing. But here in Turkey, behind the harem curtain, no one need know what a woman set her hand to.

*What is Venice to Constantinople?* Safiye said with her eyes words that must have been percolating in her heart for months, years. *That little island republic where everyone knows everyone else, clinging to their miserable swamps so as not to fall or be pushed into the sea—what is it to this vast Empire encompassing three continents, from the Atlantic to India, larger than Rome ever was, whose million subjects speak a hundred tongues? What is St. Mark's Cathedral to Aya Sophia, or the Doge's dried sun-baked hovel to the gold-lined rooms of the Topkapi palace where I sometimes live, set like a rich stone in those cool gardens—sparkling with fountains and flowers of all descriptions? I can accomplish more here by raising a finger than the Doge can by raising all his navies. His "Empire of the Sea," his trade with the East, his very bread and butter—it is all impossible, a child's dream, without our will.*

The young Venetian ambassador didn't know it, but he had just been more diplomatic making a fool of himself in front of the Eye of the Sultan than had he gone with all pomp and ceremony to the Hungarian front.

Now crimson-and-gilt-turbaned pages ceremonially washed the guests' hands and dried them with smoking incense. Then they brought mountains of food—broiled whole lamb, turkey birds, and tiny squabs nestled among heaps of well-buttered rice, either plain, yellow with saffron, or pink with pomegranate juice—on gold plate as thick as drachmas.

Little of interest would transpire during a state dinner, Safiye must have known from experience. The Christians would try to find the strange dishes appetizing, try to eat rice with their fingers, try to keep the unclean left hand carefully, clumsily hidden—this without spilling the greasy grains down their white robes of honor.

All the while, the Turks would stand by, their hands folded gracefully in front of them, maintaining a demeanor that said, "We will be good hosts, even if you are miserable excuses for guests." Their laws forbade them to eat with nonbelievers, so, gracious as they tried to be, they never failed to seem like farmers who have just slopped the pigs they fatten for slaughter.

I got the feeling Safiye found this ritual laughable. How easily she'd forgotten that she had once gone through the same discomfort.

In any case, with slightly more haste—could I say anxiety?—than I was used to seeing in her, Baffo's daughter reached for my hand and I helped her to her feet. Ghazanfer heard the stir. He held the heavy rugs back for us and I passed the woman from my hands into his, where she seemed to find deeper ease. With incongruous tenderness, the huge eunuch adjusted her veils; for this Safiye always took too little care.

The prince's favorite stretched her back against its normal curve, exaggerating her fecundity as she did so. A deep sigh filled her cramped lungs with new air, unfiltered by rugs, enlivened by the ordure of camp. The sigh caught in midbreath with a slight twinge of discomfort. She leaned into Ghazanfer for its duration, caught his eye with some meaning I couldn't fathom, and then spoke.

"The young one. Not the *bailo* himself, but his assistant." Women and their eunuchs speak notoriously in a sort of code. Between them there is no need for more; the rest of the world is intruders. "He might be the one to go through," she continued laconically. "I noticed his eyes, full of idealism and energy—"

Her thought caught, like her sigh, at the midpoint. She leaned more heavily into Ghazanfer now.

"The midwife, lady?" Ghazanfer murmured, as a man murmurs prayers.

"The midwife, my lion," was her reply.

# XXVI

"THE MIDWIFE?" I repeated in a stammer, rooted to the spot as Ghazanfer scooped his lady up and carried her to a nearby sedan.

Then, past her pain—for the moment—Safiye turned to me over the monster's shoulder with sudden impatience. "You are the densest of all *khuddam*!" she declared. But was the impatience with me or with her own condition? "The Sultan, our master, is about to become a great-grandfather." She said it as if it were no more than "the Sultan will dine on pilaf today." "And the Quince ought to be in attendance, don't you think?"

"Of course," I stammered. "Allah bless the Ottoman blood."

"No, wait . . ." And she clung to the *khadim*'s broad shoulders a moment before she found breath to continue. "Run for her, will you, Veniero? I don't want Ghazanfer to leave me until she comes."

"Of course, my lady."

"And Veniero . . ."

Just before Ghazanfer snapped the door shut over his charge, his great head bent in to receive a few more words and the clutch of a white-knuckled hand. In a moment, these translated to me as:

"And the *bailo*'s assistant. Veniero, will you?"

"I?" But what I really wanted to ask was: *Not the prince? Not the great viziers and lords of the land?*

"Yes, you. You speak the language, don't you?"

"I see. What am I to tell young Barbarigo?"

"Tell him to come and find Ghazanfer when he may. Isn't that enough?"

"Very well."

"What should be amiss if I seek a Roman priest to sprinkle my child when it is born?"

Nothing, I supposed. At least I didn't say. This was Safiye Baffo and things were allowed to her that brought the death penalty to other inmates of the harem.

I did not hesitate to run at least the first of these errands for her. The second, I put off. What business was it of the young

Venetian that there was a Baffo in the imperial harem? Or that she had been delivered of a fine, healthy boy?

I told my master instead, along with the greetings of my lady. I did not tell him what was all the talk of the harem—that Safiye had labored hardly three hours with wonderfully little pain. She was up and about the very next day, longing to be at the Sultan's Eye again, though the Quince strictly forbade it.

The moment he knew the news, Sokolli Pasha bade farewell to the young father, struck camp, and departed into Europe. He did not pause in Magnesia to take leave of his wife, which was a private grief. Soon, however, we heard that the entire army of the Faithful was united at Pazardjik. The Grand Vizier congratulated the Sultan on a great-grandson—"who favors you, my lord" and the Sultan took his privilege to name the lad the most Muslim of all Muslim names—Muhammed.

And, as soon as the midwife thought it safe, she, too, packed the mother, the infant, and three or four attendant nursemaids—but only back to Magnesia. The older woman's constant mastic-ladened mutterings ran: "Birthing a princeling in an army camp. By Allah, like some tart of a camp follower."

Here, Esmikhan got the first glimpses of her little nephew and, though tears salted her hungry eyes, she couldn't get enough of him. For days on end, she held him more than any of the nurses, certainly more than Safiye, who paced at her grille like the caged lioness she was. The main concern for her son's care, I heard the Fair One express, was a complaint that the gem-studded cradle usually used for princes of the blood was left behind in Constantinople.

"Five rams have been sacrificed for him"—Esmikhan tried to comfort her friend—"both here and in every department in the capital. The cannon will fire seven rounds from Constantinople's walls. That's instead of the three they fired when I was born."

"And I am not there to hear it!" Safiye turned with sudden ferocity on the midwife. "How can you have been such a fool to forget the cradle?" she snapped. "People will mistake him for any whore's son."

And the Quince, in silence, groped for another round, yellow comfit.

"He looks quite plain to me." Safiye appraised her son from a good safe distance.

*"Mashallah,"* Esmikhan murmured at the new mother's words, though not with disapproval. She agreed with the Turkish superstition that any praise of a child tempted the evil eye. Though she couldn't bring herself to pronounce what she found such blatant lies herself, she diligently turned any that were uttered with a constant lullaby of "Garlic, garlic. *Mashallah.*"

And she hung the infant, his cradle, the entire room, with scraps of the Koran, chunks of blue glass, quantities and quantities of garlic. Always for her own infants, she had been too weak to see to such things before the babes faded from her life. She would not fail here.

I doubted—in the richness of his swaddling, the red silk patterned with gold tulips of his tiny *shalvar,* the tasseled crimson cap that wouldn't stay put for all my lady's efforts, as well as the day-and-night vigil we kept—I seriously doubted there was the slightest danger of confusing tiny Prince Muhammed with any other infant in the empire—in the world. So, though the cradle's arches over his son's head were only intricately carved olive wood, Murad had no difficulty claiming him.

And I, too, watched with a certain reverent fascination when my lady would replace the prince in that little bed, so different from cradles at home. Not that I'd ever paid much attention to infants' affairs once I'd outgrown them myself, but I did find the long crack in the floor of the Turkish cot quite remarkable. I would have joined Safiye in complaining for a new one in a moment, thinking the wood split with age and use. The nurses didn't even seek to pad the crack much.

But I had seen how Esmikhan fit a little ceramic spout over the child's boyhood before she set him down to sleep. And I saw how, from time to time, urine was funneled through the crack and into a dish below. Later, when the first weeks of danger were passed and the cradle was set outside for air, even the dish was dispensed with, the urine allowed to trickle straight into the ground. Only feces required the laundress.

Esmikhan treated every voiding of the little boy as some regal firman, gold-infused water, no less. And I, too, watched the process with—well, let's call it the fear of God. A bitter sort of awe at the bundle of flesh between his legs—whole, uncir-cumcised, proportionately large, as it is in infants—of which the little prince was entirely and blissfully ignorant.

I felt my own loss keenly. Not just the loss of that bundle, which was only flesh, after all, but that I should never have a miniature self. I should never find—as Murad found in the lit-tle hands that fit in the hollows of his, the little life that pulsed so fiercely in the scalp's soft spot—that only sure form of im-mortality.

"Veniero. The *bailo*'s assistant." From time to time in her pac-ing, Safiye would hiss at me in Italian.

"The *bailo*'s assistant? What does she mean?" Esmikhan, un-fortunately, was not so consumed with an inspection of the small princeling's drying cord that she could ignore the new mother's words as I had being trying to do. And she had not, in the flurry of surrogate motherhood, lost any of her Italian, ei-ther.

So, when we were alone and Esmikhan, I hoped, exhausted with child care into a pleasant sort of languidness, I had to ex-plain it to her. I explained the second errand Safiye had sent me on when labor was upon her. To my surprise—and dismay—

my lady suddenly roused herself and demanded more details.

"And you have not sought out this Barbarigo?" Esmikhan sounded hurt, as hurt as if I'd neglected a request of her own.

"She wants the baby christened—at least that's what she says."

"So what's the harm in that? *Inshallah,* he'll be circumcised when the time is right, made a true believer in all earnestness. What's a little water now? The holy blade will take care of that."

*As it did with me?* I thought, but didn't say.

My lady persisted. "Can't you see Safiye is distracted?"

"I can see that." '

"Can't you do what you can to make her a happier mother?"

"Only Allah can do that."

And though my lady didn't argue with me, she didn't let me forget the request, either. "The harem," she said, "was created to cover just such contradictions arising from a woman's deepest need, to cover things that the light of day would scorch from being if it touched."

So in the end, I went.

For all the cannon fire and ram sacrifices, my word was the first the Venetian delegation, still in Magnesia, had of this birth. As I've said, affairs of the harem were no outsider's business.

Even before I opened my mouth, emotions—too many emotions—flooded my brain as I faced young Barbarigo. In that instant I remembered facing him when we both were masked, just before I thwarted his attempted elopement with Baffo's daughter that would have brought shame on my entire family. I remembered his threat of lion's mouthing me, the palpable threat of his father's power. I remembered his hatred, my jealousy that he was what I ought to be: the vigorous young Venetian nobleman into whose lap everything fell by the grace of God. And from which none dared take a thing. The same prompting came back to me as it had over and over then: "Someday you will have to fight this man for what is yours."

Lest I blow my cover and face greater shame, I suppressed all of this before I made my announcement. I sought to veil my face as with a mask once more and told him in my stiffest Turkish:

"Pray, take the message to your Governor Baffo that he is now a grandfather and may rest assured that his daughter and grandson are secure and happy."

"By St. Mark, think of it!" the young diplomat exclaimed, no inkling of conflicted emotion in him once the news sank home. "Turkey ruled by a Christian! The son of a Venetian convent girl, no less. This may well do more for the powers of Christendom than centuries of treaties."

The young man took my arm and held it so tightly that I could feel the ring bands (holding gems more showy than precious) upon his wiry fingers through my brocade sleeve. "I have been impressed," he confided, "ever since my arrival here among the Turks that this country is indeed run by Christians."

I looked at him and smelled Italian cooking on his breath. I wondered if he had ever actually left Venice at all, that he could be so naively convinced there was only one way—the Italian—of doing anything.

"I mean the janissaries," he explained, "and the pashas and the viziers—all of them, born into Christian homes. There is no reason why this empire should not be the greatest in the world, with so many well-trained members of the True Faith at the helm."

"The Turks," I told him, "say that all men are born Muslims. It is only their parents that corrupt them and raise them otherwise."

I wanted to go on and suggest that if he thought my master,

the Grand Vizier, had any vestiges of his birthplace left on him, he obviously had not been paying attention in the Divan. And what made him think, I wanted to ask, that a Turkish Christian state should be any more moral than the European ones with which he was already familiar—broken treaties, injustices, and all?

But the young man had already raised his eyebrows, startled, at my first expression of pessimism. It was, after all, only pessimism in Christian eyes. A fine Oriental fatalism had begun to impress me, in a curious mirror image, as optimism.

And I took some comfort in the knowledge that Andrea Barbarigo could not truly know Baffo's daughter, or he would have known that any true religion, Christianity or otherwise, was the farthest thing from her mind. Her child was healthy, he was male, but, most importantly, he was an Ottoman, heir to the world's greatest Empire: these were the things she cared about.

Venice, I thought, should have seen that their man Barbarigo was married and settled before sending him on this mission. His eyes, as Safiye had noted, were too full of idealism and romance. His unused lust manufactured heady visions of what must be behind the harem walls: helpless, languid females, exploited and waiting for a deliverer.

At the time, I thought there was no harm in allowing him to keep these delusions. But such images of herself played the young diplomat's intelligent but unharrowed mind right into Safiye's hands, her lily-white hands which he never actually saw, but dreamed about. They manipulated him like a puppet on strings.

# XXVII

I REMEMBER THAT first evening of autumn. There was a drizzle of rain outside, a blessing after the heat of a long and tedious summer. Esmikhan's eyes had lit up like the fire itself when she'd seen old Ali's wife bring in the tinderbox from the kitchen to fuss with the brazier for the first time that season. This was a definite sign that both Sokolli Pasha and Safiye and her young son would soon be returning to the capital, and then things would be lively again.

Such musings assured my lady there was no need to manufacture excitement that evening. The musicians and dancers she often required to pass away the hours until she could retire without arousing rumors that she was dejected or out of sorts were allowed to keep to their quarters. Surely no one would think it amiss if she spent this first rainy fall evening quietly playing chess with her eunuch.

Those who saw Esmikhan on a normal night—with her musicians and dancers—would hardly notice how four years of marriage had changed her. If anything she appeared more lively, now that all entertainments were in her control. "She's gained a little weight," might be their only remark which they would brush aside with, "That's a sure sign she's happy and well-treated."

But I had the privilege of her quiet nights, and I knew that the bright little princess for whom every day was a wonder and a joy—she was a rare visitor in our house these days. One might almost say it was a mask or a veil put on for the guests.

It was not so noticeable in winter when she had Safiye and all her old friends to keep her company. Then it was quite easy for her to be carefree and teasing again, and the color bloomed in her cheeks like forced roses. But during that summer they had faded. There was no hiding the truth: Esmikhan was not making a very happy wife. And, for some things, a eunuch was just not a good substitute.

Let me put it this way: Sokolli Pasha was not making a very good husband. I had overestimated the ability of duty to bring bliss. Or I underestimated the truth of the old Turkish proverb, "Duty never got a son."

Esmikhan liked to brush her causes for complaint off with a laugh. "Allah be praised, and He should make every woman cursed like me a daughter of the Sultan's house. I have no fear of ever being divorced for childlessness, considering who my fathers are. That is some gift."

But I was more convinced than ever that the fault was with the master, not with my lady. Sokolli Pasha had suppressed his personal desires for so long that he was no longer capable of feeling them. No wonder the sons he got had little taste for life!

Sokolli's old mother had died quietly over her needlework one day some six months after her son was married. She never said, of course, but I got the distinct feeling that she realized there was only enough of her son to be dutiful to one woman, and she had the graciousness to bow out. But what had been sufficient for a tiny, frail, old woman was hardly enough for a girl—now a budding young woman—like Esmikhan.

From the station of mere Pasha, my master had risen through a short stint as Kapudan Pasha, admiral of the fleet, until, at the death of old Ali Pasha in the previous Muslim year 972 (in the month Christians call June), he had been appointed Grand Vizier. To no higher post in the Islamic Empire can a man be named in recognition of his talents. The only post higher, that of Sultan, is a matter of birth, and takes neither labor nor talent at all.

Needless to say, Sokolli Pasha was a very busy man, keeping all of his talents in constant employ. He had little time for romantic dalliance even if he had the natural inclination for it. The duty of visiting his wife's bed the Pasha fulfilled meticulously twice a week—when he was home. But even when he did, neither he nor she got much pleasure from it.

And the three dead sons.

In no material way could it be said that Sokolli Pasha neglected his wife. Indeed, the palace in the great park had begun to make a name for itself because of the lavish parties its young mistress gave, the entertainments it offered, and the gifts presented to every comer, even the uninvited beggars at the door. Nothing made her happier than to give away time and affection thus, when she had so much to give. But she was growing wise much faster than the turn of years.

"I know," she would confide to me afterwards, "that a party is really just a lot of noise. It means nothing if there is nothing to celebrate but one's wealth. To have a birth or a circumcision or a wedding to celebrate, only then is it a real party."

And "I know these are only friends bought with money. Don't think they can fool me."

"I, too, am only bought with the master's money," I would say.

"You can't fool me, either, Abdullah," she would say, taking my hand.

And she would turn to me when all the others were gone.

That first evening in autumn, when she turned to me once more over the excuse of a chess game, Sokolli Pasha had been gone from Constantinople for six full months. He was still at his master's side, fighting the infidel across the Danube. That was where the most urgent duty lay. Who could make complaint?

But Esmikhan's womb had been empty eight months now. She mourned, but now, I think, she was almost glad to have had this time without something inside her, sapping her strength. I hoped that I came close to filling the void.

Sokolli Pasha, when he did write, had other concerns besides an heir. He wrote through the hand of a secretary, with the large margins prescribed by official documents, each letter one of any number of dutied dispatches. And more often than not, the direction was to me, not my lady at all. I always read her everything; perhaps that's what he expected.

"Your lady's grandfather"—he wrote—"may Allah always guard him, he is not the man he once was. Indeed, he has not been able to ride at the head of his troops this year. Still, he will go forward, even though it means a rough ride in a carriage. The armies of the Faith cannot win without his presence. We all feel that. Whatever happens, I avow it is Allah's will, but I suspect the campaign may not last very long this year. Should there be a ploy made for the throne or a civil war in our absence, I would rather your lady were in my house than in another's, even if that other is her caring father's. I would not alarm you, but there are those who would put her brother forward as heir instead."

"Safiye for one," my lady interjected at this point, and I nodded in agreement.

"Prince Murad does sit in Magnesia," the Grand Vizier continued, "and manages it with competence. I had a chance to see just how well this spring—when last Allah favored me with your company. Magnesia is the closest *sandjak* to the throne, after all, the seat traditionally held by crown princes. But for all his sterling qualities, Murad is still young, suceptible to manipulation. And to go against direct father-son inheritance will only open the door to malcontents, provide them with a figurehead for whatever their reasons to divide the empire are. I would not have your lady have to make the trek from Constantinople to anywhere else in uncertain times such as we may, Allah protect us, live to see."

Other letters told how old Suleiman surprised them all and, even from a carriage, continued to direct raids, stealthy maneuvers behind the enemies' backs, and great victories from the spring until this first rain.

And now, what was rain in Constantinople might well be turning to snow in the Slovakian mountains. The army would be forced to return. But they would not return early and never on account of their commander's health. That was the man Suleiman was.

It had been a very long six months.

# XXVIII

Esmikhan's plump little face caught the lamplight as she studied the game. I found her beauty not breathtaking, but soft and comfortable. Her mind was that way, too, enjoying the game not for the strategy and the thrill of brilliant plays, but for the stories it told.

"Alas, so many poor pawns' lives sacrificed on the field of battle!" she exclaimed. "I pray to Allah to have mercy on them, for they died defending the Faith.

"Oh, see how the grand Sultan forges ahead! No infidel can stand in his way!

"There's the elephant, stampeding out of control and lost in the mire. But here comes the good knight to lead him straight and help him capture that enemy soldier." (The Turks call the piece Europeans know as a bishop "the elephant.")

"And here comes the Grand Vizier. Such a clever man, sneaking through enemy lines, speaking their heathen tongues as if he'd been born there, always at the Sultan's side when he needs him. But he has left his poor princess at home on her own, and she will throw herself into enemy arms or die of boredom!"

Of course there are no female pieces on an Eastern board; that would be unseemly. It is the Grand Vizier who holds the terrific power we in the West associate with the Queen. But Esmikhan could take no interest in the game unless she could personalize it, as she had no use for stories without a heroine, and so she usually called one of the pawns herself in the disguise of a poor peasant. Her instincts of self-defense often forced her to move in ways no other player would, making all sorts of sacrifices for that one pawn. When that piece did finally make it across the board, however, off would come the disguise, the veils thrown aside to reveal a figure of such wonderful power that few fairy tales can boast similar transformations.

In spite of her novel view of the game, Esmikhan was a good player. As the game wound down to her victory this time, however, she seemed to lose interest. Several times I left my "shah" open to death, "mot" ("Shahmot" is our checkmate), and she made some silly move instead, either on purpose, to draw the game and our time together, out, or because her mind was elsewhere. She spent a lot of time pretending to study the board, but in fact it was the fire within the brazier's grate I saw reflected in her great brown eyes. If she wasn't careful, she would let me win, and capture the little pawn called Esmikhan as well.

"Esmikhan," I warned her, reaching out to touch her hand—ivory like the board it rested on. "Lady?"

She was in the middle of turning to me with a sigh when a sound in the *selamlik* below brought us both to our feet.

"Whoever can that be?" she asked, and I read in her face a curious struggle between hope and despair as she thought, *My husband!*

From the room where we sat, a window covered with a wooden lattice looked down into the main sitting room of the *selamlik*. It had been installed at Safiye's suggestion. Safiye was convinced her friend would get on better with her husband if she took an interest in his affairs and overheard some of his meetings with diplomats and ambassadors. It certainly made Safiye a more frequent visitor in our home—when she was in town. But Esmikhan had no patience with such spying, and usually the window went unused. Now we both ran to it at once.

Mejnun, the gatekeeper, opened the door and ushered a total stranger into the room below. Mejnun called for Ali, who entered and asked what he could do for the man. The man did not speak, but showed the old slave a very small object.

"It's my husband's signet ring!" Esmikhan whispered and I knew she must be right, for both Mejnun and Ali set about removing the guest's drenched and muddy wraps and making him at home.

He was a tall man, and broad. None of the width was superfluous, however. He must have been nearing thirty. Masses of dark, curly moustache had not a streak of gray. His turban must have once been white cotton, but it was now a little worse for the weather. The decorative peak in his headgear's center had lost its shape and color, so one would be hard-pressed to call it silk and not some sort of black pudding. There was a jeweled clasp in his turban, too, in which a crest of black feathers could be stuck——a crest that had long ago blown away.

It was only when his mantle was removed that his trousers above the thigh showed their true, dry, clean color——violet—— and we knew his turban peak must have originally been purple, too, a color which marked him as a *spahi-oghlan,* a member of the Sultan's standing cavalry. Still we had no indication of rank, any more than that he had at some time or other been deco- rated for valor in action. A jeweled scimitar under a cloth-of- gold vest he refused to give up to the slaves——that completed the costume.

"He looks something like you, Abdullah," Esmikhan mused.

"Yes," I replied in a scoffing whisper. "If Allah ever willed me into a spahi uniform."

"Go entertain him, Abdullah," Esmikhan said.

"Me, Lady?"

"Yes, please. Those two slaves are such dolts, and you know that's all the staff my husband left in the *selamlik.* A man with Sokolli Pasha's signet ring deserves better than that. Ali will do nothing but bring him supper, and then leave him on his own while Mejnun will simply bow and stare. But you may talk in- telligently to him, and make him feel truly welcome. You might also discover"——she finally came to the point——"why it is that he has come."

Mejnun had bowed his way back to his post, and Ali had set a fire going in the brazier and brought water for the man to make his ablutions when I entered the room. I salaamed, in- troduced myself, and said that my mistress wished the stranger welcome. The man nodded his thanks to me, but politely did not glance towards the lattice which he could not fail to notice over our heads.

It was only then that I found some ease enough to notice what a truly stunning piece of man's flesh he was. His eyes, though small and unassuming, were bright, and his jaw square and firm under several days' growth of beard. He was quite tall, and of perfect and strong proportions, even for a spahi, who takes little thought but for exercise and athletics.

He moved, however, not with a swagger like many such soldiers, but with a cautious grace as if to say, "I like nothing better than to dance, to move, to run, to leap, but I will forbear in your presence because I know it is not polite to be so self-indulgent."

Most remarkable of all was his smile. Thin, firm lips, they burst onto a perfect set of large, white teeth at the slightest provocation. Like *ataif,* wedding pancakes, I thought, over-stuffed with honey and sweet clotted cream—one had to move it quickly to one's mouth lest the sweetness spill stickily all over. Even exhausted and on guard as I could tell our guest was, the natural set of his lips was up rather than straight across or down, and little creases at the corners, quite like dimples, told me that he grinned a lot in battle, too.

"Ferhad," he said his name was, but he was very tight-lipped about it, as if he wished it were one syllable instead of two.

Ali brought warm tea, and then food, and the guest ate heartily—one might almost say ravenously, but he was too polite for that. On first impression he was careful not to let his exhaustion show lest it cause too great an imposition. I realized more and more clearly however that he had ridden long and hard before coming to rest in this place. I struck upon this detail and tried to use it to pry into conversation once his hunger was abated. He was washing his fingers in rosewater to finish, an act which did not seem at all incongruous to this soldier.

"Where did you come from today?" I asked. "Çorlu?"

"My horse came from there." He smiled. "I myself left Sofija four days ago."

"Sofija?" I said. "But that's impossible. That's more than three hundred old Roman miles as the crow flies."

The spahi smiled and shrugged his shoulders. He wasn't bragging, only stating a fact, and I knew better than to doubt him further.

"You must be on extremely urgent business," I commented.

The spahi smiled and shrugged again, but I got no more from him that night, for even as I sat there, he lay down on the divan and slept like a dead man.

When he woke the next evening, and had eaten quantities more, Esmikhan, who had refused to see any of her gossiping maids all the while he slept, sent me down to entertain him once again. I found him more relaxed and, if possible, more amiable. But he was not more communicative.

"You are, of course, welcome as our guest to stay as long as you wish," I coaxed him. "But we are only a house full of old slaves and women. Surely the quarters of the spahis in the Grand Serai would be more entertaining for a young man such as yourself."

Our guest smiled to show he forgave me my rudeness, but he said no more than, "Tell your women not to fear, my friend. Show them this ring if they are in doubt. They must recognize it."

I nodded at the plain, large agate he showed me. Yes, we knew it.

"I can only say I come from their master and mine, and that the Grand Vizier and I are bearers of a heavy burden."

Had I been listening closely, I might have guessed what his cryptic words meant, but we had to live together thus, dissatisfied, for nearly a month, before the truth was known.

# XXIX

THE WEATHER TURNED fair again, but not too hot to enjoy sitting in the garden in the afternoon. The roses, refreshed by the rain, bloomed their second bloom with a vigor I could not remember having seen in them before. Especially around my lady's pavilion were they profuse, as if they grew without leaves at all, only buds and flowers, and they filled the air with their scent.

Ferhad passed much time in the gardens, strolling with an ease and a delight that hid whatever anxieties might be weighing on his mind. My lady, too, took pleasure in the open air and often at corresponding times, though of course there was a high wall between the gardens of the *selamlik* and those of the harem.

One particular afternoon when our guest had been with us over two weeks, I left my mistress alone in her pavilion playing her oud and singing a repertoire of rather melancholic songs while I had to see about some purchases Ali had made for the kitchen. I offered to send her a maid to keep her company, but she declined, saying I needn't waken anyone from her afternoon nap on such an account; she was quite content to be alone. There are those who will say I was careless. Well, maybe so, but I certainly thought no harm.

Besides, who can struggle against the will of God?

When I reentered the garden, I remarked at once how beautiful my mistress' song had become. I had not heard her sing so beautifully, nor yet so cheerfully, in a very long time. Like a lark ascending over the garden, I thought, and other birds would surely rise in answer.

I approached the pavilion silently so as not to disturb the song. It was I who was disturbed by the scene instead.

Esmikhan sat on her pillows in the pavilion. Dressed in pink and cloth-of-gold, so becoming with her dark hair and eyes, she looked like one prize rose among all the others. Her beauty did take me aback—a long acquaintance had made me forget that she could be striking when she chose—but there was something even more disturbing about the scene. There, standing among the roses, just behind and to the left of my mistress, stood the young Ferhad.

She knew he was there. She must have known he was there—why else the change in the spirit of her song, and the high color in her cheeks? And yet she pretended she did not know. Why? Because if she gave but the slightest indication of knowing, he would have to beg pardon and flee for his life, and she would have to throw a veil over her face, and flee in the opposite direction.

So the scene stood there, poised like a butterfly on the very point of a leaf that the slightest breeze would send fluttering away. So all stood breathless in that moment (and for how many endless moments before I came?), attempting to hold it suspended there forever.

*But this cannot be,* my conscience soon caught up to my heart and said. *This is my responsibility, and eunuchs have died for allowing less.* Such destruction seemed a crime: men who think nothing of killing their fellow men are often moved to tears if they destroy a fragile butterfly. Still, it had to be done.

I kicked a pebble in the path, the young man vanished before I could blink an eye. We all took normal breath and spoke again, though the words seemed loud and harsh at first.

"How have you been?" I asked my lady tentatively.

"Fine," Esmikhan said. "Just fine," as if it were a lie. I didn't dare call her on it, but you may be certain I was twice the *khadim* after that, and I never let her out of my sight unless she was safe inside the harem.

My lady spent a lot of time over the next few days standing at the grille and looking down into the *selamlik,* even when Ferhad was not there. She called for no ladies, nor could I draw her to finish our chess game, or into a new book of poetry. Still, there is no harm done but a little palpitation of the heart, I thought. A little exercise in that direction might do Esmikhan good. *I control the doors between the worlds. We are still safe. Where there are no words, there can be but little love.* I found comfort and an excuse for apathy in such musings until one day when my mistress called me to her.

"Here, Abdullah," she said, handing me a pink rose and a pale narcissus. "Would you be so kind as to take these flowers down to the *selamlik* and place them in a vase for me." Then she added as a sort of apology, "I thought it might be more pleasant for our guest if he could have something new and bright to look at besides the same four empty walls."

"Just the two?" I asked. "Surely he would be more flattered by an armful of roses. Let me send one of the girls to the garden to cut them for you. Or perhaps a whole dish of narcissus would be nice—one of those that you so carefully forced in gravel."

"Perhaps," she said, blushing, "another day. Today I would like just these two."

I nodded and went to fulfill her wish, finding it odd, but certainly not amiss. Flowers were some diversion and one more innocent, I thought, than love poetry or long, sad songs. She was certainly not asking me to carry letters down to the *selamlik,* or anything else forbidden.

In the *selamlik,* I hunted for the fine Chinese vase in its usual place in the wall niche, but it wasn't there. I was about to call for Ali to ask where it might be when I saw it already out—placed curiously on the top of a low wooden chest. There were flowers in it, too, and they seemed very fresh. They couldn't have been cut any earlier than that very morning.

And it was a very curious bouquet altogether, not unattractive or slovenly, but very masculine. It consisted of really only one flower—an ox-eye daisy—which was flanked on one side by a leaf of a plane tree, and on the other by a sprig of cypress.

"Now I see," I thought. "My mistress has taken pity on our guest's poor hand at arranging flowers, and thought it only polite to send him others . . ."

But that thought hardly lived to take a breath before I knew it would not do, and condemned it, like some pre-Islamic father his unwanted girl-child, to the dust. In its place came, for no apparent reason, the lines of the Persian poet, so popular in the Turkish harems:

> I cried so much that I heard
>> moaning and wailing from the cypresses.
> They confided in me and said,
>> "O that your heart could find peace with us,
> For your beloved was flourishing, and so are we.
>> She was tall, and we are a hundred times taller."

Often since I'd first heard that poem recited, I had listened for "moaning and wailing from the cypresses" as a wind passed, and often thought, like the poet, of my love who was tall and fair, but now no more. And, like the poet, I had sadly whispered back to the trees:

> But what use are you to me
>> When it comes time for kisses?

So it was not strange that now, as I reached out to remove the cypress sprig from the vase, the lines should come to me again. What was strange was that I should also remember that the cypress, because it never loses its leaves like other trees, was often used by poets as a symbol of eternity.

Plane leaves and ox-eyes also have their set meanings in the intricate melodies of romantic verse: the first, because it so resembles a hand, means touch or holding, and the flower is an emblem for the beloved's face.

Now I suddenly saw clearly that there was no coincidence here at all. The odd assortment of plants had been chosen and arranged with exquisite care and the message read: plane leaf, ox-eye, cypress, "I will hold the image of my beloved's face in my hand forever."

So what did the rose and the narcissus mean—the reply that I was delivering like some furtive love letter? My mistress had sent message bouquets by me before—to other women: a bunch of rue or musk for remembrance because the scent stayed in the hand long after the flowers were gone, or a pair of pomegranates, like breasts, to felicitate a friend upon the weaning of a child. Before I had always known the code. This would be a little more difficult.

The narcissus, I knew, usually had reference to the eye, but the rose had innumerable meanings: as a bud, it was a new baby; it could represent the cheek, the face, the bosom, the nose, the lips . . .

The possible images were infinite, but when I hit upon the right one, I knew it at once. It was one of my mistress's favorite verses by the poet Manuchihri—

*The scented breeze brings news to the narcissus*
*That the rose has come out of seclusion.*

'She promises a rendezvous with you in the garden,'
   it says,
And the narcissus bows down in happiness at this
   promise.

How plainly, how perfectly the poem captured the situation, as if the poet had written with no other lovers in mind! And yet—how impossible! How eternally impossible!

"Lady," I said, turning to face the grille where I knew she was watching. (And I noticed how perfectly placed the vase was before that grille so she could not miss the message.) "Lady, I cannot do this."

There was only silence from the grille in reply. She knew I had guessed and she also knew that I could not go against what was my very reason for being—to stand as a guardian to her virtue. Yet the silence continued, and in it I read an awful thing: If I should betray her now, I might never have her confidence again as long as I lived, and that was a thought worse than death.

*Please, please put them in the vase. Just this once,* her silence seemed to ring out through the *selamlik. Don't you think I know our love is impossible? It is just the passing infatuation of a broken-hearted princess for a lonely, bored spahi. I expect nothing more. But just this one, brief exchange. Don't you know how Manuchihri's poem continues? It is not a happy ending, I know. But I still love it for its beauty. The lover is described as a cloud, the lady as a garden:*

He returned from abroad,
   His eyes brimming with tears,
And he awakened his mistress with those tears.
She reached out and tore her veil.
And emerged from hiding with her face like the full moon.
The lover gazed on his beloved from afar,
   And shouted a shout heard by all ears.

*With fire in his breast he tore his heart open*
  *So that his mistress could see his hidden fire.*
*The water of life flowed from his eyes*
*To bring forth plants from his beloved,*
*But . . . her body was ruined by the heat . . .*
  *His mistress would not bloom. . . .*

*For all our tears, I know our love is as impossible as the love of a cloud for an enclosed garden: we can never embrace. Still, just this once, Abdullah—or I shall die . . .*

I succumbed to the silence. I placed the two flowers in the vase, and even brought the leaves and the ox-eye up to my mistress so she could keep them always with her in the harem. But I determined most firmly that at this first serious trial of my duty since Chios, perhaps even since the brigands, I would not fail. I would confront our guest that very night, allowing him no more evasion, and find out just what he meant by disrupting the peace and honor of our home.

He was standing, strong and vibrant, in meditation before the vase, one finger gently circling the petals of the rose. A sudden panic filled my heart at how overwhelming the task of a eunuch was—to somehow be stronger than men who are real men—and I decided to ask Sokolli Pasha as soon as he got back if I couldn't have two or three aides.

I'll admit now that what I felt was more than the threat to my station. Jealousy. I begrudged the man every angle of his body, every battle-earned muscle. I begrudged him the way he made water. The jaundice of a Barbary pigeon crept up my back and neck and prickled under my turban like heat rash, like an infestation of lice.

Young Ferhad turned to me with a smile totally unguarded and without malice. Did he expect me to be carrying another very welcome message? I wouldn't have given him anything at that moment. Apparently he expected nothing, for he was the one who spoke first, bursting with news of his own.

"Sultan Suleiman is dead," he announced. "May Allah have mercy on his great soul."

I repeated the blessing in a murmur. "When did this dread event happen?" I asked when my thoughts came clearly again.

"A week before I arrived here to take your hospitality."

The metal of nerves that could keep such news a secret for so long shocked me more than the news itself.

"I feel I can tell you now," Ferhad continued, "for Sultan Selim, who arrived from Kutahiya three nights ago, has successfully consolidated his power in the Serai."

"Prince—I mean Sultan Selim—has arrived in Constantinople? That is curious. You may know the lady I serve is his daughter, yet she received no word from him."

"This is not the time to be placing the womenfolk in jeopardy by giving them too much knowledge. But I feel it is safe for you to know now, because Selim left early yesterday morning with a small, fast-riding guard."

"Selim come and gone and we knew nothing of it?"

"I knew your mistress is one of the Blood whom this must touch deeply, so I did feel obliged to say something as soon as possible. Still, it was best to wait 'til the new Sultan had outdistanced any enemy who might want to send word to the army before he gets there. Even so, it must not become general knowledge yet. Keep it from the gossips among your staff if possible."

I nodded.

"I hope you will convey to your mistress my profound sympathy upon the death of her grandfather, and my sincere wishes and prayers for the blessings of Allah to be on her illustrious family, now as her father rises to the throne." His tone was stilted and formulaic as if there were much he would have said, but dared not.

I nodded again to assure him I would pass on the message, even though I was certain every word had already been heard through the lattice.

"But the Sultan, may Allah have mercy on him, is—was—in Hungary leading the armies of the Faith," I protested. "Surely those men must know by now that their commander is dead. The secret cannot be kept from them."

"Our master, Sokolli Pasha, is a very brave and careful man," Ferhad replied. "The Angel of Death came quickly to Suleiman in his tent while the army was in siege around the small mountain fortress of Szigeth. The Grand Vizier, now the Bearer of the Burden, knew that if word got out, the soldiers would refuse to fight any longer, would break the siege, and all go back to their homes to wait and see if they liked the way succession came. The breaking of a siege and a retreat is not a good way to begin any man's reign, especially for the man who must follow a leader as great as Suleiman was—may his Faith be found pure before Allah.

"But Sokolli Pasha was well prepared for such an event. At once he sent a single messenger with the news in an encoded message from the camp at Szigeth. That man and another brought the word to Sofija within the week. I had been posted in Sofija, never out of sight of my horse, for months, and I did my best to carry the word as quickly yet as silently as possible here, to Constantinople, which, Allah willing, I have accomplished. Another single man met me at the gate and took it on to Kutahiya. This ring I have of your lord allowed me to stay here, enjoying your hospitality, in a place where I would not be dogged constantly for news of the front, news which, if I was tempted to tell it, could be very dangerous indeed.

"Now, as to how Sokolli Pasha managed the plot there on the

front, I will tell you what I know. He and the two physicians in attendance were the only souls who witnessed the death. I have been told the Grand Vizier himself strangled the physicians, but I personally do not think that possible. It is hard enough to keep one dead body a secret, but three?

"I think he simply refused to allow the doctors to leave the tent. He slept, guarding them, on the floor beside the dead Sultan's bed. The physicians applied embalming salts, I believe, and the cold of approaching winter in the mountains was with Sokolli Pasha to slow the rotting of his master's flesh. But for living flesh willingly to join in that chill is discipline indeed.

"To the men outside, the Grand Vizier announced, 'Our master is ill. He is resting.' When food was brought for the lord, Sokolli Pasha and the physicians partook of the small portions of a sick man so even the cooks would not suspect.

"And though all the army had to be kept at a distance for the ruse to work, Sokolli Pasha went out almost hourly with messages for the troops. These were messages he himself had penned, but which read like the words of the Sultan. They spoke encouragement and fire for the Faith. They contained orders for forays and astute maneuvers to weaken the enemy.

"Sometimes the dead body of the Sultan was painted with cinnabar to give it more life. It was propped up stiffly and, through a gauze curtain, seen by those outside to be watching the progress of the siege with interest and eternal determination.

"Well, I have since learned that within two days of the death, the fortress was taken and victory won. The dead Suleiman, through Sokolli Pasha, praised and thanked his men and handed out gifts to those who had been particularly valiant, as had always been his generous wont in life. Then the order was given that, to avoid the dangerous snows, retreat would be made from Europe until another year. Slowly, and with as much order and discipline as when they had set out with their Sultan alive, the army began following his carriage home, that carriage which, still unknown to them, had become his hearse. Every night, the Sultan's tent was pitched and the physicians carried him into it on a stretcher to rest, and back to the carriage come daylight.

"Allah willing that all continues thus smoothly, Selim should meet the army in Belgrade. Only then will rumors be allowed to leak out and proofs given. Only then, when a new Sultan is there to take over command from the corpse of his father, and receive the oaths of loyalty from his men."

"Allah willing, it will all come about as you say," I amen-ed the remarkable young spahi before me.

"Amen indeed," he said, breathing a sigh, "though it grieves me that I shall have to take leave of this lovely home tomorrow morning to ride north with further intelligence."

"It is indeed a pity," I said, able to speak now for myself as well as my mistress.

When I returned to her, "He reminds me so much of you," Esmikhan confessed, trying to laugh at her tears.

"My lady is too kind," I protested, for I had just been thinking that there were probably no two men more unalike than Ferhad, the spahi, and myself.

But the spahi's recital had filled me with wonder for another man, and that was my master. I had thought many negative things about the constraints duty put on him during the past years because of what it was doing to my mistress. But now I knew that, though duty may indeed never get a son, it could save a nation. I had seen it happen: Sokolli Pasha had single-handedly carried the entire Islamic nation over the terrible morass of potential civil war and chaos for more than a fortnight. This he had done with no hope of praise or gain for himself; he would still be no more than Grand Vizier, the Sultan's slave, when Selim got to Belgrade. No, he had done it armed with nothing but his duty. And it is one thing to be dutiful to one of the greatest, most powerful monarchs in the world; quite another when that man, like any other man, loses all force to the hands of Allah, and begins to stink.

As I sat there with my lady—she trying not to weep for her grandfather, her lover, or for both—I noticed that the chess set was still set up for play as we had left it nearly three weeks ago. Someone, perhaps one of Esmikhan's pet canaries, which she liked to let loose in the room, had knocked over the padishah, the king. But the vizier had maintained his position, strong behind the lines. The king could be set up again, and play resume where we left off.

At last, with Ferhad out the door, we did this. Esmikhan sighed, and I looked at her across the board: a little too plump, a little too happy because inside she was a little too sad. At the sacrifice of her happiness, all of the Islamic Empire had been saved.

# XXX

SULEIMAN'S DEATH WAS not made known to the general public for another whole month, not until the month of Rabi' al-Akhir and the winter season were both well underway. Only then did the great cannon boom from the Fortress in a death knell; only then did my lady remove the mirrors from her rooms, cover the walls with crepe, and dare to weep openly.

And Suleiman was laid to rest in the pillared mausoleum in the midst of the garden on the dawn-side of the mosque the great Sinan had built in his name. Finally, the Magnificent rested beside his own beloved Khurrem Sultan.

Every day for forty days, Aunt Mihrimah held a recital of the complete Koran to assist the great monarch's soul to heaven. A similar public recitation happened during the same period around the tomb at the Suleimaniye mosque. But Aunt Mihrimah's was private, for women.

And for forty days, we attended. In the courtyard through which the sedans passed, Mihrimah's vast wealth fed the poor in a charity whose merit would rise to heaven with the dead man's soul. The room upstairs drowsed with too-warm braziers and the old woman's smell of fading chrysanthemums. Downstairs was bread and pilaf; upstairs, the dainty, sweet but chalky bricks of halva. And "Bishmillah ar-Rahman ar-Rahim," the chanted names of God, were punctuated by loud sips cooling the aniseed or ginger tea. Or small cups of an infusion of jasmine, black elder, and rose petals with which the Quince dosed the season's first cold which, over the forty days, spread from one end of the company then back again. This concoction cloyed achingly just as it was, but required huge quantities of sugar to mask the true bitterness hidden beneath the outward smell.

Women chatted quietly together under the comforting—if not to say stifling—quilt of holy words. Children played together between their mother's knees. All in all, two sessions were more than enough to assure me I could expect a most soporific forty days. But then, on the third or fourth day, Nur Banu put in an appearance. What was even more startling—we thought them still in Magnesia for the winter—Safiye came with her and the young prince Muhammed.

My lady's squeals of delight totally buried an ominous recitation of the terrors of hell. And she and Safiye greeted one another with embraces and busses on both cheeks.

Crossing the room to overhear their words did seem too hovering. But without moving I could eavesdrop on Nur Banu as she greeted her own best friends.

"Yes, she has abandoned my son in Magnesia," the older woman said. " 'It is best to be in Constantinople for the health of the child,' the Fair One says. 'The Quince is here.' "

I stole a glance across the room to witness the warmth with which the midwife greeted her prize patient, then returned my attention to hear the rest of Nur Banu's recitation, competing with the Recitation of Recitations, the Koran.

" 'The center of government will be instructive for a young prince,' she says. For an infant? I don't think so. Before summer, he'll be running, *inshallah*. Where can the cool spring of my eyes run here? Besides, what can be wrong with learning how his own father runs a *sandjak*? That was the instruction I gave my Murad—may Allah keep him—when he was my grandson's age. He has turned out well, I thank the Creator. But—this is what the Fair One says, and my son believes her. *I* say she has abandoned him, but who cares what I think in all of this? Be sure I've sent Murad replacements for his bed. A number of other beauties so he will not be cold this winter. What does she say to this? What can she say? She chose to abandon him. She must live with the consequences."

One woman asked with as much tact as her curiosity would allow: "And how are things between you and her?"

Nur Banu replied smugly: "She is much humbled, thank Allah, that Selim inherited instead of Murad as she was plotting for."

"You have the Grand Vizier to thank for that."

Nur Banu scowled at the speaker and then defended her former lover with the vehemence of a current one. "Selim inherited because he is who he is, his father's only living son, not for any other reason."

"Well, I have heard Sokolli Pasha saw to it that Selim came to the throne so he—the Grand Vizier—will have a freer hand to run things his way. Selim is not a man to try to thwart him in anything."

"Don't wise ones say, 'Never trust the harem's gossip?' "

The gossiper blushed and stinted.

"It is true," Nur Banu went on, anxious to display her own knowledge of affairs, "that the Fair One curses Sokolli Pasha day and night. But she must have someone to pin blame on for her disappointment. It is Allah's will. She must learn a pious submission or she will be among the troops the angels herd hellward on Judgment Day. Of this you may be certain—and Allah knows best."

So the interest of the women in the *kadin*'s entourage returned to the recitation at hand. I helped myself to a cup of anise tea, hoping it would warm me of the chill that had suddenly crept up my back and perched there, for all the sable weighing on my shoulders. The thought of Safiye's curses turned against my master was what first set off the shivers, certainly. I knew Baffo's daughter far too well to imagine any curse she uttered consisted of no more than empty air.

I turned a protective glance in my lady's direction. Safiye had now shuttered herself against Esmikhan's friendliness, but that was the usual way of things. I detected no new threat there, though I did notice a new string of Murano glass beads around Safiye's alabaster neck. Such a necklace could cost as much as the real gems my countrymen so successfully mimicked; still, the obvious provenance was odd. Well, perhaps Murad had given them to her, a reminder of her home.

And my lady seemed in no need of consolation as she usually did upon Safiye's neglect. The young prince offered ample diversion. Little Muhammed had more personality than the creature, amorphous save for his sex, that we'd last encountered. He seemed an awfully sullen child, rewarding Esmikhan's antics with never a smile, only long, big, brown-eyed stares. But he could sit on his own now, eat more halva than was good for him with four pearls of teeth and, propped up with pillows, held a miniature divan as if already come to his inheritance.

Safiye watched the proceedings with a detached air, with less mind than she gave to an adult divan, easily—and perhaps that was where her mind wandered, after all. I heard her say very few things—and these seemed to have nothing to do with anything else happening in the room at all.

"The army is two days' march away," she said, "with Selim and the Grand Vizier. There are some that would have us set aside our grief over the loss of Suleiman our Shadow and Lawgiver. We should immediately prepare to greet Suleiman's successor with the pomp and triumph that, they say, he deserves. A large, triumphal parade of all the armed forces is planned to enter through the Golden Gate. I, for one, am not so rapidly over my sense of loss."

I detected formula and not a little sarcasm in this speech, but no one else seemed to notice. Esmikhan gave her friend a comforting squeeze. The speech had the effect, in any case, of turning the discussion to just how much of this upcoming pomp the ladies could or ought to share.

A cousin of my lady, daughter to the ill-fated Bayazid, had a house near the mosque of Yedi Kule. "That's not far from the Golden Gate on the Triumphal Way," this lady said. "From my harem's shuttered windows, we would all be able to see all the procession. Aunt Mihrimah, madam, Diadem of the Veiled Heads, we could move all of this solemnity over there and not miss a thing."

The great Mirhimah Sultan had black looks for this idea. She did not like to be moved and preferred that the world came to her instead. Nor did she care to have her hospitality overshadowed.

But other women, including my lady—though I did see the

throes of guilt to be relinquishing her mourning so soon cross her face—decided the opportunity could not be missed.

"It is for one day only, after all," justified one.

We eunuchs were consulted as to how and when our charges could be brought to the neighborhood of Yedi Kule in two days' time.

"The word of Allah," justified someone else, "is so powerful, it does not need us to go on."

"Well, I will hire reciters at my house, too," said the cousin. "There cannot be too much recitation of the Holy Word."

"Safiye, you will come, of course," my lady urged.

Safiye shrugged with what I felt to be feigned nonchalance; it was not feigned very carefully. I found it very hard to believe, particularly from one who wouldn't miss a Divan if she could help it, that she was not bursting to see which captains had won honors for themselves in the campaign, who got precedence over whom, how the various viziers fared. Yet she said, "It is up to my son's grandmother, my gracious hostess. I am at her disposal."

When consulted, Nur Banu hesitated as well, taken aback, I think by Safiye's uncustomary deference. She, too, prorogued. *She will wait to find out more precisely what Safiye wants,* I thought. *So she can act in exactly the opposite fashion.*

Then I noticed Ghazanfer's absence from the eunuch's ranks. His presence always discomforted; in the ease without him it was difficult to go looking for trouble. But when I got the chance, I asked Safiye about him, being as indifferent as possible in my phrasing.

I was pleased that she did not suspect my suspicion. She treated the matter as if I were a child asking why another child had not come to play. "He doesn't come to Mirhimah Sultan's. He doesn't like it here—for some reason. You, perhaps, may understand the caprice of a eunuch. I confess it's beyond me. At any rate, whenever I want to come to pay my respects to the great daughter of Suleiman—on whom be peace—I must depend on Nur Banu's *khuddam*."

Then, with another outward show of insouciance, I made my way around to the other side of the room and asked Nur Banu the same thing.

"I don't know," was her reply. "Something about visiting friends from his homeland. And she let him go! Safiye has no control over her eunuch, none. A slave needs to visit friends when it suits him? And he's done nothing but visit since they got here."

"What is his homeland?" I attempted one more question.

"Hungary, I believe. Some place westward, in any case."

I couldn't think of anything to ask after that.

Along towards sunset finally came the chapter contradictorily entitled "Daybreak," which rails against the mischief of weird women working magic. And then the final verse "against djinn and men," "the stealthily withdrawing whisperer who whispers in man's breast," and the day's labor was done.

The aged mother and her two daughters whose recitation we had enjoyed—they spelled one another—rose to go, accepting the thanks and small gifts of all present. They lived at the Suleimaniye mosque on the charity foundation.

"Will you see them home, Abdullah?" my lady asked. "Give them the honor of a *khadim* which usually they cannot afford? That is the least we can offer them since they refuse to stay overnight with Aunt Mihrimah—they say they do not mean to insult her hospitality, but it is a statute of their holy order."

So that is what I did, after seeing Esmikhan herself safe in Sokolli Pasha's palace. As I left the Suleimaniye, the men's recitation was just breaking up as well. I picked my way back through the dispersing crowd and as I did I suffered the odd sensation of being watched. *How can you think that?* I wondered. *Among so many hundred pairs of eyes?* And usually a sense of being watched only meant that someone averted his eyes from what discomforted him to look at—like the crippled or very deformed.

For all the bustle, the mosque's dome settled an austere calm over the gathering gloom. The air above and around me winked now with lamplight and the first stars like an inversion of the flashes of black-on-white on an ermine stole. Heaven seemed very close, grappled to earth by the chain-gray of the monument's four minarets. The casual elegance of the vast courtyard reigned like a man born to his station, like the personation of the departed monarch whose spirit so permeated the place. It hung above me like a canopy as I took the retreating steps. I had no more business. It was time to go.

Then all at once what fading light remained congealed upon a bit of white and my eye was riveted. I saw a small glass vial, set carefully on the stone sill of one of the barred arcs of window that pierced the perimeter wall. As all the world moved around me, I stood and gazed without moving a muscle at the wonder of it. How could such a delicate thing not be crushed in the press? And then I wondered, if it had attracted my attention, how had it managed not to be picked up and claimed by the first passerby.

Then I saw it was *vetro a filigrana,* the delicate canes of white glass embedded in clear that was a hallmark of the Venetian factories. I could not resist, any more than most men could resist averting their eyes from me. I picked up the bottle and claimed it as my own.

And next I knew it *was* mine. A gift. Within the vial's narrow mouth I found a scrap of paper. I tipped the fragile glass upside down and knocked the paper free.

It was too dark to see clearly. I sensed more than saw what this note might mean. With a pounding heart, I dashed to the nearest streetlamp just lit by the passing lighter with his coals and long pole, there at the boundary between the mosque's precincts and the profane world. I read. The words were Venetian. I knew the hand. It was as if I could smell my friend. Husayn. But in fact, with some sense deeper than knowing, I had expected this all along.

I gave the ascending mosque stairs quick scrutiny. Turbans drifted by in the half-light like so many bubbles, and, among them protruded plenty of round, tight felt dervish hats like so many shoals in a smooth-flowing stream. Just the crowd a Koranic recitation could be expected to attract. But among them I could not distinguish Husayn, my family's friend since I was a child, the man who, blaming himself for my sorry fate, had renounced the merchant's life and taken on that of a wandering dervish. He had taken on the part of a guardian angel as well. Now he had come again.

"The signorina plots the overthrow of the new Sultan and of your master who holds him wobbling on his throne," the note read. "Keep your lady away from the triumphal procession."

# XXXI

UPON ARRIVING HOME, I learned that a message had arrived there, too. It was from the master, addressed, as usual, to me.

"You know you could read these yourself," I told my lady who had stayed up with anxiety. She watched me break the formal seal bearing the *tugra* of the Grand Vizier with such intensity that I grew clumsy. "He means them for you."

I didn't even believe my own words. I knew by now that her scruples would never allow her to open something addressed to someone else, particularly not through the Grand Vizier's seal. But I also knew the man I served would never write directly to his wife, the daughter of his present master.

"What does he say? What does he say?" Esmikhan had to clap her hands to contain herself.

"Merely that he is at the farm he owns on the outskirts of the village of Halkali. That is less than a day's ride from here. He means to wait with the army, tomorrow see to preparations for your royal father's entry, and then be with you the evening after. That is good news, lady, isn't it?"

"But if he is less than a day's ride, why can't he come tonight? Or tomorrow at least? Be with me at night, then ride back out to his duties in the morning?"

"Duty calls him, lady. There is much he must see to with the army." More than I would tell her. More than perhaps even Sokolli Pasha knew. The small glass vial was making a very heavy lump in my sleeve.

"Go see him, Abdullah," my lady insisted. "Take him my welcome."

"Lady, not tonight." There is nothing like a day of Koranic recitation to make one feel weak and stupid. Besides, I felt the weight of the bottle—and the note it contained.

"Tomorrow, then. First thing in the morning. Abdullah, please. You must. I haven't been in his bed for seven months. Please." She cradled my naked face in her plump, soft hands.

So I agreed. "What else is a eunuch for if not to take his lady's most urgent messages to the outside world?"

And, come the morning, I felt much better about the prospect. I saw my lady safely installed with her Aunt Mihrimah and the Eternal Words. Then I rode out beyond the city walls, invigorated by the clear, cold winter air.

After having picked my way through the awkward looks an army gives a eunuch and the curdled mud they make of winter-fallow countryside, I found him as I had before. Through concentric lines of tents after identical small yellow tents splashed to the eaves with campground, I found Sokolli Pasha in the lavish pavilion beneath the flutter of seven horsetails. The Sultan was in the small farmhouse nearby. I had no idea where the farm family was.

"My eunuch!" I heard him say as I was shown in. "By Allah, that's the last thing I need right now!"

Still, he invited me to sit down, and tried to be polite in response to my deep, supplicating bow. "How are you?" His voice grew in sharpness through the speech. "How is your lady?"

"My lady rejoices at your safe return, my lord Pasha, and wishes me to ask . . ." I still stood, feeling three layers of rugs beneath my muddy boots and wooden planking beneath them.

"No. I know what you want to ask, and the answer is no. I admire your devotion, Abdullah, but the answer is still no. Now, you've ridden a long way today and you must be tired. Why don't you let my orderly find you a place where you can rest for a few hours? But I want you on that road long before the army's up and on the move tomorrow."

"Sir, may I ask why?"

"By Allah, I'd forgotten what civilian life is like. Everybody has to have a reason for everything. And you Venetians are the worst of all. Yes, how well I remember! If you must know, it's because our new Sultan, Allah help me, is a tenth of the man at forty-five that his father Suleiman—may he rest in peace—was at seventy when his bad heart confined him to a carriage."

"What do you mean, sir?" I asked. My amazement to hear these words from a man of duty would not let me remain silent.

"I mean that Selim, the son of Suleiman—yes, my dear wife's own dear father—is a roaring drunkard."

"Surely not. Alcohol is against the laws of Muhammed the Prophet."

"Yes, isn't it, though? And for good reason. But that doesn't stop Selim. Selim, the Sot, the army calls him—his own army, by Allah. Drunkenness and a strong taste for women and for boys (yes, there's that as well)—well, the army could live with that. They might even praise him for it, and 'the Sot' become something like the epithet they called his great ancestor Muhammed, 'the Conqueror.' The Turkish army is not full of scrupulous sissies, no. But worse than all of this—Selim is a coward. Do you know that in Belgrade—when we had to break Suleiman's death to the men—he refused to pass beneath their swords? Now, perhaps to a Venetian such as yourself, this custom has little meaning, just some quaint relic from the past. These Turks, you know—it's not so very long since they came riding wild off the steppes. Allah, the smell is still on them! Don't I know, I, who as Grand Vizier must be followed everywhere I go by a standard bearing the tails lopped off seven horses, never minding the flies it attracts."

"I'm sorry, sir," I admitted, "but I don't know what it means to pass under their swords."

As I would not sit, Sokolli Pasha did, amidst a rainbow arc of pillows which, save for a low table draped in correspondence and a cloak hung on a peg from the center pole, were the tent's only furnishings.

"Every new Sultan," he said, "must, upon his ascension, pass under a tunnel made of the crossed, naked swords of all the army. If any soldier does not approve of the new commander, this is his chance to let his displeasure be known. He has only to let his sword grow heavy in his hand, and drop when the pretender is beneath the blade. It's the perfect solution for a small nomadic tribe in the steppe which must move and fight as one man. Suleiman submitted to that ordeal and had the supreme devotion of all his men ever since. And he knew he could trust them, too. There were no daggers poised in the dark for him—he'd already given them their chance. Of course, that was fifty years ago, and no one in the army today was there. Still, they remember. The Muslim army never forgets its privileges, even if it forgets the difference between a left-face and a right.

"Selim refused to pass. He had already consolidated his power in Constantinople, he said. He had received the kiss of submission from the Serai staff and from the eunuchs of the harem. Well, there is the harem, and then there is the army. Selim knows very well that the janissaries have no love for him. He is Sultan only because of the death of his two brothers. The men loved Mustafa—perhaps more, even, than they loved Suleiman. And loved Bayazid because he was like Mustafa. It is for Khurrem's sake that these two favorites were killed, and her son, Selim, is a poor replacement. Well indeed might he fear the naked swords of his troops, many of whom have brothers or dear friends who died fighting on Bayazid's side at Amasia. But if he'd shown courage and respect for them, they probably would have forgiven him. To simply say, 'It does not suit the dignity of my majesty . . . !'

"If one is to rule these people, one cannot go calling such customs outdated, barbaric, or undignified, or ever—ever—put the harem before the soldiers. That is one sure way to get oneself called soft, city-piosened, and a first-class coward, and the Ottomans did not come to be masters of this great Empire by being any of those."

"Do they say so, my lord?"

"That is exactly what they're saying and, by Allah, they are right. You know, Selim had the nerve to ask that his army show their obedience to him by coming to his tent and kissing his foot, one by one, as if they were a harem full of ladies. 'Let him come and kiss our asses,' the army said.

"I tell you, I had a time of it to keep them all from deserting then and there. Even with our dead master's coffin right before their eyes, they didn't care. I had to promise them a gift of two thousand aspers when we get home."

"Two thousand each?" I was astounded.

"Two thousand aspers apiece to every cutthroat and rascal among them. I wouldn't be surprised if soldiers we never knew we had turn up for this payday, and, Allah knows, I bargained them down every way I could. But that is how edgy they are."

"Has the Sultan Selim agreed to this price?"

"Yes, Selim agreed. Well, he had to or he would walk back home seven hundred miles by himself with an ambush set at every corner. It will all but break the treasury, but what good is a treasury if you have no soldiers to guard it? He had to make another concession, too."

"What was that?"

"A group of the more pious men thought of this, and the rest went along in demanding it because it was such a supreme slap in the face of our supreme majesty. By royal decree, it suddenly became punishable by death to drink alcohol. If this caused hardship to any of the troops, they bore it gladly to think of the agony their sot of a Sultan was suffering.

"This delight got the army to their feet again, but, there we were, marching through some of the finest vineyards in the world in Eastern Serbia—and the vintage just in! Within two days the Sultan had exiled the troublesome holy men, repealed the law, and gone on a binge that saw him unable to mount a horse in the morning. He had to usurp his father's carriage as if he were about to die himself."

"But the army is here now, my lord, almost within sight of Constantinople's walls."

"Yes, they've kept going, muttering at every turn, 'Beware

the hay cart, O high and mighty. There are many, many hay carts on the roads these days.' "

" 'The hay cart'? I do not understand."

"Another ancient, time-honored Turkish custom. Whenever the army has serious grievances on the road, it contrives to find a hay cart, overturned and blocking passage. The soldiers cannot go forward, will not help clear the route, and so the impasse remains until their demands are met."

"Surely an overturned hay cart is a common occurrence in farmlands in the late fall," I remarked. "As I overheard some of the men saying, 'There are many, many hay carts on the roads.' "

"Yes. Not a good sign, that," my master said with a weary wipe at his brows, then continued.

"Farmers know well enough to keep the roads clear when the army's coming through. And if such an accident were to occur, the farmer and his family would have the road cleared in no time, or face the wrath of the whole army, when that army is in the mood to get where they're going. The hay cart is no farmer's accident, I assure you. It is carefully planned by some party in the ranks: they have stolen it, they have knocked it over, and no one can ever say who is to blame. The hay cart means neither more nor less than open rebellion. Needless to say, I have put all the hay and anything even vaguely resembling a cart under guard I can trust here on my lands."

"Praise Allah, my lord, that you are a careful man and that you are almost home without the rebellion you fear."

"We are not home yet, Abdullah," the Vizier said.

"Then, master, the news I bring may not be so difficult for you to believe." I brought the *vetro a filigrana* vial out of my sleeve and showed it, interpreting the message for him.

With the fingers of his right hand, Sokolli Pasha shoved the flesh of his sharp nose up into his eyes, a gesture of extreme exhaustion. The nose appeared much less hooked and daunting for a moment. "Abdullah, I cannot think of such things now."

"But this puts backbone to the spurts of rebellion you have seen. Murad is intended to replace his father."

"He would in any case."

"Sooner rather than later. According to the note—tomorrow. I wouldn't be surprised if the Prince is already on his way from Magnesia."

"You think a *harem* woman is orchestrating the business?"

"I know it."

"How does she do it?"

"I'm not sure. She does have a eunuch. A monster."

"Forgive me, Abdullah. A *khadim?* And a harem woman?"

"He's a Hungarian." I was desperate.

Sokolli Pasha stopped in mid-eyerub. "And what is she?"

"Venetian, my lord."

"You know this woman? You believe her capable of such things?"

I considered. My lady and his own mother were the only women this man knew. He knew that the new Sultan's heir had sired an heir. Who the mother was, he didn't know. And didn't care. He certainly didn't know Safiye Baffo. But he ought to know. This was a serious weakness in Muslim life.

"My lord, she is capable. Of this—and more."

Sokolli Pasha seemed to digest this information with a thoughtful movement inside his mouth. "Hungarian," he said, as if with a mouthful. "To move with ease among raw Hungarian troops, still restive because of the damage my late lord—may Allah receive him—wracked among them. It is the Hungarians who are most uneasy, and I thought it was no more than this. And a Venetian. That explains the reports I hear of a Venetian fleet lying just off the Dardanelles."

"My lord, I don't think she could go so far as to . . ." But I stopped to keep from contradicting myself. *She is capable. Of this—and more. And perhaps,* I swallowed. *I am partly to blame.* If Selim was as my master described him, perhaps it would take an extraordinary amount of muscle to keep him balanced on his throne. But Sokolli Pasha had, for better or worse, thrown his lot with him. Selim was my lady's father. And Safiye opposed him. My course was determined as well.

"So, master," I prompted. There had been silence in the tent for some time. "You will cancel the triumphal procession?"

"It's too late," was his final conclusion. "To back out of the procession now would seem like one more gesture of cowardice, a bad omen at the start of a reign. And we've had too many of them already.

"But you just watch the men as you pass their campfires on your return. You will see the time for praising Allah is not yet. We must still be pleading for His tender mercy."

There was indeed a sort of tension in the silence of the soldiers as if my passing were a handful of dirt to dowse their smoldering embers. But the dramatic retelling of old battle tales could just as easily cause so slight an edginess. I don't think I would have noticed had my master not told me to look for it. My ever-increasing ability to read human nature held good for affairs of the harem only. My master was the authority when it came to men.

Over and over again I recalled his final words to me: "We must allow Allah to give mankind what He wills tomorrow."

Things are different, however, for womankind.

# XXXII

"HAD HE NO message for me?" my lady asked.

Beyond the news that he couldn't see her until the morrow, there was none. And my head had been so full of his male view of things until that moment that I'd failed to manufacture something to suit her concerns. I lied now. I told her he had asked her specifically to stay away from the procession to-morrow, to spend the day enclosed safely with her Aunt Mihrimah in the swaddle of the Koran's drone. That, I hoped, would cover for him. In reality he hadn't given her that much thought at all.

But while covering for the greater neglect, I couldn't shield her from the lesser. Esmikhan's face ashed with disappoint-ment. She sucked the breath into her mouth with little clicks of the tongue in an attempt to keep back the tears. I cannot say what grieved her the most, missing the procession and the so-ciability at her cousin's, or realizing that after a seven-month reprieve, she was still in fact married to a man who gave orders like he followed them—without explanation, without a word of endearment.

I flushed with guilt for my own part in this. But I didn't dare divulge the first part of what I knew to her so I suggested, "He cannot mean it."

"Oh, he means it, all right," Esmikhan said. "You know very well my husband always means what he says. He hasn't a jok-ing bone in his body."

"Lady, surely if he realizes that this is your own father we are greeting . . ."

"You think he doesn't realize that? Abdullah, why else in the name of the Almighty did he marry me if it wasn't because my father is who he is? It's quite clear love had nothing to do with it." Her tears had broken free now and were flowing bitterly.

"Lady, Lady," I crooned, taking her plump little hands in one of mine and stroking her fine dark curls until she slept.

And in the morning, after prayers, I was relieved to find her in much better spirits. Beyond no concern to miss the procession, she even expressed a desire not to go even so far as Lady Mihrimah's that day. As little more than an afterthought she said, "But you are free to go, Abdullah, to either place, and be my eyes if you wish." I felt she was doing me a favor, not giving me an order. Her mind was elsewhere.

Perhaps her cheer had something to do with the squadron of soldiers that had appeared at our front door during the night. I met one of them in the yard. They were under Sokolli's orders, he told me, the Grand Vizier's most trusted elite, sent there, "Just in case." If Esmikhan took their presence as a decent substitute for a letter or other sign of her husband's care, who was I to contradict her?

There was so little fuss about my going that I had more than enough time to find a good seat at the cousin's near Yedi Kule. And since I didn't have my lady to accompany, I could avoid the harem and take my chances with the rest of mankind in the street below.

A high stone wall just at the first bend after the Golden Gate served me well. I watched an hour's worth of hurried preparations as carpets, flower petals, and palm branches were strewn across the roadway for the conquering heroes and their new Sultan to tread upon.

"They come! They come!" The news ran, and then, I, too,

could hear the cheers and the music—the pound of drums, the squeal of horns, and the jarring rattle of the bell standards and the cymbals—keeping time to the march of a million soldiers' feet, and the reined tripping of the cavalry. A great shout went up and we knew the first rank had reached the Golden Gate.

All eyes were straining up the road with such intensity that not a soul noticed until the crash, and then none could escape it. It looked so innocent and accidental, something that one might see any day of the week in the streets of Constantinople. But this was not any day, and it was no accident. There it was, not twenty paces in front of me, a cart spilling its mountainous yellow contents so carefully, so perfectly, in an ambush clear across the path of carpets and rose petals.

*By God,* I thought, startled into Italian. *They've put off their rebellion until they're actually within the city walls. They mean to shake the Empire to its very roots.* Even with such a thought, it was difficult to do more than simply sit and grin at the perfection of the performance.

I saw a pair of figures elbow their way through the crowd to escape the scene of their crime, but they wore heavy black cloaks so it was impossible to distinguish uniform or rank. I could not imagine how any two soldiers could have dropped out of their perfect rows what with hundreds of cheering citizens watching them. I was tempted to believe that what I saw was just a part of a general exodus that began away from the street side: children and the more prudent men drifted indoors in answer to the nervous whispers of their women.

The rest of us shifted uneasily, but stayed to see what would happen—more from indecision, I think, than from any sort of civic interest. I wished briefly that Sokolli Pasha had ordered me to stay home, too, but as it was, there was really no time to think the matter out, else more of us would have had the sense to follow the women and children behind walls.

Almost immediately, the first rank of the army, lead by a row of janissaries in feathered turbans and carrying bell standards, turned the corner and stopped in their tracks.

"Upon my word!" I heard one fellow exclaim with a very broad grin. His surprise was sarcastic and rehearsed. "If it isn't a hay cart."

"Hay cart! Hay cart!" the cry sped back through the halted troops. Somehow, by the same means, I suppose, the message was relayed forward that Selim and his guard had been halted most tantalizingly just before the Golden Gate, that portal which had stood as a triumphal arch for centuries of his predecessors, Greek and Turk alike, in the Great City. The army gave themselves quite a hearty congratulation and laughed, imagining how the Sultan's horse must be stumbling and circling anxiously, and his majesty's great red face sweating under his royal turban like raw meat.

Presently, two viziers came into view, picking their way cautiously on horseback through the clog of soldiers. I recognized the younger man as Sokolli's second, Pertu Pasha and the older as the veteran Ferhad Pasha. A coincidence of names with this second official reminded me of the young spahi whose courage and endurance had saved the empire—and nearly lost me my lady—barely a month previously. And a sudden chill along my spine made me take note rather belatedly that some of the officers whose backs and turbans I'd seen milling about our door that morning had been wearing the violet of the same elite corps. But otherwise the young officer, still with only the title Bey after his name, had nothing in common with the reverend gray-bearded gentleman who, along with his fellow pasha, controlled my attention now. And the events before me were too riveting to give place to any other concern.

"Come, come, comrades," the younger pasha said. "Your rebellion is an offense to the majesty of the Sultan."

"Good!" a voice cried from the crowd. "There is entirely too much majesty in that man."

And before anyone quite knew what had happened, the second vizier had been tumbled off his horse and into the dust. His turban tumbled after him accompanied by the cheers and a few bits of flying debris from the crowd.

Now old Ferhad Pasha spoke. "If it is revenge you want for any unknown crime," he said, "pray, take my life and no other. I am old and willingly make this sacrifice for the good and peace of my country."

The offer was refused and down Ferhad Pasha came, too, suffering no more than indignity. Now anger and violence began to move through the ranks like waves, and to rock the spectators as well. A very dangerous explosion was building—a number of stones had already been thrown, and there were drawn swords—when suddenly my master appeared.

Shoving back the massed soldiers with the butt of a lance, Sokolli Pasha made his way to the head of the column. I saw one particularly unruly man turn on the Grand Vizier after receiving a bruising whack. I think he meant to unsaddle this pasha as well, but before he got close, he was swiftly hit again, full in the face. This time, however, the weapon was not the lance but a small pouch full of aspers, and as the silver spilled to the ground, it was like cool water splashing on the very roots of the fire.

There were many more pouches where that one came from. Sokolli Pasha threw them liberally from a great sack he had slung at his side. The soldiers scrambled for the coins, and even some of the citizens managed to snatch a few, though they were at a disadvantage, being unarmed. Sokolli Pasha's steed paced forward, up and over the hill of hay with hardly a backward slide. The cart was righted in an attempt to find some coins that had rolled under it. Then it was dragged to one side and soon even the straw had been sifted away. The column was on the move again, faster, if with slightly less dignity, than before.

The spectators scurried back to their places and let their tension out in a sigh that grew to cheers by the time the Sultan and his vanguard appeared. But it was not the name of Selim they called, not that red-faced, bleary-eyed man whose great weight stodgily crushed his little pony, and whose cheap and uncontrollable flesh seemed out of place beneath the intricate luxury of the crimson, tasseled canopy, and the tight, smooth, plumed, and bejeweled turban.

"Sokolli! Sokolli Pasha!" was the cry, and my voice joined all the rest.

I was still cheering when, out of the corner of my eye, I saw a familiar sedan chair slipping out of the entrance of the cousin's harem. Moving quickly alongside with his fingers protectively touching the tightly closed shutters was the unmistakable figure of the *khadim* Ghazanfer.

# XXXIII

BACK IN THE Pasha's palace, a sacrifice was killed and all the master's favorite dishes prepared to welcome him home. Esmikhan put on her best clothes and sat in the *mabein* waiting for his return. Alas, she waited in vain, and the food was cold before it was ever eaten.

As the hour grew late, I sent a boy over to the Serai to find out what the trouble was. He brought back the word.

"The janissaries are in revolt."

"That was this morning," I told him. "The master paid them off and they gave it up."

"But they're in revolt again," the lad insisted. "They got as far as the courtyard of the Sultan's palace. Then they barred the gates and won't let Selim into his own house. Selim has had to retreat outside the walls again to one of his villas, and Allah knows what is to become of us."

"What will become of the harem?" Esmikhan asked, wringing her hands. "Do you suppose the soldiers will have the audacity to violate the harem? Oh, how I wish that Safiye were safe back in Magnesia!"

*You don't know how we all wish that,* I thought, but had worse to tell her. "There is a greater fear, lady. My lord Sokolli Pasha is also behind the gates to the palace. They are holding him hostage."

She sat up that night in her best dress, sleeping in fits and starts, not even bothering to lay her head down on a pillow, wondering (fearing? hoping?) whether she was an orphan, a widow, both, or neither. And I waited with her.

A day, a night, a day, and another night passed in the same way. We heard of perhaps a dozen deaths caused by factions brawling in the streets, but they were just the sort of eruptions, like cankers in the mouth, that indicate a general infection throughout the body. Our gatekeeper's son got a cuff at one shop and was refused service at another because they knew he was buying for Sokolli's house. But then at last we pricked up our ears and heard the boom of cannons from the fortress, not in aggressive, but in joyous rhythms, and we knew the rebellion was over. The Venetian fleet had faded back into the Mediterranean and Selim was at last safely installed behind the Sublime Porte.

"But at what a cost! What a cost!" My master shook his head wearily. We spoke together in the *selamlik* upon his final, safe return, and I had to endure several interruptions during our interview from many pressing concerns as he tied up the ends of the rebellion.

"What was the price, my lord?" I asked.

"Well, they ruined the Empire, that's all. Ruined the Empire. They couldn't see. All they cared for was their own satisfaction."

The entire treasury, I learned, was gone. All the spoils from the Kapudan Pasha's recent conquest of the island of Chios had to be handed out besides a hefty installment of the personal jewelry and real estate belonging to Esmikhan's Aunt Mihrimah. This venerable lady had made this sacrifice to ransom her drunkard brother and herself and the other women of the Serai harem from disgrace.

"Still, that is not the worst," Sokolli Pasha said.

"There is more? Allah preserve us, what more could they ask?"

"The treasury is nothing. Taxes will come in, and we will replenish it," my master said. "But they demanded concessions and they got them. The ancient laws have been changed at the very roots. Janissaries are now allowed to marry. Yes, to marry! Not only that, but they may pass their positions on to their sons. And the corps has been opened up to enlistment—to Turks as well. It is the end of the army, that's what it is. And the end of the army means the end of the Empire.

"I'll wager if you listen closely, you can hear them—the elite, hand-picked corps that once had no thought but for training and battle, the army that none in the world could defeat— I'll bet you can hear them in the streets now, wildly scrambling for brides as they scrambled for those aspers on the morning of the parade. No man's daughter is safe; they will all want a month off for honeymoons, and soon they will delight more in the bandying of sons than of lances and spears. How can you fight barbarian Christians with such a mob, I ask you? It's gone. The Empire is gone. And I was the one who bartered for her downfall."

"But wouldn't you, my lord, delight to see a son of yours join the corps you love so much?" I ventured.

"A son of mine? I have no son."

"But you might, Allah willing, some day."

Sokolli Pasha turned away, his exhaustion showing in the crow's-feet of his eyes, and in the hollows of his temples. "No, I would rather he live a quiet life as a merchant or the owner of a workshop. Especially if he is a scrawny sort of lad, which I suppose any son of mine who might deign to live would have to be. Certainly not the sort I would want protecting this Empire and any daughters Allah may see fit to give me besides. Haven't we in our present besotted Sultan, son of the great Suleiman, a perfect example of how generations rot in hereditary posts?"

"So far, master, I must compliment you. You have covered for him remarkably."

"Yes, well, I suppose I can keep the Empire going for a little while longer. If I'm left free to choose good men beneath me. And if Allah favors us. But when I am gone . . ."

"Allah willing, that dread event is many years hence."

Sokolli Pasha now turned to contemplate the future's awesomeness in silence. As focus for his meditation, the Grand Vizier happened to select the old wooden chest against the wall. My eyes followed his idly, and then they were riveted to the spot.

There, on top of the chest, was the blue and white Chinese vase filled with another singular bouquet. The rather large branch of an apple tree arced against the wall. Its leaves had turned and the three apples that still clung to it blushed pink as if the roses, now all withered in the gardens, had bequeathed their color to the apples on their deathbeds. The branch recalled at once the famous lines by Qatran:

> Red begins to show on the golden apple
>     like a blush on a lover's cheek . . .
> It looks as if camphor dust had been sprinkled on the
>     mountaintops,
>     and as if a steel sword had attacked the stream.
> The evenings become as long as the day
>     when you part from a beautiful woman,
> And the days become as short as a night of lovers' union . . .
> If tears rain down my cheeks longing for you, let them fall,
>     for rains make the garden beautiful in time to come.

It took me but a minute to decipher the message, but a moment longer to realize that young Ferhad, as I'd feared, must have been among the soldiers our master had sent to protect the house; I had seen the faces of only two or three of them, and Esmikhan had said nothing. So Ferhad had proven his worth so well during the month that Suleiman's death had had to be kept a secret that he had been trusted not to side with the rebels.

And yet here, beneath the master's very eyes, was treachery of a much deeper and more devastating variety. His choices might save the Empire. But from the point of view of the harem, they were devastating.

My master looked directly at the apple branch for a long time, but he did not see anything amiss in it. Sokolli Pasha had never been one to read poetry on the written page, much less in the symbolism of flowers. I don't think he even stopped his thoughts long enough to think what an odd bouquet a branch of withering apple made, or to wonder where it might have come from. There were no apple trees in our garden, but he never thought that it must have come from the orchards north of the city through which the army had marched. He had marched through those same orchards with them, worrying about rebellion and not love.

Fortunately, we were interrupted again at this point by another messenger with papers to be read and signed. By the time he had gone, I thought I could speak without betraying what I held in my mind.

"My uncle," I began with a slave's euphemism for "my master." "My uncle, excuse my bringing this up tonight, this first night that you've been returned to us, but I have been quite concerned lately that we should have more guardians to properly keep your harem."

"How many are you now?" Sokolli Pasha asked me in the same tone he would use for tallying men on the battlefield.

"Nearly thirty women serve your wife, my lord," I said, "including the musicians, seamstresses, maids, and cooks."

"No, I mean *khuddam,*" he said. "How many are there of you?"

"Just me, sir," I replied, surprised that he should ask. "There has always been just myself."

A brief chuckle was wrenched from my master's throat as he said, "Just you?"

"Yes, my uncle," I assured him.

Other chuckles came in the same fierce, rough way, until my master was laughing heartily, but in a clumsy, guarded manner that told me his throat was unused to such entertainment, and laughter to him was like stones dragged over tender flesh.

"Oh, forgive me, Abdullah," he said at last, gasping for breath. "I wasn't laughing at you. I was laughing at myself more than anything. And at the confounded absurdity of it all."

"My uncle?"

"I mean, here I've been the past month and a half, guarding

a dead corpse with an army of half a million, while at home I've let my wife—a woman no doubt very much alive and very bored and restless, the poor soul—go guarded with but a single *khadim,* and he hardly more than a boy. All these years I've been married—how many is it now? Three?"

"Over four, my lord."

"Four, by Allah! Well, it really is too ridiculous. If I had failed to carry out the succession, Allah forbid, history would have forgiven me. It is humanly impossible to keep such a vast empire as ours quiet and content on all fronts. Any man who's ever ruled could tell you that. But even the most common gutter sweep manages to keep his common wife in line. If one loses honor at home, it's pretty useless to hope to gain it in the Divan, but I . . ."

We were interrupted here by yet another messenger, but Sokolli Pasha waved him away. When he turned to me again, he said, "I remember the day you first came here. You seemed so young and innocent, and I saw a deep, fresh hurt in your eyes. 'By the Merciful One,' I remember thinking. 'I hope old Ali finds a good head eunuch to train this one or there will be one spoiled and skittish *khadim* on our hands.' I meant to speak to him about it later, when you were out of the room, but I see now that either he didn't hear me or I forgot to speak to him. Actually, it was probably the latter. I am so used to having to keep my own counsel that I could easily forget to give an order like that. I often find things so blatant, I assume others do, too. Then there was the business with the brigands and it turned out so well that I just assumed . . .

"I am a self-made man, you see," he interrupted himself. "Certainly Suleiman, may he rest in peace, raised me from place to place, but it was I myself who saw and did what needed to be done in order to win his favor. You are a man of the same mold, I see, and have gone ahead and made yourself indispensable, even when instruction was not given. I wonder at this, and I wonder, too, what has happened in my absence to make you think that only now, after four years alone, now you need assistance."

The hawklike stare with which he fixed me had disarmed many a more deadly schemer, but I was prepared and met it with an ease which did not betray my lady.

"When one is young," I said, carefully balancing pith with calm, "one thinks oneself capable of everything. If there is one thing I have learned in your absence, my lord, it is to dispel this youthful exuberance or at least to temper it with more caution."

Sokolli Pasha gave another ragged burst of laughter and said, "You know at twenty what I am only just beginning to learn at sixty. While on campaign this year, I decided I really must get someone to help me keep my accounts, and you will soon have to go through such a fellow with requests like this. Until then, I myself will say, certainly, buy all the *khuddam* you need. Make this the best-guarded harem in the Empire if you please. My only stipulation is, buy only fellows you can control, for I would hate to lose you as head eunuch, and I don't care what anybody says about your youth."

"Thank you, my uncle."

"And why don't you buy a likely-looking boy or two—just cut. I know the market will be glutted with them soon, just arriving with the army from our last campaign. Allah knows I don't allow it among my soldiers, but He also knows I can't be everywhere at once. You'll be able to get some very good bargains and then train them exactly as you wish. Having had no training yourself, I'm sure you'll make the best of instructors. Somewhere the tradition of a decent Ottoman household must be carried on. The Almighty knows we must stop looking to the Grand Serai for an example."

My master sighed and shook his head once again at the new

Sultan duty compelled him to sustain against his better judgment. "You mentioned this mother of Murad's son might have had something to do with this rebellion?"

"My uncle, I am sure of it."

"I suppose that is something I will never know, the archivists will never know. Only you, *khadim,* can say. And the mysteries of the harem are never spoken of in public."

"No, master."

Then a new thought came to him which I noticed had a profound effect. The normally severe lines in his face grew softer and more round—from fear? was my first impression.

"I say, Abdullah," he mused. "How fares the princess, my wife?"

"Her health is well, praise Allah."

"The child . . . ? There was a child?"

"Died just after birth, sir, early this spring you will recall."

"Yes, I assumed as much when I didn't hear. Or did I hear?"

"I think, sir, you did."

"They would have told me if I'd had a son. How many is that now? Two we've buried?"

"Three, sir."

"Well, it is Allah's will, as they say."

"Yes, my lord."

"Do you suppose, Abdullah," he hesitated. "Do you suppose she would see me this evening?"

I saw little creases of white at the corners of my master's mouth, and I suddenly got an inkling of how helpless he felt. Being surrounded and sorely outnumbered by the enemy could never have reduced him as much as this. Three days spent as hostage to his own rebellious men was nothing compared to having to face a woman, to have to think of endearments, consolations on the death of the child—things foreign to his tongue.

He would be clumsy, he knew it, and that foreknowledge would make it worse.

"Sir," I said gently, "she has been waiting for you these four days, throughout the rebellion, with naught in her heart but a prayer for your safe and speedy return to her."

I hoped my tone would recall some ancient romance he might once have heard to help him slide into the mood, but, alas, I doubt there was anything there to recall.

Sokolli Pasha smiled a smile that was timid and clumsy in the strange, new, softer lines of his face. "Tell your mistress," he cleared his throat of dryness. "Tell your mistress, my master Selim's daughter, I beg she may see me tonight."

"I shall indeed, lord Pasha," I said. "She will be most grateful." Then I bowed farewell as quickly as possible, for I hated to see such discomfort.

Esmikhan nodded when I relayed the message to her in the harem. She had been listening to all our conversation through the grille—before which she still stood in deep thought.

"My husband has begun to dye the gray in his beard," she commented.

"Has he?" I asked. "I didn't notice."

"Yes. It's dyed with henna and has a reddish cast to it that it didn't have before."

"I suppose that is to make the soldiers think he is still strong and in his vigor," I said, for it had certainly made the right impression during the rebellion. I remembered the figure he had cut while urging his horse through the ranks turning into the chaos of a riot before the hay cart and I thought I must certainly tell Esmikhan all I had seen of her husband's magnificence someday when there was more time.

"I suppose it is for the soldiers." She nodded. That it was therefore no flattery to her went unstated.

Esmikhan stood yet another moment at the grille, and I knew without following them where her eyes still lingered. Above the head of her husband, bent purposely now over some new fir-man, my lady's eyes and heart were trained on the branch of apple tree stuck in the old Chinese vase.

# XXXIV

WHEN ALL WAS calm in the capital, the new Sultan's harem was sent for, and Nur Banu soon installed herself permanently in the *haremlik* and private gardens of the Grand Serai. But her son, Murad, now heir apparent, was sent back to the *sandjak* in Magnesia after appearing suddenly and by surprise in the capital just after the rebellion. What might have been construed as insubordination was quickly changed into a formal swearing of loyalty to his sire and no more was said on the matter.

At first Murad declared he would not return unless his Safiye came, too, but his lover stood firm in her refusal to move. So then Murad made another public vow, this one being not to touch another woman until Safiye returned to him. He went with thirty witnesses to the mosque to solemnize the oath before the Mufti. After that he resigned himself with a stiff upper lip to both celibacy and political duty.

"For the sake of the woman and child I love above all else, save Allah only," he said, and departed.

He contented himself by spending half his *sandjak* earnings on messengers who ran in a steady stream across Anatolia to bring the latest word on the health of his mistress, and to carry love poems and tokens to her in return.

At the end of the mourning period for her grandfather, her womb still empty, my lady determined to make a pilgrimage to visit the saint Rumi, founder of the Mevlevi order of dervishes, in Konya. His shrine was known throughout the world (the Muslim world, I should say), for the miracles worked healing the sick, the blind, and causing the barren to bring forth fruit.

My master, too, had mentioned such a plan to me on more than one occasion. He was never a man of superstition, but perhaps he felt the need of a vacation—for my lady or for himself from my lady, I wasn't sure.

And yet there was that curious stiffness between this married couple of five full years that would not allow them to bring the subject up between them to their immediate and mutual satisfaction. Sokolli Pasha was constantly distracted by the herculean task of keeping the Empire together in spite of his master the Sultan. Even when he had attention enough to stammeringly ask his wife if there was anything her heart desired that he could give her—anything beneath the will of Allah—Esmikhan never dared mention this wish to him. To ask to cross all of Turkey without him would seem too forward and demanding of a well-brought-up Muslim girl, even one who ought, by her station as a princess of the Blood, to have been able to tell one of her father's slaves anything and everything she wanted.

"And won't people talk?" she fussed at the matter to me. "In all reason, staying here with my husband is more likely to get a child than crossing all the realm of the Turks."

"Allah's will has little to do with reason," I eased her mind.

For his part, the Grand Vizier did not wish to give offense to this daughter of the sultans. He was afraid she might go just to please him if he mentioned it, and that could open the way to gossip and silent miseries of the worst sort.

I, though skeptical of anybody's saints, had long ago determined to do what I could to help my lady towards a child she could keep. Having collected a staff of five under me, I decided that such a journey could be made with ease, without risk of my mistress' virtue, and without so much strain on me that I could not enjoy it, too. It could be a change of scenery, a little excitement, like Chios, but without the danger, without the conflict in my soul. So once I made this decision, it only remained to go between *selamlik* and *haremlik* in such a way that Sokolli Pasha thought he was doing his wife a favor and Esmikhan thought she was being obedient to her husband. Thus the trip was arranged.

I should mention that, quite by chance, I met Signor Andrea Barbarigo yet again during my flurry of preparations.

There is one thing foreign diplomats learn quickly among the Turks: If you want to know something about the government, don't ask the governors. They are either too tight-lipped, or too expensive. Ask Moshe. Between them, Moshe and his wife Esperanza had access to the best homes, *selamlik* and *haremlik* alike. They went everywhere, saw everything, and had no compunctions about telling anyone anything—for the right price—inventing tales when they had no truth to go on.

What Barbarigo had come to learn from the Jews, I do not know. I did not really care either, for within the week my lady and I were on our way south. I merely nodded at him and went about my business as he did his. I did not expect to ever see the Venetian again, and I would soon have forgotten all about the incident but for one detail.

Moshe Malchi was also known to have a private back room that could be rented—well, for whatever you had in mind. And as I turned out of the shop, I caught, in the corner of my eye, a glimpse of a familiar sedan attended by a familiar monstrous Hungarian eunuch just pulling up in the narrow alley, redolent with rats and garbage, that ran between Malchi's shop and the next.

*I always knew you for a whore, Sofia Baffo,* I sent the message silently in her direction, *going to the highest bidder in any game. But my lady and I are off, far out of your reach for months now. Good riddance.* And quietly congratulating myself that I would never have to slip and slide on such garbage after my lady's sedan, I went on my way.

Two days later we were on the road to Konya.

The ritual of praying five times a day, first enforced upon me and escaped whenever possible, had become a soothing time of rest and meditation that I now rarely missed. By no stretch of the imagination, however, did I feel converted. Rumi was considered a saint by great numbers of Eastern Christians as well as by Muslims, but I was no more anxious to take the pilgrimage as a follower of Christ than of Muhammed.

Yet even I could not escape the excitement and sense of well-being that arose as we made our way. The farther south we went, the higher we climbed, the more time turned backwards into the most delightful days of spring, fresh with plum and apricot bloom, and carpets of red anemones and wild hyacinths. And time turned backward, too, into a carefree sort of childhood for both my lady and me.

Pilgrims from three continents could be met upon the road, increasing in numbers and anticipation as we drew ever closer. They made interesting company, and their devotion was in part infectious.

One man in particular caught my attention. Any dervish, since our escape from the brigands, did, of course, but this one even more so. *Yet how can this be Husayn, my old family friend?* I thought. *Is it possible that this emaciated pile of bones was the man whose note had warned me of the hay-cart rebellion?* At least the man who delivered us from the brigands had had a body that seemed as though it ought to belong to a merchant or a well-fed civil servant.

This man wore the patchwork cloak of his order—the begging or wandering dervishes—with the crude stitches on the outside. The clothes of the previous fellow had been more like a costume thrown together to merely suggest "dervish" than anything of precise commitment. The brigand's dervish had worn a beard only a week or so old, and of a youthful black. This man's gray beard was long and dusty, and his mouth missed numerous teeth. Husayn had worn gold teeth in the place of those he lacked, for vanity. Taking on the humility of a dervish would require the gold's removal as a very first step and I remembered having seen the gaps in the brigand dervish's teeth— when, after the fact, I'd identified him as my friend. Was this the same man?

My master had once told me, "They all look alike, dervishes." Yes, but sometimes they were subtly, annoyingly different, too. If this was Husayn, he had grown into the part during the past five years in ways that hardly seemed humanly possible. No, without a sign from the dervish—or from God—first, I could not claim him.

The dervish came to beg from our company just outside the town of Aksehir. "For the love of Allah. For the love of Allah," he muttered quietly as he stumbled slowly among us.

I tossed half a loaf into his wooden bowl, for which he blessed me. He looked at me as he did so; the look, the mystical, demanding look, was the same as before. I gave him a bit of radish and onion from my shish kebab. His eyes pierced my heart like the skewer. But as he said nothing, I said nothing, and looked away.

After that, he turned up regularly among us like a stray dog one has thrown scraps to, and, though he would never take up our invitations to sit down among us, we came to think of him as "our" dervish. No doubt he was under some stern vow that prohibited any more socializing than necessary to win his bread. The more superstitious of us took his presence to be a good omen.

# XXXV

PILGRIMS LIKE TO spend their last night before reaching Konya in an old, tumbledown caravanserai called Baba Ahlam, which, it is said, gives dreams by which the pious can tell whether or not Rumi will be willing to answer their petitions. One poor, old woman of our acquaintance actually turned and went back home after that night, some dream having told her it was useless to continue on.

My lady, on the other hand, woke that morning blushing with delight. She had dreamed, she said, of a great field full of beautiful children like so many spring flowers.

"Allah be praised," she said. "It was so beautiful, I wished I could have slept forever, were it not that I must rise with haste to make it become reality."

And I welcomed the flurry of activity to pack up and be on our way, driving my subordinates to greater haste than usual because I, too, had dreamed a dream in Baba Ahlam.

In the corner of the caravanserai by the gate where I had seen his shadow, curled up like a faithful dog, last thing the night before, and all along our route that day, I kept a sharp lookout for our dervish. The old man, you see, was the object of my dreams.

In this dream, I had seen time run backwards, faster, even, than it had seemed on our journey. The old man had lost his gray and wrinkles, put weight on over his monkish austerity, and gained vain golden teeth to replace those he had lost. The dervish was the same. Not only that, but as time went further back, I saw him again as my old friend, Husayn. At least, that seemed clear in my dream, though by daylight I told myself the eerie ruin of a caravanserai must have been playing tricks on me. Only actually seeing the man again could tell me for certain.

And if Husayn was making his presence known to me, it must be to impart some life-saving information.

But now, more eerily still, he seemed to have vanished off the face of the earth.

"Did you see . . . ?" My lady drew the curtain of her sedan back ever so slightly and whispered to me.

"No, no sign of the old man," I replied.

"Who? The dervish? No, I didn't mean him. I meant . . ."

"Whom did you mean?" I asked, trying, but not succeeding very well to hide my distraction.

"Nothing." She sighed and sank back into silence and invisibility.

It was only with this hint that I happened to notice that our party had been overtaken by a regiment of young spahis. I thought nothing of it, however. The old dervish's words kept echoing in my head with strange new import, and with tones I found now familiar, for all the whistling around the gaps in his teeth. "Allah bless you, my friend."

❧

HOSTING PILGRIMS IS a religious duty enjoined upon all Muslims and, in Konya, it is a profitable business as well. So, although my first day spent looking for him turned up nothing, I was confident the dervish must be safely stowed away among the boarding houses and monasteries of the holy city. In only a matter of time I would find him.

My mistress, for her part, had many connections in Konya; her rebellious uncle had been its governor for many years. Her father—as if to wipe the name Bayazid, which they held as almost divine, forever from the townsfolk's memory—had ordered a grand new mosque built to house the saint's remains. Though it was now complete enough to worship in, the tile work was still in process. Tiles stacked everywhere bore the name "Sultan Selim"; those already on the walls were glaring and fresh and had not faded into the delicate tendrils and flowerets as they would with time and dust.

Of course, the present governor of the *sandjak* insisted we live with him for the full year of our intended stay. His wives and daughters were honored to move from the best rooms of the harem for a princess of the Blood, and I was given the head eunuch's room.

Our first day in Konya, being a Sunday, my lady spent getting used to her new surroundings and resting from the journey. I did my exploring. But we were up early on Monday and my lady spent all day in the shrine, kissing the sarcophagus, partaking of holy water, giving gifts, circumambulating, praying and listening to learned women read from the Koran, the traditions of the Prophet, and the writings of the blessed Rumi himself. I did not expect to catch a glimpse of our dervish, for Monday along with Wednesday were the two days of every week set aside in the holy places for women and their attendants alone so they could perform their devotions without infringement upon their modesty.

So it was that, though Esmikhan spent the day as if on the very precipice of ecstasy, hearing every word as if it were a present revelation to her alone, I suffered from a tedium greater than usual in a job often fraught with little more than patient waiting. Boredom I can usually bear, but not this that was mixed with anxiety about my dreams. The torment of uninterrupted thoughts there in the reverent murmur of the shrine must have quite benumbed me, else I never would have been so careless.

It was at the end of the day. As her last act before we left, Esmikhan wanted to sit upon the Stone. Set near the main portals and of plain white limestone, the Stone had a curved impression on the top where, it was said, the saint had been wont to sit while pursuing his meditations. The pilgrim, we were told, if she assumed Rumi's exact attitude, and recited the first chapter of the Koran without a mistake, could expect her fondest prayer to be answered. Esmikhan had her maids go first, and there was such blushing and giggling that the Sura, if ever they knew it, was quite forgotten, and their wishes, plainly, were much too frivolous for a saint to pay heed to: an emerald necklace or *khadin budu* for supper, perhaps.

"Now you go, Abdullah." Esmikhan touched my arm.

"I have nothing to wish for, lady," I declared.

She looked up at me, her great brown eyes moist with understanding. The only wish she could imagine for me—my manhood back—would be a mockery of Allah and his will. So Esmikhan groped for my hand, and allowed me to help her onto the Stone.

". . . Thee only do we worship, and to Thee do we cry for help . . ."

The Sura, recited with eyes clenched closed with effort, was probably never recited with more perfection, save only by the Prophet Muhammed himself. Esmikhan remained on the stone for some moments afterwards, her breath shallow with anticipation, as if she expected to be carried off into heaven by the miracle. Even her silly maids were sobered into silence as they joined their wills to hers. But soon it became clear that nothing out of the ordinary would happen. My lady groped for my hand again and we left the mosque.

"Abdullah. *Ustadh!* Peace be unto you!"

I recognized the voice, and it startled me so much that I dropped what I was holding. I was holding a corner of the large brocade curtain that allowed my lady to pass from the mosque compound to her sedan, a mere three paces across the public thoroughfare, without the public being able to see so much as her shadow. I quickly retrieved the screen, and held it much higher and tighter than usual, though I could not avoid dipping it again as I returned the greeter's bow.

A man of ordinary good manners would have stood aside when he saw what I was doing, and waited until the curtain had been folded up and packed away inside the sedan after the lady. But this man had forgotten manners in his excitement to see me—or to see what I was trying to hide. And, once the greeting had been given and the curtain dropped, the most polite thing he could do was to continue on without a pause as if the whole operation, woman, curtain, sedan, and all, were quite invisible.

The man who greeted me with such effluence and abandon was none other than the young *spahi-oghlan,* Ferhad Bey.

"I thought I recognized you on the road the day before yesterday," he said, "but we were on the march and I was unable to break rank and see. Well, how are you? How are you, my old friend?"

He proceeded to ask after my well-being, and that of everyone I knew, as if we had all day to dally in a tea shop, and as if he hadn't left the capital on his rapid march more recently than I. The only thing he did not ask me was, "How fares your lovely mistress?" but this was not so much because he was polite as because he had already seen for himself.

Ferhad spoke in detail of the duty that brought him to Konya: ". . . Disturbances on the Persian border since the Shah has learned of the death of Suleiman—Allah give his mighty soul rest. Troops are being mobilized to answer them. We have a long trek ahead over the sterile, mountainous regions of Upper Armenia and Azerbijian. We will be leaving to face this fate in another week, *inshallah*."

Some might have thought him a fool. Others would have found him indiscreet, treacherous, even, and worthy of court-martial for these confidences. But from events at the death of the great Sultan, I knew full well how Ferhad could hold his tongue when it was required of him.

No, I recognized the symptoms. He was drawn to what stood behind my curtain as a man is drawn to answer the call of the Angel of Death. He would have been content to stand there silent and to bask in what he could feel and the rest of the world was sadly numb to. But as that was impossible, guilt pricked his tongue on to such animated talk that he was hardly recognizable or sensible.

Esmikhan, however, had no difficulty recognizing him, nor of sensing the swift current that carried the flotsam-jetsam of his language on at such a rate. She stood where she was on the other side of the screen, transfixed by the vision of perfectly chiseled features. Plush, lusciously curled moustache and dark, gentle eyes so handsomely set off the brilliant purple and gold tassels of his uniform.

Esmikhan would not climb into the sedan. She stood there until my seconds shifted and coughed nervously, and my arms ached from holding the curtain. But I did not resent that physical ache. It was, I realized, as close as I would ever come to the exquisite ache of mind that knotted these two hearts I stood between.

Ferhad did not take his leave of me until the emotion had

worn him out, and he was a man trained for superhuman endurance. I was exhausted and my lady's small frame sank into the sedan at last as if she would never rise again. But there was strength enough in her to convey to me the glimmer of a thought. That tall, handsome vision of a man had been the first thing to greet her eyes when they had come, blinking, into the sunlight after the soft darkness of the mosque, and fresh from the intensity of her prayer upon the holy Stone of Rumi.

# XXXVI

TUESDAY THERE WAS relief: my lady stayed indoors. But I was all tension and vigilance when we repeated our Monday devotions on Wednesday.

Esmikhan had no desire to sit upon the Stone again. "These things take time," she explained. "One must be patient for the fulfillment. And to throw oneself too often and too violently at the saint's door is to make yourself a pest rather than a welcome guest."

Although several times I caught her eyes wandering expectantly towards the public thoroughfare where Ferhad had appeared to her, the stone and glass of the mosque her father was building remained between them.

Still, the vision enslaved her mind. Imagination, I know, can have ten times the effect on the individual as reality. But the world doesn't feel the convulsions then, when they throb in the individual's imagination. At the moment, it was the world's face I had to keep unblushing.

In spite of her imagination's abandon, Esmikhan joined me in a sigh of relief when we reached the safety of the governor's *haremlik*. She found her helplessness a discharge of burdens; she was glad she was not given the chance to make a decision she could not have made rationally. The pressure on me increased, however, and increased tenfold when my host divulged some news after dinner.

"I held Divan today. What else have the men to do when the holy places are closed to them?" He said this with a chuckle and then continued, "Besides the usual peasants with their tiresome quibbles, I found it attended by the most decorous and charming young spahi, head of a division just lately come to town. In our conversation—which, I might add, I found most enjoyable—I discovered that he knows you. His name is Ferhad Bey."

"Yes, I know him," I admitted.

"By Allah! What a happy chance!" my host exclaimed.

"He has rendered my master very useful service in the past," I said, hoping not to make too much of it.

"Ah, I knew he was a man of diligence and promise. He sat in on my judgments and made such astute observations that I would not be surprised if that young man finds himself with his own *sandjak* to rule in a very few years."

"Pray Allah he does not take yours," I said with what can only be called bitterness.

My host was startled. "Oh, I'm sure that was the farthest thing from his mind. In spite of his many qualities, he is altogether unassuming and without guile."

"Yes, I know he is," I said at once, fearing I might have spoken too bitterly. "A day at the mosque has made a philosopher of me, I suppose. I only meant to suggest that *sandjaks*, like virtue, come in limited supply. One man's gain must needs be another's loss."

"I have taken the liberty of inviting him to sup with us tomorrow night. I hope you will have no objection."

What could I say? I was only a guest and a eunuch, after all. But for the next full week there was no rest from the tension for me, either with my lady out of doors nor inside the palace. It was the first and only thing I have ever felt grateful to the Persians for: their unruly behavior that soon sent the corps marching off to the border. But even when I had seen the young horseman out of Konya with my own eyes (he considered my attention flattery), I was jumpy for a day or so. I kept imagining him to have forgotten something, to have turned coward and defected, or that peace had been most suddenly declared.

Only on that Thursday could I at last thank Allah or my lucky stars, or whatever it was that had kept my lady from finding out how her love had ingratiated himself to our host, and just how many long evenings he had spent in the *selamlik* under the same roof as her harem.

I took relief in both body and spirit, and wandered through the city on my own, ending up at the Ala ud-Din Mosque. I remembered having been there before, but the reason escaped me. In the mad flurry over Ferhad, I had forgotten about my strange dream that had driven me to search for dervishes.

And now as I entered the holy building, such a feeling of wellbeing and calm came over me that I couldn't ascribe it to the absence of the spahis alone. Seeking a rational explanation for my feeling, I began to enumerate the ways in which a mosque is different from and, at the moment, seemingly superior to a church. One has to remove one's shoes. Like Moses: "For the ground on which thou standest is holy."

I liked the great hollowness within, uncluttered by statuary, benches, and altars. I liked the feel of plush carpet beneath my bare feet and the breath of air made by the flight of an occasional pigeon which, like the people, had found sanctuary there.

The Ala ud-Din Mosque is particularly blessed in the possession of an intricately carved pulpit of great antiquity and exquisite tile work along the wall facing Mecca. Thinking it was perhaps this feature that gave the building beneath that great dome such a holy feeling, I stepped closer to investigate it. Suddenly my progress was arrested by a low murmuring at my feet. There was a man whose presence I had not noticed because he blended so perfectly with the surroundings. Sitting cross-legged on the floor, he had a lectern and a holy book before him from which he was quietly reading:

> Love burns this icy clay with mystic fire,
> And leaping mountains dance with quick desire.
> Blest is the man that drowns in seas of love,
> And finds life nourished by food from above.

They were verses from the Matsnavi Sharif of the Sufi Rumi, and their reader was dressed in the patchwork rags of the order of wandering dervishes.

My legs folded beneath me, and I sat, knee touching knee. "Tell me, my friend," I said smiling, remembering that day so long ago when we'd set sail together. "Does the saint mean 'sea' to be male or female in that line?"

Husayn—for that's who the emaciated dervish was—lifted a finger for silence and continued to read, only raising his voice a little so I should not miss a word.

He read the entire poem. His low, whistling tone and the mystical words and images soon drew me up with them until I thought the deep reds and blues of the mosque's tiles and carpets had become like the colors shed by stained glass—

wonderfully vibrant, yet of no substance one could hold—and this iridescent light moved as if with the cycle of the sun.

Husayn finished with a long pause. Then, at last, he answered my question. At least, he thought he was answering my question, and at the time, with my head still whirling from the rhythms of the poems I thought he was, too.

It was a verse from the Koran:

*And He—may the majesty of our Lord be exalted—*
*has taken no consort neither has He any offspring.*

This was followed by another pause after which Husayn slowly closed the book and the lectern, packed them under his arm and returned them to the caretaker of the mosque.

*Such a black wall of piety!* I began to think. *He has gone mad, and only the Turks in their own madness call it piety.* This thought so grieved me that I decided I must take my leave of him as quickly as possible. I cleared my throat to speak, but it was drowned out by a sound right over our heads: the muezzin in his tower calling the faithful to evening prayers. I couldn't very well run out of the mosque against all the men who would be coming in, so I dumbly followed my old friend to the fountain, copied him in making my ablutions, then returned to face Mecca, and to fall to my knees on the floor.

As I bent and straightened, knelt and prostrated like a drop of water in the vast sea of lapping Muslim waves, a memory came to my mind of the number of times I had watched Husayn eat pork and pray "Hail Mary" to hold his ducats intact. Now here I was, returning the pretense in kind. But where, a moment before in the midst of skepticism I might have chuckled at the thought, I now felt myself deeply touched. And by the time the prayers had finished, I was willing to stick by my friend's side, silence or no.

Once we had reached the courtyard of the mosque, he at last spoke words of his own. "The brethren meet tonight. Will you come?"

"Nothing," I replied, "would flatter me more."

Without another word, my friend led me away from the main streets, through a maze of alleys, monastic buildings, and rooms for the study of religion to the hall where Sufis of his order held their particular devotions.

At first I thought I would merely watch, but events proved otherwise. I did watch as first the sheikh and then the invisible spirit of their founder received obeisance from the congregation, and I watched the recitation of the first prayers, for I didn't know the words. But then, suddenly there was a squeal on a shawm and a rattle of drums, and the hall rose to its feet as one man. Before I could think, I found myself linked arm in arm with Husayn in front of me and a stranger behind me, and slowly, to the music, we began to move in a circle around the room.

Someone somewhere began to chant the ninety-nine names of Allah, over and over again. With each ninety-nine he grew faster and faster, and we moved and chanted to the rhythm he set. Faster and still faster we went until I saw nothing but a blur of whirling robes that seemed to be the physical embodiment of all the mystical names. I grew numb to the steps that had at first jarred my frame; it seemed as if I was lifted above the stumbling of my feet and I floated.

And then I felt myself truly loosing touch with reality. By God, if I kept this up much longer, I should lose my individuality altogether and fade like one drop into the great ocean of creation never to be extracted again. The thought threw me into a panic.

"No," I murmured, my head whirling. "No!" off the rhythm of the pounding names of Allah.

I broke from the circle and staggered to the edge of the hall. The dance went on without me, and I saw with reeling eyes that the circle had melted back into itself as if I'd never been in it at all. The smell and heat of bodies and the continuous pound of drums and chant were still quite overwhelming and I staggered out of the hall to escape them.

I took one or two breaths of pure air, then threw my head back to the sky. By the stars I could tell that the night was already half gone; we had been dancing for hours. Then, the stars seemed to be not only mechanical tellers of time but also the eyes of an old, old man, twinkling with compassion.

*All praise be to Allah, Lord of the worlds!*
*The Compassionate, the Merciful!*

Quietly I murmured the words Muhammed is said to have received from the Angel when he was first called to be Prophet. Then suddenly those stars became Husayn's eyes and my dream from Baba Ahlam repeated itself. The old dervish lost his gray, grew younger, and put on flesh. But the vision had another scene added to it. This time I saw Husayn as I had left him in the market five years ago when the pain and shame of my condition had been new upon me and I had been unable to feel anything beyond that.

Now I saw how my friend had left our meeting with grief and guilt heavy upon him. I felt how much he considered me and loved me as his son, and the duty he felt to protect me in the absence of all my other kin. These thoughts weighed on him for weeks and wore down his native good humor and stoicism until he was certain he would go mad. He found his family—his father-in-law, his wife, his little son, and second child as yet unborn—no consolation at all. Indeed, their affections were only salt on the wounds my fate and my bitterness had caused him.

Finally he determined he must take revenge. Denouncing my butchers to the court of the land would not suffice. He had to see that they never operated again, either in Pera or any place on earth. So one night, shielded by darkness and a heavy cloak, anger giving his stodgy figure strength and agility, my friend ambushed the wiry slave merchant Salah ud-Din and stabbed him to the heart.

And when he had removed him from humanity, he removed him from maleness as well. I had helped to wash the body; I had seen.

How I would have gloated over that hated body coiling with pain like a flimsy figure of wire in the forge. Yet Salah ud-Din died with more surprise than pain or lingering remorse. And the vision I received of this death would not even let me linger, staring with the satisfaction of revenge, but carried me on at once to the realization that Husayn was now a man with blood on his hands. No matter how foul that blood, normal society would ever be banned to him.

So he took to the secret brotherhood of dervishes. At first it was only a disguise and an excuse to be wandering without ties or means. In such a state, the hideout of brigands had been the perfect place for him.

But slowly, the true meaning of the rites began to impress him. In my vision I saw and felt the depth of his remorse as he repented of his previous sins, not only that of murder, but also the worship he had earlier paid to lucre and to trade. Completion of the great pilgrimage to Mecca, on foot and with nothing more than his begging bowl, allowed him to change his name to Hajji. One thousand and one days of initiation followed at the end of which time his rags and his bowl were no longer a disguise, but the real essence of Husayn——Hajji——to the end of his days.

Once he had found himself, Husayn had been led by dreams

and visions to find me and, having found me, he had sat and read in the mosque every day until I found him. I had, I realized, passed him by on more than one occasion even after my dream at Baba Ahlam, and not noticed him, for my mind had been burdened with the duties I owed the world. But my friend had been content to wait quietly until the world should give me peace.

The compassionate stars had whirled much closer towards dawn—the dawn of Friday, the Muslim Sabbath—before the vision and the dance were over and Husayn came out to stand quietly by my side.

"My friend," I began, wanting to blurt out all that I had seen and felt. But I realized at once by his calm demeanor, he knew it all already. Then I could say nothing but "Thank you," and, as I studied his quiet form longer, I realized that even "Thank you" was redundant.

Thus began my association with the Sufis, which continued throughout the summer. I shared their communal meals, their rites on all but the most solemn occasions. It kept me busy and entertained in a period that otherwise would have meant a great deal of lying about sipping sherbets, and listening to my lady gossip with the governor's wife. But it was more than just diversion that I found among these ragged men of Allah. I found true acceptance as I had not felt since I was still a man among the sailors on my uncle's galley.

I was a eunuch? That did not matter. "Many are made eunuchs for the love of Allah," one Sufi explained to me. "Many take vows of abstinence of their own accord—such as our brother Hajji here who first brought you among us. They realize that children and dalliance with women are mere vanities and distractions from union with the All-Merciful."

I was a slave? That, too, did not matter. "We are all—like your name—slaves to Allah."

I knew my informant meant this sincerely, but it was a simple fact that, being a slave more than just figuratively, I could not join them as completely as a free man might. Once or twice, after a particularly moving ritual, it was suggested to me, both by the brotherhood and by my soul, that I should seek to undergo initiation and begin the thousand-and-one-day noviate to become like them. But it was a simple fact—I was not free to commit myself to serve another master. I could not vow to obey every challenge the sheikh of the order might lay upon my head when the needs of my mistress might call me to her side at any time, or even out of Konya altogether. Many Sufis insist that one can and should be pious while at the same time fulfilling a profession. But it is one thing to be a shopkeeper who can pull down the shutters and lock the door when religion calls; it is quite another to have some other master stand in one's way to Allah.

"Someday," I promised my friend.

"Someday, yes." Husayn nodded quietly. "Allah willing."

# XXXVII

AFTER THE FIRST of the Muslim year, towards the end of summer, there was some disquiet. The Persians, we learned, had capitulated and sent lavish presents along with their ambassador and petitions of peace to the Sublime Porte. Besides returning the slaves, horses, and goods of the rebellious Prince Bayazid, they made gifts of more material wealth than symbolic: beautifully illuminated Korans with their covers encrusted with gold and jewels, prayer rugs of the finest Persian wools and craftsmanship, rosaries made of lumps of turquoise as big as hens' eggs.

In spite of the religious nature of the gifts, many Sunni Turks could not forget that Persians were Shi'a heretics, and the treaty was unpopular. Indeed, an attempt was made on the life of the Persian ambassador in the midst of the formal procession through the streets of Constantinople. The assassin was a holy dervish, and for a while I dared not visit my friends in the Sufi hall. My host, the governor, was contemplating whether or not a small massacre of holy men was needed to prove to the Sultan that he was capable of keeping this *sandjak* of pilgrims and shrines under control.

Fortunately, such a drastic step never became necessary. The governor, like my religious friends, built up faith from the lesson of these events: "Thanks be to Allah who showed His will in the matter by causing the assassin to be trampled to death by the ambassador's horse before any more harm could be done."

By the celebration of the Birth of the Prophet, the Persians were back to private civil war. And Turkish politics and religion had reconciled themselves to such a degree that my host thought nothing of hiring one of the members of Husayn's order to recite the tales of Muhammed as festival entertainment.

I had decided to take advantage of my option to sit in either half of the house and spend the evening with my lady in the harem. For one thing, the first snow of the year had fallen, bundling Konya up in what felt like a safe, cozy blanket. Being in the harem by the fire would exaggerate that feeling. But there was also the fact that a female reciter had been hired for that side of the curtain and, though the Sufi was my friend and justifiably well known for his performance, this woman was even better than he. Women, I have always found, can get more out of any verse than a man, for though men have been known to be carried away in ritual trances, women play with emotions like they weave color into a rug.

The women and their guests had only just begun to settle, however, when my host's young son came running in. The ladies petted him, passing him from hand to hand, commenting on his new little festival jacket, and teasing, "Where is our big boy? Our big boy said he was old enough to spend the festival with the men in the *selamlik,* but see? The festival has hardly begun and he comes running back to us."

The little lad who was no more than four bore this treatment bravely, with only a hint of tears of shame or homesickness in his eyes. As soon as he could get a word in, he insisted, "I am not a baby anymore. I have been sent by my father with an important message of state."

"Oooh," the ladies declared. " 'An important message of state!' " It seemed clear that the child had been given that lofty phrase by his father as inducement to run the errand.

The boy ignored this round of teasing and turned to me with a tone that said, "We men have no time for the silliness of women, have we?"

I did not disillusion him by suggesting that a woman's ability to call state affairs silly was one of her most valuable assets.

"*Ustadh,*" the boy said, "My father bids you come and enjoy the feast with him."

"Oh, my little uncle," I replied. "Your father is most gracious. But I have already told him I would have to ignore his invitation to spend the evening with my lady."

"But he insists," the little boy said. "There is a new arrival among our guests. You'll never guess who, so I'll tell you. It's Ferhad Bey come back to us."

My lady's great eyes caught me as I rose to leave, and filled mine with wonder. I carried it with me as a token from the harem as I entered the world of men.

The *selamlik* was still in an uproar when I arrived; a storm whirling around the center calm of the harem, it took longer to settle down here.

In the seat of honor at the governor's right sat the man who relieved me of the wonder my lady's eyes had given me. I have no doubt he read some cryptic message from the harem in me, for his getting to his feet, and his deep bow of greeting were full of tenderness, respect, and ardor. His eyes continued to prod mine for news of his love, but I avoided them by demanding of him in something close to a panic, how it was that he had come to disturb the peace of our retreat.

"I am in the service of my lord and master, the Sultan of all the Faithful," was all the reply modesty would allow him.

Our host had to supply the details. "For acts of great courage fighting against the Persians, our friend, Ferhad Bey, has been elevated to the post of Master of the Imperial Horse. Thanks be to Allah, he is to be quartered with us."

"Here in Konya?" I asked stupidly.

"Of course here in Konya," the governor replied, then continued to exalt. "All doors are suddenly opened to you, my friend."

Harem doors? I shot a glance towards my host, but his mood was too jovial to be dampened. My panic growing, I asked, "How long will you stay?"

"That depends upon the will of my lord the Sultan, and upon the beneficence of Allah," Ferhad replied.

"Allah willing," the host prayed, "it will be many joyful years."

Ferhad did not add "Allah willing" to this statement, but only smiled and nodded politely.

"Was my master, the Grand Vizier, responsible for this advancement?" I tempted.

I could not believe even Sokolli Pasha could be so careless of his harem. Fortunately, if the true reason for my question were

detected by Ferhad, he politely overlooked it as he had overlooked our host's enthusiastic tactlessness in the previous question. He assumed that I wanted news of my master, and began
to give it in great detail, describing all the foreign embassies he
had received, and with what glory.

"The name 'Sokolli' is becoming a word of fear among the
unruly elements of the country," Ferhad said.

"Do you fear it, too?" I warned him with my eyes, but I did
not interrupt his speech.

What luxurious peace we had known in Konya! Ferhad told
of things with a fierce immediacy which, had we heard of them
before, had come as idle rumors which one could easily forget.
The rebellion in Yemen with all Turkish garrisons driven out,
the sea exploits of Piali Pasha for which he had been elevated
to the station of Second Vizier, Sokolli's attempts to control all
of this in the absence of any direction from the Sultan Selim . . .

I did not interrupt this recitation, but our host did, perhaps
because he was tired of having Ferhad turn to him for opinions
which served only to show how ignorant he was of the Empire's
affairs compared with his new subordinate.

"Such a mind he has!" was our host's diversion.

"Where will you stay?" I asked then, prodding the final avenue of hope left for me.

Our host closed that avenue quickly. "He will stay here with
us, of course. There's no comfort in barracks, Allah knows, but
to rent a place would leave our friend all alone, which is even
more discomfort.

"Not that I haven't suggested to Ferhad that he marry," the
governor continued, laughing. "He should not leave the harems
altogether deprived of his fine figure. I have even suggested a
match with my eldest daughter, but he declines. Another man
would be offended, but I—I am not offended. I have not got-

ten to my age and my position without some understanding of
the politics of marriage. He's holding out. Aren't you, Ferhad?
Holding out for some better match the Sultan might someday
offer him. A slave girl of his own house, perhaps, or even a
princess of the Blood. Our Grand Vizier, Sokolli Pasha, held out,
and well he was paid for his continence. Ah, restraint! That is a
sure sign of one born to rule among the Ottomans, Allah willing.

"Yes, I have often wondered where I myself might be today
if a lust for sons had not made me fall short of a princess of the
Blood. That is something, to marry a princess of the Blood . . ."

Our host could have had no idea how uncomfortable his
speech made both Ferhad and me. Fortunately for all of us, the
governor's small son, perhaps missing the harem in truth now,
had come and climbed into his father's lap, and the governor
forgot all about the disadvantages of having children. He settled back comfortably to enjoy the festival.

I'm afraid I can't say whether the dervish gave a good performance any more than I can say whether the women enjoyed
one. I was too nervous to listen to poetry that evening. And the
coming of daylight did not improve things. Esmikhan's eyes
wandered off and glazed with dreams, but then they would
water and her cheeks would blush with guilt as she brought
them back again.

*I shall find some excuse,* I plotted. *I shall make her return to Constantinople, where we shall be safe in my master's house.*

But that was impossible, for winter had already begun and
no excuse could be worth the risk of a journey across Turkey
in the snows. And Esmikhan braved that snow there in Konya
to throw herself into a pilgrim's devotions with renewed frenzy
so that any suggestion of her boredom or wasting time was easily seen to be out of the question.

As for myself, all thought of religion and its consolations had vanished from my mind. If they did enter at all, it was in the form of some exclamation, "Oh, God, help me now," or "If You do exist, You certainly are not the Compassionate One the Muslims call You. You are rather more like the wicked boy who has caught a bird in this trap and then insists on torturing it to death!"

Then the correspondence began.

At first it came by the governor's little son, for whom Ferhad was a great favorite. I soon caught him and gave him such a scolding—all about women and honor, and did he never want to grow up to become like the hero of a popular romance? After that they began to use his sister, who was also still so young that she could go throughout the house at will. Fortunately, I was able to convince her father, in general terms, that she was old enough to begin confinement. Then they coerced one of my own seconds, and in my anger I sold him immediately and at a great loss.

Notes came in bushels of apples and went out (Allah forbid) in the family's copy of Rumi's poems. A bunch of autumn crocuses appeared in my lady's room—they could only have been picked by one with liberty to ramble about the hillside. I never was actually told who had done that rambling, but the fact that the stamens pulled from the centers of those flowers found their way into the flavorful rice upon which Ferhad broke his fast the next evening gave me a rather secure guess.

But I also began to see messages where there were none. One day I discovered a vase of forced hawthorne in my lady's room. Angrily, I had it thrown out, only to discover that she had collected it and gone to all the care and trouble to make it bloom, and set it there herself only to brighten the place. It was not from Ferhad at all. Still, between the one note I caught and the next, their love and intimacy was swollen, leapt from buds to full blooms like flowers in springtime seem to have if one fails to go in the garden every day. Some communications were still getting through, in spite of all my care.

One day I tried to present my concerns to the governor in less vague terms than I had used for the matter of his daughter.

"Our Ferhad?" he asked, incredulous. "Women are the farthest thing from his mind. Horseflesh and training, that is all that concerns him. Why, I offered him a glass of my good red wine, obtained at great trouble and great expense from Cyprus. He didn't condemn, he didn't threaten to tell the vizier or any such thing; just refused politely but firmly to even indulge in that minor infraction. By Allah, I can't drink myself with his virtue around! No doubt it's just as well for my immortal soul, but it's going to be a long, dry winter. I've no consolation but that wine improves with age."

It seemed useless to confront the lovers themselves. They knew perhaps more than I the seriousness of their actions. Ferhad was nothing if not a man of honor and Esmikhan was a woman who often sat hours with me, fingering my hand in a silence that seemed to plead with me to save her from herself. They both held high positions for which many others would envy them: the one, Grand Master of the Imperial Horse; the other, the wife of the Grand Vizier and a daughter of the Sultan. Both of them filled those posts with more devotion than many a mortal could muster, but for that devotion, their mortality made them suffer more than another.

But suffering was food to the sort of idyllic, never-consummated, never-seen-face-to-face-in-the-light-of-day sort of love they possessed. A spahi prides himself on being able to endure more than another man; a woman gets no more pleasure than from the pains of childbirth. Such was the painful, helplessness of their love.

After selling the traitor among my assistants, I could trust the rest to help me to the best of their abilities. Unfortunately, it was the *khadim* of greatest ability I had been forced to sell. I couldn't replace him until our return to Constantinople, so all I had left with me were four persons who, for all their intentions, typified the worst infamy of eunuchs: the dull, fat, lazy stereotype from which we suffer. No, this trial was a test of my strength alone.

And it was a test. That impression came strongly one day when I caught Ferhad in the hall containing the grille to the harem, where he had no right to be. Without a word he bowed and left the room. The smile he gave me as he left was full of such sportsmanlike reserve that it might have gone equally well to the man who had just defeated him fair and square in a round of wrestling.

I do not mean by allusion to the ring from which both men generally walk away unharmed to belittle the seriousness of the test I was undergoing. If I did fail, blood would be shed. That a noblewoman's virtue is sometimes set but low on men's scale of values does not erase the fact that it was my whole reason for being.

The fact that my lady and her lover, too, faced death if I failed helped me define the antagonists better. Ferhad was not the real enemy. The impossible requirements of form were the culprits, and I was like a skilled swordsman defending two babes from these invaders, defending those who could not defend themselves.

# XXXVIII

THAT YEAR THE month of Ramadhan began in the depths of winter. It seemed no hardship to fast then; one was lethargic and given to long spells of sitting cozily anyway. But by the end of the month the snows had begun to carve out rocky creeks for themselves in the back streets of Konya, and wild grape hyacinths splattered protected crannies like highly glazed tile work.

By the time the holy month neared its end, all spirits were stirring and it seemed harder and harder to fast those last few days. It would be equally difficult, I felt, for my lady and her lover to endure this time of new life without closer contact than the harem walls had so far allowed them.

Fortunately for us all, I thought, the snow was turning to mud, and the mud to dirt once more. It would only be a matter of weeks until the roads were passable and our year's pilgrimage would come to an end. I can easily keep them apart—those two lodestones—for so long.

I had proven myself. I had proven myself in a trial more difficult than facing the physical threat of brigands, the kidnappers of Chios. I exalted and thought, only a man who has slain his first enemy can appreciate how I felt.

So great was my relief and triumph that I celebrated in the best way I knew how. I escaped the harem and attended the Thursday evening services of Husayn's brotherhood again, which my winter-long tension had rarely given me commitment of spirit to do. The two or three times I did attend that season, I could never allow myself to be drawn into the dance again, but sat watching and brooding in the gallery.

But now, so great was my relief that I might have even abandoned myself to the total Sufi Union with the Divine had not a sudden image of the sword that awaited me if I should neglect my duties cut the vision at the last moment. Again I was obliged to break away from the circle, again I escaped into myself in the quiet chill of the courtyard.

And again, near dawn, Husayn came out to me alone. The moon was but a wisp, nearing the end of the holy month. We took the cloud of the Milky Way as other men may take tobacco or opium, and smoked it together silently in a pipe invisible between us.

I do not know if he read my mind. They say some dervishes cultivate that capability, and at the time it certainly seemed as if he did. But perhaps he only sensed the atmosphere with insight our shared joys and sorrows had honed keen. He spoke to it in parables.

"Elias," Husayn began, like the very voice of that sharp night, "is the wisest of all the creatures of Allah. It is said he inspired the saint of Konya, Sufi Rumi, and that he also instructed the Prophet Moses. At first Elias was skeptical that he should teach Moses anything, but Moses insisted and Elias in his wisdom also knew what a great prophet this man might become if properly instructed.

" 'Very well,' Elias said to him, 'you may come with me on my travels through the world of men. But you must not question anything I do, for the undertaking of Allah is far beyond that of men.'

"Moses replied that he would certainly comply with this request, for gaining knowledge in the Way of Allah was his only desire. So the two men went about the world and soon they came to the sea. They had no coin to pay to be ferried across, but eventually they met two poor but pious sailors who were content to have them on board for nothing.

"When they reached the other shore, Elias promptly put a great hole in the hull of this boat so it began to sink, and then he went on his way. Moses, following after, was shocked. 'These poor sailors were kind to us, and this boat is their only means of livelihood,' he thought angrily. But he didn't say anything for he had sworn not to question the deeds of this, the wisest of creatures.

"Soon the two men of Allah came to a tree and beneath the tree was a young child asleep. The child was so beautiful and peaceful and so well favored that Moses could not help but wonder. But just as he was about to form a word of praise to the Creator, Elias came and struck off the child's head in one blow.

"Now Moses was so appalled that he could not speak, even if he had wished to, and by the time he had gained his tongue again, they were far from the city, in an abandoned field. In the field was an old stone wall which was crumbling through neglect, but for this Elias stopped and had Moses spend the heat of the afternoon repairing the breach.

"At last Moses could hold his tongue no longer. 'Master,' he said, 'I do not understand. This is useless work. The wall and the field are clearly abandoned and why should we stop to do something that will benefit no one? Why, indeed, when our day has already been filled with senseless destruction and violence. To destroy those poor sailors' boat and to kill that fair-faced child surely go against all the laws of Allah. I wonder if you are Elias at all and not some satanic impostor.'

" 'How much you have to learn of the ways of Allah!' Elias sighed wearily at this breach of faith on the part of his disciple who was meant to become a prophet. 'I had you mend the wall

because beneath it is buried the inheritance of two poor or-
phaned children. Had we not mended it, others would have
come and found the treasure and taken it away before the children have grown to their majority and are able to dig it up for
themselves.

" 'You do not understand the boat, either. There are wicked
men in that city who would have stolen that only means of
livelihood from those two good sailors. They will not bother to
steal a boat with a hole in it, and by the time our friends have
made their repairs, the wicked men will be converted to Allah
and will molest them no more.'

" 'And the child?' Moses asked. 'Surely there can be no excuse to kill a child in the Mind of Allah.'

" 'But there is,' Elias replied. 'Had that child become an
adult, he would have been a very wicked man. His fair features
would have remained and he would have deceived many with
them. Not only would innocent people have had to suffer the
loss of their goods, but hundreds would have died most miserably had that small hand grown large.'

"Sometimes," Husayn concluded, "the man of Allah can best
fulfill the will of the Merciful One not by obeying His laws, but
by breaking them."

My friend and I let the story sit in silence, and then we went
without another word to eat some breakfast, for it would soon
be dawn and the fast would be upon us again.

The story stayed with me throughout the coming weeks as
the fast ended and we began to prepare to return to Constantinople. It seemed especially clear when I accompanied my lady
to the tomb of the saint on the last Wednesday of our stay. It
was as if Rumi himself, who, the dervishes say, had Elias for his
instructor, were reciting the story to me in hollow echoes from
the grave: ". . . Not by obeying His laws, but by breaking them."

When we had completed our devotions, Esmikhan indicated

that she wanted to sit in Rumi's seat one final time. I knew that repetition was believed to erase the efficacy of a wish. At first I thought she was so desperate that she didn't care, but when I helped her step down, I knew that over our stay her wish had changed. At first she had prayed for a child and the answer, so it seemed, had come in the vision of our young spahi. Her new wish I could guess at, and the way her eyes met mine made me feel that whatever power she had derived from that chair convinced her that its fulfillment lay in my good will alone.

"Not I!" I declared when she indicated again that I, too, should make a wish. My tone spoke in answer to the hope in those eyes, not to the suggestion of her tongue.

"Perhaps you have no desires, Abdallah. But can't you even pray for the happiness of your poor Esmikhan? It cannot be pleasant to serve a woman whose heart is breaking," she murmured.

Again I refused, but her words struck me with disquiet as if they had indeed come from an otherworldly source. So much so that, once I had packed her and her maids into their sedans, and sent them off with the porters and the other eunuchs, I took the first opportunity to escape even when that excuse was the appearance of none other than Ferhad himself.

I knew he would be there. He had been there in the public place outside the mosque compound every women's day since the end of Ramadhan and many before. "He mingles among the men we must govern, and discovers their feelings and their desires," our host excused him. "He is more useful to me there than he would be here while I hold court."

I was not so easily beguiled. I knew his only true desire was to catch another glimpse of my lady as she entered and exited the mosque.

My lady, too, sensed this and always sat straight and arranged her hair with care and blushed so prettily even though I made certain there always remained four or five opaque barriers between his eyes and her. If I had had any doubts before, I had none that day, for a dark afternoon drizzle had driven all the more sensible townsmen to their homes, leaving only the Master of the Imperial Horse sitting there as if he were some village halfwit. There was no one for him to spy on but the ladies. That he kept his back discreetly to us did not fool me for a moment. It only allowed me to creep up on him without his knowledge.

The face that turned to me had tears distorting its handsome angles. I pretended I thought they were only raindrops, but I could not hide my surprise to see the other out-of-character thing about him: in his right hand was an unsheathed dagger.

Now the spahis are men of war and they undergo a little ceremony when they are issued their first dagger during which they vow "to use this blade against none but the enemies of Allah and of His Shadow, the Sultan of Islam."

The enemy of Turkish society against which he now turned his knife was himself.

He had been holding it with such real intent that when my greeting startled him, he actually cut the flesh of his left wrist. It was not such a deep cut as to be dangerous but both he and I watched with startled fascination as beads of blood began to make a dainty woman's bracelet on his arm. Only the reflex of ritual greetings and pleasantries kept a morbid silence from stifling us. The pleasantries allowed him, too, to gain some degree of composure with which to chuckle as if the scratch were nothing.

"Abdullah, my friend," he said, "I have faced wild Austrians and Kurds as well as trained Persians on the frontier without a flinch. I am only wondering if I will have the courage to face what must come on Sunday next—your departure. I fear death from that, my friend, more than from any Persian lancer."

"You are mad," I wanted to tell him. "Love has made you mad."

But he knew that. He knew better than I the tragedy it was for helplessness to overcome one of Turkey's brightest hopes. So great was his intimacy with that tragedy that he could not but long for death. What use was there for appeals to reason? I spoke only more pleasantries as he bound his wrist with a scrap of his sash—"Got in the service of the Grand Vizier," he attempted a little joke—and I accompanied him back to the palace.

Surely if Allah loves His people He will not let them lose such a wonderful defender of the Faith by his own hand for the sake of a woman, I thought as we walked. Surely He could not let one of the most devoted among His women pine away the rest of her life never knowing either the love of a man, nor the pleasure of a child, even when she had crossed all of Anatolia to pray for these things.

And yet, what right had I, a Venetian, and Ferhad, born an Albanian, to second-guess the will of the God of these people among whom we were strangers? And Esmikhan, though the daughter of the Sultan, had a Circassian mother. No doubt even she was undeserving of a special dispensation from this God's age-old laws. Such thoughts kept the more rebellious ones in check.

Then, however, I thought of the sanction I had received—or thought I had received—from Husayn. A wandering dervish is considered by all to be the most beloved of Allah.

"Sometimes the man of Allah can best fulfill the will of the Merciful One not by obeying His laws but by breaking them."

Still, I was not certain Husayn's vision was altogether holiness. Sometimes, I feared, it was madness, too.

# XXXIX

THURSDAY, FRIDAY, SATURDAY came, following one another as they have since the world began. Saturday night. I surveyed my defenses as the general of a besieged town might walk along the parapet on the eve of an attack. I had insisted that my seconds keep watch through the night, waking in shifts so if the slightest noise came from the grille between the worlds, they would hear it. I tested the doors and the windows as if the enemy might try to break in with battle-axes. No, all was safe. The siege would be lifted tomorrow. We, the defenders, leaving rather than the attackers. And the only weakness was in my heart.

I went to bid my lady good night and found her weak with tears. She lay in the arms of the governor's wife and his daughters, who had vowed to spend the night with her. They thought it was leaving them that caused her such sorrow and were doing everything they could to return the compliment to so great a lady.

I helped the slaves bring out bedding and went to lower the lights, but Esmikhan protested that she had no wish for sleep that night, and darkness would only haunt her more. Then I sat on, helpless, having no desire to return to my lonely room to face my conscience burdened by her flushed face and eyes, so puffy and bruised they looked as if someone had been beating her.

Outside the lattice at the window to her room, a nightingale began to sing. It was the first any of us had heard that year—

sweet warbling like the quaver of a sob—and we all held our breath at the cool evening beauty of it. Poets say that the nightingale is the rose's lover, but the two can never meet, for the rose is guarded by jealous thorns. Hence, the exquisite sadness of the bird's song.

Had I not known it was impossible, I would have sworn this wild creature was the final farewell message of Ferhad to his own well-guarded beloved.

I have never heard a poet call the song of the nightingale the voice of Elias, and perhaps that would be considered blasphemy, but that is what it suddenly became to me. Seeming neither mortal nor yet quite divine, it taught me, or rather made me remember what I had learned the first time I stood in a head eunuch's room and saw the two doors. Being neither male nor female, I was yet able to unite the two and make them whole. What power was there! It was divine, I could call it no other: to bring together what men had torn asunder, to create harmony out of discord and joy out of sorrow. By imposing the harem and all other separations between His creatures according to class, race, nationality, and species, Allah had created the discord and sorrow. Though these were necessary, they were only to teach us the opposites. If the work and glory of the God of Islam were not to finally show compassion and mercy, then I understood nothing of my adopted religion, nor of the one I had abandoned either.

The bird's song also had a profound effect upon my lady, but, because she was only half of a whole, it sent her into a pit of even greater despair. She was too weak to give anymore force to her tears so they collapsed in upon her, and I thought perhaps she had fainted. The governor's wife and her daughters cried out with sympathetic sorrow, and began to bathe my lady's wrists and forehead with rosewater and rue.

I spoke to them, matching my words to the rhythm I heard

from the nightingale. "Perhaps, my gracious hostess, it would be better if I spent the night with my lady. It would be less wearing upon your delicate selves and less sorrowful for her."

The women were shocked and hurt. Would I deprive them of these last hours of joy and companionship? I, nothing but a cold, dowdy eunuch who can never have known true attachment even as they enjoyed between the same sex?

I was too sure of myself to be hurt by their words. I was sure and, though the others missed it, Esmikhan must have felt my confidence. She opened her eyes and met mine with the first look of interest I had seen from her in days. I replied to that look with one of calm—one might almost say pious—resolve and she sensed that, too. She found the strength to raise to her elbows and, when her attendants tried to stop her, to push them away.

"Leave us. Just a few minutes," she begged of them. "I will certainly call you back if I need you."

The women left with many doubting and grumbling glances backward. The maids, too, were waved out of the room, then my lady sat right up and asked, "Will you, Abdullah?"

"It is not a question of my will but of Allah's," I said. "But I will do what I can."

I left her then at once and found Ferhad sitting with our host in the *selamlik*.

"Why, Abdullah!" the governor greeted me. "You are just in time. Ferhad has finally agreed to join me in a glass of wine. He actually asked for it. I did not press him at all. Will you join us?"

Ferhad raised his goblet to me, giving me all the credit for his fall from perfect discipline like a naughty boy blaming his comrades. When he took a sip, I could tell he did not enjoy the burn of alcohol, but he thought it might help him face what the morrow would bring. Even at the rate he was going, I knew I had to stop him soon or he would be of no use to himself or to my lady.

I politely declined our host's invitation, and then I was inspired to say, "I'm sorry. I didn't mean to interrupt. I just had a small request. It is such a little thing, it can wait 'til we get to Constantinople. My master has a good knowledge of Persian."

"What is it, Abdullah?" the governor demanded.

"Nothing, really. Only my lady was reading some poetry and the poet makes too many classical Persian allusions for her to manage it on her own. The poem is very beautiful—an old one about the nightingale and his beloved rose—but unfortunately we can't quite make sense of it. I have the manuscript in my room and . . ."

"I'm afraid my Persian was all learned in the barracks." The governor laughed.

"But I have had experience with the poets," Ferhad said. I had guessed both answers before I asked.

"But I can see you are not in the mood," I said.

"I don't know . . . ," Ferhad began.

"If sometime tonight you do feel you could spare the time, I'll be awake all night alone in my room with the manuscript. I have packing to do . . ."

I bowed to leave but even as I did, I saw that the young spahi, so used to making cryptic love messages of his own, had had no trouble reading through mine. He set down his goblet and was abruptly his former, stalwart, hopeful self.

Back in the harem, I discovered that my lady had put on a fresh gown of deep pink and red that became her so well. She had also washed her face and fixed her hair. Had I not seen her just half an hour before with my own eyes, I would have found it hard to believe such a drastic change could come over anyone. But still, she was not altogether of one mind. The same thoughts and fears that had been plaguing me for months were now transferred to her.

"What if . . . ," she said, and that beginning was finished in

the pause by everything from . . . *he should not come or coming,
should not find me to his liking?* to . . . *we should be discovered? It is
death to commit adultery.* But such thoughts only added to the
thrills that swept cold up her back and then fired her cheeks at
intervals.

For my part, I was calmer than I had been in all those months.
The decisions were now all out of my hands and I felt wonderfully free. I took her hand and pressed it, and she surprised me
with a little kiss on the cheek. Then I left the room as if to use
the lavatory. When I returned, Esmikhan's room was empty. I
thought I would be nervous, waiting up like a mother whose
daughter is undergoing the test of virginity on her bridal night.
I thought I would start at every sound, expecting any moment
to be discovered. But I blew out the lights, unwound my sash,
set aside my dagger, and climbed into the bedding as if I were
in my own room. I fell asleep almost instantly, exhausted with
relief, and I do not think I have slept better since.

I returned to my room when I awoke in the morning. My
bedding was neatly folded as if it had not been touched, but in
the air was the definite, though delicate smell of sex, so incongruous in a eunuch's room. I opened the window and it faded
at once without a trace—like dew before sunlight. The nightingale gives way to the morning lark.

Never have I seen my lady so radiant as when I held the curtain for her to climb into her sedan to begin our long trip home.
That that night had been one of a kind did not matter. She had
been loved and cherished truly and completely and that was
more than she had ever hoped to enjoy in her life. Our host-
esses must have been somewhat insulted by the cheer with
which she could leave them now it was day. Esmikhan was so
full of joy that she sang. The notes carried through the sedan
walls and lightened the porters' steps. I think it was even heard

by Ferhad who, on pretense of a morning ride, saw us some little way out of town.

The good humor lasted for days; we made excellent time and it rubbed off on the whole party, including the maids, who were remarkably free from quarrels and grumblings about having to be kept cooped up so long.

*Whatever happens,* I told myself, *I shall never regret having done this for her.*

Such good moods, no more than spells of good weather, cannot be expected to last forever. But this one seemed to— over two weeks—and it was only stopped by something very physical. My mistress suddenly became violently ill. We stopped for a few days but she showed no signs of recovery, even with the best attendance. Finally she insisted that we try to continue, in spite of the fact that we had to stop every hour or so for her to spill her insides over the Turkish landscape. This even when there was nothing in her stomach but sour fluid to spill.

At first I thought it must be bad water, but none of the rest of us got it, and spring, when the water sources are cool and swollen with melting snow, is hardly the season for dysentery. I did not know what to think, only began to fear what the master might learn or guess. Instead of the bright, blooming rose promised him from the gardens of Konya, what I brought him was faded and brittle instead, as if it had spent the entire journey crushed in the bottom of a saddlebag.

At last we arrived in Constantinople, four days late instead of early as our progress at first had led me to hope. As soon as I saw my lady comfortable in her old *haremlik* again, I prepared to go to the *selamlik* to carry to the master the news of our safe arrival, but also to warn him that his wife was in no condition to receive him.

"No, no, Abdullah. You must not tell him that," Esmikhan

said. "You must tell him I will see him as soon as it is convenient for him."

"But my lady. You are so weak you can hardly walk."

"Still, I must. I must appear as healthy and as desirable as possible."

She made an attempt here to sit up and look in at least middling health. My face, I suppose, betrayed severe doubt, for she said, "Oh, Abdullah! Do you know so little about the woman you are meant to guard, that you cannot tell when she is pregnant?"

"My lady," I said in disbelief and then came up with a reason not to believe. "You were never this sick before."

"That is because this time it will live. I know it, Abdullah. Allah has answered my prayers."

"And sent you your wish by an illegal love."

"Yes," she said, without a note of regret.

"Then you must meet with the master. By Allah, even tonight, and he may grow suspicious."

"Yes," Esmikhan said, but there was still no fear or doubt. It was all very dutifully matter-of-fact.

## XL

As soon as we could do it without arousing suspicion, and when her sickness had eased off a bit, I went with my lady to break the good news to the others in the imperial harem. It was to be an afternoon spent pleasantly with cool drinks and gossip. The old Quince would perform all her magics by which she made babies strong and well-favored and by which she could tell the sex and the fortune. In return, Esmikhan would tell them every detail of the pilgrimage. Some favored few might even be taken by the elbow and honored, in a corner apart, with the full story of the answer to her prayers.

Esmikhan was at once sorry not to see Safiye among the women that greeted her with hugs and kisses on both cheeks. "And where is my Safiye's sweet little baby? Why, he must be a big boy by now—over two years old. How I wish to see them both!"

"Ooh, haven't you heard?" One of the girls could not blush and keep quiet like the rest. "Prince Murad has arrived in the city this morning, totally against his father's wishes."

Now there was no use for discretion and all the others joined in: "He has abandoned his *sandjak*."

"Rode day and night."

"Safiye refused all his entreaties to join him in Magnesia."

"Even after the child had grown."

"They say," giggled a maid, "the prince is quite out of his mind with desire."

"That girl," Nur Banu muttered like the plunge of an icicle from the eaves. I sensed a new cool hatred there, more than just a mild jealousy that her son had not called for her to join him in the *mabein* that afternoon as well.

At this point one of the lesser officials of the palace eunuchs drew me aside and made a request. It seemed that the veal—that special food of eunuchs which is supposed to keep us as tender as young cattle and not fire us like the red, full-grown meat men eat—had been tainted last night. Now nearly all the staff was too sick to walk, including the officers down to this man. Even he was the color of limestone with a greenish cast. My lady would be safe here in the heart of the harem, he said, but would I be so good as to come and lend a hand in the halls near the *mabein*? It would not be so bad if they were deserted as they had been for months, but since the young prince Murad had so suddenly arrived, there was much activity that had to be monitored.

"If you could only stand in a few hours until reinforcements can be brought from the old palace . . ."

"Of course, Abdullah, you should go," my lady said. "Our talk cannot be very interesting for you."

I was quickly outfitted with the white hat and green fur-trimmed cloak particular to the palace harem, and given a post, in the heart of the *mabein*. At either end of the hall, I could see one of my colleagues—leaning against the wall as the chills of the fever came over them. Usually they were set no further than ten paces apart, and did not dare to even slouch as they stood at careful attention throughout four-hour shifts. I could have called to these men in an emergency, but I'm sure I was the only one who could hear what was going on behind the door just to my right.

It was the interview between Murad and Safiye. His voice was hot with anger.

"What, I would like to know, is the infidel attraction here in Constantinople? Why do you put me off? Why must you stay here? What do you do all day that you couldn't do in Magnesia?"

"I know you are as disappointed as I am that the hay-cart rebellion was not successful. But, my prince, you must trust that I am working towards the same end in more and different ways . . ."

"Forget rebellion. It is too dangerous, for you, for our son. Besides, what do I care to be Sultan—if I can't have you there beside me."

"You could marry . . ."

Murad snapped off her last word like a pinnacle of glass. "I have promised my mother."

"And even a son makes no difference to you."

"He seems to make no damned bit of difference to you."

"Why, I care for our child . . ."

I heard a child whimper, and I knew little Muhammed must be in there as well, his first experience with his father—like being set in a pen with a charging bull.

"Go on, sweetheart. Go to your Mama."

It was another woman's voice and I knew that little Muhammed's nurse was also present. A gentle, plump woman with a husband and family of her own in Magnesia, she had been given the little prince to suckle from birth. This had given Safiye plenty of time for the pursuits she hadn't divulged to Murad— following events in the Divan, and sending her eunuch out to bring in the latest word from the quayside, the barracks, the Mufti's palace. But it also meant that the child clung to this woman rather than to his mother, especially now, with that raging bull in the room. Muhammed whimpered again as Safiye tried, clumsily, to show off her mothering skills.

"Yes, I can tell how devoted you are to him," Murad spat sarcastically. "He goes to you like a bee to honey."

The argument grew fiercer.

"There is nothing wrong with Magnesia," Murad declared. "I'll have you recall that I was born and raised there."

"Ah, yes. How often I have listened to your mother speak of those delightful days with her little Murad. Why don't you take her down there with you this time so she can mother you to her heart's content." :

"Magnesia is a nice town for a boy to grow up in. No dirt, no crowds, not like Constantinople."

"I should die of boredom."

"What did you say?"

"I said, I should die of boredom. It's so quiet there that you've forgotten how to hear."

"Boredom? You would be bored with me there?"

"You said it. I didn't."

"What's the matter? I'm not good enough for you? I am the heir to the throne of Othman! I bore you?"

"I didn't say anything." Her tone was not as innocent as her words.

"By Allah, have you been unfaithful?"

"That would be a nice trick. Here, behind these walls, crawling with dour eunuchs and your mother everywhere I turn."

"I heard tales when I was a child in the harem. I know it is sometimes done, sneaking lovers in in laundry baskets."

"If I had a lover, he would have more dignity than to go creeping around in laundry baskets. No, my lord, I have not had a lover, though I must say several nice plates of cool green cucumbers have caught my eye. I've thought of helping myself to a better . . ."

"Why, you whore! You bought-and-paid-for whore!"

There was a shocked little gasp from the nurse. She called the baby to her and must have tried to cover his ears.

Safiye laughed. "Well, what are you going to do about it? Eh? What are you going to do? I am the mother of your firstborn son. You are stuck with me. What are you going to do, kill the precious little bastard?"

Another moan from the nurse, "Allah forbid!"

"No, no. But I can have another woman. I can have any damned woman in this harem. In this country. In this world."

"Hell if I care. Have as many as you like."

"You wouldn't care?"

"I am still the mother of your firstborn son. I am still the one who taught you how to use that little old cock of yours."

"I'll show you, you bitch! Anyone in the whole damned world. I could have this woman here, right now."

"What? Our old nurse?"

"Damn it, yes! I can! I will!"

"Master! Master!" The nurse cried out in shock, then in true pain.

I shifted my feet and looked anxiously down the hall to my colleagues. One was sitting on the floor, exhausted by his sickness, and the other was rubbing his temples. The one on the floor suddenly got up and ran out of the hall to empty his stomach someplace else. They heard nothing and, caught up in their own suffering, cared less. Besides, it was none of our business what went on in the *mabein,* once we had screened those who went in.

I stood and listened. I heard the nurse's sobs and moaning pleas, "Master. No, master, please . . ."

I listened to the child whimpering for the comfort of her bosom. I heard Safiye trying to hush him in vain, then her mocking laugh, "Just look at your father, my lion. He's like a pi-dog in the streets."

"Bitch!" Murad shouted.

The door to the room burst open and the nurse, looking like a dead thing, a rat half-cat-eaten and rotted a week, threw herself out of the room and down the hall into the safety of the harem without a glance at me. Her jacket was misbuttoned and her *shalvar* twisted on awkwardly, but she didn't care.

"You're not the only one," Murad repeated. "I can have anyone, anytime."

"Yes, well, you'll have to learn not to let them get away before you go making claims like that."

The child howled.

"Take your damned brat away before I . . ."

There was a sudden, awful slap across soft baby flesh. There was a moment of horrified silence, and then the howl of pained innocence, perhaps the most dreadful sound in the world. It carried. The *khadim* at the other end of the hall stood up straight and looked at me. But before I could make any gesture of explanation, the door opened again. Safiye stuck her head out. She was flushed, panting with rage—and perhaps a little with fear, although you would never hear her admit it.

"Hello?" she said. "Oh, Veniero. Run and get someone to take this child, will you?"

She was holding the baby clumsily, not just because she was unused to the procedure, nor because the child was writhing so, but also in a vain attempt to keep the blood from a vicious cut across his face from staining her clothes.

I wanted to take the child myself. Even I, who had never held a baby before, would have done a better job of it than that.

"Not you," Safiye told me sharply. "Go get someone who knows what she's doing."

The child's scream had gone soundless with pain, but her sharp voice made him take breath in again and it came out, rending the air like doomsday. I could bear it no longer. I couldn't leave him there with his parents. I feared for his life. I snatched him away and ran, Murad's abuse and Safiye's Italian curses pursuing me all the way down the hall.

A young black nursemaid's assistant was there in the nursery trying to revive some sort of life in her superior. The rag of a woman had thrown herself in a corner, was tearing her hair, quite senseless to the pain, and moaning over and over, "O Allah, Allah, if You are Merciful, take me now. Take me before my poor Mansur finds out how he has been betrayed, O Allah!"

The minute she saw little Muhammed, however, she instantly forgot her own grief. By that time the poor child looked as if he must have lost the skin off half his face and his howls were mortifying. My arm, too, looked as if it must have sustained a grievous wound, it was so soaked with his blood.

Little Muhammed went to her and took some comfort—

either that, or finally stilled his sobs to a low hum from sheer exhaustion. The nurse cooed to him through hysterical tears of her own, and tried to mop the wound first with her sleeve, then with a kerchief the maid handed her.

"Allah, it won't stop bleeding!" she cried. "Allah, how it gapes across your poor cheek, my angel." Then, "Run for the Quince," she told her assistant. "Run, this instant!"

I stayed until the midwife came. The blood was still oozing out and the grim noises and greenish color that came from the old woman told me that her skills would be tried with this case. This made me so furious, fury above my fear, that I determined to march down to the *mabein* at once and tell the daughter of Baffo—and, the Prince, too—just what their violence had done.

I was stopped at their door. I heard sounds of their violence grown into a violence of love. My anger rotted in my stomach and made me ill.

"Ah, cursed veal!" a novice eunuch who was still staggering, exclaimed sympathetically when he saw me. He assumed by my looks that I had eaten from the tainted pot last night, too.

&#x2766;

IT WAS A week or two later when we visited the Serai again. Safiye was bright and lively, making no plans to go to Magnesia and saying no word about her son. So when I happened to see the little black nurse's assistant, I could not help but ask for news. I never stopped to think how curious it was to find her in the hot, humid, stone, and metallic world of the laundry off the nine-pillared court of the menial slaves instead of in the nursery.

She blinked at me over the great copper kettle, and I thought her tears were from the steam. I soon realized, however, that the irritation was in her heart.

"They tell me his little cheek got infected," she said. "He will always have a scar, that perfect, pure little face! They did not dress it properly, I'm sure. Maybe they even let the flies get to it. By Allah, if I were still in the nursery, I would see it cleared up. I wouldn't stop to do anything else, to gossip, to try on new clothes like those others must be doing. I would stay up all night to see that he got better."

"But surely his nurse is as dedicated to the little Prince as you are," I suggested.

"You cannot have heard."

"No, I've heard nothing."

"The nurse is no longer in the palace."

"But where has she gone?"

"Home."

"And left little Muhammed?"

"*She* made her go."

"She?"

"The Fair One, Safiye. She says it was because of the nurse's carelessness that he got that horrible wound on his cheek. By Allah, it isn't true!"

"No," I said. "I know it isn't true."

"I say it's because she's jealous. The nurse told me in dark whispers in the corner—she told me what happened, how Murad tried to . . . Well, Safiye realizes now that her position in the harem is not as secure as she thought. Murad could easily take another. Easily, easily. Why not? If only this realization would make her more careful of the little Prince. No, I refuse to call him her son. She doesn't deserve to be called a mother. If anyone does, it's my dear mistress, his nurse.

"But Safiye got jealous of her. She made her life miserable, hoping she would ask to be released. My mistress was miserable, but she would not leave the baby for anything. Safiye finally forced her to leave.

"I shall never forget the sorrow of that day. My mistress sat trying to give the lad suck 'til the very last moment. He wasn't hungry. *They*'d been plying him with sweets all day 'til I'm sure he had a bellyache. But my mistress let him play a little game they had where he'd nip at her with those little gapped baby teeth, she'd tweak his ear, then hug him close, and then they'd do it all over again. Oh, they'd laugh and laugh and laugh at that. My mistress was sobbing instead of laughing this time, but she sat, probing his little mouth with the breast until they actually dragged him from her.

" 'Go home,' the kinder folk said. 'You have children of your own and a husband at home. You haven't seen them in two years. Go to them.'

"But they still had to drag her away, so limp was she from crying, knowing she would never see her little suckling again. They took her out by the funeral door, which seems just somehow. To us in here, it is as if she had died and gone to be buried outside the walls.

"The little Prince, he set up a wail, too, to see his sobbing nurse carried away. They could not hush him. None of them had her soft, quiet ways, you know. They couldn't hold him for his struggles, and when they set him down, he tried to toddle after her, reaching out his little hands—I shall never forget it. Ever. His first steps alone were to her. And then these . . . He clung to the handle, crying, pounding, until—oh, it was hours later—he fell into a whimpering sleep. In his fit, he broke the wound open again. That's when it got infected, I'll wager. But that's when they brought me to this place, so I don't know."

Just then the head laundress came in. "You still on about it, girl?" she asked. "Still fretting about the young Prince's weaning, Allah shield him. Fie, everyone has to be weaned sooner or later. Normal women celebrate and give a little party when it finally happens for them."

"Weaning is one thing," the girl spoke up. "I swear by Allah, this will starve the Prince to death."

The laundress was a formidable woman, tall, large, with arms like a butcher's, and what gentleness might once have been in her face, the pox had ravaged. Still, she was not a cruel person, and she tried to speak with sympathy. "It is a matter we do not understand," she said.

"Because I was taken from my mother at an early age means I understand more, not less," the girl insisted.

"The gossips tell me Safiye stopped using her aloe and rue while Murad was here. I'm sure she realizes just how important her son's well-being is to her position and perhaps, if Allah wills, she may get another."

"Another she can neglect so," the maid said, angrily stabbing with her wooden pole into the steaming water.

"Now Prince Murad has returned to Magnesia. He is content that all things are well here, and that Safiye and the Prince will join him there at the end of the summer."

"I suppose it is easy to be content when one is a prince," the maid said bitterly.

"These are matters of royal love, girl. You," the laundress said with an eyebrow raised to the girl's dark skin, "and I"—she referred to her own pocked face—"will never know."

"I'd say it's ignorance of love, not knowledge, that ignores love's product."

"Come, girl, the child is young. He'll get over it. Children don't remember anything that happens to them before they're three or four."

"Yes, perhaps. And they can block out horrible things much later. But that scar on his face. That will always be there. And I'm sure whenever he touches it, no memory, perhaps, but something dark and cold. I'm sure it will haunt him 'til the day he dies."

The laundress shook her head. She tried to be kind, but she was pressed with the great responsibility of washing for five hundred souls. "Come on," she said. "Let's get this load drying. We've got three more to do today, and I don't think the sun will last, by the looks of the sky. Come on, girl."

And the maid turned from me to pull the steaming garments out of the pot. What should her pole first drag up, however, but a tiny pair of footed trousers in cream and crimson—the little Prince's. I left her burnishing her face with the back of her hand—tears, steam, and sweat into a high-polish black.

# XLI

ON OUR NEXT visit to the palace, Safiye drew my lady off to speak in private. I thought at first, and Esmikhan thought much longer than I, that the purpose of this attention was to share some wisdom about pregnancy in the fourth month, which was about all my lady had time to think about these days. But though Esmikhan was flattered by this private attention from the darling of the harem, the two were actually very different women indeed.

"Esmikhan, the great drums in the court of the janissaries have mustered the army."

"Yes," my lady replied, wistfully rubbing the swelling of her stomach. "All the cavalry has gone, too, including that from the provinces."

"I suppose you miss your husband." Safiye plied her with sympathy, but to this Esmikhan nodded rather apathetically. She bit her plump lower lip and wondered if this sudden attention from Safiye were a sign of more closeness to come, and if she should encourage it by divulging the name of her child's real father.

"They marched north this year," Safiye said.

"Did they?" Esmikhan had not cared which direction they marched, only that they had passed through Constantinople long enough for her to receive the gift of a single budding rose and then marched on.

"I find that most curious."

"The land in all directions belongs by right to Allah and His Faithful," Esmikhan said. She didn't find it curious at all.

"But you must know that your father signed a treaty of peace with Maximilian of Austria near the beginning of this year. What lies north but Austria and the plains of Hungary where our empires meet and fight? Does the Sultan mean to break his treaty? I find that hard to believe. Signing such a treaty was a terrible display of weakness. Suleiman would never have done such a thing. But because your father is not Suleiman, I also cannot believe that he would break it."

"Surely the Austrians, as Christians, must be won for Islam."

Esmikhan was trying to rise to the heights of political astuteness Safiye had set for this conversation, but her attempt only made the other woman toss her blond curls with impatience. "Well, yes, there is that. But more than that: Austria is so weak at the moment. Why bother to even treaty with them?"

"What glory is there in conquering the weak?" Esmikhan asked. "There must be someone else."

"Exactly," Safiye agreed. "But who? Who else is north?"

Esmikhan couldn't answer and showed by her shrug that she wasn't really interested. So Safiye proceeded to think aloud what had no doubt been buffeting around in her mind for days.

"Now I was certain they would go south. Yemen is in full revolt, and the rest of Arabia is threatening to follow them. Even your father, weak as he is . . ."

"My father isn't weak. He is the Shadow of Allah."

"Forgive me, Esmikhan—exactly. He could not risk the loss of face rebellion in the Holy Cities and Medina would cause."

Esmikhan gave a pious nod.

"But Arabia is south."

"Is it?"

"Of course. That's the direction we turn when we pray."

"Oh, yes."

"And I had Ghazanfer follow them a full day's march. Do you know Ghazanfer, my eunuch? Bright, ambitious, yet at the same time very discreet."

She said these words with a sharp punctuation in my direction. Obviously these were things I was not, at least, not sufficient to her liking. And she wished I would stand elsewhere—out of earshot, preferably. I smiled and refused to comply with her unspoken wish. Since she couldn't get Esmikhan to take the hint and order me away, she had to continue with the real purpose of all this talk.

"And you know something else curious Ghazanfer told me? He told me that several thousand of the homeless refugees that clog the slums of Constantinople went off with more janissaries by ship into the Black Sea at the same time.

"Where have they gone?" Safiye demanded again and, before Esmikhan could plead that it really was none of her business, she explained why indeed it was her business. "If your father knows where they have gone, he said nothing in his speech when he saw the troops off. Ghazanfer gave me that speech almost word for word. Unlike his father, Suleiman, your father takes no interest in war. His speech was all pious clichés the

Mufti must have taught him and nothing more. Then he refused to join them! Even on his deathbed, Suleiman would not have done that. No, even if he does know, I'm sure your father had nothing to do with the decision and his mind is so far from the battlefield that I can't hope he'll let it drop within hearing of Ghazanfer or any of the other *khuddam* I can trust. So, Esmikhan, if your father is not running the army, who is?"

"Don't worry, Safiye," my lady said. "The army of the Faithful is well directed. My husband is at their head and there is no Muslim more capable than he."

"You catch my drift!" Safiye said, and with an unsaid sigh. *At last!* "Now your husband, the most glorious Grand Vizier, said nothing of this in the Divan."

"How do you know this, Safiye?" Esmikhan asked.

"If I do not have time to go to the Eye of the Sultan and hear for myself, I send Ghazanfer—every day."

"Ghazanfer seems to be everywhere."

"I told you he was a good *khadim*," Safiye said.

"Where did you find him?"

"I can't stop and tell you now. Maybe another time. What I need you to tell me is whether or not they held the war council at your house. For security reasons, perhaps. It is clear they did not hold it here."

Esmikhan said she couldn't remember. "He holds so many meetings, you know," she said. "I hardly notice anymore."

"The Master of the Imperial Horse would have been there," Safiye prompted.

Esmikhan blushed. "Yes, now that you mention it, there was . . ."

"Go on. He did meet with Sokolli, then, at your house."

Safiye encouraged Esmikhan's blushes and hesitation. "The general of the janissaries would have been at this particular meeting, too."

*And the other viziers and Kapudan Pasha because the navy was used,* I filled in to myself, for I remembered the meeting well. *And the Mufti, the Sheikh al-Islam, was there. He had to give his blessing to this course, for it is somewhat irregular. Of course he did in the end. How could he refuse the reconquest of lands that had once belonged to Islam but which, in the last ten years, had fallen into Russian Christian hands?* But I said nothing aloud.

"Well, I suppose I do remember such a meeting—vaguely," Esmikhan confessed after more prodding. "But I don't remember talk of war. All I remember was some talk of canals—building canals—and that is the work of peace."

"Canals?" Safiye mused. "I know that building a great canal to join the Mediterranean and the Red Sea is a favorite project of Sokolli Pasha. He believes the Faithful could control all trade from India, China, and points beyond with such a short water route through Suez. Who in Europe would then buy from the Portuguese or Spanish who must sail months around Africa when we could offer such a cut rate?"

"My husband is a very wise man," Esmikhan said.

"He is indeed," Safiye replied. "But no one in their right mind is sailing on the Red Sea these days, what with all Yemen in revolt, throttling it off at the neck."

Esmikhan had no very clear notion of geography but the notion that a sea might have a neck that could be throttled was very touching to her.

While she mused on this with pathos, Safiye continued, "And since the army has gone north, not south, it seems clear Sokolli Pasha does not mean to try and pacify things there so he can build his canal in Egypt."

Esmikhan shrugged helplessly. "I thought they were talking about canals."

I was quite amazed at how closely Safiye's thoughts followed the actual discussion. It was almost frightening how little had avoided first assimilation into her mind, and then the acuteness of her conclusions. As a matter of fact, however, Esmikhan was right. The major topic of discussion had been canals. Lala Mustafa Pasha, the Second Vizier, had interests in Syria and Egypt and he had spoken almost word for word those arguments we had just heard Safiye give to try to persuade the army to march in full force against Yemen that year. The Mufti, too, spoke in favor of saving the Holy Cities from falling into the hands of the Yemeni heretics.

But then my master had produced a great old book, one of the many I often saw him pouring over late at night when nerves wouldn't let him sleep. It was in Greek, at which the Mufti had coughed and declared, "A godless tongue," but Sokolli Pasha had insisted on translating for them anyway.

"In the days of the Empire of Alexander the Great, a man named Seleucus Nicator had proposed the building of a canal between the Don and Volga Rivers."

"Worse than a Christian," the Mufti had said. "A pagan."

Lala Mustafa Pasha, a man addicted to power, had been more cautious once someone had pronounced the magic, tantalizing words "Empire of Alexander the Great." Still he had questioned, "What would be the use of such a canal in such a faraway land? It would take years to build, and to what purpose?"

"It would not take so long as all that," Sokolli Pasha had insisted. "There is a point where the two rivers come within but thirty thousand paces of each other. A man can walk that in a day and the ground between them is all but level."

"I still do not see to what purpose this is."

Sokolli Pasha had pulled out a map and showed them. "The River Don flows into the Black Sea, easily accessible to us here in Constantinople. Our ships could sail up the river, across the canal, and into the Volga which flows into . . ."

"The Caspian Sea!" Lala Mustafa had exclaimed for himself.

"Which puts us right at the heart of . . ."

"Persia!"

"Exactly. Remember how many men we have lost over the years because of the dangerous and rugged crossing that must now be made across land, through Armenia and Kurdistan. Any time we wish to fight Persia, we must lose so many men, untold animals and supplies——and time!——all before we even see their banners flying. Two months, more or less, coming and going each time. And that's once the snows have melted somewhat."

"And we never had much success getting heavy cannon and artillery through the mountain passes," Lala Mustafa had admitted.

"What rejoicing there would be in heaven and on earth if we could make the heretic Persians submit to the true Sunna!" Even the Mufti had seen the logic of the plan.

"Not only that, but beyond Persia——access to the Volga leads us right into the heart of Asia. It would be a water route almost equal to that to be gained by splicing the Suez, with less strain and manpower. The benefits of such a monopoly would make our land rich for all centuries to come."

"Allah willing," the Mufti had been careful to interject.

"Such a project would mean we'd have to control Astrakhan," Lala Mustafa had mused.

"Yes," Sokolli had agreed. "Once the proud, strong land of the Tartars, our brothers both in faith and in the Turkish tongue. Ten years ago Astrakhan fell to the Russian barbarians. The dead remain unavenged, the captives still in chains, and our cities full of the refugees charity cannot support, yet who have lost the land of their fathers so they cannot support themselves, nor send us the rich gifts they were wont to."

"They will fight like demons for their land," Lala Mustafa agreed, "and they will willingly join us in building the canal. Afterwards I don't think they would be at all opposed to increasing the tribute gifts in order to gain the privilege of joining their rich land to our empire."

It had not taken much more talk for the plan to find unanimous favor and the blessing of all. I knew all of this as I watched Safiye probe my mistress for details she couldn't remember, but I said nothing. Esmikhan, too, soon lost patience and tried to change the subject.

"Where is my sweet little nephew, Muhammed, Safiye?"

"Oh, somewhere inside. I'm sure his nurse is taking good care of him."

"How is his little cheek healing? Will there be a scar?"

"Yes, I'm afraid so."

"Allah defend him!" Esmikhan exclaimed in sympathy.

"My dear, there is nothing either you or I can do about it now," Safiye said impatiently, "so you might as well help me find out what you can about the army's movements this year. It does make me angry when your husband keeps things a secret like this."

"No doubt he is afraid of spies."

"No doubt, but I am not a spy. My interest is all with the Ottomans. I have the future of my son to think about."

"It seems to me you might do better for your son if you were with him more." Esmikhan said this cautiously. She was still very much in awe of Safiye, for all their years of friendship. Beautiful women can have that effect on their own sex as well as on men. Eunuchs alone can learn immunity, and that only with concentrated effort.

"When—if Allah wills—my son grows to be a man, he will be the Sultan. He will have to know about the Divan and janissaries and war—all such things. Allah willing, he will not be a monarch who sits home idling with the harem favorites when the army marches."

"You might wish him to idle with his mother, however," Esmikhan suggested.

"But how can I teach him if I don't know about these things myself?"

Esmikhan was silent, for she knew no answer to this except, perhaps, one she carried like her unborn child, close to her heart, and whose time had not yet come.

As we turned to rejoin the rest of the women, Safiye happened to catch my eye with her sharp brown ones. She paused, then spoke in Italian. "You know, don't you, Veniero? You were there when they held that meeting, and you did not have babies on the brain."

I smiled quietly.

"Tell me," she pleaded. "Tell me where they have gone and why."

"I think my lady is right," I said in Turkish. "You would do better to spend more time with your child."

# XLII

NOT HALF AN hour after I'd sent the messenger on his way to Astrakhan with a notice for the Grand Vizier that his wife had come to her time, another man arrived with news from the front. They must have passed one another in the streets by the quay, and perhaps even salaamed and wished each other "A joyful arrival."

Yet the news from the front was as different from the good tidings of home as night is from day. The invasion of Astrakhan had woefully miscarried. Although it was at first successful, a force of a mere fifteen thousand Russians had come upon the Turks as they worked, unarmed at the canal, and put them to a dreadful, confused flight. The hand of Allah seemed to be against the expedition, too, for even of those who had managed to reach the safety of the boats without being ambushed and hacked to pieces, a mere seven thousand were returning. An early, sudden winter storm had surprised the ships at sea and sunk half the fleet.

Sokolli Pasha, the messenger said, knew that the disastrous news would proceed him into Constantinople, and he wanted his wife not to fear unduly. She should know that he, at least, thanks be to Allah, was safe and would be home as soon as he could.

I waited as long as I dared after the messenger had gone to his barracks before going up to the birthing room. I had decided I would not break the news until after the child was born, but my lady read my face, and then it was better that she knew all than that she be kept guessing with nothing.

She gave a little cry when I had finished, whether from the labor or my words, I knew not.

"Please, do not fear, lady," I said. "Your husband sends word that he, by the mercy of Allah, was spared."

"But what about . . . ?"

Pain, or again, perhaps dread, cut her words short, but I knew she could not help but think of the child's father.

"I'm sorry, lady. I do not know. I will try and find out and let you know as soon as I can."

Tears pressed silently from her eyes, but she nodded gratefully as I left.

I returned to the house at nightfall, having heard nothing.

Even the disaster was as yet unknown in the streets.

"She's having a hard time of it," the Quince greeted me.

The midwife had poured gunpowder in a thin line across the threshold, and I knew if I crossed it, I could not come out of the birthing room again, for it was believed I would take the strength of pangs with me. They would only torment and bring forth nothing, so I stayed without and only peered in from time to time. The room was dark, and made darker still by the thick clouds of burning sandalwood and frankincense that were to make the labor sweet. I wondered, rather, how Esmikhan could even breathe, and I shrank when I imagined the incense drying in a still, suffocating mask on sweat and tears. I could barely make out the glimmer of the gilded cover of the great Koran the Quince had hung as a talisman above the point where the baby should be born. I couldn't distinguish the figure of my lady huddling on the birthing stool beneath it from those of the other women—her maids and some from the Serai—who were in attendance to give her encouragement.

The women had set up a rhythmic chant of *"Allah akhbar,* God is great!" Esmikhan was encouraged to join in as she could, and all of them let their words blur into one long, sustained wail when the contractions came.

"The baby is buttocks first," the midwife elaborated, "and I have so far been unable to get it turned around."

Although my notion of a woman's insides was very vague, I knew a slave girl in the palace had died from just such a difficulty within the last six months. The thought made me viscerally sick. But as there was nothing I could do, I went to my room and tried to spend an evening as usual.

Echoes of the women's chant pursued me to my room and I found I could neither eat nor sleep nor read. My assistants and the *khuddam* who had come with the women from the palace were finding distraction in the general room by singing, telling tales, and playing chess. Careless clouds of laughter timed to the wails of the chant helped them forget that they were half women; that if the demon of childbirth brought death, they would find themselves on the slave block again.

Still, let them escape as they can, I thought, though I could not join them.

I let the women's wails chase me out of the house, through the garden, and into the dark streets. Their echoes even seemed to come to me in the refuge I took in the hollow mosque at the end of the street. There I alternately prayed, paced, and wept, returning always to the weeping again (unmanly, but that did not bother me) whenever realization of my true helplessness struck me again.

I was not alone in the mosque. I joined a man, a tinsmith by trade, who with his two young sons, bundled in blankets and trying to sleep, was also waiting for a woman to deliver—his wife of their sixth. He came and spoke to me quite merrily of children, begetting and bearing. There was nothing to it, he assured me.

Had his wife never had any difficulties at all? I asked.

"The first was not so easy," he admitted, tousling the head of the eldest son. "Before it was over, I was called into the room and she relinquished all claims she had on me if only my seed would stop hurting her and come forth. After that bit of magic, the child came readily enough, Allah be praised. Since then, I could divorce her at my heart's desire without having to return the brideprice to her father or anything. But why should I bother? She is a good wife, Allah bless her, and now produces with the ease and fecundity of a rabbit."

I grew angry at the man for such careless talk, and for latching onto me when I would have rather been alone. But he did know how to make time pass. And when his daughter came to announce the successful birth of yet another son and he left me with wishes for equal joy, I was pleased to discover it was already after midnight.

But nobody came with glad tidings for me.

I considered taking a description of the little ritual that had delivered the tinsmith's wife of her first child to Esmikhan's midwife. But this, I decided, was madness. First of all, the Quince was the best money could buy. If there was any good in this practice, no doubt she would have already tried it. Secondly, what man should be called in to acquit her? Even if Sokolli Pasha were in town, I knew, Esmikhan knew, perhaps even the midwife knew, that it was not his seed. Whether Ferhad was among the thousands dead in Astrakhan was not yet known. Assuming that he was, my mind played with the scenario that he was in Paradise, still had control over his seed, and was attempting to bring his true love to the other world to join him. Martyrs for the faith on the battlefield go straight to Paradise, they say, whatever their sins. So do women who die bringing forth Muslim children.

This thought caused me such sorrow that I startled the silent mosque with a sob. What about myself? I thought. On no account was I guaranteed to be in Paradise with her. In this confusion of paternity, where did I fit? Neither legally nor physically had I any claim upon this child struggling to be born. Both were so impossible as to be laughable.

But the memory came to me as I sat in that great empty mosque, of a night some few weeks ago as Esmikhan and I had sat by the fire playing chess. I reminded her of just such a night three years previous when she had first laid eyes on Ferhad. I mentioned it laconically, for there were others in the room, and at first her silence made me suppose she, too, had missed my meaning.

But at length she smiled slightly and said, with equal cryptics, "You know, Abdullah, my first thought when I saw him was how much he looked like you."

"If I were a man."

"Yes."

Esmikhan made a move then, a very astute play which I had totally overlooked. But before I could condemn my stupidity or she could gloat, she cried out, "Oh, Abdullah! it moved! The baby moved! Come and feel. There it goes again! It's always lively in the evening. Come on, Abdullah, don't be shy."

And I went around the table and let her place my hand on that great mound—like bread set to rise. By kneeling, my face had been brought very close to hers. I remember staring at the round, pink curve of her cheek and being more amazed at the life I saw there than at that I felt beneath my hand. She was so pleased to feel life within her that she was blushing. But even as I stooped there, waiting for the next infant kick, there passed through my mind the image of the hollow bones beneath that cheek as if I were being given a vision of what the future held and how my same, blushing lady would someday rot in the grave.

I had since, perhaps in self-defense, extracted a different meaning from this moment of vision than that of a morbid prophecy it seemed at first to warrant. Life at its most intense is often found in contrast to death, for it's by opposition that opposites take on meaning. And when the light and angle between two poles is so perfectly set, as they seemed to be on that evening, then, like two mirrors, they reflect one another and whatever is caught between them is thrown likewise into the depths of eternity.

The real, enduring Esmikhan, I decided, was neither the physical, living body who had bloomed and caught Ferhad's young eyes, nor the thing that hung like a dead weight from

Sokolli Pasha's marriage contract. Her essence was something else again, no easier to describe than the nature of a reflection. I remembered the first evening I'd met her, dressed as a bride, and that secret, invisible thing that had passed between us on the road from Kutahiya which has made me say on occasion that we were married, she and I. Being neither male nor female, but having in me the attributes of both, it was I who was most qualified to love the eternal reflection of my lady that was neither living nor dead. Indeed, I believe, when there is true love between mortals of any sex or between man and God, that is the part that is loved. If so, then I was, in a certain way, the child's father more than either of those two men who were away, fighting their wars, and neither of whom bothered to sit quietly on a winter's evening, feeling the child's first movements, and being reflected in eternity's mirrors.

And, too, I was responsible in a very acute way for the terrible pain that was tearing my lady apart at just that moment. It was not sheer blind vengeance that made husbands kill the eunuchs as well as the adulterous wife when the crime was discovered. If it were that this strange God Allah, whose will I had, perhaps, misunderstood, were taking it upon Himself to punish the sin even when it was still a secret to mortal eyes, He would have revenge on me as well. I was certain I could not live if Esmikhan were dead and that reflected, eternal part of her beyond my reach. If Sokolli Pasha did not have me killed, I would, I decided alone in the mosque, be obliged to kill myself.

When the morning call to prayer brought ranks of men to interrupt my sanctuary, I participated, but without much faith, as if this Allah were a capricious master I could not trust. Then I went back to the house.

During the night, the child had begun its descent down the birth canal.

"Thanks be to Allah," I blurted.

The Quince shook her head soberly but wearily. She had had no time to enjoy her own drugs, and reality, more than the long hours, was telling on her.

"Now your lady is so exhausted she cannot push. The pains come like swift waves and merely wear her away like the crumbling of a shoreline. I do not know if she can do it. Allah alone knows."

I escaped this news into the streets of Constantinople once more. Making some attempt to learn word of the army was diversion, although very little and seemingly very useless. By evening the rumors had begun to have a common tint, which spoke of some truth, behind them. There had been disaster. Some ships of the fleet had been sighted off Pera, but they were loathe to enter the harbor before nightfall.

"Sokolli Pasha dares not show his face by daylight in this city," one man said. "You mark my words, the Sultan will replace him for this."

There was no word of joy I could take home with me, nor did I meet one at the birthing room door.

"It is useless," the Quince said. "We can do no more. She cannot even hold herself up on the birthing stool. She will die in any case. As Allah is my witness, I have no choice but to cut the child out."

To cut the child out, to murder the mother. "I will take that same knife and use it, still warm, on myself when you have done that!" I cried.

So saying, I pushed the old woman out of the way, sending the numerous charms on her headdress and bosom ajangle. I stepped over the gunpowder in one great stride: in a moment or two we could all come and go as we pleased, for my lady would be dead and the gunpowder of no earthly purpose but to fill cannon and cause more death. I passed the bundles of dead-weary women, whose *"Allah akhbars"* were no more than sighs, and whose hands fanned themselves instead of the woman in labor. I picked Esmikhan up off the floor. She lay there like some discarded rag with all life drained from her, but when I moved her, the increased pain brought some stiffness of life in her limbs.

"Abdul . . . ," she murmured.

Her lips were white, cracked, and dried as if they were made of mosaic. Her face had begun to take on in reality the aspects of the death mask I had envisioned several weeks before, but I ignored it, searching for the life that still glimmered in the other mirror. I grasped my own elbows around her distended waist and squatted to the floor, holding her tightly between my thighs. I felt a spasm of pain go through her, and I took it on myself.

"Push, my lady."

"Can't."

"You must."

"Hurts."

"You must. You will die if you don't."

"Already . . ."

"No, by Allah. Think of the child," I hissed in her ear, hoping the other women would not be listening, but of course they were. "Think how it was conceived. Think of Rumi's Stone in Konya and the blessings of the Almighty. Think of the nightingale's song."

"Uh-uh," she gave a little grunt of refusal.

I could feel the swell of another pain building in her and I countered it with the vise of my arms.

"Esmikhan," I shouted. "Push! Push!"

"Allah's will . . ."

"Esmikhan. I will not let you die. If you die, I will die as well. By all that is holy, I swear it. I will not live without you. I love you, Esmikhan. More than life. Do not kill me as well."

I think she could feel my tears hot upon her neck where the sweat was already clammy as a corpse.

"Abd . . ." She began to say my name, but turned her strength into a push instead.

"That's it," I exclaimed. "Again. Once more."

"No . . . ," she said, but she did, sucking strength from my arms until they felt as weak as mint jelly.

"Again."

She did, and suddenly there was a sound of rushing water. Through my slippers, my feet got wet. And a tiny wriggle of white and red slipped out into the Quince's hands.

The attendants opened their mouths to rejoice as if they had witnessed a miracle. They shut them again immediately and went about their work in silence. Whatever the miracle of life, etiquette would not allow them to jubilate.

"What . . . What . . . ?" Esmikhan found strength to ask, for the Quince was keeping the child to herself for a moment—a long moment of internal struggle, or so it seemed.

The Quince blinked away some nagging thought and then said, with a faint smile, "I'm just tying off the cord, lady. She's a perfectly healthy girl, Allah shield her. There, the cord's all done."

"Don't remember . . . ," Esmikhan murmured with confusion and gratitude. But then she fainted dead away.

Her body was as limp as if she had pushed her own life from her as well as that of the child. Between breast and thighs she was so misshapen as to be unrecognizable as human, but her breath still came in shallow little tugs. I laid her down on a mattress and tried to give her senselessness some comfort. Shyly, tenderly, I planted a kiss on either bruised eyelid. Then I bent my head and wept, harmonizing with the dry, healthy yells of the baby.

"Shall I go tell the master?"

It was one of my seconds who addressed me, everyone coming and going over the gunpowder now as they pleased. At first I couldn't imagine whom he meant by "the master."

"Sokolli Pasha," he said. "He's come home, Allah be praised. Been in the house this hour or more."

"No, no. I'll go," I said, groping for water to wash away my tears.

"My lady wishes to announce to you that her face is black. It is Allah's will." I stood and faced the tall figure of a man whose beard seemed to have gone completely white since I'd last seen him. He had not bothered to dye it during the last month or so.

He looked at me closely as if trying to read something more in my message than the traditional way of saying, "The baby is a girl." Then he smiled and said, "He who allows dark shadows to settle on his face when a girl is born to him, or decides to keep her only with disgrace—does it not say in the Koran that his judgment is faulty?"

"Then may I offer my congratulations, Master?" I asked.

"Congratulations?" Sokolli Pasha laughed a very dry, horrible laugh. "Congratulations. We have lost Astrakhan and for this I get congratulations?"

"Master, I meant . . ."

"Abdullah, I know."

There was an uncomfortable silence, which Sokolli Pasha soon stirred as a mother may rock the cradle of her silent child to see it stir and comfort herself that it only sleeps.

"The young men fell like rain," he said, "thousands of them. I may not be vizier tomorrow morning, you may as well know that, Abdullah. Then I shall be obliged to divorce your mistress and the child . . . And all because of that Lala Mustafa, may Allah plague him. Yes, he has his beady black eye on my post. He would like nothing better than to be Grand Vizier himself. He's been plotting for it ever since the business with Bayazid. That handsome young son of Suleiman's would never have rebelled if Lala Mustafa had not meddled with the correspondence between Constantinople and Bayazid's *sandjak*. Though lively and popular, Bayazid was not a rebellious son. But Lala Mustafa and the boy's mother, that Russian . . ."

Sokolli Pasha stopped here as if he were afraid to say more. Then he smiled at me.

"I know what gossip among slaves is like," he said. "I am a slave myself and was once the lowest of the pages in the palace. Gossip may lose me favor in Selim's eyes faster than a drunken rage could. So I'd thank you, Abdullah, if you'd let it be known among whomever you gossip with the truth about Lala Mustafa in Astrakhan. Although he pretended to be behind it, he wanted the mission to fail for no other reason than that he knew how dear it was to my heart. From the moment we marched off, he was among the soldiers, whispering.

" 'What is this land of Russia we must fight?' he asked. 'It is a land where the nights are unnaturally long in winter and the days too long in summer. In order to keep Allah's laws and to pray, both after sunset and before dawn, one must deprive oneself of healthful sleep. During the month of fasting, when food and water may be taken only during the nighttime hours, surely the long days will kill us. This is a land Allah created to remain in heathen hands, for clearly, one cannot be a good Muslim in Russia.' "

"He got the Mufti convinced of this philosophy, too. By the time we were set upon, the men had no will to fight and defend themselves. Allah's will was against it, they thought, so what good were their arms? Even Selim the Sot had known better than to come to that forsaken place. They were cut down miserably as they fled. Now we shall never have that canal, the only thing that could have broken this deadlock between Per-

sia and our empire. Now we will fight against each other with
no progress on either side until we are both weak and exhausted
and open prey for Christians. You mark my words, some day . . .
And for all of this, you congratulate me?"

Sokolli Pasha sighed wearily and shook his head. But then he
remembered where he was, my presence, and the news I had
just brought him.

"But how can I be downcast?" he asked, trying to fight the
sarcasm inherent in his words. "This night I have become a father at last. Good Abdullah, send my best wishes to my wife. I
shall come and have a look at the child whenever you think it
wise. In the meantime, here. Here is a little present for the girl."

Sokolli Pasha laid a little wooden figure in my hand. It was
round-bodied and colorfully painted—very un-Muslim. The
body opened to reveal another figure inside, and another and
another—seven little dolls nesting cozily all together. I raised
my head from this toy's examination to smile in amazement at
my master. Who would have thought the Grand Vizier capable
of such things?

The smile he returned to me was honest enough, but it
seemed to hide some disturbing nuance I couldn't quite place.
"It's not my doing," he apologized about the gift. "Did I have time
for such things with the army falling apart on me? You'll go
shopping for me, Abdullah, and get whatever is needed for the
celebration we must give in ten days' time. Sweets for the
guests, something nice for the mother and the little girl from
the" (he cleared his throat—on purpose?) "Father. Whatever you
like. Whatever is customary. I don't know."

I looked again at the little wooden dolls, almost afraid to ask.
Sokolli Pasha answered my look and my hung head. "That came
from the Master of the Imperial Horse. A remarkable young
man. He and his squad managed to surprise a group of Russians,
killing scores of them and rifling their saddlebags. This, he said,

was my cut of the booty. He would be obliged if I gave it to my child with his best wishes."

And Sokolli Pasha fixed such an eye on me that I had to bow at once and escape the room.

I fled into the harem, where I found my lady, sleeping with her daughter in her arms. Quietly, I set the wooden dolls between them where they would find them when they awoke. Then I sat in the shadows on the opposite divan and simply watched them sleep. Mother and daughter were somehow like nesting dolls themselves, a brief glimpse of eternity in the shifting patches of latticed sunlight. For though both faces seemed crushed and bruised with exertion, their identical dark curls plastered with sweat to their foreheads, there was the peace of paradise there between them.

*And I,* I thought, *of all the men that new babe might ever know, I alone could sit and watch them sleep like this.*

*All praise be to Allah, Lord of the worlds!*
*The Compassionate, the Merciful.*

Unbidden, the words of the Sura came to my lips. And unbidden, I thanked whatever Power there might be for the fate It had sent me.

*For a complimentary copy of the Ann Chamberlin newsletter, please send your name and address to:*

Ann Chamberlin Newsletter
PO Box 711114
Salt Lake City, UT
84171-1114

# Available by mail from

**TOR**
**FORGE**

---

**1812 • David Nevin**
The War of 1812 would either make America a global power sweeping to the pacific or break it into small pieces bound to mighty England. Only the courage of James Madison, Andrew Jackson, and their wives could determine the nation's fate.

**PRIDE OF LIONS • Morgan Llywelyn**
*Pride of Lions*, the sequel to the immensely popular *Lion of Ireland*, is a stunningly realistic novel of the dreams and bloodshed, passion and treachery, of eleventh-century Ireland and its lusty people.

**WALTZING IN RAGTIME • Eileen Charbonneau**
The daughter of a lumber baron is struggling to make it as a journalist in turn-of-the-century San Francisco when she meets ranger Matthew Hart, whose passion for nature challenges her deepest held beliefs.

**BUFFALO SOLDIERS • Tom Willard**
Former slaves had proven they could fight valiantly for their freedom, but in the West they were to fight for the freedom and security of the white settlers who often despised them.

**THIN MOON AND COLD MIST • Kathleen O'Neal Gear**
Robin Heatherton, a spy for the Confederacy, flees with her son to the Colorado Territory, hoping to escape from Union Army Major Corley, obsessed with her ever since her espionage work led to the death of his brother.

**SEMINOLE SONG • Vella Munn**
"As the U.S. Army surrounds their reservation in the Florida Everglades, a Seminole warrior chief clings to the slave girl who once saved his life after fleeing from her master, a wife-murderer who is out for blood." —*Hot Picks*

**THE OVERLAND TRAIL • Wendi Lee**
Based on the authentic diaries of the women who crossed the country in the late 1840s. America, a widowed pioneer, and Dancing Feather, a young Paiute, set out to recover America's kidnapped infant daughter—and to forge a bridge between their two worlds.

---

Historical fiction available from

### PEOPLE OF THE LIGHTNING • Kathleen O'Neal Gear and W. Michael Gear

A breathtaking epic of heartbreak and passion, warfare and nature's violence—set 8,000 years ago in the gorgeous land we call Florida.

### FIRE ALONG THE SKY • Robert Moss

A sweeping novel of America's first frontier. "There is not a single stuffy moment in this splendidly researched and wildly amusing historical adventure."
—*Kirkus Reviews*

### THE EAGLES' DAUGHTER • Judith Tarr

War and romance in the Holy Roman Empire! "Seduction, power and politics are the order of the day."—*Library Journal*

### MOHAWK WOMAN • Barbara Riefe

This unforgettable third novel in the compelling Iroquois series tells the poignant tale of a young Iroquois woman who must learn what is means to become a warrior in both heart and soul.

### DEATH COMES AS EPIPHANY • Sharan Newman

"A spectacular tale made even more exotic by its rich historical setting. Newman's characters are beautifully drawn."—Faye Kellerman, author of The Quality of Mercy

### NOT OF WAR ONLY • Norman Zollinger

"A grand epic of passion, political intrigue, and battle. History about as vivid as it gets."
—David Morell